Henry Craik, Sir Henry Craik

The Life of Jonathan Swift

Henry Craik, Sir Henry Craik

The Life of Jonathan Swift

ISBN/EAN: 9783743389403

Manufactured in Europe, USA, Canada, Australia, Japa

Cover: Foto ©Raphael Reischuk / pixelio.de

Manufactured and distributed by brebook publishing software (www.brebook.com)

Henry Craik, Sir Henry Craik

The Life of Jonathan Swift

Presented to the
LIBRARY *of the*
UNIVERSITY OF TORONTO
by
The Estate of the late
PROFESSOR A. S. P. WOODHOUSE
Head of the
Department of English
University College
1944–1964

THE LIFE

OF

JONATHAN SWIFT

Swift
in later years
from the Portrait prefixed to Lord Orrery's Remarks.

THE LIFE

OF

JONATHAN SWIFT

DEAN OF ST. PATRICK'S, DUBLIN

BY

HENRY CRAIK

SECOND EDITION.   WITH PORTRAITS

VOL. II

London

MACMILLAN AND CO

AND NEW YORK

1894

CONTENTS

CHAPTER XII

SWIFT IN RETIREMENT

Effect of the quiet time at Letcombe—Disgust with politics—Libels that pursued Swift's retirement—The spurious *Essays*—His position in Dublin and at Laracor—Troubles as Vicar and as Dean—The completed triumph of the Whigs—Swift to Oxford, on his fall—The fellowship of slavery—Parties in Ireland—Swift suspected of Jacobitism—The "English Garrison" in Ireland—Toleration Act—Swift's views of it—Union against a common danger—His occupation—Literary schemes—Reviving interests—Vanessa—The relations between her and Swift—*Cadenus and Vanessa*—Vanessa at Celbridge—The letter to Stella—Vanessa's death—Her will and letters—Stella—The nature of her bond to Swift—Restraints imposed on it—The Marriage—What it meant to each   Page 1

CHAPTER XIII

SWIFT AS IRISH PATRIOT

Growth of an Irish party—Swift joins it from hatred to the Whigs—The ills of Ireland—Absentees or Out-liers—Neglect of former restrictive statutes—Degradation of resident landlords—Wretchedness of the tenants—Professional Beggars—Irish affairs between 1714 and 1720—Swift as Irish Patriot—The *Universal Use of Irish Manufactures*—Prosecution of the Printer—Duke of Grafton stays proceedings—Swift's *Apologia* to Pope—Swift against an Irish Bank—The Copper Coinage—

Wood's Patent—Outcry against it—M. B. *Drapier*—The details of the patent—The Committee of Inquiry—The *Second Letter*—The *Third Letter*—Are the Irish slaves?—The *Fourth Letter*—The *Drapier's* Protest—Proclamation against the Author—Carteret as Lord-Lieutenant—Swift's letter to him—The *Letter* to Lord Midleton—The Bill of Indictment against the printer thrown out by the Grand Jury—The *Drapier's* Fame—The *Fifth Letter*—Walpole's New Scheme for Ireland—Archbishop Boulter and his rule   .   Page 48

CHAPTER XIV

SWIFT AGAIN AMONG THE WITS—GULLIVER'S TRAVELS

Swift's attractions to England—Invitations from Bolingbroke, Gay, and Pope—The occupations of his friends—His visit in 1726—Bolingbroke in later life—Arbuthnot—Pope—Gay—Atterbury and his banishment—Bathurst—Congreve—Peterborough—Swift and the Temple family—His reception by his friends—Dawley and Twickenham—Leicester House—Illness of Esther Johnson—Swift's anxiety—The recovery—Swift and Walpole—The Story of their dealings—Hopes of conciliation dispelled—Return to barbarism—Swift's reception in Dublin—*Gulliver's Travels*—The stratagem about the manuscript—Conditions under which the book was written—Its motives—Comparison of the different parts—Swift back in England (1727)—Bathurst—Pulteney—Voltaire—Swift as ally of the Opposition—The death of George I.—Walpole's power maintained—Swift's anxieties for Esther Johnson—Her relapse—Back to his "lair"—The *Journal* at Holyhead—Swift in solitude—His last sight of England   .   .   .   Page 91

CHAPTER XV

THE LAST CHAPTER IN SWIFT'S PUBLIC WORK

Swift's autumn in Ireland—Stella's approaching end—Their relations in the last scene—Stella's will—Her death—The funeral

—The blank in Swift's life—"Only a woman's hair"—Swift
on Irish politics—Statement of Irish wrongs—The remedies
proposed by others than Swift—Lord Molesworth—Thomas
Prior—Arthur Dobbs—Swift's place in these discussions—
Answer to a Memorial, &c.—*Maxims controlled in Ireland*—
A Short view of the State of Ireland—*A Modest Proposal*, &c. .
—*Answer to the Craftsman*—Swift and the Corporation—
Traulus—Swift's speech at the Guildhall—*Advice to the
Freemen of Dublin*—Swift and the defence of the Church—
The Bills for residence and for division of benefices—Swift's
anger with the Bishops—*Modus* for the Tithe on Hemp—The
tithe on Agistment—Swift and the *Legion Club*—Swift and
English politics—Sympathy with the professions of Boling-
broke and Pulteney—Swift's *Proposal for virtue* .   Page 136

CHAPTER XVI

PERSONAL LIFE AND SURROUNDINGS OF THESE YEARS

The inner side of Swift's life—His summer excursions throughout
Ireland—Gaulstown—Quilca—Market Hill—Dublin under
Carteret—His Tory leanings and Swift's *Vindication* of his
action—Carteret's recall—The Duke of Dorset—Swift's in-
creasing gloom—His money cares—Wide influence—Cathedral
administration—Badges to beggars—Loans to Tradesmen—His
intimates—Sheridan—Helsham—Delany—Ford—Faulkner
—Friends at Howth—Bindon's portrait—Dublin foes—Provost
Baldwin—Ambrose Philips—Arbuckle—Amory—His claim of
Swift's acquaintance—Learned Ladies—Mrs. Sican—Mrs.
Grierson—Mrs. Barber—Other literary aspirants—William
Dunkin—Matthew Pilkington and his wife—Mrs. Pendarves—
The link of association between her and Swift—The Schomberg
monument—Bettesworth and his threats—Bishop Hort and
Faulkner—Increasing depression—Friendship for Lord Orrery
—Anxiety about his will—Its provisions, and the later changes
in these—Ending of Swift's work—"Years and ill-health have
got possession of me"   .   .   .   .   .   Page 168

CHAPTER XVII

LATER LITERARY WORK AND CORRESPONDENCE

The circle of Swift's friends in London—Their attitude towards the Government—The *Beggars' Opera*—Its rapid popularity—Gay and his new fame—The *Dunciad*—Swift's hopes of rejoining the circle—Gaps by death—Congreve—Gay—Arbuthnot—Swift's correspondence with Bathurst—Relations with Bolingbroke and Pope—Swift's contempt for their philosophy—" *Orna me* "—Lady Betty Germaine—The Countess of Suffolk—Swift's complaints against her—Petty annoyances—Mrs. Barber and the counterfeit letter to the Queen—The Pilkingtons—Later literary efforts— *Verses on the death of Dr. Swift*—*The Beasts' Confession*—*The Place of the Damned*—*The Day of Judgment*—*The Rhapsody on Poetry*—*Polite Conversations*—*Directions to Servants*—Faulkner's edition of the Works—*Verses to a Lady*—Walpole's irritation—Swift's increasing melancholy—The remnants of the old circle—The *History of the Four Last Years*, and its reception by his friends—Swift's work closed . . . . Page 200

CHAPTER XVIII

THE CLOSING SCENE

Added gloom and loneliness of Swift's later years—Removal and death of Sheridan—Increase of disease—Waste of bodily strength—Longing for death—Swift and Samuel Johnson—A fruitless request—Swift's interest in his last literary ventures—A final struggle for his Church—Clouds and thick darkness—Pope's dishonesty to Swift—The publication of the letters—The last glimmerings of reason—Outbursts of violence—Curators appointed—Wilson and his insults—The crisis of the disease—The long struggle over—The repose of apathy—Death in life—The final seizure—The end—The nation's grief—Estimate of Swift's character and genius . . . Page 238

APPENDICES

I. FRAGMENT OF AUTOBIOGRAPHY 277

II. NOTE ON *A TALE OF A TUB* 288

III. AUTHORSHIP OF *FOUR LAST YEARS OF THE QUEEN* 290

IV. THE MARRIAGE OF SWIFT AND STELLA . . 298

V. SWIFT'S OFFER TO ANNOUNCE THE MARRIAGE . 308

VI. WOOD'S HALFPENCE 313

VII. PROCLAMATION AGAINST THE *DRAPIER* . . 315

VIII. EDITIONS OF *GULLIVER'S TRAVELS* . . 316

IX. JOURNAL OF 1727 319

X. THE WILL OF ESTHER JOHNSON 330

XI. *CHARACTER OF MRS. JOHNSON* 332

XII. LETTERS FROM THE MSS. OF THE EARL OF CORK . 342

XIII. SWIFT'S DISEASE 349

CHAPTER XII

SWIFT IN RETIREMENT

1714–1720

ÆTAT. 46–52

Effect of the quiet time at Letcombe—Disgust with politics—
Libels that pursued Swift's retirement—The spurious *Essays*
—His position in Dublin and at Laracor—Troubles as Vicar
and as Dean—The completed triumph of the Whigs—Swift to
Oxford, on his fall—The fellowship of slavery—Parties in
Ireland—Swift suspected of Jacobitism—The "English
Garrison" in Ireland—Toleration Act—Swift's views of it—
Union against a common danger—His occupation—Literary
schemes—Reviving interests—Vanessa—The relations between
her and Swift—*Cadenus and Vanessa*—Vanessa at Celbridge
—The letter to Stella—Vanessa's death—Her will and letters
—Stella—The nature of her bond to Swift—Restraints im-
posed on it—The Marriage—What it meant to each.

THESE quiet weeks at Letcombe, after the storm and
turmoil of political struggle, were of critical importance in Swift's life. At the end of the four years
of ceaseless excitement, in which gratified ambition
had been chequered by doubt and impatience, and
occasional disgust, he had to balance the results of
his life so far. Looking back on the early years of

dependence and self-distrust: on the early pride and ambition: on the mistaken literary efforts that had preceded the first product of his full exuberance of genius in the *Tale of a Tub*, his was a strange experience. Scarcely had he discovered the richest vein of his genius, before he had found the dangers it was likely to involve. His boldness of speech had been misconstrued. The humour with which he set forth the ludicrous inconsistencies in all vulgar conceptions of the supernatural, had puzzled the timid and conventional thought of his time. To restrain that humour, he had turned to what he might suppose the safest of all spheres, that of religious, social, and political essay-writing. He sought to make himself, above all, simple, clear, and logical in his method. Theory and speculation he set aside as fanciful and absurd. But in spite of himself, his humour would break out. With almost wayward exaggeration, he had thrown all his energies into the political struggle: and now, when the crash came, he was left "a poor cast courtier," whose aims and ambitions seemed suddenly to have slipped from his grasp, and all that he had gained from the struggle was a contempt for the trickery of politics. Vexed with the imposture, he had carved out new literary schemes, and formed deep and lasting literary friendships. With this legacy from the past he had now to find new aims, and to achieve new influence.

Swift never sought to cover his retreat by any assumptions of philosophical indifference. To leave England was a grief to him: to leave his friends, still more so. "When I leave a country without probability of returning," he writes to Pope, "I think as seldom as I can of what I loved or esteemed in it, to avoid the desiderium which of all things makes life most uneasy." From a position of enormous influence he had now sunk into one which made it prudent for his friends to avoid him. Thus Addison conveys his fear, through Jervas, to Pope.[1] "He owns he was afraid," writes Jervas, "Dr. Swift might have carried you too far among the enemy during the heat of the animosity : but now all is safe, and you are escaped, even in his opinion."

Pope resented this expression of alarm : but others might not be so indifferent : and such suspicion no doubt aggravated Swift's lot. That was not made more bearable by the fact that he was pursued by the utmost bitterness of lampooners. One of their productions was *The Hue and Cry after Dean Swift*, borrowing its title from a tract written in the interest of the late Ministry, called *The Hue and Cry after the Pretender*. Its ribaldry and insult were made all the more pointed by extracts from what professed to be his *Journal*. These extracts, not unlike in style to those in which he parodied the last scenes of Bishop Burnet's life, are curious chiefly for the strange accuracy with which they repeat some of the features of the letters to Esther Johnson and Rebecca Dingley, portraying some of those personal foibles which Swift loved to detect in himself as well as in others, and which he exposed with an almost

---

[1] *Jervas to Pope*, Aug. 20, 1714.

morbid frankness.   Save for the difficulty of believing that it could be so, one is tempted to think that some treacherous friend had obtained access to the letters, and used their contents to give point to the satire.

Another ingenious plan for mortifying Swift, was the production of a volume of "*Essays, Divine, Moral and Political, by the author of a Tale of a Tub.*"[1]   Subscribed with his own line, "In State Opinions *à la mode*," the frontispiece represents Swift breaking off at the gate of St. Patrick's Deanery, from the divines, with whom he had been riding, as the phrase was, "tantivy to Rome."   The essays were a parody of works by Swift, the authorship of which had at various times crept out.   The Dedication to Prince Posterity, suggested of course by the introduction to the *Tale of a Tub*, gave a defence of Swift, which really amounted to an indictment against him ; and it was largely composed of tags and sentences out of his own works.   The Essays on Religion piece together more of the same kind of fragments, representing it as his intention to show that Religion is worthless ; Christianity is ridiculed through phrases taken from the *Argument against abolishing Christian-*

---

[1] Mr. Dilke may very probably be right in ascribing these to Steele.   The plan is not unlike that which would suggest itself to Steele : the intimacy which he once enjoyed with Swift would account for the startling fidelity with which they often reflect Swift's own thoughts.   But still more strong is the indication of authorship given by the stress which is laid in the Essay on Friendship, on the circumstances of the breach with Steele : and by the frequent reference to what was Steele's peculiar hobby, the necessity of the dismantling of Dunkirk.

ity : and Priests are satirized by a similar juxtaposition of various scattered remarks. The Moral Essays ascribe to him not only a contempt for virtue and for the ties of friendship, but even scandalous immorality. Those on Politics chiefly aim at proving Swift's flagrant inconsistency.

His actual surroundings, so far as we can picture them to ourselves, were embarrassing and cheerless enough. In his own words :—

> " My state of health none cares to learn,
> My life is here no soul's concern,
> And those with whom I now converse
> Without a tear will tend my hearse.
> Some formal visits, looks and words,
> What mere humanity affords,
> I meet perhaps from three or four,
> From whom I once expected more.
>
> .   .   .   .
>
> My life is now a burden grown
> To others, ere it be my own."

He was in debt to his predecessor Sterne for a large rambling, useless house; the expenses of installation cost something more; and the thousand pounds, which he was to receive from the Queen's last Ministry, to meet these and other debts, were withheld upon their fall. His home was dismal: and already the best part of Dublin society was being driven from the liberty of St. Patrick's by the unhealthy dampness which may well have aggravated Swift's maladies in later years.

At Laracor he found things looking gloomy enough to suit with the prevailing melancholy of his mood.

"The wall of my own apartment," he writes to Bolingbroke, "is fallen down, and I want mud to rebuild it, and straw to thatch it. Besides, a spiteful neighbour has seized on six feet of ground, carried off my trees, and spoiled my grove." He has plenty of occupation indeed, in visiting his parishes, and looking after his tithes and farms; but it is occupation of a sort that contrasts unpleasantly with the scenes in which he had lately borne a part.

Both as Vicar, and as Dean, he had petty troubles. At Laracor a Dissenting chapel was set up, and fallen as Swift was, he wasted energy in resisting this insult on his Church, as at once immoral and illegal. With St. Patrick's chapter he was involved in even more serious disputes, where he had the mortification of finding that Archbishop King supported his opponents. His authority was not, indeed, likely to be very gently administered: and when he applied to Bishop Atterbury for advice, even that fiery prelate counselled moderation.

In England, meanwhile, matters were moving fast against Swift's friends. A Parliament, mainly Whig, met in March, $17\frac{14}{15}$. A committee of secrecy was appointed: and before its report was issued, Bolingbroke suddenly withdrew, and took service with the Pretender: Ormond waited for his impeachment, and then fled: and Oxford was thrown into the Tower.

All seemed lost: and it was now that Swift showed his fidelity to his friends. To Oxford he wrote as follows :—

"DUBLIN, *July* 19, 1715.

"MY LORD,

"It may look like an idle or officious thing in me, to give your Lordship any interruption under your present circum- stances; yet I could never forgive myself, if, after being treated for several years with the greatest kindness and distinction, by a person of your Lordship's virtue, I should omit making you at this time the humblest offers of my poor service and attend- ance. It is the first time I ever solicited you in my own behalf; and if I am refused, it will be the first request you ever refused me. I do not think myself obliged to regulate my opinions by the proceedings of a House of Lords or Commons; and therefore, however they may acquit themselves in your Lordship's case, I shall take the liberty of thinking and calling your Lordship the ablest and faithfullest Minister, and truest lover of your country, that this age has produced. . . . I have seen your Lordship labouring under great difficulties, and exposed to great dangers, and overcoming both, by the providence of God, and your own wisdom and courage. Your life has been already attempted by private malice; it is now pursued by public resentment. Nothing else remained. . . . God Almighty protect you, and continue to you that fortitude and magnani- mity he has endowed you with! Farewell.

"JON. SWIFT."

"No misfortunes," the Duchess of Ormond writes in answer to his letter sent on the downfall of the Duke, "can lessen your friendship, which is so great as to blind you on the side of your friends' faults, and make you believe you see virtues in them, it were happy for them they enjoyed in any degree." So too, Lady Bolingbroke, who had even more serious ills to bear than her husband's loss of power and office, found comfort in Swift's fidelity: "Your letter," she says, "came in very good time to me, when I was full of vexation and trouble, which all vanishes, finding that you were so good to remember me under my afflictions, which have been not greater than you can think, but much greater than I can express." Knowing what were the troubles of her married life, there is a touch of pathos for us in what she adds, with a confidence which she could repose in Swift: "As to my temper, if it is possible, I am more insipid and dull than ever, except in some places, and there I am a little fury, especially if they dare mention my dear lord without respect, which sometimes happens."

Swift did not lower either his standard of fidelity to friends, or the sternness of his front to foes. Suspected, and even in danger as he must have known himself to be, he never swerved from the decisiveness of his opposition to the new order of things. He valued the Protestant succession and would have tampered with no schemes to upset it : but he was enraged to find what claimed to be a guarantee of liberty made the excuse for its curtailment.

Rightly or wrongly, Swift became thoroughly impressed with the idea that, in the name of Protestant liberty, true liberty was being destroyed. This determined his attitude when he again set his hand to active conflict : and the first note of what animated his life hereafter was struck in the fierce irony expressed in a letter to Atterbury of April, 1716.[1]

"I congratulate with England for joining with us here in the fellowship of slavery. It is not so terrible a thing as you imagine : we have long lived under it : and whenever you are disposed to know how to behave yourself in your new condition,

---

[1] *Swift to Atterbury*, April 18, 1716.

you need go no further than me for a director. But, because we are resolved to go beyond you, we have transmitted a Bill to England, to be returned here, giving the Government and six of the Council power for three years to imprison whom they please for three months, without any trial or examination : and I expect to be among the first of those upon whom this law will be executed."

The bitterness of indignation that breathes through these words, represents Swift's fixed opinion on the new order of things. "The scene and the times," he tells Pope,[1] "have depressed me wonderfully." "As to your friends," Arbuthnot assures him, "though the world is changed to them, they are not changed to you." But no assurances would tempt him back to England, and in Ireland he stood, as yet, listlessly aloof. He interfered occasionally in appointments, in regard to which he fancied that his position gave him some right to have a voice : but it was an interference prompted only by the desire to serve his friends, and stimulated only by the determination not to bate one jot of his privileges. "They shall be deceived," he writes to Walls of those in power,[2] "as far as my power reaches, and shall not find me altogether so great a cully as they would willingly make me." But except for this, he stood as yet apart and apathetic.

Ireland had adopted with no long delay the new order of things. Sunderland was Lord-Lieutenant, and in his absence, the Lords Justices were chosen from amongst the pronounced enemies of the late Govern-

---

[1] *Swift to Pope*, Aug. 30, 1716.
[2] *Swift to Walls*, May 5, 1715 (Mr Murray's MSS.)

ment. Instead of Archbishop Lindsay, a Tory and High Churchman who, in 1713, had obtained the primacy through Swift's aid, Archbishop King, who owed Swift a grudge for being passed over, was now chosen as one of these Lords Justices : and for a time the feeling between him and Swift was one of absolute estrangement. King led a section of the Church which so far accepted the new order of things. But another party amongst the clergy were fierce in their denunciations of all that was allied with the Whigs, and carried their Tory principles to the verge of Jacobitism. Small sparks were enough to kindle flame between these sections. A long discussion, which violently agitated the Church, had been opened by Dr. Browne, Bishop of Cork, in a sermon [1] preached against drinking in remembrance of the dead. The contention was nominally doctrinal, but was in reality directed against the Whig custom of drinking to the immortal memory of William III. : and those who had neither doctrinal scruples, nor Jacobite sympathies, yet took the side of the Bishop of Cork from mere antipathy to the Whigs. On the other side Dr. Synge, Bishop of Raphoe,[2] defended the custom : and opinion varied according to the political bias of each

---

[1] "*Of Drinking in Remembrance of the Dead : a Discourse delivered to the Clergy of the Diocese of Cork, by Peter, Lord Bishop of Cork,*" Nov. 4, 1713.

[2] "*Defence of Eating and Drinking in Remembrance of the Dead, by Edward, Lord Bishop of Raphoe.*" This was followed by a rejoinder from Dr. Browne : and the controversy became general. Swift's well-known answer, when asked to drink to Irish commerce, that "he never drank in memory of the dead," is of course explained by the controversy.

theologian. For the opposition, Swift's friend Delany, in *A long History of a Short Session of Parliament, in a Certain Kingdom*, showed how the remissness of the Tories, and the eager zeal of the Whigs, had changed what was originally a Tory, into a Whig, Parliament, bent on the destruction of the Church. He was followed by a crowd of pamphleteers on his own side : and those of the Whigs were as numerous as the Tories. In 1714[1] we have a doggerel poem, reflecting on the late Government, as *Perkin's Cabal or the Mock Ministry*, and holding up to ridicule the lewdness of Bolingbroke, the dull crassness of Bromley, the scoundrelism of Prior and Moore, the "true prelatic pride" of Atterbury, and Phipps, as

> "The very Jeffries of his age,
> Frantic and wild with party rage."

In 1715 we have *The Last Will and Testament of the Pretender*,[2] bequeathing to his supposed adherents the legacies most suitable for each. Atterbury is to have "a troop of dragoons to be mounted by Irish Papists" : Prior, "all the empty and full bottles found in my house" : and Swift, "the liberty of writing a second part of the *Tale of a Tub*, with as much blasphemy as he shall think proper."

Amidst this violence of controversy, the following letter to Archbishop King shows that Swift was exposed to a danger not hitherto suspected by his biographers.

---

[1] Irish Academy Pamphlets, vol. xxx.   [2] *Ibid.* vol. xxxii.

"My Lord,

"I received yesterday a letter from Mr. Manley, giving an account of the seizing of a parcel of treasonable papers with one Jefferies directed to Dr. Swift. I acquainted my Lord-Lieutenant with it, who was very well pleased with this fresh instance of your Grace's diligence and zeal in the King's service, which cannot fail of being highly acceptable to his Majesty. His Excellency commanded me to give you his thanks for it, and he hopes that if there appear enough against the Doctor to justify it, he is kept in confinement, and Mr. Houghton also : but how far that may be justifiable your Grace is best able to judge. I presume they are at least held to very good and sufficient bail. If anything can add to your Grace's character this application to the public service will undoubtedly heighten it in the esteem of all good men, which like all other things that may happen to your advantage will give a particular satisfaction to, my Lord, your Grace's most dutiful and most obedient servant,   Charles Delafaye.[1]

"Bath, *May* 25, 1715."

The suspicion led to no such steps as King's correspondent desired, and its baselessness needs no elaborate proof. It is evidence of the fact, indeed, that Swift had more warrant for supposing his letters to have been tampered with in the Post-Office than has generally been thought; but it is evidence of nothing else. A man is scarcely to be held responsible for all that is addressed to him in the midst of a doubtful and turbulent political crisis. No one doubts that there were Jacobites amongst Swift's friends : still more amongst his casual correspondents ; but this did not make him one himself. His own words to King give a candid description of his

---

[1] This letter, from Archbishop King's MSS. in the possession of Dr. Lyons, was printed in the Report of the Records Commissioners, 1871.

position, although he was doubtless deceived as to the inclination of one at least amongst his patrons :[1]—

"Had there been ever the least overture or intent of bringing in the Pretender, during my acquaintance with the Ministry, I think I must have been very stupid not to have picked out some discoveries or suspicions. And although I am not sure I should have turned informer, yet I am certain I should have dropped some general cautions, and immediately have retired. When people say things were not ripe at the Queen's death, they say they know not what. Things were rotten : and had the Ministers any such thoughts, they should have begun three years before ; and they who say otherwise, understand nothing of the state of the kingdom at that time.

"But whether I am mistaken or not in other men, I beg your Grace to believe, that I am not mistaken in myself. I always professed to be against the Pretender ; and am so still. And this is not to make my court (which I know is vain), for I own myself full of doubts, fears, and dissatisfactions ; which I think on as seldom as I can : yet if I were of any value, the public may safely rely on my loyalty : because I look upon the coming of the Pretender as a greater evil, than any we are likely to suffer under the worst Whig Ministry that can be found."

Swift felt annoyed that his rectitude should be doubted by one for whose sake he had risked the suspicion of his former friends as unduly favourable to a Whig. He had striven to put the best interpretation on King's conduct to Lord Oxford : and now King was the first to accuse him of having been ready to go all lengths with a treasonable Ministry. On the 22nd of November, 1716, the Archbishop wrote :[2] "We have a strong report that my Lord Bolingbroke

---

[1] *Swift to King*, Dec. 16, 1716.
[2] *King to Swift*, Nov. 22, 1716.

will return here and be pardoned : certainly it must not be for nothing. *I hope he can tell no ill story of you.*" The insinuation was one which might fairly rouse Swift's indignation. It not only charged himself with treason, but charged Bolingbroke, his friend and patron, with a readiness to purchase his own safety by betraying one whom he had himself misled. In the letter already partly quoted, he expresses surprise that his Grace could for so many years act along with him and be his correspondent, while believing him to be "a most false and vile man." The sting so rankles in Swift's mind that he speaks of it even in a business letter to Archdeacon Walls.[1] He has received, he says, a letter from the Archbishop, which was

"Civil and friendly except in one article, for which I will be revenged by an answer : he says 'tis confidently reported that Lord Bolingbroke is returning : that the consideration must be to discover secrets : and his Grace hopes that my Lord has no ill things to say of me. By which the Archbishop plainly lets me know that he believes all I have said of myself and the late Ministry with relation to the Pretender to be Court lies."

But while Swift refused to accept the tenets of the Jacobites, he held firmly to the Opposition, as representing his former friends. King attempted what was scarcely a very creditable device for breaking Swift's credit with them. In a letter written shortly before (Nov. 13, 1716), Swift had spoken frankly of the schemes of the Non-jurors as "a complication of as much folly, madness, hypocrisy, and mistake, as was ever offered to the world." He hinted even that

---

[1] *Swift to Walls*, Dec. 19, 1716 (Mr. Murray's MSS.)

the new Government might find in these mistakes an opportunity for recovering influence with the Irish clergy, by a little well-timed attention. Any personal view was the last present to Swift's mind in the suggestion. But King quoted the letter in London, as a proof that Swift was ready to change "to principles more in fashion, and wherein he might better find his account."[1] The report came to the ears of Erasmus Lewis and Bishop Atterbury : and to them Swift cleared himself, with warmth that was fully justified, of an accusation as hurtful to his honour as the charge of Jacobitism would have been to his political judgment.

For two or three years Swift stood apart and suspected as one of the small clique of Tories and High Churchmen who were fighting against the party of the Whigs and Moderates. But fierce as the battle was, it exhausted itself. Antipathies died out in the presence of a danger that threatened both sides alike, and that changed the face of Irish politics. This change is the most marked feature of these six years, from 1714 to 1720. The English Government had found, or fancied that it had found, a better way of governing Ireland than by raising one party against another. Support was now to be sought from none but the peculiarly "English party" : any thought of national feeling in Ireland was to be rigidly excluded from consideration. Even men like Archbishop King found themselves set aside. Nothing was left for

---

[1] The words occur in a letter from Swift to Atterbury, July 18, 1717.

such men but to strike a truce with those whose enemies they had hitherto been. There was no longer to be room in Ireland for two parties.

Beginning with this principle, the English Government aimed at preventing any Irish institution from becoming imbued with Irish ideas, and from thus growing too powerful. The Presbyterians were to be encouraged, because their encouragement tended to weaken the Irish Church: and the Irish Church was to be impregnated with the leaven of English Whiggism, which would leave its administration in the hands of unswerving and paid adherents of the Government.

In 1719 the Government pressed forward the Bill granting toleration to the Presbyterians. It was fiercely opposed: and in the Council passed only by the Lord-Lieutenant's casting vote. In the House of Lords the bench of Bishops almost unanimously opposed it: Archbishop King of Dublin, Archbishop Synge of Tuam, and Bishop Sterne of Clogher [1] united against it. But it passed by the votes of those whom King calls "our brethren lately sent us out of England": [2] and became the forerunner of a long series of Acts passed by the same means, and in pursuance of the same policy.

In common opposition to this policy, old enmities were buried. Swift and King came together once more. Swift strained every nerve to give the Church of Ireland a national spirit of her own, distinct from

---

[1] Sterne, Swift's predecessor at St. Patrick's, had been moved from Dromore to Clogher, on the death of Dr. St. George Ashe, in 1717.

[2] *Archbishop King to Archbishop of Canterbury*, Nov. 10, 1719.

that imposed on her by Walpole. It seemed to him, at that time, no hopeless task : but he soon found he had to fight against the deliberate machinations of the English Ministry, who designed to permit no such influence to the Church. It was thus that, beginning in 1714 as the adherent of a discomfited party, he became, in 1720, the champion of Irish nationality, the vindicator of Irish liberty, against the stratagems of the English Whigs.

Before we turn to his work in that capacity, we have to look to other sides of his life. During a part of these six years he was busily occupied with the arrangement of his business affairs.[1] He descends into the details of these with an almost painful minuteness, finding refuge in this, it would seem, from more painful thoughts. When he came to the Deanery he came with a burden of debt. Even debt did not prevent his making a benefaction to his own parish of Laracor, in the shape of some glebe lands ; but it gave him the absorbing desire to increase his store, and to make himself secure against that most grinding form of dependence which poverty brings.

He was not, however, without other interest. As time went on he recovered from the first crushing weight of the blow that had fallen on himself and his friends. He renewed his correspondence with Pope,

---

[1] The MS. letters to Archdeacon Walls have, as will be seen, been made use of wherever they could throw any light on Swift's life. But to produce voluminous directions as to the letting of his farms, the packing of his clothes, the management of his servants, and the storage of his wine, seemed scarcely worth the space which it would have demanded.

with Bolingbroke, with Arbuthnot, and even with
one from whom he had been parted by political differences, Addison. From the first, indeed, the tone of
Swift and his friends in regard to the new order of
things is one of uncompromising hatred and contempt.
The country, so one gathers from their letters, seemed
to them given over to hypocrisy, slavery, and the
dunces. There was no place in its public business
for an honest man ; no favour to be expected from it
for one who thought for himself, and respected his
own independence. But one influence after another
came to mitigate this. An attitude of despairing
contempt is not very enduring: it is apt to relax
itself. Swift was perhaps the first to suggest how
the dunces could be made use of: and to find in
them "tools as necessary for a good writer, as pens,
ink, and paper."[1] Literary schemes recovered their
interest. Swift renewed his own reading, and was
busy in bringing slowly to full ripeness the work
that was to attract his widest audience.[2] He suggested
to Gay a new type of humour, in a travesty of pastoral
poetry, which should give us pastorals for the Quakers,
for the Chairmen, and even for Newgate. Prior was
helping out the slender resources which his extrava-

---

[1] *Swift to Pope*, Aug. 30, 1716.

[2] There are several indications that *Gulliver* was written during
these years, and completed, in something like its present shape, in
1720. Vanessa is found alluding to an incident in the book about
that time. At the close of the fourth part Gulliver casts anchor
in the Downs, on 5th Dec., 1715 ; a few lines further on he says,
"At the time I am writing, it is five years since my last return to
England."—Scott's *Swift*, vol. xi. p. 369. Swift's imaginary dates
are generally fixed by the time at which he wrote.

gance had left him, by publishing a subscription edition
of his poems : and Swift, like others, was busy helping
the poet's scheme.   And at the same time that new
interests were arising, the political horizon was clear-
ing.   Lord Oxford's trial began with all the usual
deadly paraphernalia, and ended only in smoke.[1]
He was once more greeted with cheers in the streets
of London.   The Government was weakened by dis-
sension in its own ranks.   Opposition was threatening
in and out of Parliament.   Bolingbroke's banishment
promised to come to an end.   The wits found that,
even without the aid of patronage, they could hold
their own against the dunces.   The hopes of Swift
and of his associates became more bright.   Writing
to Bolingbroke, near the end of 1719,[2] Swift speaks
of the decay of his own powers : but it is in the half-
jocular tone, which indicates rather an unsatisfied
thirst for active employment than a fear of unfitness
for it.

"I am six years older and twenty years duller. . . . I have
gone the round of all my stories with the younger people, and
begin them again . . . I lay traps for people to desire I would
show them some things I have written, but cannot succeed.
. . . If I can prevail on any one to personate a hearer and
admirer, you would wonder what a favourite he grows."

When Swift wrote this, he was feeling the need of
a more stirring arena of work.   The circle of his
friends was drawing together again : they were urging
him to join them : and the invitation was not without
its effect.   The dangers that had threatened those

---

[1] July 1, 1717.   [2] *Swift to Bolingbroke*, Dec. 19, 1719.

whom he had supported, were now past : and the virulence of the libels on himself had lost some of its bitterness. The Government which he detested, and whose continued power seemed to him a continued triumph for hypocrisy, a continued exaltation of the dunces over the wits, was showing signs of weakness. Ireland, which had been broken into parties after the model of those in England, and where for a time the adherents of the Government had carried the day, was now uniting in one strong spirit of antagonism to a Government that expressed itself more and more through the mouthpiece of a narrow English clique, and in a policy disgracefully selfish. In politics and in literature at once, Swift was ready for a new start : and the opportunity for it was not long in coming.

But before we leave this intermediate halting-place in Swift's career, there is another aspect of his life to be dealt with. The darkest passage in that life is the one which has gathered about it most of human interest : and the drama now passed through an important phase. To deal with this completely, it will be necessary to anticipate, for this purpose only, two or three of the years which followed Swift's return to active public life. These years complete the story of Vanessa.

It is needless to say that in the records of Swift's life as in the memory of men, the names of Stella and Vanessa are indissolubly linked together. They both present something of the same picture, so old in its pathos, and yet so fresh in its interest, of a woman's tenderness and a woman's passion beating against the loneliness, often the self-absorbed loneliness, of genius. His relations to both bring out the same strange contrast in his character—its sensitivity along with its fierce cynicism. Both are victims of the wounds which morbid gloom like that of Swift's inflicts on others, and on itself—wounds in the sharp pang of which its own weary burden finds a strange sort of relief, cruelly as they cut into the hearts of others. Once or twice Stella and Vanessa crossed one another's path. For years they shared Swift's interest. But, beyond this, there is no real reason why their stories should be told together. They worked on different moods, they touched on different parts of his life, they stood in totally different relations to him. To trace in the growth of one intimacy any conscious infidelity to the other, and to concoct a history of Swift's feeling, and its changes from Esther Johnson to Hester Vanhomrigh, is a task which nothing but the imagination of Swift's biographers has suggested to them. With other men such a process might have some fitness; but the peculiar aspects of Swift's relations to women have been made the subject of so much curious conjecture, that he may at least, in common fairness, claim to be acquitted of a vulgar and thoughtless infidelity. We see the truth about Stella and Vanessa, only when we look at them apart: and we must cast aside the inveterate habit which one biographer has borrowed from another, of considering them only as if their history made two sides of one story, two aspects of one passion.

We have already seen how, on the eve of quitting England in 1713, Swift had learned the truth about Vanessa's passion. At first he had attempted to turn it aside, as most men would have done, by affecting to treat it as scarcely serious. But when he came back to London in the same year, it was to renew, almost in spite of himself, his former intimacy with Vanessa. She knew, and had learned to sympathise with, his political interests. Her circle was the same as his. She threw herself on his assistance and advice : and she sought his guidance in her studies. When she found him again near her, she probably forbore the more marked expression of her passion, likely at once to have alienated and to have alarmed him. But the intimacy was renewed, and the recollection of the few letters written to him when absent, perhaps made Swift more tender to the feeling which had prompted them, however unwise that might be. To have checked it would have been doubtless wiser : but the dangers were less visible to Swift than they would have been to other men. So matters drifted on, till the midsummer of 1714, when Swift quitted London for the solitude of Mr. Gery's house at Letcombe. His first letter thence was to Vanessa, probably for no other reason than that she knew most of his movements, and had followed most closely his recent hopes and fears. But he soon became cautious. She pressed him for advice as to her family troubles. Her mother was dead and had left debts : her younger sister was not strong : her surviving brother was a good-for-nothing spendthrift: and her own fortune was in danger. Swift gives her such advice as he can, and obtains for her an advance of money: but ruthlessly hints a doubt that some of her troubles were swelled by affectation; possibly, even, he may have thought, expressly intended to draw the bonds of their intimacy more close. When about to leave for Ireland after the Queen's death, he writes to Vanessa with the utmost caution: "his letters will be few," and if she comes over, "he will see her very seldom." He knows how sharp is the tongue of scandal, and he has no wish that it should be busy with her name or his own. When she does come to look after her property, his letters continue to have the same cautious tone, inconsistent with the notion either that he was throwing off, for Vanessa's sake, any former bond, or that he was suggesting to her any hopes of a closer tie in the future. "I say all this," he adds, after one of his cautions, "out of the perfect esteem and friendship I have for you." These are words that no man could use to wipe out the memory of an accepted passion; they could be intended only to prevent its growth. Settling in Ireland, she lived partly in Dublin, and partly at Marlay Abbey, near Celbridge, which she had inherited from her father: and his earlier letters after her arrival prove that he was almost jestingly deprecating a passion which he called indiscreet, and which he fancied, however wrongly, was not absolutely sincere. This coldness inflames her the more: she urges his presence on the old excuse of wanting his advice. "What can be wrong," she asks, "in seeing and advising an unhappy young woman?" "Counterfeit," she says, "that indulgent friend you once were;"—still without a hint that he had ever encouraged other thoughts than those of friendship. He is provoked at times to anger at what he holds to be a whimsical folly: but his anger only goads her passion still more. "Treat me as you do," she says, "and you will not be made uneasy by me long." "See me and speak kindly," she cries; without that kindness there is "something in your look so awful, that it strikes me dumb." Swift might have been wiser to have been still cold and restrained in his reply: but he could force himself to no more than a kindly assurance, as far as possible removed either from the ardour of a lover, or the effusive insincerity of one who was conscious that he had wronged her, in word or deed. When she changes to threatenings he meets it only by banter: when scandal begins to be busy, he plainly tells her—again neither like the ardent nor the faithless lover—"that it was what he had foreseen: that it must be submitted to: and that by the help of discretion it would wear off."

What, then, was it that Vanessa's friendship meant for Swift? He might have been wiser to crush it at once and for ever: instead of that, for nearly eight years, he strove alternately to humour or to keep it in check, and failed hopelessly in the end. During these years what side of his nature was it that this friendship laid hold of?

Not, we fear it must be said, the best. When

Swift was absorbed with the outside homage that was paid to him : when he put his pen, however honestly, yet unreservedly, at the service of a party ; when he was elated with a somewhat truculent triumph, then it was that Vanessa's friendship grew, and with these scenes it was chiefly associated. She flattered his weakest side : she learned the catchwords of his party, and, unlike Stella, she became, as she fancied to please Swift, a "politician."[1] From very hatred of cant, Swift at times professed that creed of worldly selfishness, which despair often suggests to every man, but of which no man desires to have a reminder at his hand. The maxims of such a creed are repeated for behoof of Vanessa, much as they might have been for Matthew Prior, with his motto of "Vive la bagatelle !" "Live for the good that the present moment can give :" "riches are nine-tenths of happiness, and health is the other tenth :" "converse with fools, and let them help you to avoid the spleen "—these, and the like, are the phrases scattered through the letters written to Vanessa. They serve, along with other signs, to show us that the friendship, bred in the heated air of political faction, satisfied, after all, only a small part of Swift's nature. The cynic rarely loves to have his cynicism returned upon his hands. Cynicism Swift had in plenty : it was not this that a woman's love ought to have brought to

---

[1] Contrast this with what he says to Stella, "I never knew whether you were Whigs or Tories" (the *Journal* always speaks as if to Stella and Rebecca Dingley together) ; "and I value your conversation the more that it never turned on politics."

him. But Vanessa's love involved little more than the ambition to have her passion returned, and the desire to attain her end by humouring a mood that needed rather to be soothed and changed. The friendship had begun in literary guidance: it was strengthened by flattery: it lived on a cold and almost stern repression, fed by confidences as to literary schemes, and by occasional literary compliments: but it never came to have a real hold over Swift's heart.

Slight as was its hold, however, when Vanessa had settled down in Ireland, when she had extorted from Swift, by the very vehemence of her passion, some tender apologies for his seeming harshness, the evil was done. Vanessa continued to pour forth her passion, jealous of anything that implied disbelief in its reality, indignant with any jest that seemed to smile at it. In 1716, its limits were even more definitely fixed. Swift and Stella then entered into that formal bond which seemed to one or to both to express most fitly the relation in which they stood to one another.[1] That tie, the truest and most tender that was ever to bind Swift, was henceforth safe, he might deem, from intrusion or comparison. It was a tie as to the outward signs of which all the world was free to judge: but the real meaning of which was hidden from the public gaze. The friendship for Vanessa was suffered to drift on, but all outward signs of it were most carefully dissembled. His

---

[1] The circumstances of the marriage are noticed further on. The evidence for it will be found in Appendix IV.

relations to Vanessa might, as Swift clearly feared, become the source of a vulgar scandal from which his pride revolted. The affection for Stella was avowed; but beyond was a sacred region, into the mystery of which he would not suffer the world to pry.

On this limited footing the friendship for Vanessa continued. It played only on the outside of Swift's life. Its course continued the same: on Vanessa's side, the fervency of passion: on Swift's, at times, a burst of real tenderness, occasionally a tribute of almost exaggerated compliment, varied now and then, by an impulse of uncontrollable impatience. Foolish his action may have been; but it was not unnatural. Moody and ill-at-ease as he then was, he was ready to accept as the best solution of a difficulty, a make-shift state of things, by which Vanessa was soothed. He attempted, indeed, what was an easy, but not a very complimentary, expedient, to attract Vanessa's love into another channel. The younger Sheridan tells us of a certain Dean Winter who was brought to pay his suit to Vanessa: and Deane Swift adds as another suitor, Dr Price, who became Bishop of Meath, and afterwards Archbishop of Cashel.[1] But Vanessa's passion had at least so much of the dignity of truth, that it would not be fooled out of its chosen aim. The old intimacy, on something of the old terms, was allowed to run on. The tie to Stella had been

[1] Delany mentions neither: so the reader must judge for himself on the probability of the story, for which the evidence is certainly not very strong.

rivetted by what was only a formal and secret ceremonial; and Swift perhaps conceived that a friendship, flattering to Vanessa's passion, might, without wrong, be added to it.

When the intimacy had thus gained a new lease of life for want of the resolution that might have broken it off, Swift revived one of its earlier associations.   In 1713 he had written the poem of *Cadenus and Vanessa*,[1] which remains as the monument of the ill-fated passion. It had been written when the first revelation of Vanessa's passion had struck him with

"Shame, disappointment, guilt, remorse."

This poem he now revised;[2] and as it is the revised form which we may conclude has come down to us, the examination of it will not be without its use.

Originally the poem was no doubt intended to recount, for Vanessa's ear alone, the story of her passion.   But it is not a narrative only : we may read it rather as an attempt to account for that passion in the way least wounding to Vanessa's pride.   Her gifts and endowments of mind and body are set forth : she is the chosen object of the gods' attention : her advent is to test the discernment of the world : her infatuation for the Dean is explained as the suspension of judgment with which an angry goddess visits the

---

[1] It is scarcely necessary to say that Cadenus is a transposition for Decanus or the Dean.   Vanessa is "Hessy" or "Missessy," with the first syllable of Vanhomrigh prefixed.

[2] This revision has been hitherto overlooked : but it is not without importance.   In a letter of May 12, 1719, he writes : "Vous aurez vos vers à revoir quand j'aurai mes pensées et mon temps libre : la muse viendra."

resistance to her sway. But strong as the passion might be, its open declaration too had to be explained : and it is thus the explanation comes.

> " Two maxims she could still produce,
> And sad experience taught their use :
> That virtue, pleased by being shown,
> Knows nothing which it dares not own ;
> Can make us without fear disclose
> Our inmost secrets to our foes :
> That common forms were not designed
> Directors to a noble mind."

In these verses Lord Orrery finds an expression of the extraordinary opinion that vice turns to virtue when it loses shame. Delany rightly deems this a distortion of their meaning : and surely we may see in them only a bold and hazardous truth, whose motive is the justification, *to Vanessa*, of Vanessa's own avowal. There are other verses which Lord Orrery and Delany unite in condemning.

> " Where never blush was called in aid,
> That spurious virtue in a maid,
> A virtue best at second-hand ;
> They blush, because they understand."

But this too, we are entitled to excuse, as a truth, however one-sided, which Swift hazarded only that he might defend Vanessa's self-respect.

Then comes a passage in the poem, which may perhaps be accepted as an addition made by Swift, when the poem was revised in 1719. The Dean now saw that the passion was not a transient one. Not its rise only, but its continuance and its deeper meaning

must be touched upon.   Vanessa may have demanded
a solution of her doubts : and Swift had before him a
delicate task which he managed with his usual want of
skill to gauge a woman's heart.   It is Cadenus who
now becomes—unlike the context of the poem—the
pupil whose crass stupidity lags behind Vanessa's
teaching :

> "Her scholar is not apt to learn :
> Or wants capacity to reach
> The science she designs to teach :
> Wherein his genius was below,
> The skill of every common beau,
> Who, though he cannot spell, is wise
> Enough to read a lady's eyes,
> And will each accidental glance
> Interpret for a kind advance."

Then come the hardest and most disputed lines of
all :—

> "But what success Vanessa met
> Is to the world a secret yet.
> Whether the nymph, to please her swain,
> Talks in a high romantic strain :
> Or whether he at last descends
> To act with less seraphic ends :
> Or, to compound the business, whether
> They temper love and books together :
> Must never to mankind be told,
> Nor shall the conscious Muse unfold."

No lines more unfortunate were ever penned : so
much we are bound to allow.   To defend them is impossible : but the coarsest suggestion that may be
drawn from them, is not unlikely only, it is impossible.
The poem was published at Vanessa's wish : a wish that
would never have arisen, had it hinted at her shame.

We must find another meaning, and it is not hard to
do so. Swift had before suggested a mere intellectual
friendship, in place of that complete union to which
Vanessa's passion clearly tended. These were the
evident alternatives : and he hints at a third as a
compromise, perhaps soothing to Vanessa, which
might have linked the intellectual friendship with
something of a closer tie. If a doubt of its honour is
suggested by the ambiguity of the words, we must remember for whose ears it was destined. The poem
was written, not for the public, but for Vanessa and
for her only. She knew what was the truth : and
Swift clearly tells her that the secret must remain
their own. It would have been well for her memory
had she remembered his advice. Whether that
advice involved disloyalty to Stella, or was excused .
by the embarrassment in which Swift found himself,
is a point of casuistry which each reader must determine for himself.

This understanding reached, the letters became
more cordial. Swift soothes her with compliments,
which it is possible that he did not expect to be interpreted too literally. She is told of her superiority
to other women, whose caprices Swift despised. She
receives his literary confidences.[1] She is promised a

---

[1] In a letter written shortly before her death, she makes a clear
reference to a scene in *Gulliver's Travels*, the MS. of which she
must therefore have seen. "One of these animals was so pleased
with me, that it seized me with such a panic that I apprehended
nothing less than being carried up to the top of the house and
served as a friend of yours was." The reference is plainly to
Gulliver's adventure when carried to the house-top by the monkey
in Brobdingnag.—Scott's *Swift*, vol. xi. p. 156.

sequel to *Cadenus and Vanessa* which should celebrate the history of their friendship. But, in spite of cordiality, he trusted neither his own name nor hers to scandal. He seems never, till a year or two before her death, to have visited her at Celbridge. With a friendship so limited, her passion could not rest satisfied. In 1720, she allows it to break forth in a torrent of remonstrance. For ten weeks she has not seen him. "It is not in the power of time or accidents to lessen her inexpressible passion." "The love I bear you is not seated only in my soul: there is not a single atom of my frame that is not blended with it." Religion cannot comfort her: "were I an enthusiast, you would be the deity I should worship." "Sometimes you strike me with that prodigious awe, I tremble with fear: at other times a charming compassion shines through your countenance which revives my soul." To outbursts like these Swift replies only by calm advice, which shows how little he returned the passion. "Esteem, love, and value," are the words he uses—words cold enough in such a connexion: but he entreats that she "would not make herself or him unhappy by imaginations."

These words revealed to Vanessa the real hopelessness of her long struggle. We need not, in excusing Swift, blind ourselves to the pathos of the last scene of all. She seems to have been at Dublin when this letter came: but she at once retired to Marlay Abbey, which was some ten miles off, and which remains to this day the monument of a love which no recklessness, no folly, no self-abandonment

can deprive of the tragic dignity of its end.[1]   For
the first time jealousy is allowed to have its course :
she puts her fate to the touch and writes to Stella to
ask whether she is the wife of Swift.   Stella, secure
in her own assured position, however little that
position had been asserted, avowed her marriage to
Vanessa, and sent the letter on to Swift.   She could
have chosen no method more certain to crush a rival
whose claims she had hitherto disdainfully ignored.
Vanessa must have felt that her last card was
played : that she had defied a rival whose shadow
had ever lain across her path.   On receiving the
letter, Swift rode, in bitter anger, to Marlay Abbey.
He entered unannounced : without a word threw on
the table an envelope containing Vanessa's own
letter : and riding back to the Deanery, saw her no
more.   Years of irresolution on his own part, of
hopeless passion on Vanessa's, of perhaps undue resignation on the part of Stella, had done their work.
Each felt that a tragedy, not to be wiped out of their

[1] Marlay Abbey stands close to the village of Celbridge and beside the Liffey, which flows through the estate.   The river is in
this place broken up by islets and rocks, and runs between high
wooded banks.   The slopes on either side are covered with fine
old trees, chiefly beeches and elms.   Close to the house, between
it and the river, there stands a fine Oriental palm, which must
have been there before Vanessa's day.   Across the river and beyond the garden the chief feature of the grounds is a splendid yew
plantation, the growth of centuries—more notable surely than the
laurels which Scott's informant found the characteristic of the
place, as they certainly are not now.   Going up the river side, a
path leads to a point in the rocks, where there is a seat with steps
leading down to the water.   It is quiet and shady, and has a
pleasant outlook upon the river rushing broad and full amongst its
rocks.   This is the spot which local tradition represents as the
seat where Swift and Vanessa used to read together.

lives, had run its course. Its first victim was Vanessa, whose crushed and baffled passion brought her death.

She lived only for a few weeks after the crushing blow had fallen. Before her death she had time only to collect her forces for such vengeance as was in her power. In the interval, if we believe the common account—and the date of her existing will perhaps confirms that account—she revoked a will in favour of Swift, and appointed as her executors and residuary legatees, Judge Marshall and Bishop Berkeley of Cloyne. Swift was not named even amongst the smaller legatees who were remembered by gifts of a few pounds to buy a ring. The omission could not have been accidental: and each must judge for himself what was the feeling with which that omission was made, and what was the strength of love that sought this way of satisfying its vengeance. Common report added, but added falsely, another condition to the will. Vanessa was said to have left injunctions to her executors to publish the letters between Swift and herself, and to give to the world the poem of *Cadenus and Vanessa*. The will contains no such injunction: but it is hardly possible to suppose that the letters were left to the executors without some implied injunction of the kind. Bishop Berkeley wisely decided to suppress the correspondence: and it never saw the light till Sir Walter Scott was able to publish the letters from a transcript made by Judge Marley, which passed into the hands of Scott's friend, Mr. Berwick. The poem was published soon after Vanessa's death, which took place at the close of May, 1723. The best proof that Swift saw and dreaded the interpretation which the world might place upon the verses, is to be found in the shock the publication caused him. Angry with himself, tortured at once by remorse and by indignation at the tangle of circumstance that had woven itself round him, he withdrew for a time to the South of Ireland, and left Stella to wait, alone, for the time when his remorse would seek consolation from herself.[1]

Side by side with, and yet distinct from, the story of Vanessa with its strange mixture of vanity and tragedy, there runs the far more intricate story of Swift and Stella. We have seen the limitations of the bond that held him to Vanessa. But Stella's love was based on no chance intimacy. It was entwined with the memory of his earliest hopes, and in spite of passing clouds, it retained to the end its living power over him. There is here no story with imprudence for its origin, irresolution to confirm it, and mingled harshness and delusion for its close ; there is in it rather the working of his heart, the central tenderness that gave a bright lining to all his gloom. But, not less important in his biography, it tells also

---

[1] An anecdote is told of her reference on one occasion to the poem : almost the solitary instance of her jealousy. A gentleman in her presence remarked that Vanessa must be an extraordinary woman that could inspire the Dean to write so finely upon her. Stella smiled, and said she thought it scarcely so clear : "the Dean, it was known, could write finely on a broomstick."— Delany's *Observations*, p. 58. And these words must have been spoken after Vanessa's death.

of the tortures which a morbid obedience to rashly formed and perverse resolves, continued to inflict both on Swift himself and on her who was dearest to him. Without the story of Vanessa, Swift's life would have stood out, more clear, more complete, and less ambiguous : [1] without the story of Stella, it would have been a maimed and lopped fragment, with one-half of the man's nature wanting. Round this incident the liveliest human interest, the most natural human feeling, spent upon his history, must ever gather : and we cannot, therefore, afford lightly either to discard or to accept any fragment of evidence bearing on the point.

We have seen how that tie was first formed, on the simplest and most easy foundation. Dissect as we may that early life with Sir William Temple, we cannot get beyond a few simple facts that tell us all we need care to know about it. A somewhat vain, imperious, and irritable master : a youth whose pride was all the more fiery because it was necessarily restrained, and whose natural melancholy was deepened by dependence. On the other side a girl, still more likely to be overawed by the dignity of her distant kinsman, companionless in the staid and solemn household, save for the youth to whom she owed all that she had learned, whose character must even then have moulded her own, and about whose future she must already have had mysterious anticipations. The

---

[1] So entirely is the evidence wanting, as I hold, to prove what Sheridan, for instance, maintains, that the love of Vanessa was a real passion with Swift, which did interfere with, and might easily have overwhelmed, his feeling for Stella.

Pindarics would be read by her without too great critical severity. She must have watched, perhaps with special guidance, the part Swift played in the literary controversy that occupied her master's leisure. Under Swift's tuition, her mind received that masculine simplicity which he prized for its contrast to what he held, with morbid relentlessness of insight, to be the tricks and disguises of the other sex. She had learned to regard him as her guide and protector: she had virtually, in retiring to Ireland after Temple's death, placed her life's happiness in his keeping: and henceforward she became his chosen companion and friend. The choice was one he never affected to conceal, though he fenced the companionship round with the safeguards that might keep scandal at a distance. When another sought for Stella's love, Swift repelled the intrusion, yet without breaking through those limitations on his own friendship that had made such intrusion possible. For a time the relations between them were accepted without misgiving by Stella. She had all his thoughts to herself. Glimpses of ambition were opening, which she no doubt shared: and these early years at Laracor, with occasional visits to London, were years of peace for both. Stella was buoyed up with hope: and Swift was soured by none of the misanthropy of his later years. When he went to London on the memorable visit that began in 1710, it was reluctantly that he quitted Stella and Laracor—the canal, the willows, the fishpond—all associated with her companionship. For two years at least, all his thoughts are hers. His chief desire is to return : his aim is confined to bringing his mission to a successful issue, that will make the Church his debtor : his ambition to attaining a future that will be easy for himself and Stella.   But presently, his life becomes more crowded.   The intense desire of power was roused again within him. The companion of Ministers, the champion of a party, the guide of a policy, he became immersed in the excitement of the game of politics, and lost all but the sense of the stakes.   All this raises a veil between him and Stella, and seems to set her image further from him.   We need not assume that Vanessa ever usurped Stella's place in his regard : but yet Vanessa was inevitably associated with the scene in which he played so large a part, and the thought of which was so flattering to his pride.   When he came back to Ireland in 1713, it was only for a short banishment, during which all his thoughts were of England ; and when he returned finally in August, 1714, it was in a spirit of disappointed ambition, and despairing gloom.   The real union between himself and Stella, which may have seemed near in 1710, and which an earlier satisfaction of his ambition might probably have brought about, was now more distant than ever : and all the more that he now found himself embarrassed by Vanessa's passionate pursuit.

It is clear indeed that, although there was no estrangement, no very special warmth attended the meeting of Stella and Swift on his return to Dublin. His correspondence gives no evidence even of their frequent intercourse in the period that immediately succeeded: and in the unpublished letters to Archdeacon Walls during the three or four years beginning with 1714, messages ·are indirectly given through Walls, which convey no impression of very intimate relations. "My service to Gossip Doll (Walls' wife) and the *ladies*" is the phrase with which most of the letters close. "Pray show the enclosed," he says, in a letter of 1716, referring to a snub administered by himself to a would-be wit, "to Mrs. Johnson, to see whether she be of my opinion." The wish to know her opinion shows that there was no breach, but the asking it through another as surely shows that their intercourse was by no means regular. In another letter,[1] he speaks of reproaches from the "ladies" for his not going to Dromore : and the excuse is again indirectly sent : "Gossip Doll" is to tell the ladies that he will write soon, but "as for coming down, 'tis impossible." "Your black privy counsellor," he says again playfully to Archdeacon Walls ;[2]—"do not be alarmed, I mean only Mrs. Johnson." Elsewhere he speaks of enclosing a letter for Mrs. Johnson, in one to Walls. Scattered phrases like these show that Swift was in no regular correspondence with Stella : that the fact of their marriage was unknown to Walls : but that, indirect as their intercourse now was, it was yet easy and friendly enough.

Just then, while still humouring Vanessa's passion, Swift was joined by the formal rites of marriage,

---

[1] *Swift to Walls*, Dec. 30, 1716 (Mr. Murray's MSS.)
[2] *Ibid.*, June 18, 1716 (Mr. Murray's MSS.)

with Stella.[1] In his mysterious life, no action was more mysterious than this. A proneness to tender emotion, along with a constitutional thinness of temperament that allows the emotion easily to die away, is no possible explanation of the alternate tenderness and coldness in Swift. But we must' expect to find him in his life, something the same as he is in his books. In the latter he often applies the scalpel with an unnatural and cynical serenity, to the very sufferings of humanity that have excited—nay, are at the moment exciting,—his pity. So it is with his own life. His feelings are strong : but a certain intensity of will, a force of intellectual passion, is perpetually torturing and crushing them. So dealt with, by what was undoubtedly a morbid perversity, these feelings, keen as they were to begin with, became cold and dead under the chilling influence of a gloomy misanthropy. The result never shows itself more clearly, in the havoc it wrought on himself and others, than in the story of which we have now to seek the clue.

There were not wanting motives that might make Stella inclined to the step. In 1716, she could not fail to see that the tie that bound them together must be closer or must end. She had waited long and patiently : but she had found that her patience was rewarded only by seeing the love for which she had given up her life, growing cold amidst the calls of

---

[1] The fact of the marriage is a disputed one : but the reasons which lead me to think that it admits of no doubt, are given in Appendix IV. Meanwhile for the purpose of the narrative this fact is assumed as true.

ambition, and colder still in the gloom that followed defeat. The meeting after four years of separation had shown her that Swift had formed plans in which she had little share, and that he either could not or would not accept her love as satisfaction for the blank that defeat of these plans brought. She must doubtless have suspected the passion pressed on Swift by Vanessa, and the degree to which Swift had humoured it. The gradual fading of the hope that she had cherished so long, told on her health, and Swift was not so blind as not to perceive Stella's suffering. In these circumstances Swift employed, it seems, his friend and old college tutor, Dr. St. George Ashe, Bishop of Clogher, to inquire from Stella the reason of her sadness. He may himself have shrunk from the interview, in the thought of the wrong done to Stella by his weakness in suffering Vanessa's love. He can scarcely have failed to know what Stella had hoped for, and what her steadfast devotion now gave her the right to claim. Stella told the Bishop that she had waited patiently while it had seemed that there might be reason, in Swift's interest, for delay : but that now her waiting was rewarded only by coldness and neglect. Such indifference gave slander a ground for attacking her good name : in one way only could that slander be met.

Swift agreed to make Stella his wife, so far as the formal ceremony of marriage could do so : but upon the condition that they should be to one another only as they had been before, and that the world should know nothing of the new bond. The ceremony was performed in the garden of the Deanery, by the same friend, who had been the bearer of the message, the Bishop of Clogher, in the year 1716. The Dean and Stella continued to live in separate houses. No concealment was attempted of the fact that they were to each other friends of no common nearness : but slander was kept at a distance by the care with which Swift fenced round their intercourse. They never met except in the presence of a third person, and Swift, as we have seen, often chose an indirect channel to convey a message to his wife. No woman's constancy would have stood a harder trial : only an empty ceremony had rewarded her years of lonely endurance, and even that ceremony was to be a secret assurance to herself that calumny was baseless, not an open pledge behind the conditions of which the world would have no right to pry. Slander was still to be fenced against, not defied. So far as their lifetime was concerned, the conditions imposed on the ceremony made it useless for any purpose whatever. How could calumny be stopped, by a formality, and a secret formality, whose hollowness Stella herself knew, and of whose existence the world knew nothing? Stella may have had other motives for her original request : but in accepting Swift's conditions, her only hope, beyond mere compliance with his wish, must have been that some day, if posterity should suspect her honour, the eventual announcement of her marriage might prove its suspicions baseless.

What, then, were the motives that prompted,

on Swift's side, a compromise so strange, and in what mood did each accept it ? Swift had doubtless at one time looked on Stella as his future wife. But such thoughts had now passed away. Disappointment was pressing heavily on him. Defeat had just befallen him, and he had not yet recast his weapons for a new fight, or roused his genius to new efforts. His friends were at a distance, some of them scattered in exile. He felt himself thrust, perhaps permanently, into obscurity. It was scarcely wonderful that thoughts which might have been cherished in other days, when his hopes were high, should now grow dim and fade. He had striven, too, for pecuniary independence as a means by which he might make himself free in action: and the fruit of his long efforts was a burden of debt. We have seen how, prompted by the memory of his early days, and the endless embarrassments with which scanty means torture a proud man, Swift had fixed for himself, with almost morbid pertinacity, a rigid rule of parsimony. That parsimony involved no sordid avarice, because at this very time he was sinking some of his means in a gift to his parish. But it determined him never to entangle either himself, or one dear to him, in the endless petty cares of domestic poverty.

Weighed down by circumstances as he was, many men might have sought the quiet of marriage, as a resting-place from his toils. It was not so with Swift. Defeated, powerless, growing old, attacked on every side by virulent enemies, he set aside, with a morbid self-torture, not so rare that it need astonish us, the quiet comfort that married life might have brought. He exaggerated the difficulties in its way. Nor were other motives wanting to increase his sullen determination. Married life might have seemed to involve an oblivion more complete than his ambition desired, of all the stormy scenes he had left. He might reject the prospect of settling down into the monotonous life of an Irish ecclesiastic, amidst a people whom he despised. He might still see fights before him, where it would be better that he should stand unencumbered and alone. His health, too, was filling him with terrible forebodings: worn by the *saeva indignatio* that wasted his life, wearied by the struggle, burdened by warnings of decay, he might feel that side of his nature which a woman's love could touch, leaning more and more to the cold impassiveness, to which it had ever been inclined. Swift tells a friend, even in earlier life, that his temperament was cold, and that this was a safeguard to his heart. His biographers have not unfairly accepted his own account, and have explained by its means the mystery of his relation to Stella. With some reservations this may be true: but the reservations are worth remark. A very little knowledge of human nature tells us, that men do not commonly proclaim their coldness of temperament, when it is so marked as to provoke ridicule rather than inspire respect. Nor are the qualities we find in Swift, exactly those we should expect to find in a nature over which passion had no sway. But without ascribing to Swift all that a strained interpretation of his own words has been thought to convey, we may still find in him one of the most striking instances of a phase of human nature that is not uncommon, where the very force of intellectual passion acts with the expulsive power of a new emotion upon other feelings. It was the consuming intensity of his hate and scorn that left so little room for feelings that with most men are so strong. With the growth of his satiric vehemence, these other feelings became even more straitened and more cold.

To all these motives for Swift's action, we must add the entanglement in which he found himself from suffering Vanessa's passion to live on. This would not argue in Swift any real division of feeling between Stella and Vanessa, and much less any idea of conscious deception of the latter. But he had rashly allowed her passion to continue: he knew how quick slander was: and he was certain that his announced marriage would rouse Vanessa's rancour, and make his name a jest. Prudence, natural indeed though scarcely dignified, was added to his other motives for keeping secret the concession that he made to Stella's wish.

On Stella's side, whatever her own hopes had been, it was enough that Swift willed it so. Moulded by his teaching, inured to patience, used to accept his will as law, she submitted to the conditions he imposed. Had she any stings of jealousy, these might now be quieted by the thought that, formal as was her own tie to him, it was closer than any other. But she had, indeed, little choice in the matter. She had asked security for her reputation. Swift gave it; and its secrecy was a condition which, harsh as it was, might fairly be said not to lessen its efficacy to soothe her conscientious scruples.

She bowed to the conditions, and allowed no outward sign, at least, of her discontent, to show itself. Their intercourse remained at once as limited, and yet as easy, as before. She was addressed by Swift, and addressed him, in a tone of cordial and often affectionate friendliness. To the world no change appeared in her manner to him who had been "her early and her only guide," and whose wife she now was.

Swift's determination may have been mistaken, morbid, even callous: but this need not lessen our reverence for Stella's devotion. It was not hers to criticise his motives: it was hers only to be loyal to his decision. She knew that the secret of her rightful place as his wife was safe in the keeping of a very few chosen friends. Before her death others might share it: in the end the world might know it: but meanwhile it need go no further.

A few years later—about the year 1723—Swift's decision seems to have relented. It is to that year that it seems proper to assign a story which we may infer to have been told to Dr. Sheridan by Stella on her deathbed. She then announced to one whose honesty she could entirely trust, the secret of her life. But she told him also that about 1723, Swift had been ready to undo the conditions. By that time his hopes had revived, and the morbid gloom was lessened. Further, Vanessa as we have already seen, had drawn upon herself the announcement of the marriage, and, at the same time, the wrath of Swift. To soothe Stella's just indignation, Swift may well have offered to proclaim to the world the position of his wife.[1]

But her own health was now gone. Her years of patient loyalty, she may have thought, might now be prolonged to the end. She feared, and feared with reason, that the place to which he called her was one which she could scarcely hope to fill. The offer was what she must have chiefly prized: and that she now had. She voluntarily resigned her rights: and answered that it was now "too late." A few weeks more brought the death of Vanessa, the publication of *Cadenus and Vanessa*, with all its ambiguous phrases: and the noisy rumours which would only have been kept alive by any publication of her own marriage to the Dean. Stella wisely resolved to wait and trust her cause to the judgment of posterity.

[1] See Appendix V. for an examination of the evidence on which this narrative of Swift's offered announcement of the marriage is based.

CHAPTER XIII

SWIFT AS IRISH PATRIOT

1720–1725

ÆTAT. 52–57

Growth of an Irish party—Swift joins it from hatred to the Whigs—
The ills of Ireland—Absentees or Out-liers—Neglect of former
restrictive statutes—Degradation of resident landlords—
Wretchedness of the tenants—Professional Beggars—Irish
affairs between 1714 and 1720—Swift as Irish Patriot—The
Universal Use of Irish Manufactures—Prosecution of the
Printer—Duke of Grafton stays proceedings—Swift's *Apologia*
to Pope—Swift against an Irish Bank—The Copper Coinage—
Wood's Patent—Outcry against it—M. B. *Drapier*—The
details of the patent—The Committee of Inquiry—The
Second Letter—The *Third Letter*—Are the Irish slaves ?—
The *Fourth Letter*—The *Drapier's* Protest—Proclamation
against the Author—Carteret as Lord-Lieutenant—Swift's
letter to him—The *Letter* to Lord Midleton—The Bill of
Indictment against the printer thrown out by the Grand Jury
—The Drapier's Fame—The *Fifth Letter*—Walpole's New
Scheme for Ireland—Archbishop Boulter and his rule.

WE have seen how, in 1720, the position of parties
in Ireland had been modified, and smaller differences
forgotten.   For us the central interest now lies in the
struggle maintained against that narrow and exclusive
clique which governed Ireland in avowed contempt of
all phases of Irish opinion, and which considered

itself as placed there only to subordinate the good of the country to English interests.

Amidst the struggles of contending factions the real evils of the country had been overlooked: the need of reform had occupied the attention only of an insignificant handful. None had yet succeeded in rousing a national spirit to resist the nation's wrongs. Over-insistence on these wrongs was looked upon as veiled Jacobitism. The theorists proposed their schemes timidly, and the Government neither accepted responsibility for the wrongs, nor troubled themselves to find a remedy.

In putting on his armour for a new fight, Swift's first motive was probably merely opposition to the Whigs. He looked back with bitterness to the fall of his friends. He detested what he held to be the cant of the Whigs, and their travesty of liberty. He was imbued with the fervent hatred of the Whig party that inspired his own literary clique. He was angry at his own banishment. Irish questions had, indeed, previous to this, occasionally excited his attention: but his real interest in Irish politics only now begins.

His attitude in this new struggle is not hard to define. He scorned Jacobitism as little more than a frivolity. He set himself to decry the rampant bitterness of the High Church zealots. He had nothing but contempt for doctrines of divine right and absolute prerogative.[1] But he was opposed to the landlords

---

[1] "He was reckoned by his friends," says Deane Swift in a MS. letter in Lord Cork's possession, "to be a republican." Rash as the expression is, it doubtless expressed a partial truth, as

on account of their aggressive selfishness towards his own Church. He denounced Presbyterian encroachments from his life-long detestation of the fanaticism and doctrinal bigotry which he held them to express. He believed the Whig government of Ireland to be a government founded on corruption. All these motives went to swell the current of his indignation against Irish wrongs.

It is no part of the biography of Swift to give a full account of the economic history of Ireland in his time. But to illustrate his work, it is absolutely necessary to know something of the condition of national ruin and semi-barbarism which produced at once the motive in Swift, and the ready response in his audience. We may take the picture of this condition, as given us in the contemporary memoirs, in the pamphlets of Swift himself, and in others that dealt at the same time with the same questions, and were almost certainly familiar to the circle amidst which he moved.

In Swift's day the most palpable evil in Irish life was that of which, ever since, so much has been heard—the number of absentee landlords, or "outliers," as they were called. In former days, under sovereigns who looked to the grantees of lands in Ireland for the defence of the kingdom against sudden rebellion, there had been a summary remedy for absenteeism. Again and again, the English kings, from the Plantagenets to the Tudors, had been obliged

regards the bold front which Swift maintained against authority unjustly exercised.

to equip costly armies to stamp out rebellion, to which the absence of the English landlords had been an inducement. The burden on the Treasury was unwelcome, and statutes of increasing severity had marked their sense of this breach of contract on the part of these English owners. By a statute of Richard II., two-thirds of the estate of an absentee were forfeited to the Crown. The Lancastrian kings had proceeded on the same policy : and Henry VIII. had summarily resumed the whole Irish estates of some English nobles who were habitual absentees. Even under the early Stuarts the same course was pursued : and security was at least taken that absenteeism should not free a landlord from contributing heavily to the revenues of the country upon whose resources he preyed : while the holding of Irish offices was burdened with the requirement of residence in Ireland. But more recently a change had sprung up. Residence had not been encouraged. Statutes to enforce it still remained in the statute-book : but they were a dead letter. The landlord drew his rent from Ireland, but did not help to pay her taxes. He spent the rent in England : and, since lavish ostentation might help to social consideration one whose Irish blood would otherwise have been a bar to him, he frequently spent more than his rent, and left his estate encumbered with mortgages in the hands of English mortgagees. The holder of an Irish office thought only of its emoluments, and was indignant at any ill-timed suggestion of a visit to the country burdened with his support, and nominally entitled to his services.

There were stories of those who had landed at Ring-send on Saturday night, had received the sacrament at the nearest parish church on Sunday, taken the oaths on Monday morning in the Courts, and set sail for England in the afternoon, leaving no trace of their existence in Ireland save their names on her Civil List as recipients of a salary.[1]

By this custom it was calculated that at least £600,000 per annum, out of a total rental of £1,800,000, left the country, and was spent in England. The blame for it is not to be laid altogether at the landlord's door. There was little to encourage re-sidence : and much, on the other hand, to make the life of a resident landlord unendurable. Scorned by those who had more freshly arrived from England, and who endeavoured to hold their Irish connexion as loosely as possible, the Irish landlord found himself reduced to a level in society that wounded his pride at every turn. He knew that to his exertions, and the exer-tions of those who went before him, the English tenure of Ireland owed its continuance. Yet no political career was open to him : the offices in his own country went to strangers : he was classed, in an uncalculating and indiscriminating contempt, along with those of an alien and conquered race. Scorned in the society of the English emissaries, he might withdraw to his own estate : but his presence there did little good. He was without education, without any intellectual interest, and he could only strive to cover the wounds inflicted on his pride by a lavish

---

[1] *List of Absentees*, 2nd ed., p. 27.

display of coarse and brutal luxury. In a house neglected, dirty, and sordid, he spent his rents in endless carouses, whose only redeeming feature was a half-savage hospitality. His house swarmed with unkempt hangers-on, who might be seen cutting their food from the ox that was roasting whole in the hall, and quenching their thirst from the tankard on their master's table. If any luxuries of furniture were, perchance, admitted, the false pride, which aped what it detested, was sure to prompt their purchase in the English market, and of English manufacture.[1]

Despised themselves, the landlords repaid their contempt upon the tenants. Thriftless themselves, they provided for their needs by forcing thriftlessness on others. All the thought of the tenant was to contrive means for meeting the recurring fines for renewal, careless how the indebtedness so incurred could be wiped out. Nor could the tenants help themselves. The vast majority were Roman Catholics,[2] and as such felt themselves to be scarcely within

---

[1] It is useless to quote chapter and verse for each of the features of Irish society here depicted. But those who have studied the masses of Irish pamphlets on the questions of the day will recognize them as drawn from the pages of these contemporary records.

[2] There is scarcely any point on which the evidence is more various than that which bears on the comparative numbers of Protestants and Roman Catholics. Boulter reckons the latter as 5 to 1 (vol. i. p. 210): in a MS. letter in the British Museum from Bishop Clayton of Killala to Lady Sundon, I find them reckoned at 8 to 1: whereas in the earlier tract "*On the Conduct of the Purse of Ireland*" (1714) they are reckoned to be, in all except northern parts, as 20 to 1. The discrepancy is constant. The author of the *Scheme of the Proportion which the Protestants of Ireland may probably bear to the Papists* reckons the former to be as about 6 to 14.

the protection of the law. They were entirely without education, and no other calling than that of an almost barbarous husbandry, was open to them. They were sunk in an abyss of poverty. "The people," we are told,[1] "go bare legged half the year, and rarely touch flesh meat." So wretched was Irish tillage that it was cheaper to import English corn than to use Irish, even with the expense of freight.[2] Their own occupation would scarcely have kept the tenants above starvation point, and it was consequently little more than a pretence. As soon as the potatoes were planted, the hut was closed, and the family went forth on the more profitable employment of begging.[3] Idle, lazy, and incorrigible, they wandered from house to house, often extorting a sort of black mail, and thus providing for the needs of winter. So profitable did this become, in the absence of any restraint, or in the apathy which prevented the local magistrates from enforcing the law, that begging became a recognized profession.[4] Adepts were hired to complete the family group, and these adepts shared the spoils of the season at its close. Girls were debauched in order that they might, as fictitious widows, move compassion, and earn an alms. As the summer drew to a close, they came back,

---

[1] *List of Absentees*, 2nd ed. p. 32.

[2] See Swift's *Proposal for Universal use of Irish Manufactures:* and *Considerations for promoting the Agriculture of Ireland*, by R (obert) L (ord) V (iscount) M (olesworth) (1723).

[3] *Essay on the Trade and Improvement of Ireland*, by Arthur Dobbs. Dublin, 1729, 2nd Part.

[4] Arthur Dobbs computes the number of able-bodied persons thus drawn from labour, as 30,000 annually.—*Trade and Improvement of Ireland.*

gathered in the potato crop, and then lived during the winter months an existence little above that of brutes. A class like this soon produced a class even lower and more dangerous than itself. The country was cursed with a brood of hedgers, born of adultery and incest, herding together in troops where the ties of relationship were as completely lost as in a herd of cattle. They were thievish and revengeful, enemies to the industrious, an intolerable burden and plague-spot on the land. But in no other country could they have led a life so free from interference. The English clique at the Castle were too much occupied in checking fancied disaffection, and in dispensing patronage so as to secure support amongst hungry partizans, to care for the welfare of the masses, to whom Whig and Tory were meaningless names. The local gentry, despised by the governing clique, threw off the responsibilities of their position, and allowed matters to drift from bad to worse. The better population of the North, who had still their own energy to save them from despair, left the country in emigrant ships for the West Indies, where they were landed only to lead the life of slaves to those who bound them by chains of debt.[1]

To combat such ills Swift stepped from the seclusion in which he had remained since 1714. The

---

[1] See Archbishop Boulter's *Letters*, vol. i. p. 260. A few years later, in 1736, Bishop Clayton writes from Cork that the North, where the linen industry flourishes, is sending forth emigrants, while the South, whose hempen manufactures a new Act of the English Parliament had destroyed, found no such energy in her people.—Sundon MSS., British Museum.

history of Ireland had not meanwhile been eventful. But it had been marked by at least two events of some importance—the rise of the dispute as to the finality of the decisions of the Irish House of Lords,[1] and the passing of the Act giving back toleration to the Presbyterians, of which they had been deprived in 1703.

It was in the year 1720, that Swift entered upon this new era of his life. Rarely has it happened to any man to exercise decisive influence in so many widely separated spheres of action. Few could have foreseen that the disheartened politician, the misread satirist, the broken pamphleteer, was yet to appear in two new capacities—enough alone to have won for him a great name—as the Irish patriot, and as the author of the most comprehensive satire that the world has ever seen. Anger first roused him : he saw all the wrongs of Ireland as the work of the Whig Government. He felt himself that this was the history of his own impulse. "I do profess without affectation," he writes to Pope a few years later,[2] "that your kind opinion of me as a patriot, since you call it so, is what I do not deserve ; because what I do is owing to perfect rage and resentment, and the mortifying sight of slavery, folly, and baseness about me, among which I am forced to live."

The wrongs of Ireland were undoubtedly deepen-

---

[1] By the passing, on March 26, 1720, of a Bill for *the Better Securing the Dependency of Ireland on the Crown of Great Britain*, by which the appellate jurisdiction of the Irish House of Lords was actually taken away.

[2] *Swift to Pope*, June 1, 1728.

ing. But that which first stirred Swift's pen, was not new. Since the days of Charles II. the Irish had been forbidden to seek a market in England for their cattle. Since the last years of William III. the most iniquitous of a long series of iniquitous laws had crushed out the Irish woollen manufacture by refusing it the liberty of exportation, and by restricting it to the narrow and precarious market formed by the contraband trade to France. Every year, however, increased the pressure. The exasperation waited only for a voice to utter it.

This was the function now assumed by Swift. The pamphlet which bore the name of "*A Proposal for the Universal use of Irish Manufactures*" was published in 1720. It proposes, in effect, a reprisal on England for her restrictions, by a refusal to use anything that comes thence. A confederation is to be formed, pledged to use nothing that is not of Irish manufacture. Everything, he trusts, will be burned that comes from England, except the people and the coals. This is the basis of the paper : but as it proceeds his indignation waxes warmer. That indignation is preserved, according to one of the most unique secrets of Swift's art, without a trace of the monotonous invective that palls upon the reader. Its power lies in its variety. Indignant earnestness is subtly varied by sarcasm, straight blows of invective by delicate irony. The anger comes out in short, pithy, and telling sentences, which are abruptly closed, and leave a sense of power in reserve. Take for instance, a sentence like this :—

"The Scripture tells us 'that oppression makes a wise man mad:' therefore, consequently speaking, the reason why some men are not mad is that they are not wise. However, it were to be wished that oppression would in time teach a little wisdom to fools."

The paragraph has no close connexion with what goes before: and just as little with the ironical complaint that follows, bewailing the wrongs that England suffers because Ireland is audacious enough to use a few of her own products. But we are arrested, as it were, by the concentrated force of these words, simple in themselves, but pregnant with a cynical pity that it would be hard to surpass.

The irony of his description of the sufferings of England from the fact that her tyranny is not quite complete: the contempt poured out upon a slavish adulation of English fashions: the picture of the English nobody who passes for a celebrity in Ireland [1] —all these carry us beyond the range of the particular proposal, into a wider region, where human nature is satirized.   Swift's proposal was faulty in political economy.   Of this the age knew little, and Swift cared nothing for it.   He anticipated its maxims only to ridicule them.   For him "maxims were controlled" in Ireland ; or, as a modern writer might have phrased it, the general truths of political economy had no

---

[1] "Another, who has been for thirty years the common standard of stupidity in England, where he was never heard a minute in any assembly or by any party, with common Christian treatment : yet, upon his arrival here, could put on a face of importance and authority, talk more than six, without either gracefulness, propriety or meaning, and, at the same time, be admired and followed as the pattern of eloquence and wisdom."

application. It is the general maladministration of Ireland that is the real object of his attack; and the tyranny of slaves to slaves, that landlords show, is still more fiercely satirized.

> "I know not how it comes to pass (*and yet perhaps I know well enough*), that slaves have a natural disposition to be tyrants : and that when my betters give me a kick, I am apt to revenge it with six upon my footman, although perhaps he may be an honest and diligent fellow."

What follows is rigidly characteristic in its simple force, wasting no word by redundancy, marring the effect by no overwrought effort.

> "I have heard great divines affirm, that nothing is so likely to call down a universal judgment from Heaven upon a nation as universal oppression : and whether this be not already verified in part, their worships, the landlords, are now at full leisure to consider. Whoever travels this country, and observes the face of nature, or the faces, and habits, and dwellings of the natives, will hardly think himself in a land where law, religion, or common humanity, is professed."

No Government, not swayed by folly as well as injustice, would have accepted the pamphlet as anything else than a fair statement of Irish grievances. To have these grievances stated might, indeed, be a danger, but for this the Government themselves were surely responsible. No law was attacked. The irony of the tract accepted the worst of the laws, as facts against which there could be no appeal. That feelings were deeply stirred was due only to the consummate skill with which the case was set forth. But the Government were insane enough to place upon the tract precisely the meaning that Swift would have wished, but which their own interests would have bid them ignore. They took it as an attack upon themselves.[1] The Lord Chief Justice Whiteshed was urged forward : a prosecution against Waters, the printer, was instituted, and the Grand Jury were induced to find a true Bill. But when the trial came on, the jury refused to find a verdict of guilty. Whiteshed bullied, and coaxed, and browbeat them by turns. He laid his hand on his breast and swore that the author's intention was to bring in the Pretender. The jury were stubborn : but at length from very weariness they brought in a special verdict which enabled the proceedings to be prolonged. Whiteshed did not relax his efforts : but they were in vain, and when the Duke of Grafton assumed the functions of Lord - Lieutenant in the autumn, he stopped the prosecution by a writ of *nolle prosequi*.

Having thus put his hand anew to the plough, Swift paused. In a letter to Pope, of 10th January, 17$\frac{22}{21}$,[2] he reviews his position : possibly for the sake of his friendship with Pope : more probably perhaps merely as a record of his consistency, for his own

[1] The Government adherents endeavoured without much success to answer the pamphlet. Amongst the tracts belonging to the Royal Irish Academy, I find one reply published in 1720, in which Swift is bitterly attacked for kindling ill feeling between England and Ireland, as he had before done between England and her allies. The writer is orthodoxly humble. "The Protestants of Ireland," he says, " are sensible that nature and circumstances as well as Constitution and original right, have placed them under a dependence on their mother country." Swift is one of the "*labia latrantia* " whose barking keeps off peace.

[2] The date 17$\frac{21}{20}$ given by Scott is erroneous, seeing that the Duke of Grafton's arrival in Dublin as Lord - Lieutenant, which took place in August, 1721, is referred to.

satisfaction.[1] He declares his utter ignorance of the conditions of the political world since his retirement. But, although aloof from the strife of party, he finds himself the object of its bitter abuse. He resents this all the more because, when his favour was at its height, he never sought to do otherwise than save merit from being proscribed on merely political grounds. He had been taunted by his Tory patrons as a Whig: now he is stigmatized as the most rabid of Tory partizans. On the other hand, he wishes to make no court to the new Whig powers: "for the new principles fixed to those of that denomination I did then, and do now, from my heart abhor, detest, and abjure, as wholly degenerate from their predecessors."[2] He desires only to be suffered "to run quietly among the common herd of people, whose opinions

---

[1] Pope declared that he never received the letter : and, if we could trust Pope's word, it seems not impossible that the letter was written only, and not sent.

[2] "He means particularly," says Warburton on this passage, "the principle at that time charged upon them by their enemies of an intention to proscribe the Tories." Warburton's assumption is as absolutely without foundation as his assumptions usually are, and the implied charge against Swift of hating the Whigs only because the Whigs were unwilling to receive him into favour, might well be disregarded. But it is more serious to find Mr. Elwin apparently accepting Warburton's interpretation as correct. I can find no warrant for this interpretation either in the words themselves, in the context of the letter, or in the whole tenor of Swift's life. He left the Whigs, as he now says, and as every incident in his life shows, because they developed views to which he could not adhere ; because they seemed to impair the privileges of his Church: because their conduct was factious and intolerant. In all this his judgment may have been mistaken : but that is no excuse for the often repeated charge of political inconsistency. That inconsistency has no reality save to those whose continuity of principle is nothing more than servile submission to all the tenets that pass current under a certain party name.

unfortunately differ from those which lead to favour and preferment." Are his opinions so dangerous as to give warrant for the attacks made on him? He has ever been against a Popish successor: he has ever justified the Revolution: he has attached no weight to the mere right of inheritance other than that given it by law and by popular opinion, both of which must yield to political expediency. He has always had a mortal antipathy against standing armies in time of peace.[1] He has always desired that Parliaments should be annual.[2] He disliked the monied interest in its opposition to the territorial, which he thought the safer basis for government. He feared the growth of the National debt. He feared still more the encroachments on the liberty of the subject,[3] by which the Government, whose excuse was the preservation of liberty, was compelled to defend itself. These were his opinions, "when he was in the world": if he has any, these are his opinions still: and he wishes only that a political catechism were published once a quarter by authority. Otherwise he may strive to make his court by uttering Whig

---

[1] It need not be said that Swift spoke in this with the prejudice of his day. But an opinion which has been forgiven to many modern politicians, although maintained against the experience of two centuries, need not surely be much of a reproach to Swift, maintained, as he maintained it, in common with nine-tenths of his contemporaries, and under the natural alarm which an innovation excites.

[2] This is one of the tenets to which Swift adhered: and his advocacy of it is an early proof of that scheme of parliamentary reform, coupled with a popular basis for monarchical government, by which he and those who sympathized with him, hoped to counteract the tyranny of the Whig oligarchy.

[3] Such as the suspension of *Habeas Corpus* in 1715 and 1716.

principles, and find that they have been exploded a month before, and that their utterance proves him only "a disaffected person."

Having thus given an account of his political faith, Swift turned again to his work for Ireland. He touched upon her follies as well as her wrongs. A proposal was now mooted for establishing a national Bank for Ireland. It provoked controversy and jealousy against the monied interest, which was the chief support of the Whig party. Suspicion of stock-jobbers, and of "funds of credit," and knowledge of the evils of the South Sea Company, probably supplied the motives of Swift's opposition to the scheme. Amongst other means of ridiculing it, he wrote a tract proposing to establish "A Swearer's Bank," the profits of which were to consist of fines rigorously exacted for the use of profane language. By much casuistry he justifies the project: he gravely meets objections, such as its possible encouragement of swearing. But his contributions to the controversy, in which he chose his side with some rashness, are otherwise of no more than passing interest. His next interference in Irish affairs had issues far more serious. There was at this time, admittedly, a very serious lack of copper coin in Ireland. It was so great as to hamper the small transactions of the poor, and render the payment of weekly or daily wages a matter of difficulty. The lack of coin seems to have dated only a few years back,[1]

---

[1] Prior, in his "*Observations on Coin in General, with some Proposals for regulating the Value of Coin in Ireland*" (Dublin, 1729), states that twenty years before, the copper coinage had been good and abundant.

and it was caused by the fact that the copper coinage was undervalued in the currency, and had consequently left the country.   Its place had been supplied
by a host of worthless coins, the private tokens used in
payment of wages, and the " raps " which were current amongst the lower peasantry. The want had
been duly reported to the English Cabinet: and it
was taken up there, not as a real grievance to be met
with speedy and scrupulous justice, but as a new opportunity for a job.   We only increase the difficulty
of understanding what follows, if we seek for too
great exactness of information, and expect to find,
either in the theories of 1720, a correct estimate of
political economy, or in the fierce invectives of partizans, a strict adherence to truth.   The patent to make
a new copper coinage was granted by the English
Government to one William Wood, who had some
connexion with the iron trade, and whose antecedents,
it appears, were not very creditable.   Naturally, according to the habit of the day, various officials had
to levy black mail on the transaction : and the amount
of the coinage had to be sufficiently large to enable
Wood to recoup himself and make his own profit.
It was fixed at £108,000 : an amount altogether
absurd, according to any estimate, unless the copper
coinage was to have more than its proper place in the
currency of the country.[1]   The greatest share of the

---

[1] In a *Scheme of the Money Matters of Ireland*, by John Browne
(Dublin, 1729), the total currency is reckoned at £514,000, of
which the gold is £500,000, the silver only £10,000, and the
copper £4,000. This is exclusive of the paper currency consisting
of bankers' notes, reckoned at £400,000. But Browne's authority

plunder was to fall to a lady, whose position was not without sufficient precedent at Court: but in whose case the somewhat blunt moral sense of the time had been stimulated into severity by party feeling. The Duchess of Kendal was to receive £10,000 from Wood. The patent had to pass through various offices, and receive various signatures: at each stage in its progress, and to each signatory, some gratification had doubtless to be paid. Finally, the plunder of Wood —whose claim, or whose hold, upon the Government it would be useless to attempt to explain—was to be so large that when the patent was finally recalled the compensation allowed to him was a pension of £3,000 a year for eight years.[1] These facts are sufficient proof that the groundwork, at least, of a somewhat scandalous job was here.

The patent passed on the 12th of July 1722. As an additional insult to Ireland, it appears to have been passed without any consultation with those responsible for her government, even though the Lord-Lieutenant happened to be in London at the time. The full facts could not become known all at once. It was not till more than a year afterwards that the two Houses of the Irish Parliament were so stirred by public feeling as to vary their usual submissive-

---

is not very trustworthy: and the author of a reply to one of his tracts (*Considerations on Seasonable Remarks*) denies that the currency, all included, can exceed £600,000.

[1] How far this was to cover the sums he had disbursed, including the bribes he had paid, it is impossible to say. It is not likely that any of the money that went to the Duchess of Kendal ever was repaid. The nation had probably to recoup Wood for his useless bribes.

ness by presenting memorials against the patent.
Wood published a reply in the *Flying Post* of 8th
October, 1723, which was only an aggravation of the
original offence. He claimed for the Prerogative
" the power to make the money of what metal, weight,
fineness, and denomination the King in his great
wisdom shall think fit ; to enforce its currency : and to
give the profit arising from the coinage to whom he
pleaseth." He confesses with astonishing effrontery,
that the coinage may not be all the Irish could wish :
but do they want to be like starving wretches who
will not take food that is not cooked exactly according to their fancy ?

So matters went on during the winter, the ill-will
gradually swelling. The Government began to awake
to a sense, not of the injustice, but of the inconveni-
ence that the injustice might bring. In March, 17$\frac{24}{23}$,
communications were passing between Lord Carteret,
as Secretary of State, and the Duke of Grafton as
Lord-Lieutenant, in regard to an inquiry: and on the
9th of April, 1724, that inquiry was at length opened
before a Committee of Privy Council at the Cockpit,
Whitehall. The memorials from both Houses had
been followed by addresses from Corporations, from
Quarter Sessions, from Trades Guilds. But some
more articulate, more definite, and more independent
mouthpiece for the common indignation, was wanted.
Then, and then only, was it that Swift stept in. The
indignation had already risen to boiling pitch : he
gave it voice, but it is not to be supposed that he
created the universal force of feeling which soon ani-

mated all Irishmen, merely by a skilful exaggeration of a fictitious grievance.

Swift's first pamphlet, published while the Committee of Inquiry was sitting in London, took the form of a letter written in the character of M. B. Drapier, directly to the Irish people. It was, so the title-page declared, "Very proper to be kept in every family": and, to promote its circulation, the author says he had "ordered the printer to sell it at the lowest rate."[1] The letter shows all the art that enabled Swift to sway at will the passions of men. In describing the patent, he uses the same sort of exaggeration that had been found in the memorials of the Irish Parliament. "If you beat down twelve English pence," he tells the Irish, "and carry the copper to the brazier, he will give you the nominal value, with but one penny of abatement. Do the same with Wood's halfpence, and you will get no more than a penny for your twelve pence." It is absurd to suppose either that this was true, or that Swift thought that it was true. His object was simply to put a scandalous transaction in the grossest aspect possible. Just as absurd are some of the pictures that he draws —of purchasers who will have to pay their debts in cartloads of Wood's trash, of two hundred and fifty

---

[1] The price was twopence: and both printing and paper are of the very poorest. There is a tradition at Delvill that the vault now to be found underneath the summer-house which was adorned with Stella's portrait, was used for the purpose of clandestine printing : and the tradition was confirmed by the finding of some type there, about forty years ago. But the story rests on no very sure foundation ; and it seems to imply an unnecessary caution, seeing that the publication of the letters was perfectly open.

horses that will be required to bring up to Dublin the half-yearly rental of Squire Conolly.[1] Swift wished to drag a political scandal to light; he chose to picture as immediate realities what were only to be conceived as remotely possible results. The device was one of the ordinary and recognized methods of political controversy then: later ages may judge whether it has since been discarded.

But apart from exaggeration, there was enough of real injustice in the matter. In the reign of James II.—no very severe comparison—a patent for copper coinage was granted, allowing thirty-two pence to be coined from each pound of copper, which was then intrinsically worth 18d. Wood's patent allowed thirty pence out of each pound, the pound being in 1723, intrinsically worth 12d. only. This was bad enough: but there was no guarantee that the coin should even reach the prescribed value. As a fact there were several varieties of Wood's coinage. Assays were of little value, especially as the Comptroller was to be paid by Wood himself. More than this, there was no real limit of the quantity issued. In previous patents, a clause had been inserted compelling the patentee to exchange his copper for its nominal value in the currency. Previous patents had, indeed, been little more than extensions of the custom common

---

[1] The mention of Conolly's name is not accidental. Conolly was Speaker of the House of Commons: was a close adherent of the Government: and had directed the action of the Duke of Grafton, then Lord-Lieutenant, when he was openly thwarted by Viscount Midleton, the Chancellor, whose advice he refused to follow, and who opposed the patent.

during the seventeenth century in Ireland, of private coinages. Wood's patent was not so limited: the moment the coinage passed from his hands, he had no further concern in it. With a silver coinage so scarce as it now was, it was easy to set afloat the copper coinage: it might be trusted, in the mass of heterogeneous coins, to tell few tales.

But even in the first letter, Swift enlarges the question from the details of the coinage. The half-pence are bad: but how, he asks, has this come about? He answers his own question: "because you in Ireland are far from the ear of the King, and cannot mislead him like Wood and his friends." "You must suffer unheard: your good coin will leave you, and you will be compelled to barter your goods against this dross." With a boldness of inconsistency that few but Swift could have ventured, he turns round to the cottar's point of view. The shopkeeper has been warned how his goods will go: now the cottar is warned that, with this dross as his only coin, he will find that he can buy nothing from the shop-keeper. "Do you fancy that we will part with our goods for a coinage that might as well be made of old kettles or pebbles?"

All classes will be wronged: and the wrong will be suffered because we are so helpless. What then is to be done? The answer is easy. Refuse this trash. Let it be the accursed thing in Israel. Have no fear of the royal prerogative: a prerogative strained is a thing which is not: and to give it heed is but dishonouring the King. You are bound by statute to take gold and silver : but it is at your option to take copper.   It is at your peril, as sane men, that you will take this trash.   The nation as one man, must bind itself to refuse : even the peasant should rather cling to his "raps" than accept this badge of slavery and starve.

The Report of the Committee of Inquiry was dated the 24th of July, 1724.   It is singularly inconclusive in its defence of the patent.   It compares the patents of former days : and urges as a justification for this, that whereas former patentees had paid £16 a year to the Crown and Comptroller, Wood—that is to say, the Irish people—was to pay £1000.   The assay is adduced as proving the soundness of the coin : but the only coins assayed were those coined after Lady-day, 1723, whereas all in circulation were coined before that date.[1]   Irish officials, it is admitted, were not consulted : but there was no reason, it is asserted, why they should be.   The main ground of accusation, in the flagrant disregard of Irish interests, and of Irish views, is absolutely ignored.   And yet this elaborate defence ends with the recommendation that this beneficial and necessary coinage should be limited to £40,000.

Before the Report of the Committee was published, a forecast of it and of the action of the Government was published in a London paper, and repeated in Harding's Newspaper, in Dublin, on the 1st of

---

[1] Mr. Southwell, one of the assayers, told Archbishop King that the orders were strict which limited the inquiry to the later date.

August, 1724.   The paragraph may have been meant as an assistance by a clumsy friend, or it may have been the attack of a more skilful enemy, of Wood. Wood, it was asserted, was willing to take goods for his coin, if silver were not forthcoming : he would restrict the amount to 5½d. in each payment, and it was hinted that unreasonable obstinacy might be met by exercise of the prerogative.

Swift had here just what he desired.   The Drapier's Second Letter is addressed on the 4th of August, 1724, to Harding, the printer, on the occasion of the paragraph.   The merits and details of the question are now laid aside.   Even Wood is almost forgotten in the vehemence of rage that a nation should be exposed to the menaces or to the mercy of such as he. He will restrict, forsooth !   So that our boasted freedom is held by the grace of Wood !   And there is talk of a proclamation !   If it comes, every honest citizen is bound to ignore what will be no more than a fiction based on error.   Once for all, resist: or waste no labour, but accept your inevitable yoke of slavery.

The Second Letter prepared men's minds for the Report.   That Report reached Dublin when the letter had suggested the indignation which Swift meant that the Report should kindle, and the third letter, of 25th August, fell on ground well prepared. This time the " Nobility and Gentry of Ireland " were addressed : and the tone adopted was very different from that of the previous papers.   The purpose of Swift in this letter is no longer to argue against a scheme which is universally condemned.

With a grave irony, he shows the utter absurdity of the position.   Is it true that the profit of an obscure mechanic is to be preferred "not only before the interests, but the very safety and being of a great Kingdom, and a Kingdom distinguished for its loyalty, perhaps above all others upon Earth?"

"Are not," he asks, "the people of Ireland born as free as those of England?   How have they forfeited their freedom?   Is not their Parliament as fair a representative of the people as that of England?   And has not their Privy Council as great, or a greater share in the administration of public affairs?   Are not they subjects of the same King?   Does not the same sun shine upon them?   And have they not the same God for their protector?   Am I a freeman in England and do I become a slave in six hours by crossing the Channel?"

The lies of the witnesses, the dishonesty of the patentee, the rottenness of the coinage—all these are cast aside, as if they were proved and needed no more said of them.   The independence of Ireland is what he insists on : and the duty resting upon the men of leading in her midst, to assert that independence. The King has granted the patent.   He cannot, it seems, withdraw it.   " Well then, it rests with us to consult his dignity by doing for him what he cannot do for himself, and accordingly to refuse every farthing of this worthless dross.   The well-being of Ireland clearly points to one course : it is for you to lead on it."

Swift probably guessed when he wrote this letter, with its tone of suppressed indignation, that it assumed an independence of spirit which did not really exist.   It was skilfully drawn so as to prepare men for a new appeal, and was far from a last word. For two months he waited: and on the 13th of October, 1724, the fourth and far the greatest of the Letters appeared. It was addressed "To the whole People of Ireland." Again it casts aside the lesser controversy as to the coinage and its conditions. Ireland is summoned to assert her independence, no longer as a decent and reasonable interpretation of her relations to England, but with the indignant voice of a nation that has borne her yoke of slavery to a degraded tyrant, far too long. She is to wrench her freedom from the crumbling and mouldy corruption of English misrule. There is not a line of the whole letter that is not instinct with life, and thrilling with sarcastic force. The flimsy technicalities of debate are torn to pieces. The phrase "depending kingdom," which, as applied to Ireland, had been made to justify any stretch of power, is "but a modern term of art": were it ten times true, it would be inapplicable here.

"Let who ever thinks otherwise,[1] I, M. B. Drapier, desire to be excepted: for I declare next under God, I depend only on the King my sovereign, and on the laws of my own country. And I am so far from depending upon the people of England, that if they should ever rebel against my sovereign (which God forbid !) I would be ready, at the first command from his Majesty, to take up arms against them, as some of my countrymen did against theirs at Preston. And if such a rebellion

---

[1] Expressions as faulty in point of grammar as this are not rare in Swift's prose, the strength of which lies in its clearness and flexibility rather than in technical correctness: but in the Drapier's letter, flaws had of course a special appropriateness which they had not elsewhere.

should prove so successful as to fix the Pretender on the throne of England, I would venture to transgress that Statute so far, as to lose every drop of my blood to hinder him from being King of Ireland." [1]

He is sick to death of the cant that one English governor has repeated after another. We are to be told, eternally, "to think of some good bills for encouraging of trade, and setting the poor to work; some further Acts against Popery, and for uniting Protestants." We all know the mixture of wheedling, flattery, and solemn promises, that would follow. But you can corrupt us no longer: you have wasted the wherewithal to bribe. You can betray us no longer: we must betray ourselves, if we be longer slaves. "But God be thanked, the best of them are only our fellow-subjects, and not our masters." Are we in Ireland to be the victims of a strained prerogative, long forgotten in England? Are we to be at the mercy of men ignorant of our wants, who "look upon us as a sort of savage Irish, whom our ancestors conquered several hundred years ago"? We need waste no words. The question is simply one of

---

[1] The manœuvre by which Swift managed to associate a suspicion of Jacobitism with his opponents, is one peculiarly characteristic: and so is the skill with which, in the next letter, he meets the objections to this paragraph, by half offering an extent of submission that might equally be embarrassing—a submission even to Jacobitism, if Jacobitism were to become strong enough. He does not commit himself, however: he fears a "spiteful interpretation." In short, he places the English Cabinet on the horns of a dilemma. "Am I to resist Jacobitism? Then what becomes of your doctrine of Ireland's dependency?" or, "Am I to become a Jacobite, if England bids me? Then, what becomes of your Protestant succession? Must even that give way to your desire to tyrannize?"

might against right, a question as old as human nature, but never brought into shorter compass. "The arguments on both sides are invincible: for, in reason, all Government without the consent of the governed is the very definition of slavery: but, in fact, eleven men well armed will certainly subdue one single man in his shirt." Force us then if you can: but so long as we have the power, we shall be free. We will take your coin, when, as your patentee threatens, it is melted down, and poured into our throats: but not till then.

If the English Government found in this letter a note of open defiance, they had themselves to blame. Their scheme, whether in its first suggestion good or bad for Ireland, had been carried out in a way to outrage all the decencies of government. Swift had at first poured his sarcasm on Wood: and the dangerous questions in the background might have been avoided by abandoning the scheme. Even after the Report was issued, he had ascribed its mistakes to Wood and his accomplices. The Government had remained obstinate: and now they found themselves confronted by open defiance all along the line. Unable to retrace their steps, they saw no way open to them but prosecution.

A proclamation was accordingly issued.[1] Harding, the printer of the letter, was thrown into prison, as if to shame the undoubted author into surrender. Ireland was now under a new rule. The Duke of Grafton, honest and well intentioned, but proud and

<hr>

[1] See Appendix VII.

dull, had failed to solve the difficulty, and had indeed been little trusted by the English Cabinet.[1] He had been thwarted at every turn by Viscount Midleton, who had sought to provide for his popularity in Ireland, by opposing the coinage, although he had been careful to keep on good terms with Walpole. The Duke was now recalled, and in his place, Lord Carteret was sent from the Secretaryship of State, into what was to him little less than banishment. He was sent to manage a difficulty which he had perhaps done something to foment. Whatever his faults, he was at least free from those of Grafton. If Grafton failed from dulness and timidity, it was his brilliant recklessness that prevented Carteret from reaching the highest pinnacle of success. He was versatile beyond all men of his day: and his versatility bewildered duller men. He had a breadth of scholarly and literary sympathy that forbade his absorption in the sphere of politics, and those for whom that sphere was everything, looked askance on his aberrations. He had a keenness of insight that detected tricks and corruption wherever they prevailed: but he met them chiefly with the sneer of the cynic. He refused to believe a Tory to be necessarily a traitor, and conceived an administration possible, which should strengthen itself by alliances amongst all moderate men, and not confine itself to those who bound themselves by party ties founded

---

[1] "A fair-weather pilot, that knew not what he had to do, when the first storm arose," are the words in which Walpole describes him.

as much on accident as reason. His talents enabled him to dispense with labour : his recklessness led him to despise it. Even when carrying out the behests of his own party, he refused to shut his eyes to their abuse of power, and neglected the maxims of orthodox Whiggism in the distribution of his patronage. Such had been his administration, hitherto, in England : and, as such, in Ireland it gained him the regard of Swift, the suspicion of Walpole. The vice-royalty of Carteret became an epoch in the life of Swift.

When Carteret had been nominated as Lord-Lieutenant in April, 1724, Swift had used the privilege of an old friend to write to him very freely on the subject of the coinage. Such a letter would in itself dispel the notion that Swift's only object was to find an excuse for a partizan attack upon the Government. For a month he awaited a reply : and then addressed Lord Carteret in a second letter, which is a masterpiece in its kind. "I have been long out of the world," he writes, "but have not forgotten what used to pass among those I lived with while I was in it : and I can say that during the experience of many years, and many changes in affairs, your Excellency, and one more,[1] who is not worthy to be compared to you, are the only great persons that ever refused to answer a letter from me, without regard to business, party, or greatness : and if I had

---

[1] This may have been the Duke of Chandos, though the Dean's principal complaint against that nobleman belonged to a later date. (See Scott's *Swift*, xviii. 224.)

not a peculiar esteem for your personal qualities, I should think myself to be acting a very inferior part, in making this complaint."

Fortunately for both, Lord Carteret did not seek to pursue the quarrel. He wrote in terms that more than soothed the ruffled feelings of Swift : and their friendly relations were renewed before Carteret's actual administration of Ireland began.[1]

Enraged at the proclamation, Swift met Carteret, soon after his arrival,[2] with angry expostulations. Carteret excused himself by the Virgilian quotation—

> Res dura, et regni novitas, me talia cogunt
> Moliri.

On this or some such occasion, it may have been that Swift replied by the not uncomplimentary outburst, "What in God's name, do *you* here ? Get you gone, and send us our boobies again."

The proclamation was issued on the 27th of October ; and Swift took a bold method of meeting it. This was a letter[3] addressed to Lord Midleton,

---

[1] The relations between the two were those of sympathy, interrupted only by the occasional jars which circumstances forced on, and in which each learned to respect the other's wit. On one occasion Swift was kept waiting for an audience, and is said to have written on the window of the waiting-room, the lines

> " My very good lord, 'tis a very hard task,
>   For a man to wait here, who has nothing to ask,"

under which Carteret wrote the reply,

> " My very good dean, there are few who come here,
>   But have something to ask, or something to fear."

[2] October 22nd.

[3] This letter Scott prints out of the proper order, as the sixth letter. He heads the letter, which in his edition professes to be printed from the Dublin edition of 1735, "Deanery House, Oct., 1724." The Dublin edition however dates it, at the end, "Deanery

the Lord Chancellor, defending the Drapier, and almost acknowledging himself the author of the letters. That the letter was actually sent there seems no reason to doubt, although it was not printed till more than ten years had passed. The fitness of its destination is clear. Midleton, although a Whig, had not concealed his dislike to the coinage. His office had however compelled him to be the first signatory to the proclamation. For years Swift and he had stood aloof : but now a common sympathy had brought them together, even though Midleton's official duties made him the direct agent of the oppression he disliked.

In this letter Swift takes up two accusations against the Drapier. He had estranged, so it was said, the Irish and the English nations from one another : and he had spoken injuriously of the royal prerogative. The first he dismisses briefly. He fears that the estrangement had a foundation other than the Drapier's words. Ignorance, disregard, contempt—these were the only means by which, hitherto, England had sought to bind Ireland to herself.

"As to Ireland, they know little more of it than they do of Mexico ; farther than that it is a country subject to the King of England, full of bogs, inhabited by wild Irish papists, who are kept in awe by mercenary troops sent from thence : and their general opinion is, that it were better for England if the whole island were sunk into the sea. . . . I have seen the grossest suppositions passed upon them ; that the wild Irish

House, Oct. 26, 1724." Swift may have known of the proclamation a day or two before its formal issue : or he may either in error, or with some purpose, have dated the letter a day or two before it was written.

were taken in toils : but that in some time they would grow so tame as to eat out of your hands."[1]

As for the prerogative, he is at a loss to see what crime the Drapier has committed. He will submit to be silent, if forced to be : but he will still "go and whisper among the reeds, not any reflection upon the wisdom of my countrymen, but only these few words, BEWARE OF WOOD'S HALFPENCE."[2]

The bill against Harding came before the Grand

[1] That this was not a mere rhetorical exaggeration of the Englishman's belief, is shown by the following passage from Burdy's *Life of Skelton.*   (Works, i., lxiii.)   "When he was in London, there was a man from the parish of Derriaghy, he assured us, that passed there for a wild Irishman, and was exhibited as a public show, dressed up with a false beard, artificial wings, and the like. Hundreds from all parts flocked to see a strange spectacle, which they had often heard of before : and among others, a Derriaghy man, who happened to be in London, came in the crowd, and saw the wild Irishman, a hideous figure, with a chain about him, cutting his capers before a gaping multitude. Yet notwithstanding his disguise, he soon discovered, that this wild Irishman was a neighbour's son, a sober civilised young man, who had left Derriaghy a little before him. When the show was finished, he went behind the scene, and cried out so as to be heard by his countryman, 'Derriaghy, Derriaghy.' Upon this the seeming wild Irishman, staring with surprise, spoke aloud, ' I'll go any place for Derriaghy.' They had then a private meeting, when he told him, that being destitute of money, he took that method of gulling the English, and succeeded far beyond his expectations."

[2] The stories repeated by Scott, of Swift's fear of detection by his servant, Blakeley, and of his having visited Harding in prison in the disguise of a clown, are foolish inventions. Swift was absolutely secure against detection, for the best of all reasons, that there was nothing to detect. His authorship of the Drapier's letters was notorious : and it is curious that Scott should have repeated stories like these, while on pages immediately following, he gives abundant evidence that the Dean was recognized as the Drapier by every street boy in Dublin. The question was only one of legal proof. Archbishop King all but told Lord Carteret that Swift was the author, and hinted that he was about formally to announce it.

Jury early in the Michaelmas term. By a letter of "Seasonable Advice," on the 11th of November the Drapier warned them of what was expected of them. "Shall *Jonathan* die," ran the Scriptural quotation, now in every one's mouth, "who hath wrought this great salvation in Israel? God forbid: as the Lord liveth, there shall not one hair of his head fall to the ground; for he hath wrought with God this day." Whiteshed, the Chief Justice, again attempted, as he had in Waters's case, to browbeat the jury. But it was in vain. The bill was thrown out: and Whiteshed could only show his resentment by the questionable means of dissolving the Grand Jury. Another Grand Jury was formed: but its elements were the same. The vindication of the Drapier was not enough: the war was carried into the enemy's camp by a present-ment against the halfpence. The City of Dublin was now fully roused. Authority was scouted: the agencies of the law had been made ridiculous by Whiteshed's impotent attempt to override the rules and customs of his office. It remained for Swift to follow up his triumph. He could afford to assume an apologetic tone: he had no longer to create an impression, but to confirm one created. The mob was on his side. The addresses of more august assemblies were now supplemented by those of the sworn associations of butchers and brewers, by the "Flying stationers" or newsboys, and by the Black Guard. At every street corner broad-sheets and ballads in his honour were sold. Every tavern had its club to celebrate the Drapier, and every convivial meeting rang with choruses in his honour. Some of the doggerel that was written in contempt of Wood, and in honour of the Patriot Drapier, was sorry enough. But other writings than those avowed by the Drapier, either came from his hand, or passed under his revision. At the most critical juncture, lines of his own were addressed to the people, urging resistance to the tyranny closing in upon them, and concluding thus :—

> "If yet to virtue you have some pretence,
> If yet ye are not lost to common-sense,
> Assist your patriot in your own defence.
> That stupid cant, 'he went too far,' despise,
> And know that to be brave is to be wise :
> Think how he struggled for your liberty,
> And give him freedom, whilst yourselves are free."

His friend Sheridan came to his assistance with a piece called "Tom Punsibi's dream," which represented the sufferings of Ireland from her more powerful neighbour, and hinted in no very obscure way at the parts played by the Duchess of Kendal and Walpole, in the affair of Wood. Other pieces held up White-shed to ridicule with such success that the vexation is said to have shortened his life.

It was in this full tide of triumph, that Swift published, on the 14th of December, 1724, his fifth letter, addressed to Viscount Molesworth,[1] closing the series for the present. Its tone is one of humble apology. "He is aware of his gross presumption in

---

[1] Lord Molesworth was one of those whose Whig connexions did not prevent his sympathy with the Drapier.

attempting to vindicate liberty with weapons so poor as he has at command. He must have been misled by trusting to the bad guidance of authors who fancied that the monarchy, either of England or of Ireland, was not quite a tyranny. But he is so deplorably ignorant, that he cannot even now withdraw the points found fault with." He is like "the dumb boy whose tongue found a passage for speech by the horror of seeing a dagger at his father's throat." "This," he goes on, "may lessen the wonder that a Tradesman, hid in privacy and silence, should cry out when the life and being of his political mother are attempted before his face, and by so infamous a hand." He can only promise that for the future he will bury at the bottom of his chest all the writings that treat of liberty : will never presume while in Ireland to bring them to the light of day : and will never forget the "climate I am in." Hitherto he has not shaken off the impression left by the works of Lord Molesworth himself, of Locke, and Molyneux, and Sidney, who talked of liberty as a common blessing. But now he will "grow wiser, and learn to consider my driver, the road I am in, and with whom I am yoked."

The Ministry were compelled to yield. As the controversy was closing for Swift, new pamphlets from his imitators continued to come forth. The description of the supposed execution of Wood was given, with his dying speech upon the scaffold. Dreary jokes were played upon his name, and the street cries on the subject were repeated in pamphlets to suit the taste of the day.[1]   Others took up a more dangerous line, and improved the triumph over the Government in the interests of the Jacobites.   "Honest" Shippen, the doughty champion of the cause, brought forward the affair of Wood in the English Parliament as a means of stirring ill-will against the Government of Walpole.   It was a use of his victory that Swift would scarcely have encouraged.   He strove to make it yield other fruit: and for at least ten years after the end of the Drapier's fight, he stood foremost amongst those whose advice and whose labour were spent in striving to right the wrongs which weighed down Ireland from within and from without.   The beginning of his work in this direction may be said to date from the Drapier's so-called seventh letter,[2] which although written about this time, did not appear till 1735.   It is much more a start on a new course, than a continuation of the past struggle.

Swift's future place and work in Ireland, belong, however, to another chapter.   At present it is well to look to the state of English administration there, as it was shaped by the struggle just ended.

The fierceness of the attack on his administration,

[1] Scott has published (vol. vii.) several pamphlets, which cannot be considered authentic, and which present no intrinsic evidence of Swift's authorship.   They not only repeat his arguments, and travel over ground which he had covered, but they are without any of his wit or humour.   Of those printed from p. 58 to p. 92, some are certainly not by Swift, including the "Short Defence" (p. 58), "The true State of the Case" (p. 64), the "Letter to Wood from his only Friend in Ireland" (p. 73), and the "Letter to Wood from a Quaker."   Others are doubtful.

[2] It forms the seventh in the series, only if we reckon the letter written from the Deanery House, and not in the character of the Drapier, as sixth.

led by Swift, had made Walpole resolve on a new course in Irish politics. The attack had been on two points in which he was most vitally concerned. One of these was the chief excellence, the other was the chief defect of his administration. There was nothing in which his administration was more able than its finance : there was nothing by which it was more deeply stained than its corruption. Swift's onslaught attacked a point of pride, because it decried a scheme which was connected with finance. It attacked a point of disgrace, because it exposed the corruption which entwined itself with the whole system of which Walpole was the head. Walpole disliked the exposure, but perhaps still more the financial defeat ; and the dislike prompted his new scheme for the government of Ireland. It was a novel version of the system of " thorough " familiarly associated with the names of Strafford and of Laud.

Walpole's plan was soon laid. Lord Carteret, as Lord-Lieutenant, was to be the governor of Ireland only in name. Some patronage might be exercised by him, though under the eye of criticism. The direction of the immediate steps to be taken might be in his hands, though in obedience to the dictates of general policy from England. The settlement of matters calling for the exercise of delicate tact on the spot might be left to him. But another influence was to be stronger. Carteret had really been dismissed from the Secretaryship of State, and Walpole had found in his appointment as Lord-Lieutenant at once a refined revenge for Carteret's opposition, and a satisfactory means of providing for Irish government.

Soon after Lord Carteret's appointment another vacancy occurred, that of the Primacy and the Archbishopric of Armagh. It had been held by Lindsay, who was appointed through Swift's influence, shortly before the death of the Queen. He had brought to the office a rigid Toryism that was suspected even of a Jacobite stain. His successor was a man of another cast. This was Dr. Hugh Boulter, before Bishop of Bristol and Dean of Christ Church, Oxford, who for nineteen years to come, is one of the most prominent figures in Irish history.

He was a man of undoubted vigour, and of admirable business powers. No detail escaped him. His vigilance was incessant. He noted every symptom of failing health in the holder of any office, whether high or low, and was ready betimes to recommend to his masters in England some scheme for changing, settling, re-arranging, all the placemen concerned, so as to lie more ready to his hand. He was in no way confined to the affairs natural to his calling, but subordinated these to political considerations, with absolute callousness. He had a keen eye for what was expedient in matters of finance, or trade, or law. More than this, we are bound to admit that he was a faithful, even a pertinacious, friend. If he took a man under his care, he never tired till he got him settled in some post. He never fretted when his favourites were repulsed : but quietly returned to the charge. He was without spiteful remembrance or ill-will. When any one who had opposed him yielded—and not a few did so yield—he was ready to receive him into favour, and to bury all grudges. Finally, he had no ignobly selfish ends. For nearly nineteen years, he held the garrison in Ireland : and during that time he amassed no private fortune, and compassed no material advantage for himself.

On the other hand, when we look at him as governor of Ireland, his whole attitude appears that of one who mocked at real justice. From first to last, through the correspondence in which for fourteen years he sets forth, with striking perspicacity, his views on Irish politics for the benefit of his masters at St. James's, there is but one tone with respect to the country he is set to govern. He came without one grain of Irish sympathy, and he never obtained or sought to obtain it. To him, an Englishman who had struck root in Irish soil was on the same footing with an Irishman, who by race, language, and religion, was an alien. "The English Party" ; "the English interest" ; "the friends of England,"—these words are ever recurring : nothing is to be done for the good of Ireland till it be shown that the good of England is concerned the same way. If Ireland is to be prosperous, it is only because Ireland prosperous is a benefit to England.

He recognizes perfectly what his own position is. "Many of our own original," he confesses at the outset, "esteem us Englishmen as intruders." He early discerns how widely spread is the notion of the "independency of this kingdom." He has few around him whom he can trust, and has to struggle almost single-handed.   It was a bold though not a very noble struggle.   It would not do to be too severe at first : and with some tact he was to urge that, good as the coinage was, it might, on the whole, wisely be withdrawn.   When the withdrawal came, he had to help in giving dignity to the retreat; and it was with some difficulty that he obtained a vote, thanking the King,—not for the "*wisdom*" of the act, as the Opposition were desirous of having it, so as to express their sense of the foolishness of the original design,—but, in more courtly terms, for his "*condescension.*"

This first difficulty got over, the policy he advocated was that of increasing, at all hazards, the English interest.   "All the great places must be filled with Englishmen, if we are to have quiet here." Over and over again this is the theme he urges. Even dissent has at times to be encouraged, in order to prevent Irish churchmen from waxing independent.

Set to govern Ireland, Boulter had clearness of vision enough to see that the task would be easier if Ireland were more prosperous.   To accomplish this, he set himself, with the dogged determination of a man who has a work to do, not with the ardour of a reformer.   He is instrumental in getting an Act passed enforcing the tillage of five acres out of every hundred.[1]   He strives to meet the distress caused by three successive bad harvests (1726, 1727, 1728),

---

[1] *Letters,* vol. i. p. 221.

by charitable distribution of bread and corn. He sees in the increasing emigration of many of the most industrious classes of Ireland not only a danger to the English interest, but a source of misery to those who, under false expectations, were carried as slaves to the American plantations; and, other means failing, he would fain stop it by the high hand of force. To counteract the spread at once of pauperism and of Roman Catholicism, he labours hard to strengthen the chartered schools, which sought to meet the difficulties by tearing asunder the natural bonds of the family, and dividing children from their parents. He was sincere so far as he went: but he handled even matters meant to benefit Ireland only from an English point of view. When a Bill essentially affecting the well-being of an Irish manufacture is rejected by the English Council, he finds matter for thanks to the English Ministers in the fact " that the rejection was not based *solely* on disregard for Ireland, but *also to some extent* on the notion that rejection would benefit England !"[1] And this he writes with no thought of sarcasm.

Such was the man who, during the whole of Swift's remaining years of activity, and through the viceroyalty of three governors, virtually ruled Ireland. It was exactly the sort of rule—narrow, obstinate, blind to all merit but submission—which most irritated a man like Swift. But it was wise in its day and generation. Each year confirmed Boulter's hold. "For five years," he can write in 1729, " the

---

[1] *Letters*, vol. ii. p. 62.

Government has been in English hands."   He gained
his ends : and even when a new proposal was broached
in reference to the coinage, in opposition to which
Swift took a strong part, Boulter carried the day
against the Drapier, and Swift could only show his
indignation by hanging out a black flag from his
Cathedral for the benefit of the Kevin Bail ![1]

[1] *Letters*, vol. ii. p. 246.   The Kevin Bail was the name given
to the mob of Swift's Liberty of St. Patrick's.   The name survives
in Kevin Street.

CHAPTER XIV

Swift's attractions to England—Invitations from Bolingbroke, Gay,
and Pope—The occupations of his friends—His visit in 1726
—Bolingbroke in later life—Arbuthnot—Pope—Gay—Atter-
bury and his banishment—Bathurst—Congreve—Peterborough
—Swift and the Temple family—His reception by his friends
—Dawley and Twickenham—Leicester House—Illness of
Esther Johnson—Swift's anxiety—The recovery—Swift and
Walpole—The Story of their dealings—Hopes of conciliation
dispelled—Return to barbarism—Swift's reception in Dublin
—*Gulliver's Travels*—The stratagem about the manuscript—
Conditions under which the book was written—Its motives
—Comparison of the different parts—Swift back in England
(1727)—Bathurst—Pulteney—Voltaire—Swift as ally of the
Opposition—The death of George I.—Walpole's power main-
tained—Swift's anxieties for Esther Johnson—Her relapse—
Back to his "lair"—The *Journal* at Holyhead—Swift in
solitude—His last sight of England.

EVEN during the early years of his residence in
Ireland, Swift had ever turned fondly to his associations in England : and as the fierceness of the
Drapier struggle was wearing off, these associations
were claiming a stronger hold upon him.   His

correspondence with one or other of the circle had never entirely ceased : and, during the recent years, that circle had come together again, had acquired additional strength in their literary position, and were not without hope of political influence as well. They were now beginning to look 'forward to Swift's rejoining them : and he had himself never abandoned the hope of being back amongst those friends with whom the most brilliant period of his life had been spent. During his years of retirement, he had been occupied on a work for which due appreciation would be found only in that circle, and the plan of which he had already imparted to some of them. As time goes on the correspondence increases : Swift looks forward to another visit to England : even though he feels that there is something in himself which may make the renewal of these old associations less pleasant. He knows how moods that he would fain check are asserting their power over him. He dwells over, perhaps exaggerates, these moods, with something of a morbid severity of self-judgment. The reaction after the years of excitement in England, and the comparatively slight interest which he could take in the scenes around him now, even when they yielded to him the excitement of the fray, had produced an increased inclination to dwell on trifles, to avoid exertion, to seek for the paltry pleasure of worthless flattery. "Nothing has convinced me so much," he writes to Bolingbroke,[1] before he had dipped actively into Irish politics, "that I am of a little subaltern

[1] Dec. 19, 1719.

spirit, *inopis atque pusilli animi*, as to reflect how I am forced into the most trifling friendships, to divert the vexation of former thoughts, and present objects." After he had begun his struggle for Irish independence, and was outwardly defying the Government, this mood was exchanged for one quite as morbid, and strangely in contrast with the bold attitude which Swift maintained to the world. "I, who am sunk under the prejudices of another education," so he writes to Pope,[1] "and am every day persuading myself that a dagger is at my throat, a halter about my neck, or chains about my feet, all prepared by those in power, can never arrive at the serenity of mind you possess." He felt the encroachments of that undue occupation about money, which his friends also remarked, but which was much more the effect of an exaggerated rigidity of self-discipline, than the product of avarice in the ordinary sense. He himself did not judge it tenderly. He confessed it nakedly to Bolingbroke : and received in return an edifying lecture on the subject from that' spendthrift philosopher and rakish moraliser.[2] His perception of these infirmities perhaps held him back for a time from the visit. But the attraction is too strong to be resisted. Everything calls him to England : "there" he says, "I made my friendships, there I left my desires."[3] In Ireland, "he had distributed his friendships in pennyworths to those about him that dis-

---

[1] Sept. 20, 1723.

[2] *Bolingbroke to Swift*, July 28, 1721.

[3] *Swift to Gay*, Jan. 8, 17$\frac{2\,7}{2\,8}$.

pleased him least ": but he had never ceased to consider it as a place of banishment, and the feeling
did not diminish, or wear off, with time.

Bolingbroke urged, as early as July, 1721, that
Swift should come to him in France ; and the invitation of Bolingbroke was followed before long by
invitations from others of the old circle.   At the close
of 1722, Gay renewed a correspondence long interrupted,[1] and impressed on Swift how his presence
was desired.   The letter stirred some feelings that
Swift had perhaps tried to quell.   "This humdrum
way of life," he says, "would be passable enough, if
you would let me alone."   He is almost angry at the
disturbance, which it will take him three months to
get rid of, and to school himself again into apathetic
dulness.   But in 1723, the invitations become more
persistent.   His friends will take no refusal.   In
June of that year, Bolingbroke returned from exile,
to fill a position even more prominent in the circle
than that vacated by Bishop Atterbury, whose banishment began at the same time that Bolingbroke's
ceased.[2]   Gay and Pope are occupied with new
literary schemes, on which they seek Swift's advice.
His old friends have again gathered round London,
and if the hopes of snatching power from the hands of

---

[1] *Gay to Swift*, Dec. 22, 1722.

[2] According to Atterbury's belief, Bolingbroke and he "were
exchanged." The opinion was one he continued to entertain :
but, although Mr. Elwin is disposed to think that it might not be
entirely without grounds, there seems scarcely to be such evidence
as would warrant us either in fixing a new stain on Bolingbroke's
character, or attributing to the English Government a singularly
objectless and foolish bargain.

Walpole were not very great, at least the danger of molestation in their own pursuits was past. Before Lord Oxford died, he seems to have been the centre of considerable political influence.[1] His death came in May, 1724. By his son, the father's invitation to Swift was renewed: and Swift can only answer that the scene in England might be sadly changed, and that the subsequent return to Ireland would be still more hard.[2] But in spite of hesitation the visit draws nearer. "You are getting into our vortex," Pope tells him: and each of the circle paints, after his own fashion, the new scene that will meet Swift. "So much of the old world and the old man in each of us has been altered that scarce a single thought of the one, any more than a single atom of the other, remains just the same"—so says Pope. "They are to meet together as mariners after a storm"—says Arbuthnot. At length, at the close of 1725, Swift made up his mind to the voyage; and in March $17\frac{2}{2}\frac{6}{5}$ he set out for London after an absence of twelve years.

Of that company, into the midst of whom Swift now returned, the most conspicuous member, Bolingbroke, was already aspiring, as the prospects of office

---

[1] See a letter from *Prior to Swift*, April 25, 1721.

[2] "I have many years frequently resolved to go for England, but was discouraged by considering what a scene I must expect to find by the death and exile of my friends, and a thousand other disgusting circumstances: and after all, to return back again into this enslaved country to which I am condemned during existence —for I cannot call it life—would be a mortification hard to support."—*Letter from Swift to the 2nd Lord Oxford*, Nov. 27, 1724. This letter is one of those amongst the Oxford MSS., for copies of which I am indebted to Mr. Elwin.

became more dim, to fill that place, described in his epitaph as "something more and better."[1]   He never was more assiduous in cultivating that gift of insincere moralizing with which he attempted to deceive others, and perhaps even himself, as to his real character.   In judging the moral standard of that Alcibiades of Queen Anne's age, there are many counts that we would have to add to the indictment which, by Swift, were either unnoticed or condoned. But even setting aside all the stains which rest upon the record of his public life, there remains much in the character and utterances of Bolingbroke that must have jarred on Swift.   Able as he was, Bolingbroke never could subdue that feeblest of all vanities, that leads a man to assume airs of affectation towards one, who, as he knows, can detect the transparent folly of his deception.   His pretentious philosophy went for nothing with Swift, who "doubted pretenders to retirement."   His vanity led him to indulge his inclination for a thin and superficial scepticism even in writing to the Dean, who turned upon him with some vigour of rebuke, unwilling as he always was to speak to his friends "as a divine."   Bolingbroke defended himself in terms that can scarcely have been more palatable to Swift, whose orthodoxy, sound as he persuaded himself that it was, at least required some management.   The offence which Bolingbroke gave by the empty mouthings that only

---

[1] "Here lies Henry St. John, in the reign of Queen Anne, Secretary of War, Secretary of State, and Viscount Bolingbroke: in the days of George I. and George II., something more and better."—*Epitaph in Battersea Church.*

irritated and disturbed, without satisfying any human soul, was not likely to be wiped out by still more flimsy defences of his religious attitude, by contemptuous patronizings of Christianity, and by his condemnations of the higher philosophy whose principles he understood as little as he practised the dictates of religion.[1]   In short he amused himself with a quasi-philosophical religion much as he did in devising inscriptions for his greenhouse, or decorations for Dawley Farm ; and his assumption of the part of theological amateur was little fitted to be pleasing to Swift.

Arbuthnot still retained his old central place amidst the company of wits, chiefly by the moral qualities that made him the superior of the others. By them his humour was rated more highly than their own, although to the world at large it was almost an unknown gift. Arbuthnot was forgetful of himself; he was indifferent to the ambitions that prompted jealousy amongst the rest.   He watched with the keenest interest the success of his brethren ; he guided, suggested, helped : but he remained careless about his own fame.   Convinced that amid the crowd of dunces, the best genius of the age was concentred in his own friends, he yet must have seen, as clearly as their detractors, the flaws in the character of each.   In the annals of our literature there are not a few men who have filled something of the part that he did : but none who has filled it with such complete success of self-abnegation.   It is a part that earns no

---

[1] See his letter to Swift of Sept. 12, 1724, throughout.

wide or high-sounding fame : but it is something in
an age of such envenomed detraction, and such vehemence of party hate, to have lived revered and
cherished by its men of "light and leading" : to have
trained their talents, to have condoned their faults :
to have died without losing their esteem : and yet
without one stain, in the midst of very general
corruption, on which the keen eyes of political partizans could fasten.

With Swift, however, Arbuthnot's influence was
specially strong. He had the rare tact of balancing
dangerous tendencies in a friend without having recourse to the certain irritation of rebuke. With
Swift's cynicism Arbuthnot had an underlying sympathy. In both men their cynicism was connected
closely with the most characteristic trait of their
genius, their peculiar humour, born of the age and
its experiences. The dominion of religious hypocrisy
was not yet forgotten : the loathing of the cant that
had made religious fervour of all kinds repulsive, was
still strong upon men's minds. But they were nause-
ated yet more by what had succeeded to that cant,
by the folly of the Wit-woulds who fancied that they
had crushed hypocrisy under their flaunting vice, and
whose foppery seemed to themselves wisdom. Between the two, men like Swift and Arbuthnot took
refuge in a peculiar humour that necessarily engen-
dered cynicism. In Swift we know to what that cynicism led, and what havoc it wrought : in Arbuthnot
its fruit was only a quiet and ironic apathy. He
never let it eat into his soul with the corroding force

from which Swift suffered. Full of affection, he knew how to bear trial with resignation, how to preserve his quiet gaiety even amid bodily torments. His very faults were those which never lost any man a friend. "He is not without fault," says Swift:[1] "there is a passage in Bede highly commending the piety and learning of the Irish in that age, where, after abundance of praises, he overthrows them all, by lamenting that, alas! they kept Easter at a wrong time of the year. So our doctor has every quality and virtue that can make a man amiable or useful: but alas! he hath a sort of slouch in his walk." No wonder, with a friend who knew his infirmities and his strength so well, that Swift held fast to the bond between them. "If there were a dozen Arbuthnots, I would burn my *Travels*," he says, after telling how the main motive of Gulliver is depreciation of mankind. To Arbuthnot, in turn, Swift's depth of feeling, cynical as it was, came as a relief after the superficial brilliancy of others in the circle. His own geniality had no need to dread contact with the growing harshness of Swift's temper, and his own dignity was too well preserved to be in danger from the onslaughts of Swift's arrogance of manner.

Passing to others in that circle, the intimacy between Pope and Swift has unquestionably a far greater place in our literary history. It was now at its closest. Before Swift had left England in 1714, he had already befriended Pope. To Pope as a Roman Catholic, the Whig party was naturally repug-

[1] *Swift to Pope*, Sept. 29, 1725.

nant: and this feeling had been strengthened by the help and admiration of Swift, and increased by the suspicions which, rightly or wrongly, Pope had conceived against Addison. When Swift returned, it was to find Pope completely estranged from those literary allies who belonged to the Whigs, and ready to join him in that natural infirmity of a literary clique, which flatters its own exclusiveness by banning the spirit of the times.

For Swift, his friendship with Pope stands midway between that with Arbuthnot and with Bolingbroke. It is not so mixed with suspicion as is the latter, not so full of kindly sympathy as the former. Swift was not blind to the ingrained insincerity which had taken deep root in Pope's nature, and here and there hints a little ridicule of his affectations. But the full extent of Pope's twists and contrivances was known to none of his contemporaries, and Swift was of all others the most likely to ignore or think lightly of them. They jarred on none of his own moods: they were too far removed from him to let him follow all their ramifications, or trace their hidden motives. And, apart from them, there was much in Pope's character to attract Swift. His very weakness appealed to Swift's strength. His keenness of temperament, his combination of sensitive tenderness with sarcastic virulence, his unfailing tendency to impress on every dispute some personal aspect, to find in his adherents personal friends, in his opponents personal enemies—all these had their counterpart in the more masculine character of Swift. Pope's eager attachment to the little circle amid which he moved, his violent condemnation of all that did not enter into their likes and dislikes—these, too, suited with the misanthropy of Swift, tempered as it was by love for his own friends.   Pope's literary models were just those that Swift admired, widely different as was the use each made of them.   Pope's absolute mastery of literary form; his strict limitation of subject: the unrivalled clearness and polish of his truisms,—all suited with Swift's preference for lucid and well-defined expression, for perfect common-sense, over cloudy abstraction, strained paradox, laboured intricacy, and their attendant absurdities.   But Pope accepted as a mere literary canon what was to Swift a deep-seated contempt for the limitations of human knowledge and of human power.

The two were now to meet at what may be deemed, in some respects, the height of their fame: and it was perhaps well for both that the meeting was not more prolonged, and the intercourse not more constant.   As it was they came together with the attraction of common tastes, common genius, common literary schemes; of gratitude on Pope's side for early and helpful introductions: of admiration on Swift's side for a lightness and gracefulness of touch which he could appreciate, but could not rival.

There was another of the circle whose character wins from posterity, as it did from his contemporaries, the leniency due to childlikeness and simplicity.   In early days, when Scriblerus was being planned, Swift saw in Gay the most likely assistant next to Arbuthnot, had he not been too young. But youth had passed without changing poor Gay, or weaning him from his carelessness, his imprudence, his want of self-respect. Swift, however, never judged friends too hardly. Gay's slovenly sensuality, his frivolity, his petty selfishness, his exaggerated self-importance, were all occasionally trying to his friends, Swift included. But he never upbraids Gay for his indecent complaints that patrons have not opened their purse-strings wide enough. He never grudges the poet the marvellous success that a year later made him the talk of the town. He only seeks to preserve for him, out of the clutches of his own thriftlessness, some of the solid fruits which that success brought. When Gay poses as a martyr, Swift admits his claim : perhaps all the more readily that it helped him to deal a blow at political enemies.

One other there was, now gone from the circle, and remembered only as a token of the persecution which genius was supposed wrongfully to have suffered at the hand of Walpole. Swift, at least, honestly believed that Atterbury was guiltless of Jacobite plottings. He ridiculed the episode of the dog Harlequin, through which the missing link in the proof of Atterbury's guilt was established : but ridiculed it in perfect good faith. There is no doubt now as to Atterbury's guilt : but it was then concealed from his friends by a process of Jesuitical prevarication, which leaves on Atterbury's character a worse stain even than that of treason, especially in a case where treason might be so far conscientious, and was at least not uncommon.   But Jesuitical as he was in this episode of his life, insincerity was not Atterbury's common failing.   He had left amongst the circle a memory which was not without its lasting effect. From him they had imbibed that refusal to subscribe to the tenet of the Whigs which regarded the Revolution as the beginning and end of the Constitution. From his whole character, his love of extremes, his anxiety to play a sensational part in some exciting drama, his resolute refusal to regard prudence or expediency in his bigoted attachment to a cause, even from his fiery vanity, the Bishop was fitted to make a deep and lasting impression upon those amongst whom his life had lain.   Warm and loving in all his private relations, with the tenderness of a woman, and the courage, if not the calm judgment, of a man, he held his place in the hearts of his friends, and made it impossible for them to believe that his public acts could be stained by duplicity and treason : and not a little of their indignant protest against the Government of Walpole, not a little of their claim to be the assertors of liberty in an age which bowed before a political autocrat, is to be traced to the work, to the spirit, to the trial, and to the banishment of Atterbury.

Others survived to remind Swift of the old brilliant days.   Lord Bathurst was full of gaiety now, at forty, as he remained when more than ninety years had passed over him, and had seen him the friend of Goldsmith and Sterne, as he had been of

Pope and Swift. Congreve, for whom Swift had made Tory powers propitious, when the stars were against Congreve's friends, the Whigs, was still as genial a companion as ever, in spite of increasing years, failing health, and the degrading patronage with which the Duchess of Marlborough, the daughter and heiress of the great duke, had enveloped him. Peterborough was still one of the company : still as fond of roaming as ever, still as warm in his friend-ships, still as full of eccentricities.

Arriving in March, 1726, Swift met with a reception that pleased and cheered him. There was one old tie, which had long been irksome, and which was finally broken, just before his arrival in London. The family of Sir William Temple had little of Swift's love. His relations with Lady Giffard, Temple's sister, had been avowedly hostile. Swift now addressed a letter to another of the Temple family, Lord Palmerston, on a trumpery matter connected with the occupation of certain rooms in Trinity College, which Lord Palmer-ston could assign, and from which a friend of the Dean found himself likely to be removed. Swift's letter was undoubtedly written in terms not unlikely to be offensive to Lord Palmerston, although the want of courtesy in the manner of urging the claim was probably caused only by Swift's morbid fear of being supposed to show undue subserviency. Lord Palmer-ston resented the tone of the letter : and with still worse taste reminded Swift of the regard due "to a family he owed so much to." This was precisely the phrase most certain to revive the rankling sore which early dependence had left in the mind of Swift: and in the state of Swift's mood at the time, it was sure to be resented. He turns upon his assailant in a letter which professes to be one of calm contempt, but which in reality shows in every line how deeply the shaft had wounded. Lord Palmerston's letter he describes, in terms of wild exaggeration, as "full of foul invectives, open reproaches, jesting flirts, and contumelious terms." "I own myself indebted to Sir William Temple," he proceeds, "for recommending me to the late King, although without success, and for his choice of me to take care of his posthumous writings. But I hope you will not charge my living in his family as an obligation, for I was educated to little purpose, if I retired to his house, on any other motives than the benefit of his conversation and advice, and the opportunity of pursuing my studies. For, being born to no fortune, I was at his death as far to seek as ever, and perhaps you will allow that I was of some use to him. This I will venture to say, that in the time when I had some little credit, I did fifty times more for fifty people, from whom I never received the least service or assistance."

Unquestionably Swift was not here so much resenting an actual injury as seizing on the opportunity offered him to pay off old scores. His relation to Sir William Temple had been—and no discussion of this or that phrase will get us beyond this—one in which poverty and genius had found themselves unwilling debtors to wealth, position, and complacent mediocrity. The results had been those which such relations always

have had, and always will have.   Swift paid his debt
by attention, respect, and care for his patron's memory.
But the family of Temple had abused him, and had
dropped hints of the material advantage derived by
Swift from the friendship, of his entire dependence
on Sir William, and of base ingratitude on his part.
This new offence was the spark which set the smoulder-
ing ashes ablaze.   The episode closed that chapter
in Swift's life, and left him free to dismiss it entirely
from his mind.

But otherwise his reception in England was
pleasant.   As one of his correspondents remarked to
him, "he was like the man who had hung all night
from a bush, and with the daylight found that his
heels were only two inches from the ground."   He
had dreamed, or had imagined that he dreamed, of
imprisonment and halters : but he found himself no
longer shunned as a dangerous associate.   The asperi-
ties of party had lessened in his absence.   He writes
on the 16th of April to Tickell : "I am here now a
month picking up the remnant of my old acquaintance, and descending to take new ones.   Your people
(*i.e.* the adherents of the Government) are very civil,
and I meet a thousand times better usage from them
than from that denomination in Ireland."   Gracious,
however, as was his reception in political circles, it
was elsewhere that his interest was centred.   Bolingbroke's new house at Dawley[1] was open to him,

---

[1] Dawley House, a remnant of which yet stands amidst a
dreary network of brickfield, and railway, and canal, lay between
West Drayton and Hayes.   It still bears traces of the picturesque
quaintness peculiar to the age when it was built ; but the char.

where the disappointed politician was, in Pope's words, "labouring to be unambitious, but labouring in unwilling soil"; was fitfully striving to repair the ravages of debauchery by a fare of ostentatious frugality, and was aping philosophy by a sort of stage idyllicism. Within a few miles was the village at Twickenham, where Pope was busy with freaks of miniature landscape gardening. Swift lived at first with Gay in his lodgings at Whitehall: and then during June and July he stayed, along with Gay, at Pope's villa. During these months, the three "Yahoos," as Bolingbroke, borrowing from Gulliver's phraseology by anticipation, called them, were busy over literary projects. Swift, Pope, and Arbuthnot, were planning the issue of their "Miscellanies." Gay, too, was busy over his Fables, which were to appear at Christmas. He was also working up the scheme suggested by Swift, of a Newgate pastoral, at length to take shape in the Beggar's Opera. Pope's genius was finding a new channel for itself in his "Dulness," which appeared two years later as the *Dunciad*. *Gulliver's Travels*, the fruit of Swift's years of retirement, were now receiving their finishing touches, and were canvassed and quoted amongst the company. At times, the friends rambled together through the country, renewing those memories of English life and

acteristic monument of Bolingbroke's occuption is the great Dawley wall, with which the estate was girt, still testifying to the solidity of the original workmanship. What surprises us chiefly in this and other houses of the time is, that with so much to choose from, Swift's contemporaries should have selected just that part of the neighbourhood of London which seems least capable of attracting any whose love of the country was real and not assumed.

scenery which Swift had gathered long ago.   At other times Congreve and Bolingbroke joined them at Twickenham, or they passed to Arbuthnot's lodgings in town.   Through Arbuthnot's influence, Swift opened a connection with the opposition court of the Prince and Princess of Wales, which seemed to offer new hopes of political influence, but led to passages in Swift's life which a biographer would fain omit.

This visit, brightened as it was by friendships renewed, was darkened by anxiety.   Stella's health was breaking, and he soon received news of her that caused him much alarm.   Those round her strove to hide the truth from Swift.   Mistress Dingley, blundering when blunders were possible, made Swift's anxiety ten times greater by suspense.   He wrote to Sheridan and Worrall, begging for news, quick, frequent, and above all, *true*.   In his letters to them and to Dr. Stopford the same mood is shown, eager to hide the truth from himself, yet determined to know the worst : unmanned by the thought of his possible loss, but yet forcing himself to look forwards, that he may arrange for the closing scene of that life, broken and tangled for his sake, in such a way as to keep scandal at a distance.   "For my part," he writes to Stopford,[1] "as I value life very little, so the poor casual remains of it, after such a loss, would be a burden that I must heartily beg God Almighty to enable me to bear. . . . They have writ me deceiving letters ; but Mr. Worrall has been so just and prudent as to tell me

---

[1] *Swift to Stopford,* July 20, 1726.

the truth : which, however racking, is better than to be struck on a sudden.—*Dear Jim, pardon me, I know not what I am saying : but believe me that violent friendship is much more lasting, and as much engaging, as violent love.*" The attention on Swift's part, at such a crisis, to outside decorum, has been blamed as heartless : "in case the matter should be desperate," he writes to Worrall,[1] "I would have you advise, if they come to town, that they should be lodged in some airy, healthy part, and not in the Deanery : which besides, you know, cannot but be a very improper thing for that house to breathe her last in."[2] Undoubtedly the words leave a grating sense of ill-timed and callous calculation : but we need not judge them too harshly. Into the secret of that long friendship we can never penetrate : but we know sufficiently its formal conditions. The letters show clearly enough how Swift is distracted by his grief. At the same time he is penetrated by the fear that a wrong word or act may give a false aspect to a tie which is the most sacred in his life. He is in a state of nervous anxiety. As each suggestion presents itself, as each precaution occurs to him, it is put down without waiting to think of its effect. " Forgive the inconsistencies," he says to Worrall, knowing how contending feelings have distracted him while he wrote, and how strange must seem the attitude in which he stood to Stella. Not for the first time, but now more completely than

---

[1] *Swift to Worrall*, July 15, 1726.

[2] The Deanery was in the most unhealthy district in Dublin, and was damp and ill-drained. The atmosphere in the Cathedral was dangerous to the health even of those who worshipped there.

ever, Swift's clear masculine perspicacity and his strong energy fail him, as the fibre of tenderness is touched in him.[1] "I look upon this to be the greatest event that can ever happen to me : but all my preparations will not suffice to let me bear it like a philosopher, nor altogether like a Christian." For the present, however, the blow which Swift dreaded, did not fall; and for a time Stella regained some strength.

Besides his literary and personal occupations, Swift had other thoughts during his visit. As regards politics, he was encouraged to hope that without loss either of honour or consistency, it was open to him to make terms with the new powers. In the end, the result proved that he either over-estimated his own capacity of surrendering his independence, or under-estimated the terms that would be exacted. His dealings during this visit, with Walpole, have been so much canvassed by opponents, that, for his justification, they demand a careful review.

Fortunately we have evidence enough to dispose of all doubt in the matter, and to save us from resorting to the ill-natured stories of the gossips.[2] From this evidence it appears, in the first place, that, whatever might be Swift's views with respect to

[1] Compare for similar but lesser incidents in his life, the death of his mother (vol. i. p. 248) ; of Mistress Long (p. 292) ; of young Harrison (p. 327) ; of Lady Ashburnham (p. 326) ; and, subsequently, of Gay (ii. p. 209).

[2] Our chief guides are : (1) a letter from Swift to Lady Betty Germaine, of 8th January, 173$\frac{5}{6}$: (2) one from Pope to Swift, of 3rd September, 1726 : (3) letters between Lord Peterborough and Swift in April, 1726 ; and (4) one from Swift to Dr. Stopford of 20th July, 1726.

Walpole, it was not Swift who first opened communications. " I was twice with the chief minister," he writes to Stopford on the 20th of July, "*the first time by invitation; the second time* at my desire, for an hour." When the first invitation came, Swift saw no reason to decline it. He had been specially careful not to attack Walpole personally, during the Drapier controversy. He had spoken with respect of Walpole's abilities. He had been well received by many of Walpole's own party. The violent pique which his literary friends formed against Walpole had not yet affected Swift. He still claimed to be an adherent of true Whiggism. But, further, he desired to make representations on behalf of Ireland: and he had a friend to help in Gay. On the other hand Walpole had heard of Swift's proposed visit to England. Archbishop Boulter,[1] Walpole's special emissary in Ireland, had written to give warning of it, and to urge that due watch should be kept over his motions while in England. Walpole may well have thought that he could improve on the advice of his emissary, by changing a powerful foe into a friend. Apparently the form which the first overtures took, was an invitation on the part of Walpole, to Swift and some of his friends, to dine with him at Chelsea.[2] The Dean accepted, and made a friendly remonstrance on the Minister's suspicion of innocent persons. He alluded, in all but name, to Gay, whom Walpole

---

[1] See *Boulter's Letters*, vol. i. p. 62.

[2] " He invited me and some of my friends to dine with him at Chelsea."—*Swift to Lady Betty Germaine*, Jan. 8, 173¾.

suspected to be the author of a libel against him, and who was thus debarred from Court favour. Walpole doubtless understood the allusion well enough : but he was shrewd enough to treasure up this undefined application, for use at a future time. At a dinner of this sort, grave political questions could scarcely, with propriety, be touched upon: but Swift had grave political questions to urge; and for this, amongst other reasons, he pursued the acquaintance. At this moment the ill-government of Ireland was his strongest thought. He had even pressed his views on the Princess of Wales, and had obtained her permission to renew his complaints, if she should come to be Queen.[1] It was for this, then, that he sought, through Lord Peterborough, a formal interview with Walpole. It was granted with a readiness, and with a choice of days, that Prime Ministers do not, one would fancy, generally grant to men whom they understand to come as suitors for favours.[2] Swift had no personal request to make. He came as the representative of Ireland, to ask the redress of her grievances as a right, and feeling that the boldness of his advice would be the best claim on the gratitude of the Minister. Walpole received him, not because he thought these grievances should be redressed, but because he wished, as a prudent Minister, to learn the nature of the charges, and, as a man of the world, to gain Swift. The interview led to nothing. "We

---

[1] *Swift to Lady Suffolk*, July 27, 1731. The original in the British Museum shows that Scott misprints the date slightly.
[2] *Lord Peterborough to Swift*, undated letter of April, 1726.

differed," says Swift, "on every point."   An account
of the interview was sent to Lord Peterborough, the
next day, by Swift, with a request that he would
show it to Sir Robert Walpole.[1]   This version of the
conversation must therefore be received as expressing
the absolute truth.

From it we learn that Swift, when the interview
began, at once approached the subject of Ireland.
Both he and Walpole seem to have been perfectly
frank with one another : but they quickly saw that
there was no basis for agreement.   Swift found that
Walpole, as he says, " had conceived opinions which I
could not reconcile to the notions I had of liberty."
There was nothing for it but to part : and in his letter
to Peterborough Swift sums up, as in a last word, the
grievances which he has so often urged elsewhere,[2]
that they may be again laid before Walpole.   There
is something significant in the closing argument
which Swift gives for consideration of these wrongs :
" because they have been all brought upon that
kingdom (Ireland) since the Revolution : which, however, is a blessing annually celebrated there with the
greatest zeal and sincerity."   These words, with their
cynical hint, exhibit a feeling which was coming over

[1] Walpole had been knighted, on the revival of the order of the
Bath, in June, 1725, referred to by Swift in his Ballad on
Quadrille.

> " The king of late drew forth his sword
>   (Thank God, 'twas not in wrath),
> And made of many a squire and lord
>   An unwashed Knight of Bath," etc.

[2] The grievances, like almost all those against which Swift
wrote and spoke, are all put forward from the point of view of the
English and Protestant settlers, not of the great mass of the Roman
Catholics of Ireland.   *Their* benefit was at most only incidental.

others besides Swift, as time went on. Neither he nor they would formally admit that their adherence to the principles of the Revolution was one whit less strong than it had been. But the conviction was none the less surely making way, that these benefits had been, in Ireland above all, purchased at no small cost. It was this growing conviction that drew Swift more widely apart from Walpole and the Whigs than he was ready to confess even to himself; and the divergence was quickly increased by association with the literary band, the first principle of whose creed was condemnation of all Walpole's acts.

An interview so important and so widely known as that of Swift and Walpole, was sure to breed a swarm of rumours. Swift, it was said, had been bought : the Drapier would be heard no more : some snug berth would be found where he could slumber in supreme content : and finally, it was said, the Bishopric of Cloyne had been given to him. Such rumours served Walpole's purpose admirably, and the spark of gossip was fanned into flame by him and his under-strappers. Presently Swift found that his hint for Gay at the Chelsea dinner was represented as a mean attempt to crave pardon for himself.[1] Swift spared no pains to make the real circumstances clear. Not only has he not sought promotion, but he will not, he says, accept it "except upon conditions that would not be granted."[2]

The hope of reconciliation, never strong, was now

---

[1] *Swift to Lady Betty Germaine*, Jan. 8, 173⅘.
[2] *Swift to Stopford*, July 20, 1726.

completely dead. "I absolutely broke with the first Minister," he says to Stopford, "and have never seen him since." The only result of the attempt was to estrange Swift from others indirectly connected with Walpole. Swift fancied that even with Lord Carteret, he could no longer be on friendly terms: "I am all to pieces," he says, "with the Lord-Lieutenant." He is "weary of being among Ministers whom he cannot govern, who are all rank Tories in Government, and worse than Whigs in Church."[1] But, strong as was Swift's conviction that the hopes of reconciliation were at an end, the overtures were renewed by Walpole. The renewal disposes, if need were, of any suspicion of undue compliance on the part of Swift. Writing on the 3rd of September, soon after Swift's departure from London, Pope, who was still on fairly good terms with Walpole, reported a conversation with him, in which the Minister had regretted Swift's premature departure, and had hinted at a possible remove to England.[2] It was then too late. Swift was already in communication with Pulteney, Walpole's most relentless foe.

Thus end the dealings between the two. It would be a speculation, not without an odd interest, to attempt to trace the possible results in our literature and in our politics of a closer union between the Drapier and the all-powerful Minister. It was perhaps fortunate for both that the scheme ended so soon as it did. When Swift was on the eve of another journey

[1] *Swift to Tickell*, July 7, 1726.
[2] *Pope to Swift*, Sept. 3, 1726.

to London, next year, he alludes almost jocularly to Walpole, and threatens that, failing better treatment, *vengeance ecclésiastique* will be his.[1] It is reasonable to interpret this as the expression of a broken amnesty : but even if we take it as a hint for renewing overtures of peace, it is scarcely such a renewal as would be hinted by a compliant and yet repulsed petitioner for the crumbs of ministerial favour.

Such are the plain facts of an important episode in Swift's career. They have been distorted by his enemies so as to bear an aspect to which nothing in Swift's conduct is akin. Proud, overbearing, prejudiced, in certain ways ambitious, and not seldom unjust—all these epithets no fair biographer can deny to be applicable to Swift. But weakly compliant he could not be, without ceasing to be himself. Distortion has been helped out by gossip. Chesterfield told a college tutor that he knew Swift had made an offer of his pen to Walpole as the price of preferment. The foundation of his knowledge was the report of Colonel Chartres, the man whose battered and noisome debauchery was of all things vilest in Swift's eyes. The story shows its own baselessness at every step, even were it not disproved by what we know. Other legends of the same kind copy one another so as to betray the unity of their fictitious origin. One of these tells of Walpole answering Swift's request for a change to England by pointing to a tree which transplantation had destroyed. Another puts the

---

[1] See *Swift to Mrs. Howard*, Nov. 17, 1726 ; also *Swift to Mrs. Howard*, Feb. 1, 17$\frac{26}{7}$.

metaphor of the tree in the mouth of Swift : and this time it is a falling tree to which Swift compares himself, meeting with rebuke from Walpole for having imitated the tree by leaning on a falling wall.

Leaving politics and literature behind, Swift faced the journey back to Ireland, with better hopes of Stella. Bolingbroke urged him to winter at Montpelier, and had it not been for anxieties at home, and for the gloomy warnings of his own lifelong malady which excitement aggravated, Swift might have agreed. He left London on the 15th of August, and after a journey of only seven days found himself in a scene "as unknown as the antipodes," where he could only dream of those he had left behind.[1] His departure was lamented by Pope in a letter which, strained as it is, shows clearly enough how Pope's feminine weakness clung for support to the stronger and more masculine intellect that was now dominating his own, and making his genius work according to its will.

On his return to Dublin Swift had striking evidence of the estimation in which he was held in the country whose love and reverence he held so lightly. A quick journey had carried him, as he deemed, from civilization to barbarism. When his ship was signalled in Dublin Bay, the citizens turned out to do him honour. The Corporation met the ship in wherries : the quays were decked with bunting : the bells were rung : and the city received, in gala fashion, her most beloved citizen. The contrast was strange, to the time when

---

[1] *Swift to Pope*, Aug. 30, 1726, wrongly dated Oct. 30, 1727, in the Dublin quarto, and in Scott.

he had taken possession of his deanery amidst insults, and had been avoided in the streets as a dangerous, because a fallen, man.

But the most pleasing circumstance to Swift was the fact that his absence from England was not to be long. He was to return in spring, and meanwhile he keeps up a brisk intercourse by letter with Gay, Pope, and Bolingbroke ; with Arbuthnot, Mrs. Howard, and Mr. Pulteney. The first were the partners in his literary schemes : Mrs. Howard gave him a hold on the centre of Opposition in Leicester House :[1] and Pulteney was cultivating his friendship, as the champion whose aid might best compass the organization of Walpole's foes.

But something of more lively interest to us connects itself with this visit to England. Swift left on the 15th of August : and early in November, *Gulliver's Travels* appeared.

In regard to no one of Swift's works was there, even from the first, so little real secrecy, as about this. For years before they were published, the *Travels* had been talked about, as familiarly known, amongst his friends.[2] Vanessa had read them : Bolingbroke, Gay, Pope, and Arbuthnot had joked on their episodes without reserve : and even Mrs. Howard

[1] The residence of the Prince of Wales.

[2] Miss Vanhomrigh refers to an incident in the *Travels* in a letter written about 1721 or 1722 : Bolingbroke speaks of them in a Letter to Swift of Jan. 1, 17$\frac{23}{24}$: again in a Letter of July 24, 1725 : Pope in a Letter of Sept. 14, 1725 : and Swift himself in a Letter to Pope of Sept. 29, 1725. As the time of their appearance approaches, the references become even more frequent in the correspondence of Swift and his friends.

writes to Swift as she could not have written without knowing that his authorship was an open secret. About the *Travels of Gulliver* almost the only mystery is the fact that the manuscript was conveyed to the printer by a secret channel. Swift felt some misgivings as to the effect of the book upon the political powers that were. He was little disposed to recoil from their avowed enmity : but neither did he wish, unnecessarily, to make the breach irreparable. The hesitation, on political grounds, was strengthened by another cause. Swift entertained doubts as to the vigour of his own powers. He never felt himself fitted to criticize his own works. Age had crept over, him, and his anxiety lest age should bring mental decay, was morbid in its intensity. The publication of *Gulliver* roused in him these misgivings. He paused before giving it to the world. When it was launched, he looked with nervous interest for the criticisms of his friends. He had, by the stratagem about the manuscript, left himself free to change and recast what might be condemned. This literary bashfulness, then, combined with political caution, supplied a reason for some slight concealment : but both arguments soon lost their strength. He had soon no terms to keep with the Government : fears ceased to disturb him as to the merits of the book.

Swift made no secret of his motive. He wrote, *Gulliver*, as he says, " to vex the world, rather than to divert it." [1] He " hated and detested that animal called man." As age grew on him, Swift's love of

---

[1] *Swift to Pope*, Sept. 29, 1725.

individuals had increased, but his general misanthropy had also deepened. "I love only individuals," he says. No one saw more clearly than himself, the ravages of that disease, misanthropy. He knew how ignoble it was. He was vexed with himself for the contempt he wasted on the poor Irish, whose sufferings and degradation he saw, and whose vindicator he had been. He envied those whose minds were free from the "fierce indignation that lacerated his heart."[1] Bitter against mankind, he could neither confine, nor master, his hatred. Thus upon the "foundation of misanthropy," to use Swift's own words, the "whole building of his *Travels* was erected." But plainly as he has told us the leading motive of the book, powerfully as that motive is stamped on it as a whole, vivid as is the impression which it leaves, our best means of gathering its full significance, of fixing its place in Swift's biography, is to compare one part with another. To trace the possible sources of suggestion, to estimate the indebtedness of Swift to his predecessors in the same line of allegory, is the business of a commentary and not of a biography. But the book itself must be examined, if we are to master an important chapter in the story of Swift's life.

[1] "A friend of his found him in this condition (weary of life) one day : and Swift, putting the question to him, whether corruptions and villanies of men in power, did not eat his flesh and exhaust his spirits? he answered, that in truth they did not : he then asked in a fury, Why—why—how can you help it, how can you avoid it? His friend calmly replied, Because I am commanded to the contrary, 'Fret not thyself because of the ungodly.' This raised a smile and changed the conversation to something less severe and sour."—Delany's *Observations on Lord Orrery's Remarks*, p. 148.

The scheme was one of those which took birth in the councils of Scriblerus, and many of its outlines must have been drawn even before Swift ceased to form one of that congenial circle. In the earlier and more aimless years of his banishment, these outlines were filled in: and the book received its finishing touches after that fierce struggle, which stirred Swift's energy once more, but which left him face to face with approaching old age, with the fire of his consuming indignation burning more fiercely than before. As we might expect each of these moods is reflected in the book.

It is in Lilliput that the original conception of the book is most apparent. It was intended to parody the style in which travels were dressed out for the public by the literary hacks of the day: and though it was not in Swift's nature to confine himself entirely to such an aim, he adheres to it with some fidelity. He carefully maintains the circumstantiality of the narrative: and preserves, with elaborate accuracy, the due proportion between the pigmies and their surroundings. He cannot refrain altogether from references to contemporary affairs: but his side strokes at Walpole, at the French wars, at the divisions of party and of sect, are occasional only, and not systematic. Mankind are ridiculed by the travesty of their works and ways in the court of Lilliput: but there is nothing unkindly in the laughter: and the humour with which Gulliver is made to accept in all good faith the honours and precedence which the pigmies of Lilliput confer, is much more apparent than any satiric bitterness.   It is only towards the close that Swift's words reveal the vehemence of anger against party divisions, bred in him during these weary years of banishment.

In Brobdingnag, the humour is not less, but the satire is far more bitter and intense.   Brobdingnag is not merely Lilliput seen, as Scott puts it, through the other end of the telescope.   To ridicule mankind by comparing them with pigmies was one thing: to make them contemptible by using them as a means of elevating a superior order of beings, was quite another.   In Lilliput the humour is on the surface: the satire is only occasional: in Brobdingnag the satire never allows itself to be forgotten long.   Human nature seemed to Swift contemptible chiefly for its infinite pettiness and triviality, for its endless and futile restlessness: for its pigmy strainings to create difficulties, for the blind folly with which it entangled itself in labours beyond its strength.   In the natives of Brobdingnag the leading feature is that massive simplicity after which Swift's soul longed.   Political science they deem a waste of time.   They have ceased to multiply books.   Of philosophy they are fortunate in having no conception.   To pursue legal niceties is, with them, a capital crime.   They are wise enough to see their own counterpart in creatures so contemptible as human beings, and are not blind to their own faults, reflected in these, "the most pernicious race of little odious vermin, that nature ever suffered to crawl upon the surface of the earth."   But human nature, in Gulliver, is content "to wink at its own

littleness," and to forget the gulf between itself and
the giants by which it is surrounded.

Yet bitter as is the drift of the satire in Brobdingnag, it is not without relief. We are carried on
by the story, and in amusement at the mishaps of
Gulliver we forget that we are laughing at ourselves.
But in Laputa, and the Houyhnhnms, we advance a
step further. The spirit of the allegory is changed.
We miss the nicely - adjusted proportions, and the
careful construction of the preceding voyages. ·It
is not without purpose that Gulliver is made to
return from Lilliput and Brobdingnag, by vaguely
described and almost miraculous means ; while from
Laputa he sails to the allied empire of Japan, and
from the Houyhnhnms prepares for his homeward
voyage as he would have done in starting from
Rotherhithe.   In the latter region we are no longer
in realms of pure fancy, but only in places where the
ordinary laws of nature are confounded in a bewil-
dering jumble. Fancy and reality are constantly
intermingled. As the Academy of Lagado comes
nearer to the type of human crotchet-mongers, and
as the Yahoo typifies more closely humanity, so the construction of the allegory fails, but so also the directness of the satire is increased.   In Lagado we are
in the midst of our familiar wits and Greshamites :
in Glubbdubdrib we see the falsities of our own
history exposed : in the Struldbrugs of Luggnagg
we see the hideousness that human nature would
present, were it but permitted to ripen to full maturity. So in the Yahoos we see a counterpart of

human nature, free only from the dangerous ingredient of "a little reason," which makes humanity more detestable. Swift speaks no longer with the mouth of Scriblerus, but with a voice whose reality falsifies the original scheme, and from a heart torn by that fierce anger that he vented on his kind.

The voyage to Laputa is especially full of faults of construction. Its strokes are constantly delivered, not with the impartiality of fable, but with the directness of personal spleen. The flaws in Atterbury's indictment might have served to give point to a political pamphlet,[1] but had no place in a satire on humanity. No medium of parable was necessary to prove that crazy and self-absorbed projectors were contemptible : but if, on the other hand, Swift meant to satirize anything else than the *abuse* of human powers of scientific investigation, his satire stands condemned by the logic of facts.

But, notwithstanding, this third voyage tells us much both of Swift's opinions and of his mood. It is there that he "is filled with melancholy" to find one class of projectors without repute—those who sought to make the public weal prevail. It is there that the confessions of those summoned from the grave repeat for us Swift's views on the notabilities of the past. Above all it is there that Gulliver finds the Struldbrugs, the unmitigated gloom of whose

---

[1] As a fact, the incident of the dog sent over to Atterbury, which was made much of in his trial, and which Swift makes Gulliver suggest to the Laputans as worthy of their attention, has been since proved to have suggested to the prosecution a correct train of evidence.

existence reflects the morbid despair with which Swift awaited old age.

If it is the voyages to Lilliput and to Brobdingnag, in which no thought of the satire they contain mingles with the interest of the story, that have proved most attractive to children, it is the voyage to the Houyhnhnms which is likely to excite most interest amongst men. On its coarseness we need not dwell. But beyond that fault, we may admit that the fable is clumsy: that the comparison between the Houyhnhnms and their counterparts is often mere verbal quibbling: that in the fancy of horses ruling men, there is no great depth of satiric force. We may admit further that Swift deserts matter of general concern, and here also attacks particular classes from motives of personal irritation. But all this fails to affect the real interest of the satire. Its central feature is contrast between the Houyhnhnm, representing, in himself, and as the negation of all human attributes, the type of Stoical and impassive dignity; and the Yahoo, as the picture of degradation, the points of distinction between whom and human beings gradually drop away, leaving humanity without one shred of defence for its own self-respect. Step by step the force of the contrast gains upon us: from a picture full of warning, it changes into a sentence of despair: with ruthless hand it throws down the fancied dignity of humanity, strips off the trappings and disguises with which we deceive ourselves, and leaves us face to face with the stern realities of our nature and our lot. Scathing, indeed, must have been the contempt for his kind, unrelenting the clearness of vision, that had to seek relief from smooth conventionalities by pitiless delineation such as this. But a further question still remains. We can scarcely doubt that Swift summed up the book in this contrast between Houyhnhnm and Yahoo. But did he satisfy himself with the ideal Houyhnhnm? Was the formal Stoicism, typified in the ruling caste, Swift's conception of the highest morality? Was that absence of passion and emotion, that negation of natural affection, that level and unlovable monotony, what Swift most admired? If it was so, then his ideals were shaped in a mould strangely different from anything in his own consciousness. If it was not so, was this picture but another ply of the satire on humanity, whose best ideals could be attained only by eliminating all that made life worth living, but whose passions and emotions, when ripened to full maturity, ended only in the loathsomeness of the Yahoo?

There was no long doubt as to the reception of the book. It was quickly in the mouths of all. By the highest and the lowest it was read, from the Cabinet Council to the nursery. Even the Duchess of Marlborough confesses that she has made a life-long mistake in treating its author as her foe.[1] If he is supposed to be the author, Gay tells him, he is not much injured by the belief. So Pope tells him,"he needed not have been so secret."[2] With what is

---

[1] *Gay to Swift*, Nov. 17, 1726.
[2] *Pope to Swift*, Nov. 16, 1726.

clearly nothing more than an affected ignorance, Pope repeats the story of the publication. "Motte received his copy, he tells me, he knew not from whence nor from whom, dropped at his house in the dark from a hackney coach : by computing the time, I find it was after you left England : so, for my part, I suspend my judgment."[1] Before the month was out Lord Peterborough and Mrs. Howard had written to Swift as to the author, the last signing herself by the name given to a maid of honour by *Gulliver*, as "Sieve Yahoo."[2] Swift answered her letter in a disguise that was pretty plainly an assumed one.[3]

The reception of the book pretty clearly proved that there were in Swift no signs of failing originality. And as for danger, Swift had followed his own

---

[1] It is surely not unreasonable to suppose that Pope himself may have been the friend who dropped the manuscript from the coach, and who takes this means of informing Swift how he had carried out his commission. From the *Dublin Weekly Journal*, it is possible to fix exactly the date when the first Dublin edition appeared. The *Journal* of Nov. 26, 1726, contains an advertisement of the book, as "in the press, and will be published next week." The *Journal* of Dec. 3 repeats the advertisement, with the heading "Just published." According to Gay's letter of Nov. 17, the London edition was issued about the 7th or 8th Nov. The intervening period is scarcely long enough for a pirated edition : and we are almost forced to conclude that Swift may have given help to the speedy issue of the book in Dublin.

[2] The names are inconsistent, one belonging to the third voyage, the other to the fourth.

[3] Swift's answer is amongst the Suffolk MSS. in the British Museum : and enables us to correct the form which it bears in Scott's edition. The date, not doubtful as Scott represents it, is *Nov.* 28, 1726 : the letter is written in a character much larger than Swift ordinarily used, and with some slight pretence of disguise, which could deceive no one accustomed to his handwriting : and lastly, it is signed, not "Jon. Swift," as Scott's edition represents, but "Lemuel Gulliver."

maxim too well to be troubled on that head. " In the
Attic Commonwealth," he says elsewhere,[1] "it was
the privilege and birthright of every citizen and poet
to rail aloud and in public, or to expose upon the
stage by name any person they pleased, though of
the greatest figure, whether a Cleon, an Hyperbolus,
an Alcibiades, or a Demosthenes : but, on the other
side, the least reflecting word let fall against the
people in general was immediately caught up and
revenged upon the authors, however considerable for
their quality or their merits. Whereas in England,
it is just the reverse of all this." Obedience to
the maxim saved the complacency and avoided the
anger of individuals. "None accuse it of particular
reflections," say Pope and Gay, using, curiously
enough, the very same words. Some, no doubt, like
the Lord ——, of whom Gay speaks ironically, were
offended that humanity, so honoured in having produced them, should be scurvily treated by Gulliver.
Others, like the dapper critic Lord Orrery at a later
day, were shocked that any man should be able to
find in himself the material for such a picture. But
for the most part men were amused, not hurt. The
cap fitted so well in general that it was assumed by
none in particular, and hung upon its pole, to the
delectation of the passers-by.

Some of his friends offered criticism on this or
that passage : a few thought Laputa dull : but all
read : and what pleased Swift even more, some
readers were persuaded of the actual truth of the story.

---

[1] The Author's Preface to the *Tale of a Tub*.

Arbuthnot had an acquaintance who sought for
Lilliput on the map. Another told him that he had
fallen in with a shipmaster who knew Gulliver well,
but found that the printer had made a mistake : he
lived in Wapping, not in Rotherhithe. An Irish
Bishop, Swift heard, thought the book full of lies,
and piqued himself on the discernment that "hardly
believed a word of it." Arbuthnot expects a run for
the book as great as that of *Bunyan :* Gulliver, he
thinks, is a happy man that at his age can write such
a merry book. As a merry book, it has been in
great measure accepted : and what was written to vex
mankind, has been largely read to amuse children.

When *Gulliver* had already taken the world by
storm, and was passing rapidly through new editions ;[1]
when the Miscellanies of Swift and Pope were almost
ready for issue,[2] Swift returned to England on the
9th of April, 1727. He was to be absent from
Dublin for six months, and meant to try the waters
of Aix-la-Chapelle. Arriving, he was seized on by
his friends as men seize a recovered treasure. Pope
longed to renew their rambles, to wander over Lord

---

[1] Even in France, parts of the book had already been dramatized, and appeared in the theatres.—*Lady Bolingbroke to Swift,*
about February, 172⅞. As to the editions of *Gulliver,* see
Appendix VIII.

[2] Pope announces to Swift (letter of March 8, 17⅞⅞) that the
"Miscellany is now quite printed." Pope was "prodigiously
pleased with the volume," in which he and Swift were "to walk
hand in hand down to posterity." It was one of an issue of three
volumes, which Ford, when afterwards writing to Swift, and
pressing the need of a collected edition of his works, calls "that
jumble with Pope, &c., in three volumes, which put me in a rage
whenever I meet them."—*Ford to Swift,* Nov. 6, 1733.

Bathurst's woods at Cirencester, to linger with him in the Grotto, and to plan new literary ventures. Pulteney and Bolingbroke were eager to brace him for new political struggles. Peterborough was bent on patching up the broken communications with Walpole. Arbuthnot sought him for pure friendship, Chesterfield for wit, and a greater than any, Voltaire, was now to cultivate the acquaintance of Gulliver, by delicate flattery. Leicester House was open to him, and by the ladies there he was encouraged to renew something of those habits of brow-beating that had been his privilege in the Court of Queen Anne. To the world, Swift's fame stood at its height. To himself, he was a prisoner who had but for a moment broken his prison bars to tantalize his eyes with a vision of freedom. He was a lonely old man, with ·affections all tangled, hope all gone, despair mastering him, the cloud of a great dread hanging over him, and bringing its gloom ever more closely over his life.

For the politics of the Opposition, Swift had little inclination. He was too old for the struggle, and it was only occasionally that he could rouse himself to it. But in the hopes and fears excited by the sudden death of George I. on the 11th of June, Swift did so far share. Leicester House was now the Court of St. James's. For the moment Walpole's power seemed to be at an end. Mrs. Howard, George the Second's mistress, so long cultivated by the wits, was now to be the dispenser of Court favour. Sir Spencer Compton became Minister, apparently for no other reason than that the Minister of George I. could scarcely be the Minister of his son. Walpole had, however, but a short time to wait. Compton was soon thrown aside for incapacity. Mrs. Howard soon showed how little real influence was hers. The Queen and Walpole became the real possessors of all power. The hopes of the Opposition dwindled away more quickly than they had grown.

To Swift the disappointment was not much. Harder blows were falling on him. His malady recurred with a fierceness it had never shown before. He felt his memory dulled, his brain benumbed, his reason threatened. And to add to this, news came to him in August, that Stella's health was again declining. Her strength was completely undermined: the momentary flicker had died away, and her end was near. To Sheridan and Worrall, Swift writes in language of even more bitter anguish than that of the year before. He cannot face the blow: he cannot come to see her die. Let them tell him only the bare fact, with no circumstances: these he could not bear to read. Why should he struggle against his own malady? Was he to live only that he might lose all that made life worth having? "What," he cries, "am I to do in this world? I am able to hold up my sorry head no longer."

The blow lingers yet before it falls. His own malady lightens. But his hopes and interest in English politics were ended. All called him to Dublin, where his home was, where he may be near, if not present at, Stella's death-bed, where he may creep to his own lair when reason fails. Even the society of those he most prized in England became irksome, and he abruptly quitted Pope's house at Twickenham, where he had been staying, for London. About the middle of September, with grief and foreboding at his heart, he quits, for the last time, the circles that he loved so well.

By a curious chance there has turned up a memorial of Swift, on this sad journey homewards, which gives us a picture, drawn for no eye but his own, of his state of mind in this gloomiest moment of a gloomy life. It is rarely that we can get any utterances of a man's mind so completely natural—casual stones, as it were, cast aside, that might have gone to the construction of something greater : the wayward freaks of fancy that show us how Swift's pen was moved by each passing whim.[1] Reaching Holyhead on the 24th of September (1727), he found that the packet had left ; and stress of weather as well as the want of passengers prevented his crossing for more than a week. During that week, he wrote, in a little notebook that he had picked up from George Dodington's desk, and that is now preserved at South Kensington, an account of his lonely thoughts from day to day. Here and there, he cannot avoid recurring "to the suspense he is in about his dearest friend"; but, for the most part, the notebook, where it does not bear upon his own doings during these dismal days, is occupied with the woes of the country to which he is doomed, and reflections on the literary

---

[1] For the contents of the Notebook, see Appendix IX.

topics which he has discussed with his friends at Dawley, and Twickenham, and Whitehall. It is thus he breaks out in regard to Ireland :—

> " Remove me from this land of slaves,
>   Where all are fools, and all are knaves.
>   Where every fool and knave is bought,
>   Yet kindly sells himself for nought.
>   Where Whig and Tory fiercely fight
>   Who's in the wrong, who in the right,
>   And when their country lies at stake
>   They only fight for fighting's sake ;
>   While English sharpers take the pay,
>   And then stand by to see fair play.
>   Meantime the Whig is always winner,
>   And for his courage gets—a dinner."

Reflection over the literary schemes which occupied the mind of Pope, and which had doubtless formed the subject of much earnest discussion in the evenings at the Twickenham villa, leads Swift in his solitude to pen these memorable lines, as a testament to posterity :

"I do hereby give notice to posterity, that having been the author of several writings, both in prose and verse, which have passed with good success, it hath drawn upon me the censure of innumerable attempters and imitators and censurers, many of whose names I know, but shall in this be wiser than Virgil and Horace, by not delivering their names down to future ages ; and at the same time disappoint that tribe of writers whose chief end next to that of getting bread, was an ambition of getting their names upon record, by answering or retorting their scurrilities : and would slily have made use of my resentment to let the future world know that there were such persons now in being. I do therefore charge my successors in fame, by virtue of being an Ancient two hundred years hence, to follow the same method. Dennis, Blackmore, Bentley, and several

others, will reap great advantage by those who have not
observed my rule.   And Heaven forgive Mr. Pope, who hath so
grievously transgressed it, by transmitting so many names of
forgotten memory, full at length, to be known by readers in
succeeding times, who perhaps may be seduced to Duck Lane
and Grub Street, and there find some of the very treatises he
mentions in his Satires.   I heartily applaud my own innocency
and prudence upon this occasion, who never named above six
authors of remarkable worthlessness.   Let the fame of the rest
be upon Mr. Pope and his children.   Mr. Gay, although more
sparingly, hath gone upon the same mistake."

The *Journal* itself, with its minute record of these
days, is a curious proof of self-inspection.   We see
even in this glimpse of his inner mood how utterly
impossible it was for him to rest.   The minutest
circumstance is tortured into an occupation.   He
discusses his own relations to the homely figures
round him : he sees them moving like ghosts about
him, as strange and as insignificant to him, as he is to
them.   "By my conscience," he says, "I believe even
Cæsar would be the same without his army at his
back."[1]   Powerful as was the weapon he wielded in
his satire, he is forced to confess it powerless here.
He amuses himself by planning how he would act,
were it always thus with him.   His dreams carry him
back to Pope and Bolingbroke, strangely jumbled up
with anticipations of his Dublin life.   He sees them
in his Cathedral, where nothing was as it ought to be,
where no servants were at hand, and all the surplices

[1] There is a curious parallel to these words of the *Journal*, to
be found in the voyage to Brobdingnag.   Speaking of an indignity
he had to suffer in his solitude amidst the giants, "the King of
Great Britain himself," Gulliver says, "in my condition, must
have undergone the same distress."

were locked up, and the pews broken. To crown all, Bolingbroke was preaching from his pulpit; and vexing Swift by quoting Wycherley by name.

Amidst such phantoms of those that cherished him, and to whom his thoughts were so ready to turn back: amidst such gloomy anticipations of the home that awaited him for what remained of his life; in anxiety, in restlessness, in gloom; Swift passed for the last time out of the brilliant circle in England, and came again to take his place at the head of the small band that were struggling against the wrongs of Ireland.

CHAPTER XV

THE LAST CHAPTER IN SWIFT'S PUBLIC WORK

1727–1737

ÆTAT. 60–70

Swift's autumn in Ireland—Stella's approaching end—Their rela-
tions in the last scene—Stella's Will—Her death—The funeral
—The blank in Swift's life—" Only a woman's hair "—Swift
on Irish politics—Statement of Irish wrongs—The remedies
proposed by others than Swift—Lord Molesworth—Thomas
Prior—Arthur Dobbs—Swift's place in these discussions—
Answer to a Memorial, &c.—*Maxims controlled in Ireland*—
A Short view of the State of Ireland—*A Modest Proposal, &c.*
—*Answer to the Craftsman*—Swift and the Corporation—
Traulus—Swift's speech at the Guildhall—*Advice to the
Freemen of Dublin*—Swift and the defence of the Church—
The Bills for residence and for division of benefices—Swift's
anger with the Bishops—*Modus* for the Tithe on Hemp—The
tithe on Agistment—Swift and the *Legion Club*—Swift and
English politics—Sympathy with the professions of Boling-
broke and Pulteney—Swift's *Proposal for virtue.*

SWIFT had quitted Pope's house at Twickenham
with a haste that looked like flight. He had buried
himself for a short time in London and then left
England for ever. A cloud was hanging over him,
under the gloom of which he must suffer alone. The
brilliant affectations of Dawley, the keen and self-
absorbed satire of Twickenham, were no medicines fit

for his disease. Disappointments had now brought their last, and by far their worst, result, in deep-rooted misanthropy, strengthening its grasp upon his whole nature year by year. Ill-health and infirmities were forcing him to feel that he was a drag upon the society of the wits. Lastly, and more than all, he feared that his maladies might have results for which he could not ask their sympathy without possibly provoking their sneers. Dreary as it was, there was no place for him but home.

In his lonely Deanery House Swift passed an autumn that must have been sad enough. The blow that had been lifted for a short time, was now surely descending on her to whom his heart clung most earnestly of all on earth. There could be no ending but one to the consumption that had laid its grasp on her : and for these few months Swift waited, with what torturing grief we know by the letters he had written when absent in London.[1]

---

[1] It is curious how little of reference there is to Esther Johnson, in Swift's correspondence with his literary friends. Only Boling-broke, whose taste was none of the most fastidious, mentions the name of Stella two or three times ; and then with words of fashionable cant, entirely incongruous in the circumstances. In Sept. 1724, he desires to hear Swift

" Inter vina fugam Stellæ mærere protervæ."

"Your *Star*," he writes in July 1725, "will probably hinder you from taking the journey" (to England). With still more gross vulgarity, he sends (in Feb. 172$\frac{4}{5}$) some fans which Swift is to "dispose of to the present Stella, whoever she may be." Esther Johnson had then just rallied from an almost fatal illness, so we may guess how Swift received such jests. In no letter to Boling-broke does Swift mention her name. Even Addison knew her only in Ireland.

Of the last scene of that life, whose faithful love and devotion have won for themselves immortality, we know but little. Stories have been told of what passed between Esther Johnson and the Dean, so inconsistent that we are left to choose between them, on the best grounds that we may.[1] What seems in some respects a fairly well authenticated story, represents their parting to have had some added bitterness from the harshness of Swift. It is Sheridan who tells us that, on the approach of death, Stella besought Swift to acknowledge their marriage before the world: that his only answer was to turn on his heel, and quit her presence for ever: and that her last hours were spent in inveighing against the cruelty of him on whom all her life's devotion had been spent. If the evidence, however, has been satisfactorily dealt with, in its own place, we are entitled to set aside a story which would reflect on Swift more hardly than any other recorded incident. Without repeating here the details of argument, it is enough to sum up the impression which the various traditions give us of the general features of Stella's last days. The final scene in what had been a long mystery, whose full meaning was perhaps not clear even to the chief actors themselves, was now approaching. Stella had been content to fulfil her part of the bond by unquestioning and unfailing love. Swift had paid her by an affection, which, severe and abnormal as was the restraint he placed on it, was the warmest

---

[1] These are dealt with, in detail, and the evidence for each is examined, in Appendix No. V.

feeling of his life. That bond had been sealed by a formal union, kept secret from the world. The refusal to announce it came, originally, from Swift: and whether or not he made any offer of an avowal, as time went on, and as the way seemed open for it, this would not affect the painful impression which the original refusal must have left on Stella. In her last hours, this impression may have recurred with peculiar bitterness: and not from resentment, or from unwillingness to accede to her dying request, but only from the pain that her regrets would cause, Swift may have withdrawn from a death-bed, whose pangs he could do nothing to alleviate. That he watched the course of the last struggle, that he longed passionately for any gleam of hope, and that when the end came, he looked back on the past with no feeling but the bitterest sorrow, on the future with no prospect but of loneliness and gloom, we believe to be as certain as any fact recorded in Swift's biography. But with all his sensitivity, and amid all his gloom, Swift's later words never once reveal remorse, or suggest that different action of his own might have broken through, or even lightened, the decree of fate.

The end did not come very rapidly. Pain and asthmatic oppression did their work slowly. On the 30th of December, Esther Johnson made a Will,[1] in which she bequeathed the interest of her fortune to her mother, Mrs. Mose, still living at Farnham, and to her sister Ann, now Mrs. Filby: after the death of both to go towards the stipend of a chaplain in Dr.

---

[1] See Appendix X.

Steevens's Hospital in Dublin. The Will contains but little reference to Swift, save as it leaves to him certain papers, which we may presume included his own letters : and entrusts him with the duty of acting as trustee for his own cousin, Mrs. Honoria Swanson, in respect of a small legacy which Esther Johnson left her.   But on the other hand, this very trust seems to preclude the idea of anger on Stella's part ; and the provisions of the Will are precisely those with which Swift indicated his agreement in a letter written from London more than a year before.[1]   If any inference is to be drawn from the Will itself, it is certainly not that Esther Johnson wrote it when moved by resentment against Swift : but rather that she faithfully fulfilled his directions, both as to its main provisions, and as to those minor points, with which his name is connected.

At six o'clock on the evening of Sunday, the 28th of January, 17$\frac{2}{2}\frac{8}{7}$, the end came.   It appears from the paper which Swift began to write the same night, that he had some company with him at dinner, according to his usual custom.[2]   A note was brought to him at eight in the evening : but it was only at eleven o'clock that he found himself alone with his grief, with no solace but to think on what he had lost— "the truest, most virtuous, and valuable friend, that

---

[1] *Swift to Worrall*, July 15, 1726.

[2] The entertainments of Dublin society seemed to have been apportioned with a certain regularity.   The dinners at the Deanery took place on Sundays : and Thursdays were the regular nights on which Dr. Helsham and Dr. Delany entertained at Delville.   See Mrs. Delany's Autobiography.

I, or perhaps any other person, was ever blessed with." [1]
In words that were perhaps never meant for any eye
but his own, he wrote down his feelings, and the record
of her character, beginning that night, and continuing
from day to day, save when "his head aches, and he
can write no more."

On the evening of Tuesday, the 30th of January,
Stella was buried in St. Patrick's, according to the
directions of her Will. Following the custom of the
time, the funeral took place late at night : and from
the situation of the grave, near the southern door of
the Cathedral, the lights of the attendants at the
last ceremony gleamed through the window opposite
the Deanery. Swift, though he had her body placed
where her ashes might one day lie side by side with
his own, [2] was too ill to be present at the funeral, and
could not bear even the ordeal of seeing the lights
which told of the work going on within the church.
They "removed him into another apartment," that
he might not see the gleam that lighted that grave
in which was laid the long and faithful devotion of
a lifetime, and in whose silence reposes that secret
of Swift's life which, whether for compassion or for indignant blame, has roused so much of human interest. [3]

Henceforward he must strive and suffer alone.
The tenderness, of which his attachment to Stella had

[1] Character of Mrs. Johnson. See Appendix XI. Born on the
13th of March, 16$\frac{81}{82}$, Stella had not completed her forty-sixth year
at the time of her death.

[2] Quite recently a fresh excavation in the Cathedral revealed a
coffin which contained the bones both of the Dean and Stella.

[3] The epitaph on the tablet, which now hangs near that of Swift,
is poor, and the work of an unknown hand later than Swift's day.

been the strongest symptom, deeply as it had struck its roots into his nature, withered into cynicism. But a lock of Stella's hair is said to have been found in Swift's desk, when his own fight was ended, and on the paper in which it was wrapt were written words that have become proverbial for the burden of pathos that their forced brevity seems to hide—" Only a woman's hair." To comment on them would be inept and futile : it is for each reader to read his own meaning into them. But can they cover only the cold sneer of heartless cynicism? Was it cynicism that conjured up in his loneliness the ghosts of the love, and tenderness, and devotion, that had come like rays of light across the tragedy of his life? Was it a sneer that prompted the passionate confession of helplessness to utter all the meaning that lay in that little lock of hair?

Lonely, suffering, and comfortless, in the great Deanery House, that seemed a type of the gloom that lay before him, Swift felt with morbid bitterness the blank that had fallen on his life. All that was good was leaving him : his interests were dying out : his letters are filled with reflections on himself : his hatred of those amongst whom his lot was cast, became more and more irrepressible, although he admits how unreasonable it was. All his harshness, all his prejudices, all his impatience of contradiction, all his love of money, increased tenfold. · But crushed, as we know he was, Swift seems to have shown but little of his inner feelings to the world. Throughout his life he bore his burdens with much secrecy. He allowed his friends to speak of that malady that filled him with such ghastly forebodings, in the tone of light comment, that suited their own passing ailments. Dark as his future was to himself, he did not show its full gloom to his friends. He still amused himself with their affairs : he still sought to have a bright place in their regard : he continued, even, to give hopes of coming back to them some day : and meanwhile he affected an interest in the success of the literary schemes on which they were busy, and from which they were gathering new renown.

For himself, he turns again, with some concentration, to the work of an Irish patriot. The Drapier's letters had achieved for him a position of commanding authority : he had now to drive that authority home.

Both the evils and the proposed remedies had reached a new development since we glanced at them in the years that preceded the Drapier's letters. Few, even amongst the narrow clique that ruled her, doubted that the state of Ireland was utterly wrong, and called imperiously for a remedy : and we have already seen how the need of reform had been urged even before the Drapier's letters appeared. These letters had lifted the struggle on to a new platform ; but they had been only the beginning of the later struggle. Bold assertions of Ireland's independence had been made : one victory, at least, over the tyranny of the official clique had been won. It remained to guide that victory in the right direction, and to show its effects all along the line.

Others than Swift saw the evils and brought

forward proposals of reform. Foremost amongst these was Viscount Molesworth, who, in 1723, had discussed the radical ills of Ireland drastically enough.[1] The "whole economy of agriculture," he says, "is neglected." He sees the first blot in the land system, in the rack-renting, which made it impossible for the tenant to improve, knowing as he did, that every penny laid out on the land was not only lost, but would ultimately go to increase his rent, or the fine for renewal of his lease, when the lease expired. Not venturing to appeal to the stringent remedy of law, he would bring a powerful public opinion to tell upon an unreasonable landlord. "If," he says, "a landlord turns out a good, old, improving tenant, let him suffer under the obloquy of his country."[2] He denounces the conduct of the landlords in destroying roads; in taking advantage of the disabilities of Roman Catholic tenants : in failing to make themselves, in any way, the guides or leaders of the classes dependent on them. But for the tenants, too, he has reforms to propose. Large farms of three or four hundred acres were commonly taken by the tenants only from motives of a mistaken pride; and, unable to stock or work them, the tenants sublet to others lower than themselves—those "cottagers," whose rent was drained from their life's blood, and who could keep

---

[1] *Some Considerations for the Promoting of Agriculture and Employing the Poor*, by R(obert) L(ord) V(iscount) M(olesworth), 1723.

[2] It is curious to note, in this proposal of Viscount Molesworth, the germs of the custom of boycotting which has so developed in our own day, as to have acquired a name which will puzzle future etymologists.

themselves alive only by being thieves or the harbourers of thieves. Hence had arisen those curses of the land, the land-jobbers, who ground the tenants more hardly than the landlords themselves. The holdings, Lord Molesworth maintains, must be strictly limited; they must be for definite terms; and all subletting must be forbidden. He would extend still further a sort of paternal government. Instead of hunting down the Roman Catholic priest, and compelling him to subsist on precarious alms extorted from a starving peasantry, he boldly proposes that Government should undertake the payment of the priests, and thus provide for their loyalty more surely than by a hundred penal Acts. He would establish a school of agriculture in each county : and would teach the rudiments of the art to children instead of their primer. The custom of gleaning, or "leasing," as it was called, had spread so far as to be a real burden on the farmer, who found one-tenth or more of his crops carried off by the hordes of thieving mendicants, who plundered before his eyes, and who were only to be driven away by main force. They were a pest, like that of the Egyptian locusts, and their idle sorning called for the severe action of the law. The too numerous holidays of the Roman Catholic Church must be limited. The crowds of hedgers and vagabonds must be shipped off by compulsory emigration. Fisheries must be fostered : all restrictive monopolies removed : and encouragement given to Irish trade. And finally, Parliamentary representation must be improved by giving the suffrage to the leaseholders, instead of confining it to the freeholders, who were often men of inferior wealth and station.

The tract of Lord Molesworth was answered by one who bore more hardly on the landlords, and stated with greater energy of invective the sufferings of the tenants.[1]　Others took a lower tone.　They spoke with bated breath, and with humble apology, of the wrongs of Ireland.　They found the sole hope of remedy in proving that her weal might benefit England, and craved for her the liberty to exist, because her existence might be good for the mother country. But Lord Molesworth's lead was followed by others of a better type, and amongst these were Thomas Prior, the author of the *List of Absentees*, and Arthur Dobbs, who wrote an *Essay on the Trade of Ireland*, in 1729.

The specific which the latter urges above all, is to create a yeomanry by means of fixed tenures. "Would the landlords," he says, "fix the tenures and possessions of their tenants upon a lasting and certain foundation, by leases of lives renewable or fee-farms, I would not doubt to find our people soon become industrious, and frugal to the utmost."　He knows that the nobility and gentry will object: but if the land is to be improved, if pauperism is to be checked, if landlords are to be anything else than reckless squireens grinding an uncertain income out of a starving tenantry, if the vampires of middlemen are to be stamped out, thus, and thus only, can it be done. But with fixed tenures imposed on the landlords, he

---

[1] *Considerations upon Considerations for promoting of Agriculture.*　1724.

would have restrictions for tenants too.   Farms must
be neither less than forty, nor more than one hundred
and sixty acres.   They are not to be divisible.   Each
is to have but one farmhouse.   Subletting is to be
illegal.   The scheme was bold enough : but it still
presupposed a national energy, to rouse which something more than theoretic proposals was needed.

Alongside of these there were a crowd of lesser
proposals.   Some urged the use of tormentil for bark
in tanning, so as to preserve an industry which was
dying out for lack of timber.[1]   Others urged the
use of Kilkenny coal, so as to stop the importation
from Whitehaven.[2]   Others again urged the establishment of "Lombards" or money-lending offices, secured
by the public credit, and under Government inspection.
All these schemes showed rather the ferment in men's
minds, than the existence of any settled plan of
reform, or any confidence in the resources of national
energy and independence.

In all those appeals for reform, one thing must not
be forgotten.   They were spoken, not from the heart
of Ireland, but from those who were in great measure
mere outsiders.   The mass of the Roman Catholic
population was slipping, past all hope of reclamation,
out of the hands of the ruling class.   Here and there,
moderate schemes of toleration were proposed,[3] which

---

[1] *The Method of Tanning without Bark.*   Dublin, 1729.

[2] *The Case of many Thousand Poor Inhabitants of Dublin.*
Dublin, 1729.

[3] As by Edward Synge, who as Prebendary of St. Patrick's
preached a sermon in October, 1725 (on the anniversary of the
Irish Rebellion), urging a modified toleration, as a step towards
proselytizing.

might enlist the sympathies and loyalty of Roman Catholics. But such proposals were rare : and for the most part, the dense mass behind the smaller divisions, and sects, and parties of the English minority, is unheeded and unknown, except by the few, like Swift, whose view reached out beyond the little intricacies of party struggles, into the darkness beyond.

On almost every one of the proposals that we have mentioned, Swift had something to say. By the Drapier's letters he had roused a feeling that all the other reformers together could not have kindled. Theories, and nostrums, and fancied remedies were all well in their way : Swift had given the one thing needful in the motive power that had galvanized into life the dead national feeling ; and this new energy it was his object to keep alive.

Swift's tracts themselves best explain their purpose. In one bearing the title, *An Answer to a Paper called a Memorial of the poor Inhabitants, Tradesmen, and Labourers of the Kingdom of Ireland*,[1] he states broadly the evils which had their foundation in the very necessity of things. What now meets his view, is—

"The fair issue of things begun upon party rage, while some sacrificed the public to fury, and others to ambition : while a spirit of faction and oppression reigned in every part of the

---

[1] In Scott's edition, which is more faulty in regard to these Irish pamphlets than in almost any other point, this is dated 1738, instead of 1728. The date is correct in the Dublin edition of 1735 : and it is further proved by the reference, which the *Answer* contains, to the "lately produced" paper on *The State of Ireland*, which was printed in 1727.

country, where gentlemen, instead of consulting the ease of their tenants, or cultivating their lands, were worrying one another upon points of Whig and Tory, of High Church and Low Church : which no more concerned them than the long and famous controversy of strops for razors : while agriculture was wholly discouraged, and consequently half the farmers and labourers, and poorer tradesmen, forced to beggary or banishment. 'Wisdom crieth in the streets : Because I have called on you : I have stretched out my hand and no man regarded : but ye have set at nought all my counsels, and would none of my reproof : I also will laugh at your calamity, and mock when your fear cometh.'"

With these words he casts aside their puny theories : "I have done with your memorial,"[1] he says ; "you have spoken as a stranger, and as of a country which is left at liberty to enjoy the benefits of nature, and to make the best of those advantages which God has given it, in soil, climate and situation."

On such an assumption they cannot but be wrong, for no such privilege belongs to Ireland : it is not hers to enjoy the "benefits of nature." Only utter ignorance could have assumed it : and on the ground that this privilege is denied her, Swift takes up the battle in her name.

With absolute calmness of logic, but with unrelenting force of sarcasm, he lays bare her wrongs. There is no mincing of matters : no softening of the stern reality. "Every squire, almost to a man, is an

---

[1] The memorial was written by John Browne, who turns up in various guises in all these Irish disputes : and the confusion into which the editor, who acted in Scott's name, has fallen, is nowhere more conspicuous than here. First came the memorial : then Swift's answer printed by Scott : then, lastly, the apology of Browne, which Scott prints before Swift's answer to the Memorial, although it is dated ten days after, and is intelligible only as a reply to Swift.

oppressor of the clergy, a racker of his tenants, a
jobber of all public works, very proud, and generally
illiterate." Thus he begins a page of description:
and it may be taken as a specimen of his tone. The
absentees are not only wrong: he absolutely over-
whelms in sarcasm their craven abnegation of their
birthright, their servile imitation of English fashions.
They go to England, "to be preceded by thousands,
and neglected by millions." No hope, then, may be
looked for from the landed gentry. But still, slaves
as we Irish are, we may stand together. "Nature
has instructed even a brood of goslings to stick
together, while the kite is hovering over their heads."
Ireland must be her own saviour and must work out
her own redemption. Let us only have the brute
instinct, to be true to our own kind.

Swift's insistence on Irish grievances was neither
that of the political agitator, nor that of the theorist,
who entered into the details of possible improvements.
His purpose was too sincere, his knowledge of Irish
wrongs too real, to allow him to become an agitator;
his sarcasm was too fierce, to allow him to become a
theoretical reformer. What strikes us most in all
these tracts is the deliberate incisiveness of their
irony, the despairing bitterness that gives them finish
and completeness. In another tract, published as
early as 1724,[1] he shows, one by one, how the ordinary rules that guide us in regard to other nations
are utterly fallacious when applied to Ireland. In

---

[1] *Maxims controlled in Ireland.* In modern language, this might
well have been entitled, "The theories of political economy proved
to have no application to Ireland."

a third,[1] he catalogues in regular order the possible adjuncts and conditions of prosperity, and shows how the very negative of each is present in Ireland. "If we flourish, it is against every law of nature and of reason : like the thorn of Glastonbury, which blossoms in the midst of winter." He draws a fanciful picture of what Ireland might seem to a stranger, favoured as she is by nature : but he breaks from it in despair.

"My heart is too heavy to continue this irony longer : for it is manifest, that whatever stranger took such a journey, would be apt to think himself travelling in Lapland or Iceland, rather than in a country so favoured by nature as ours, both in fruitfulness of soil, and temperature of climate. The miserable dens, and diet, and dwelling of the people : the general desolation in most parts of the Kingdom : the old seats of the nobility and gentry all in ruins, and no new ones in their stead : the families of farmers, who pay great rents, living in filth and nastiness upon butter-milk and potatoes, without a shoe or stocking to their feet, or a house as convenient as an English hogsty, to receive them. These may indeed be comfortable sights to an English spectator, who comes for a short time, only to learn the language, and returns back to his own country, whither he finds all his wealth transmitted. *Nostra miseria magna est.*"

Nothing shows Swift's genius in these Irish tracts more conclusively than the marvellously simple materials with which he maintains their force. He enters into the questions with no intricacy, he treats them with no variety of view. Setting aside all those tracts which careful scrutiny shows to be falsely ascribed to Swift, it is surprising how small is the range amongst the rest.[2] They have all one end and one

---

[1] *A Short View of the State of Ireland*, 1727.
[2] This is a matter which could be fully dealt with only in re-

aim: "Be independent." Law cannot help: theory is futile: English selfishness has left us little. But if we can gain anything we can gain it by self-assertion, and by that alone. Swift is quite well acquainted with the current nostrums. He names almost all of them. He speaks of Prior with approbation.[1] He deals out a patronizing nod to this or that scheme. But he never lingers long over any one. He saw that the evil lay deeper, and that it could be cured only by giving to Ireland the motive power of independence, by kindling her energy through withering sarcasm, derisive scorn, and fiercest indignation. The sarcasm and the indignation are for the English selfishness: the scorn for Irish imbecility and weakness. He repeats over and over again the same advice. "Quit yourselves like men; be strong. Curb your follies, and resist the fantastic taste for foreign luxuries. Know that your strength is in the plough and not in the depopulated pasture lands." "Ajax was mad, when he mistook a flock of sheep for his enemies: but we shall never be sober until we have the same way of thinking."

Perhaps the greatest, certainly the most characteristic, of Swift's efforts in this direction, is his "*Modest*

editing the works. But again it must be pointed out, that we should err widely in accepting all the tracts as genuine which Scott's edition attributes to Swift. The descriptive notes, which preface the tracts in that edition, are frequently contradicted by the tracts themselves. On the authority of that odd pedant, Dr. Barrett, tracts are accepted by Scott's amanuensis, which are often inconsistent with Swift's views, feeble travesties of his style, and which scarcely pretend even to imitate his wit.

[1] *Proposal that the Ladies wear Irish Manufactures.* See Scott's *Swift* (2nd edit.), vol. vii. p. 260.

Proposal for preventing the Children of Poor People in Ireland from being a Burden to their Parents or the Country." It was published in 1729, when, even from Archbishop Boulter's letters, we learn that people were starving in hundreds through the famine, and that the dead were left unburied before their own doors. English civilization was shamed by the sight, and to Swift at least it seemed no moment to be silent. His sarcasm was never applied with more deadly seriousness of purpose. With the grave and decent self-respect of a reformer, who knows the value of the proposal he has to make, Swift propounds his scheme. There is no strain in the language with which the state of matters is described : but the very simplicity and matter-of-fact tone that are assumed, make the description all the more telling. Of a million and a half inhabitants, about two hundred thousand may be the number of those who are bringing children into the world : of these about thirty thousand can provide for their children. There remain one hundred and seventy thousand whose case has to be met : and the pamphlet assumes as an admitted truth, that no method yet proposed can meet that case. Agriculture and handicrafts, we have not : and though stealing offers an employment, yet complete proficiency in that calling is not often attained under the age of six. What then has to be done ?

With the calm deliberation of a statistician calculating the food supply of the country, Swift brings forward his suggestion. He has inquired into the facts : and finds that a well-grown child of a year old, is a most delicious, nourishing, and wholesome food, whether stewed, roasted, baked, or boiled : and he makes no doubt that it will equally serve in a fricassee or a ragout. The charge for nourishing such a child, in the present scale, will be about two shillings per annum, "rags included" : and " he believes no gentle-man will repine to give ten shillings for the carcase of a good fat child." The mother will have eight shillings net profit.

In the same tone, he dilates upon the advantages of the scheme. Refinements have been suggested to him. The flesh of young lads and maidens, too, might, it is thought, be put to the same use. But with all respect, he sees difficulties : and chiefly because "some scrupulous persons might be apt to censure such a practice (though indeed very unjustly) as a little bordering upon cruelty : which, I confess, has always been with me the strongest objection against any project, how well soever intended." As he concludes with an earnest, but modest enforcement of his scheme, he is careful to add that he has no personal motive ; his own children are all past the age when he could make a profit of them.

No work of Swift's has been more canvassed : none more variously estimated : and none more grievously misunderstood. Some have esteemed it a heartless piece of ridicule, a callous laugh raised out of abject misery. Men who might have been expected to see more clearly, have shuddered, in well-simulated horror, at a cynicism which they have found too strong for their nerves. So to interpret it, is to misread it as entirely as the Frenchman did, who took it as a grave and practical suggestion, and who fancied that Swift in sober earnest proposed that infants in Ireland should be used for food. In truth, the ridicule is but a thin disguise. From beginning to end, it is laden with grave and torturing bitterness. Each touch of calm and ghastly humour, is added with the gravity of the surgeon who probes a wound to the quick. Swift's clearness of vision laid the woes of Ireland bare to him; he has left them on record for all time. Molesworth, and Dobbs, and Prior, and Browne, are all forgotten : can England ever forget what lies on her conscience, while Swift's *Modest Proposal* continues to be read ?

Alongside of the *Modest Proposal* we may read another tract which has much the same character, though with application more restricted. In 1730, the *Craftsman* had made some strong remarks on the facilities recently given for the recruiting of the French army in Ireland. The incident, as we see from Archbishop Boulter's letters,[1] had caused some alarm amongst the Government adherents, who found their own transaction wearing an untoward aspect. The *Craftsman* had seized the opportunity: and Swift, whose sympathies were with the *Craftsman*, added to the agitation by his ironical reply. "Why hinder the recruiting ?" he asks, in all simplicity. "Do you not know how the loss of these recruits will benefit Ireland ? Elsewhere, no doubt, men are the sinews

[1] See Boulter's *Letters*, vol. ii. p. 30.

of a nation : but this is a maxim 'controlled' in Ireland. What we want is depopulation. Make Ireland a desert, and all will be well. Have a grazier and his family for every 2000 acres, and then we shall be as England wishes us to be. If the army is idle, let it find employment in gathering taxes. If we still need more depletion, take our surplus to the colonies and employ them as a screen between his Majesty's subjects and their savage neighbours. When our island is a desert, we will send all our raw material to England, and receive from her all our manufactured articles. A leather coinage will be all we want, separated, as we shall then be, from all human kind. We shall have lost all : but we may be left in peace, as we shall have no more to tempt the plunderer." The *Modest Proposal* has had thousands of readers for one that this *Answer to the Craftsman* has had. The *Proposal* needs much less knowledge of Irish affairs for its apprehension : but, special as is its object, the irony of the *Answer* is as perfect in its way.

With one or two other leaders of what was so far a National Party in Ireland, Swift became an oracle in all matters affecting the public weal. Whatever differences might before have divided them, Swift and Archbishop King were now entirely united as Irish patriots.[1] Disputes and perplexities were sub-

---

[1] King's bitterness, in his old age, was almost equal to that of Swift himself. Burdy, in his *Life of Skelton*, tells a story of King, which shows how he regarded the Irish authorities. A young nobleman, who had just taken his degree, was brought to be introduced to the Archbishop, who sat propt up with pillows.

mitted to their decision, and to Swift, above all, an unstinted reverence was paid. A reference to some incidents in which he was concerned, may help to give us an idea of the position that he held in these later years. In 1729 he received the freedom of the city from the Corporation. Permanently settled in Ireland for life, he began to accept, with a pretence of gratification, the homage of praise so lavishly offered to him. The days of prosecution were ended: but instead, the snarling of opponents fretted him, and he seems to have resolved, by the acceptance of proffered honour, and by ostensibly assuming the place which general report assigned to him as Irish Patriot, to check their backbiting and slanders. The freedom of the city was an honour conferred rarely, and only on men high in place and power: in the case of Swift, it was the spontaneous offering of Ireland to the Drapier. In his speech of thanks[1] he accepted the authorship of the Drapier's letters. He set forth his claims to have deserved well of the State. He repudiated with indignation the assertion that he was a Jacobite, or false to the Protestant succession, although he claimed the right, "with many wise and good men," to dislike some things in the public proceedings in both kingdoms. An ill-advised and crack-brained Irish peer, named Lord

"One piece of advice I have to give to you, my Lord," said he: "be as unlike the rest of the Lords of Ireland as you can, and you'll do very well."—Burdy's *Life of Skelton* : Works, vol. i. p. 118.

[1] See *The substance of what was said by the Dean of St. Patrick's to the Lord Mayor and some of the Aldermen of the city of Dublin, when his Lordship came to present the said Dean with his freedom in a gold box.*—Scott's *Swift* vol. vii. p. 272.

Allen, who had sought Swift's friendship in and out of season, had been rash enough to upbraid the Corporation with their treasonable extravagance, in conferring such an honour on the enemy of King George. This gave Swift the opportunity he desired. In a public advertisement he gave the lie to Lord Allen: he held him up to public indignation in the speech of thanks: and not content with this, he gibbets him to an unenviable immortality, as "Traulus." He invents for him the excuse of madness, but only to disallow its sufficiency to cover his misdeeds. His madness is "but the pimp to his vices."

> "Positive and overbearing,
>   Changing still, and still adhering:
>   Spiteful, peevish, rude, untoward,
>   Fierce in tongue, in heart a coward;
>   Reputation ever tearing,
>   Ever dearest friendship swearing:
>   Judgment weak and passion strong,
>   Always various, always wrong:
>   Provocation never waits,
>   Where he loves, or where he hates:
>   Talks whatever comes in his head:
>   Wishes it were all unsaid."

He traces other vices from his father's line:

> "Hence the mean and sordid soul
>   Like his body, rank and foul:
>   Hence that wild suspicious peep
>   Like a rogue that steals a sheep:
>   Hence he learnt your butcher's guile,
>   How to cut your throat and smile:
>   Like a butcher, doomed, for life,
>   In his mouth to wear a knife:
>   Hence he draws his daily food,
>   From his tenants' vital blood."

Six years later, Swift uttered a few words in public, which have come down to us, and which show us how he viewed Irish affairs, when the struggle was passing from his hands, and when, in old age and decrepitude, he was forced to give it up to others. On the 24th of April, 1736, an assembly of merchants met at the Guildhall to draw up a petition to the Lord-Lieutenant on the lowering of the coin : and Swift addressed them in the following words :[1]

"Gentlemen,
"I beg you will consider and very well weigh in your hearts what I am going to say and what I have often said before.   There are several bodies of men, among whom the power of this kingdom is divided—1st, The Lord-Lieutenant, Lords Justices and Council ; next to these, my Lords the Bishops ; there is likewise my Lord Chancellor, and my Lords the Judges of the Land—with other eminent persons in the land, who have employments and great salaries annexed.   To these must be added the Commissioners of the Revenue, with all their under officers : and lastly, their honours of the Army, of all degrees.

"Now, Gentlemen, I beg you again to consider that none of these persons above named, can ever suffer the loss of one farthing by all the miseries under which the kingdom groans at present.   For, first, until the kingdom be entirely ruined, the Lord - Lieutenant and Lords Justices must have their salaries.   My Lords the Bishops, whose lands are set at a fourth part value, will be sure of their rents and their fines.   My Lords the Judges and those of other employments in the

---

[1] The speech is referred to in a letter from Mrs. Whiteway to Dr. Sheridan, of the same day, telling how the Drapier had been to a meeting and made a long speech, "for which he will be reckoned a Jacobite."   It is also referred to in the *Advice to the Freemen of Dublin* (Scott's *Swift*, vol. vii. p. 364) ; but it has not been printed in any edition of Swift's works.   I was fortunate enough to find it on the fly-leaf of one of the tracts bound in vol. 126 of the Collection in the Royal Irish Academy.

country must likewise have their salaries. The gentlemen of the revenue will pay themselves ; and as to the officers of the army, the consequence of not paying them is obvious enough. Nay, so far will those persons I have already mentioned be from suffering, that, on the contrary, their revenues being no way lessened by the fall of money, and the price of all commodities considerably sunk thereby, they must be great gainers. Therefore, Gentlemen, I do entreat you that as long as you live, you will look on all persons who are for lowering the gold, or any other coin, as no friends to this poor kingdom, but such, who find their private account in what will be most detrimental to Ireland. And as the absentees are, in the strongest view, our greatest enemies, first by consuming above one-half of the rents of this nation abroad, and secondly by turning the weight, by their absence, so much on the Popish side, by weakening the Protestant interest, can there be a greater folly than to pave a bridge of gold at your own expense, to support them in their luxury and vanity abroad, while hundreds of thousands are starving at home for want of employment."[1]

Only a few days later, Swift published one of the last, if not the very last, of his tracts on Irish politics. It was an *Advice to the Freemen of Dublin in the choice of a Member to represent them in Parliament.* He urges upon them the absolute necessity of choosing their

---

[1] The occasion of the agitation in which Swift thus took part was an intention on the part of Archbishop Boulter to take steps for the lowering of the gold coin. The speech was uttered in anticipation of the proclamation, and Swift was accused by the Archbishop of being the author of the popular excitement, and was threatened perhaps with the displeasure of the Government. " If I were but to lift my finger," the Dean is reported to have answered, "they would tear you to pieces." When the order was actually given, Swift showed his anger by hoisting a black flag over the Cathedral (Boulter's *Letters*, vol. ii. p. 246). Side by side with this there was a new introduction of £2000 worth of copper coin, which, trifling as was the amount, served to rouse Swift's old indignation from its likeness to the famous patent of Wood. There was little reason in his protest. Indeed, he avows to Lord Orrery (MS. Letter, 31st March, 1737), " I quarrel not with the coin, but with the indignity of its not being coined here."

own Lord Mayor, in preference to another candidate, who held office under the Government. No one, he says, who holds such office can be independent. Is he to displease those to whose good-will he owes his bread ? "Believe me," says Swift, "these are not times to expect such an exalted degree of virtue from mortal men. Blazing stars are much more frequently seen than such heroical virtues." "Count upon it as a truth next to your creed, that no one person in office, of which he is master for life, whether born here or in England, will ever hazard that office for the good of his country." Swift speaks as a sort of civic Nestor : and whatever hopes of conciliation there may once have been between him and Walpole, these last words are a plain trumpet-note of defiance to those who made themselves the tools of Walpole's Irish policy.

Such are specimens of Swift's work in Irish politics. Doubtless he began with little thought of Ireland, impelled by a hatred for the Whig domination, by his own exclusion from the scenes he cared for, by the disappointment that soured himself, and by the cloud that weighed upon his friends. But he kindled to the work as it went on. The luxury of moving masses of men roused the only appetite that was very strong in Swift. The reality of Irish wrongs became more vivid to him, and his honest

Strange to say, Faulkner, who had published a protest from Swift, was summoned before the Council : and Swift himself thought he had so much cause to fear prosecution, that he sent away his papers (same MS. Letter). The alarm was probably due to the nervousness of old age and ill-health.

indignation more intense. His claims, indeed, were for the English born in Ireland as against the freshly imported emissaries of Walpole; and not for the native Irish themselves. But in spite of the narrow standpoint of his time, Swift reached out farther, and he could not be blind to the misery of the Irish Catholics. "*Nostra miseria magna est:*" simple and full of meaning as the words are, they derive their force chiefly from the thought, not of comparatively well-to-do English settlers who failed to gain Government posts, but of starving Irish, to whom were denied the very rights of men.

But the freedom and privileges of his Church: its independence of Bishops who were little else than paid political agents of Walpole: the maintenance of its property against the selfish encroachments of the greedy Irish squirearchy—these, too, were objects which lay close to Swift's heart, and seemed to him a part of the fight against Irish wrongs.

In 1731 two Bills were brought forward relating to the Church, one enforcing residence on the clergy, along with the burden of building houses : the other intended to promote the subdividing of large benefices. Swift was unsparing in his denunciation of both, as directly planned to degrade and pauperize the clergy. He poured out his satire upon the Bishops who supported them, who felt not for the first time the lash of his sarcasm.[1] Writing to Bishop Sterne, in July 1733, when the Bills were already things of the

---

[1] Swift's traditional description of the Irish Bishops of Walpole's making has become almost hackneyed. "Excellent and moral men have been selected on every occasion of vacancy. But

past, Swift speaks of them as "two abominable Bills, for enslaving and beggaring the clergy, which took their birth from Hell." "I call God to witness," he goes on, "that I did then and do now, and shall for ever firmly believe, that every bishop who gave his vote for either of these Bills, did it with no other view, bating farther promotion, than a premeditated design, from the spirit of ambition and love of arbitrary power, to make the whole body of the clergy their slaves and vassals till the day of judgment, under the load of poverty and contempt." If there is anything else involved in the Bills, it is, in Swift's view, a desire to give an impulse to the Sectaries.

Other Bills roused Swift's indignation on behalf of his Church, not against the Bishops, but against the landowners of Ireland. That the latter acted with selfishness and extortion, in order to supply themselves with means of riotous waste, there can be no doubt : and what they could not obtain from their tenants, they sought to grind from the Church. By a Bill of 1733, it was proposed to change the tithe on hemp, for a fixed payment, or *Modus*, as it was called, of less value : and Swift entered the lists against it so effectively, that the Bill was lost. In 1736, another Bill, even more directly aimed by the landowners at the property of the Church, sought to

it fortunately has uniformly happened, that as these worthy divines crossed Hounslow Heath on their way to Ireland to take possession of their bishoprics, they have been regularly robbed and murdered by the highwaymen frequenting that common, who seized upon their robes and patents, came over to Ireland, and are consequently bishops in their stead."

get rid of the tithe of agistment, or the payment which was due to the clergy on pasture land. It had been long the subject of lawsuits, which had uniformly been decided for the clergy : but in 1737, the House of Commons, composed in large measure of land-owners, attempted to set aside the tithe by a resolu-tion of their own. It was in answer to this attempt that Swift wrote the last, but most withering of all his poetic satires, *The Legion Club*. His fury bursts all bounds in the storm of abuse and ridicule and utter scorn that he pours upon the august assembly, that met

> " In the building large and lofty
> Scarce a bowshot from the college,
> Half the globe from sense and knowledge."

As each image is exhausted a new one is brought on : and so vivid is the imaginative power of his descriptions, that, as we read, we seem to see the gibbering of the madmen, twisting their straws, tugging at their chains, and making the place hideous with their foul and loathsome bestialities. So fierce is the indignation, so unsparing its expression, that we may well believe what is told us by Lord Orrery[1] of its results upon the author. "In the year 1736," says Lord Orrery, "I remember him seized with a violent fit of giddiness. He was at that time writing the . . . *Legion Club*, but he found the effects of the

---

[1] Remarks, Letter XXI. Though Lord Orrery speaks of this as a matter of his own recollection, it appears he got the information from Deane Swift. It is given by him in a letter to Lord Orrery of March 23, 1750 (Lord Cork's MSS.) The sentences that follow in Orrery's narrative are taken from the letter.

giddiness so dreadful, that he left the poem un-
finished."   His old enemies were coming in greater
force : and the last scene of his life was begun.[1]

One other topic must be touched on before we leave
the last chapter of Swift's public work.   During all
these years, distant as he was from the arena, he
never lost sight of the battle of English politics.
Every step which confirmed Walpole's power, which
made the Whig supremacy seem more firmly founded,
caused new hopelessness in Swift.   But he refused to
consider his opposition to Walpole and the Whigs to
be merely that of the partisan.   He claimed to base his
resistance on his hatred of corruption, on his love of
liberty, on his desire to see the Constitution resting
once more on what he called " the Gothic institution
of limited monarchy," with the bulwarks of popular
support, and of virtue, for its defence.   It was the
same theory which furnished Bolingbroke with the
specious maxims of his Patriot King, and which inspired the eloquence of Pulteney.   The Opposition,
to which all Swift's friends belonged, were, or claimed
to be, the maintainers of national virtue, the resisters
of corruption, the defenders of liberty against arbi-

---

[1] It is worth noticing in connexion with Swift's later efforts for
his Church, that Skelton's anonymous tract, with the title " *Some
Proposals for the Revival of Christianity*," published in 1736, was
ascribed to Swift.   It is rather a ponderous imitation of Swift's
ironical style : and we are told that when the tract was brought to
Swift, his only remark was, "The author of this has not continued the irony to the end."—Burdy's *Life of Skelton :* Works,
vol. i. p. 42.   Of Skelton's efforts in that kind of literature, his own
unique biographer is compelled to say, " His attempts at wit are
certainly laudable, but not so successful as I could wish."

trary rule.   The plea was a specious one : and, apart from the somewhat palpable insincerity of such maxims in the mouth of Bolingbroke, the political theory was one admirably fitted to prevail, as it did ultimately prevail, against the selfish narrowness of the Whig aristocracy.   It is more than likely that Swift may have suggested, during his last visit to London, some of the lines on which Bolingbroke and Pulteney worked. [1]   But however this may be, most

[1] This finds some confirmation, from the following heads of a tract, which I have found in a memorandum in Swift's handwriting.   The memorandum belongs to Mr. Frederick Locker, who kindly permitted me to use his papers, the same which came from Theophilus Swift into Scott's possession.   But the interest of this memorandum escaped Scott's notice.

" Proposal for Virtue."

"Every little fellow who has a vote now corrupted.

"An arithmetical computation, how much spent in election of Commons, and pensions and foreign courts : how then can our debts be paid ?

"No fear that gentlemen will not stand and serve without Pensions, and that they will let the Kingdom be invaded for want of fleets and armies, or bring in Pretender, etc.

"How K(ing) will ensure his own interest as well as the Publick : he is now forced to keep himself bare, etc., at least, late King was.

"Perpetual expedients, stop gaps, etc., at long run must terminate in something fatal, as it does in private estates.

"There may be probably 10,000 landed men in England fit for Parliament.   This would reduce Parliament to consist of real landed men, which is full as necessary for Senates as for Juries.   What do the other 9000 do for want of pensions ?

". . . In private life, virtue may be difficult, by passions, infirmities, temptations, want of pence, strong opposition, etc.   But not in public administration : there it makes all things easy.

"Form the Scheme.   Suppose a King of England would resolve to give no pension for party, etc., and call a Parliament, perfectly free, as he could.

"What can a K. reasonably ask that a Parliament will refuse ? When they are resty, it is by corrupt ministers, who have designs dangerous to the State, and must therefore support themselves by bribing, etc.

"Open, fair dealing the best.

"A contemptuous character of Court art.   How different from true politics.   For, comparing the talents of two professions that are very

certainly Swift humoured the pretences of his friends.
He never writes to Pulteney, without reminding him
of the prevailing corruption, and the hopes that are
centred in him, as the saviour of the country.   He,
and he alone "has preserved the spirit of liberty."
He has "resisted the corruption of politics."   He is
the " *Ultimus Britannorum :*" and he is the "chief
support of liberty to his country."   The same tone is
kept up to Bolingbroke and Pope : they are the
narrow band who are to storm the citadel of corruption, which a too powerful Minister has built.   The
pretence was perhaps all the more specious to Swift,
on account of his distance from the scene, and the
glamour which that distance threw over the professions of political virtue made by his friends.

different, I cannot but think, that in the present sense of the word Politician, a common sharper or pickpocket, has every quality that can be required in the other, and accordingly I have personally known more than half a dozen in their hour esteemed equally to excell in both.'

These notes are interesting, both as showing from whom Bolingbroke and Pulteney may have drawn some of their topics, and as
giving us a type of Swift's method of laying down the outline of
what he meant to write.

CHAPTER XVI

PERSONAL LIFE AND SURROUNDINGS OF THESE YEARS

1727–1737

ÆTAT. 60–70

The inner side of Swift's life—His summer excursions throughout Ireland—Gaulstown—Quilca—Market Hill—Dublin under Carteret—His Tory leanings and Swift's *Vindication* of his action—Carteret's recall—The Duke of Dorset—Swift's increasing gloom—His money cares—Wide influence—Cathedral administration—Badges to beggars—Loans to Tradesmen—His intimates—Sheridan—Helsham—Delany—Ford—Faulkner—Friends at Howth—Bindon's portrait—Dublin foes—Provost Baldwin—Ambrose Philips—Arbuckle—Amory—His claim to Swift's acquaintance—Learned Ladies—Mrs. Sican—Mrs. Grierson—Mrs. Barber—Other literary aspirants—William Dunkin—Matthew Pilkington and his wife—Mrs. Pendarves—The link of association between her and Swift—The Schomberg monument—Bettesworth and his threats—Bishop Hort and Faulkner—Increasing depression—Friendship for Lord Orrery—Anxiety about his will—Its provisions, and the later changes in these—End of Swift's work—" Years and ill-health have got possession of me."

THE active part which Swift played in the Irish controversies of the first decade of George the Second's reign, does not by any means complete the story of his life during these years.   Over and above this there are personal incidents which stand out with more distinctness now that he is living full in the eyes of men, with the main portion of his life behind him.   Any difficulty in following this part of his career cannot at least arise from want of material, which crowds upon us with almost embarrassing profusion.   When we have attempted its arrangement, there is still another aspect in which we must consider him during these years—that of the busy correspondent, alive to most of what was stirring the English capital, and affecting the literary circles there with something more than a memory of the past.

During the years that had passed since Swift broke from retirement, and began his work as Irish patriot, he had not only been extending his influence in Ireland, but his acquaintance with the country.   In 1721 and 1722 he had spent some time with the Rochforts at Gaulstown.[1]   In 1723, after Vanessa's death, when he sought escape from remorse and scandal in absence from his usual haunts, he had travelled for a time in the South of Ireland.   Even the western wildnesses of Connaught were not unknown to him.[2]

Most of the summers of 1724 and 1725, he spent at Quilca, the quiet country retreat which Dr. Sheridan had made for himself in a bleak spot

[1] The Rochforts, afterwards ennobled as Lords Kilmaine, held the properties of Gaulstown and Belvidere, stretching along Lough Ennel, within a few miles of Mullingar.   Here also the Swift family held considerable property—a part of which still remains in the hands of their descendants.   The Rochforts' house stands in a fine situation overlooking the lake, which was the scene of adventures humorously described by Swift in some of his occasional verses.

[2] *Lady Howth to Swift*, Aug. 6, 1736.

amongst the wildest of the Cavan heaths. It stood close to a little lake, and the care of its proprietor is still visible in the splendid avenues of trees which compass it, even in its decay. Round it have clung many traditions of its owner, of Swift, and of their amusements. The stretch along which Sheridan was wont, as it is said, to attempt a revival of the Roman chariot races : the slope close by the lake which he used for a theatre : the seat in the garden where Swift's arbour stood : the lake itself where Sheridan is said to have constructed an impromptu island out of osier twigs and turf to astonish Swift—all these have their place in the stories that haunt the neighbourhood, with a vitality strange when we consider how completely the surrounding inhabitants are separated from the class for whom Swift wrote and spoke. Not far off is the House of Rantavan, near the Street of Mullagh, the home, in Swift's days, of Henry Brook (the Fool of Quality), where, according to tradition, Brook's mother showed her superiority to the general fear of the Dean, by meeting Swift on his own ground of sarcasm. The ease and quiet of the place—in spite of poor Sheridan's scolding wife—and the whims and humour of his host, made Swift love Quilca, even though he has perpetuated in verse the memory of its disorder, its dilapidations, and the general shortcomings in which it reflected its owner's character.

Some months after Stella's death, he went to the house of Sir Arthur Acheson, at Market Hill, where he stayed no less than eight months, returning to

Dublin only in February 17$\frac{29}{28}$. The inmates of Market Hill pleased him—the quiet and indolent ease of Sir Arthur, and still more the readiness of his wife to submit to the caprices of her guest. Political sympathies had begun the intimacy : and Lady Acheson was glad to receive from Swift that instruction and literary guidance which it was always pleasing to him to give. As the friendship ripened Swift showed more of the capricious whims by which he was wont to display his independence of conventional restraints. He issued his orders for the cutting down of trees, without deigning to wait for the owner's consent. He indulged his taste for composing half humorous, half sarcastic, trifles, on the surroundings of Market Hill : and although these seem to have been taken by his hosts in the spirit their author intended, they got abroad, were exaggerated, and were reported, even amongst Swift's London friends, as violations of the rights of hospitality. The story serves only to show the malignant curiosity to which Swift was exposed even in regard to his personal intimacies in these later days.[1] So friendly, indeed, were his relations with the Achesons, that he planned the building of a house for himself in the neighbourhood of Market Hill.

Swift came back to Dublin in February 17$\frac{29}{28}$. One presence that had been more than all others to him was gone : but he still had, both in Dublin and throughout Ireland, friends enough to prevent any

---

[1] " My Lady shows every mortal the libels I have writ against her " : which proves she did not consider these libels in a very serious light.—*Swift to Sheridan*, September 18, 1728.

outward loneliness.   Adverse as he was to Walpole's Government, Swift held a position too strong to fear attack.   More than this, he had, so long as Lord Carteret continued to be Lord-Lieutenant, a friend in high place.   In the early days of his Viceroyality, Carteret had been compelled to take measures against the Drapier.   But these measures had failed : the Drapier had defied the Government, and the Government left him alone.   Carteret was free to indulge his own sympathies ; and he chose to stand aloof from the keenest of Walpole's partisans, and to associate with men who were reckoned amongst the Opposition.   His scholarly tastes had attracted him to Sheridan, with whom his evenings were often spent, and at whose house he witnessed the performance of a Greek play by the boys of Sheridan's school.   But Sheridan was a Tory : so was Dr. Delany, so was Dr. Stopford, and so, finally, was Swift : yet in the society of all these, this Whig Lord-Lieutenant was found to take pleasure. The Whig zealots shook their heads, dreaded a Roman Catholic restoration, and pretended to believe that a Jacobite rising was at hand.   Swift undertook the vindication of Lord Carteret.[1]   He showed that literature and polite tastes and a preference for companionable friends over bores, were frailties, culpable indeed, but yet worthy of mercy : that the Greek tragedy which Lord Carteret had witnessed, was not known to contain any Jacobite principles in disguise : that evenings of social enjoyment, which preserved

---

[1] *A Vindication of his Excellency, John, Lord Carteret, from the Charge of favouring none but Tories, High Churchmen, and Jacobites.*   1730.

some tincture of scholarship, opposed as they were to Whiggish notions, might yet be pardoned. The favour shown to Tories he admits to be great. No doubt benefices of £100 a year had been given to Dr. Sheridan, Dr. Stopford, and Dr. Delany : and a contract worth £11 a year had been given to Sir Arthur Acheson. But, on the other hand, the Whigs were not quite without their rewards. They have had some £10,000 a year in bishoprics, and nearly twice as much more in civil and military commands. Worthy as they are, the Whigs cannot say they have been altogether forgotten.

The *Vindication* turned the laugh against Lord Carteret's assailants. But it availed nothing with Walpole. Carteret had been humiliated : and now, as his patience had not revolted, he must be made to go. In May, 1730, this Lord - Lieutenant, who so strangely combined the character of friend of Swift and representative of Walpole, surrendered his post. The change was a serious one for Swift. He had formerly waged a severe struggle with Lord Carteret and his Government. But underlying the struggle there had always been a certain sympathy : and as Swift said afterwards, in Carteret he had hated the governor, not the man. When people asked Carteret how he had governed Ireland,—so he wrote at a later day to Swift,—his reply was that he "had pleased Dr. Swift."[1]

Carteret was succeeded by the Duke of Dorset, and the Castle patronage of Swift's circle was over.

---

[1] *Lord Carteret to Swift*, March 24, 173⅞.

There was no special ground of jealousy between himself and the new governor, and through the influence of Lady Betty Germaine, the way was opened for friendly relations. In old days the Duke and he had some acquaintance, and though Swift feared that the friendship of the Duke for Lady Allen, the wife of "Traulus," would necessitate a breach with himself, it does not appear that this was the case.[1] But intimacy or close sympathy was impossible. Dorset came to be a tool in the hands of Boulter; and nothing could reconcile Swift to what tended to increase the Primate's power. Swift, during these years, had a great place in the Dublin world : but it was one cut off from all easy intercourse with the dispensers of patronage and the holders of office. He was thrown back upon the circle of his own intimates in Dublin and around it, and upon those whom he still held to be his fittest companions, the remaining members of the old group that knew the story of the days of Queen Anne. Some day he still hoped again to see them : meanwhile, he enjoyed their letters—to use his own frequent metaphor—as the usufruct of a capital sunk perhaps for life.

Powerful as he was as the Dictator of Dublin society, as the avowed Censor of the Government, and as the disdainful recipient of a homage lavishly yielded to him, Swift was gloomy and morose in spirits ; annoyed by petty troubles : and sought relief from disappointment, ill-health, and misanthropy, in occasional outbursts of almost childish humour. There

---

[1] *Swift to Pope*, May 2, 1730.

is no need to dwell on the anecdotes of escapades and practical jokes which have gathered about the name of Swift, and have served to do duty as the biography of these later years.[1]   How he badgered his intimates ; how he bullied his servants ; how he personified a helpless usher in order to bring down upon himself the pompous contempt of one new to Dublin society, whose dire terror, when he afterwards recognized in the Dean the butt of his sarcasm, gave sport to Swift and his friends ; how he domineered in society, and put the timid to the blush : how he went in the disguise of a fiddler to a beggar's wedding, and detected the subterfuges that served to impose on the pity of the charitable — stories of this kind might be endlessly multiplied, were we to draw upon the various reminiscences that have come down to us.   It may be questioned, however, if they do not give us a false idea of Swift.   Their authority is, at the best, more than doubtful.   They often give proof of their own origin in the readiness to attribute to a man of wit all stories that wanted a paternity, and seemed to find a suitable one in being attached to his name. At the most, they show us that Swift varied his gloom by occasional outbursts of boisterous mirth : that he did not spare even his friends when the fit of sarcasm

---

[1] Swift's earlier biographers dealt strangely with these anecdotes. They borrowed many, without acknowledgment, from the narrative of poor Mrs. Pilkington, while repudiating her authority : and instead of using them in order to throw light on Swift's character, and to illustrate his life, they were content to throw them together in one unconnected series at the close of their story, taking but little pains to ascertain their truth.   Sheridan is good enough to call this the Plutarchian method.

was upon him : and that though his contempt for affectation was often carried beyond the bounds of courtesy, he was yet ready to submit to, and even to enjoy, his own discomfiture, when, instead of submission, he met with a smart repartee. But after all, the real picture of a man like Swift is to be drawn from his more serious, and not his lighter, moments.

One source of annoyance increased on Swift as time went on. The memory of early years of privation made him feel with overwhelming force the need of money as an aid to independence : and this need made the love of money take an undue hold on him. His letters during this time recur again and again to money troubles, to unpaid rents, to vexatious lawsuits, to scanty revenues. Yet he was clearly saving money with sufficient rapidity. When he came to Ireland in 1714, in spite of debts incurred by his long stay in London, and in spite of heavy dues on his installation, he still had money to spare : and before his death, he had saved more than eleven thousand pounds—in those days no contemptible sum. His income as Dean, and Vicar of Laracor and the conjoined cures, was £700 or £800 a year, and fell little below that of the superior judges in the Dublin Courts. He lived plainly, and though he kept two or three horses, in the selection of which he is said to have been careful, he never, unless we accept a story of his last days,[1]

---

[1] Bishop Rundle, the latitudinarian divine whose promotion caused so much excitement in Swift's later days, tells in a letter how Swift had vowed to set up a coach when Walpole fell : how news came to rouse him from his lethargy, telling that the fall had actually happened : and how he kept his vow, only to lay aside

kept the equipage which was in Dublin considered an almost necessary requisite for those who held any considerable position.   He was, in his own words, the poorest man in Ireland who dined off plate, and the richest who did not drive his carriage. His house was a capacious one, situated in the centre of what was still a rich quarter of the city.   His complaints of poverty, and his anxieties as to money, were indeed rather signs of general disappointment and ill-health, than the results of any pressure of pecuniary embarrassment.

Isolated as he was from the officially great, yet Swift's authority and countenance were sought in every project of importance.   He ruled his Cathedral with a firm hand.   He organized a system of restricting the pauperism that was eating into the vitals of Ireland, by granting badges to licensed beggars and dealing severely with the able-bodied vagabonds that infested the streets.[1]   To maintain his hold over the tradespeople, and at the same time to increase the prospects of success for industry, he kept a certain sum of money to be used in giving loans to strugglers in their early efforts, without destroying their sense of independence.[2]   In each and every sphere, in short, the force of his imperious will was felt: and the

the equipage and sink back into greater gloom when a later packet brought a contradiction of the rumour.

[1] See the tracts beginning at p. 382 of vol. vii. of Scott's 2nd edition.

[2] Johnson has spoken with bitterness of this trait, as "an employment of the catchpole, under the appearance of charity." Prejudice apart, Johnson could scarcely have blinded himself to the need of encouraging in Ireland the self-reliance which Swift saw to be the nation's chief want.

disappointment that breathes through so many of his letters is due to the smallness of the stage on which he acted, not to the smallness of the part he played.

Round him there was grouped a circle of intimates, amongst whom his authority was absolute, and by whom his caprices were submissively accepted. The closest of these was perhaps Sheridan, whose wit and humour, as well as his easy, kindly, unworldly character, attracted Swift. His horseplay sometimes offended,[1] and "his chief shining quality," in the words of Swift, "was that of a schoolmaster"; but he had other qualities that endeared him to the Dean. He had not a little of the theatrical taste, which bore fruit in his more famous descendant. He was a good musician, and ready either to be the butt of Swift's lighter hours of merriment, or to meet him with some rhyming impromptu by way of repartee. Without injury to his temper, poor Sheridan bore the afflictions of a termagant wife and sluttish daughter; and far from repining over his domestic troubles, he even joined with Swift in extracting from them an aid to merriment. Even from him, Swift at last found cause of alienation : but the separation did not come till Sheridan was near his end, and till Swift had passed into that darkness which forestalled his death. Before that, Swift had shared with Sheridan not his trifling enjoyments only, but his deeper cares and sorrows. Sheridan knew more than any other of the secret between the Dean and Stella : and to him the Dean had trusted chiefly for news, at a time

---

[1] *Swift to Delany*, Nov. 10, 1718. S. Kensington MSS.

when Stella lay on what seemed likely to be her death-bed.

But the same ease and lightness of heart that made Sheridan so pleasant as a friend, stood sadly in his way throughout life. Swift obtained for him Carteret's patronage. He was made Chaplain, and seemed in a fair way of promotion. But as ill luck would have it, he chose for a text, on the day when he was to celebrate the accession of the House of Hanover, "Sufficient for the day is the evil thereof." "Poor Sheridan," as Swift puts it, "by mere chance-medley, shot his own fortune dead with a single text."[1] "What business," says Swift to him, quoting Don Quixote, "had you to speak of a halter in a family where one of it was hanged?"[2] Swift strives to teach him what was perhaps a little more than even worldly wisdom, as an antidote to his too guileless confidence. "Think and deal with every man as a villain, without calling him so, or valuing him the less, or flying from him. This is an old true lesson." But while he lectures his poor friend on his folly, he will not let him escape on the plea of surpassing unselfishness. "I believe you value your temporal interest as much as anybody, but you have not the art of pursuing it." Advice fell with slight effect on Sheridan. To the end of his life he was never out of trouble. He brought down on himself the wrath of the Presbyterians by attacking their fanatical dislike to music from the pulpit at St. Patrick's : and provoked, in reply,

[1] See *Vindication of Lord Carteret* (Scott's *Swift*, vol. vii. p. 303).

[2] *Swift to Sheridan*, September 11, 1725.

their ridicule of "the merrymaking worship at the
Cathedral, on St. Cecilia's day," and of the musical
festivals, "that turned a Christian church into a play-
house." Through carelessness, errors, disputes, and
misfortunes, Sheridan preserved his unruffled temper
to the last : and finally died in poverty, having missed
a dozen chances of competence and even wealth.

Two others who stood close to Swift, though they
neither shared so completely his confidence, nor submitted so humbly to his caprice, were Dr. Helsham
and Dr. Delany, Fellows of Trinity College. They
had together built the house of Hel-Del-Ville as it
was at first called, and they gathered round them
there a circle which comprised Swift, and in the
earlier days, Stella, to whose memory the house afterwards became a sort of shrine, when it was tenanted
by Dr. Delany, and his wife, Mary Granville.[1] Of
Helsham we have a description in Swift's own words.[2]
"An ingenious good-humoured physician, a fine
gentleman, an excellent scholar, easy in his fortunes,
kind to everybody, has abundance of friends, enter-

---

[1] Delville still remains as it was in the occupation of Mrs.
Delany. It was by her hands that the elaborate shell decorations
of the ceilings were executed, and to her perhaps is due the device
of the star (Stella), that is inlaid in marble in the floor of almost
every room : as well as the star-shaped window in the little oratory
which opens off what was then the library. The garden remains
much as it was when Swift spent his hours of leisure there, and
enforced his tuition on Mrs. Pilkington (if we are to believe her
story) by no gentle arguments. In the garden, the "Temple"
has been rebuilt in the shape it stood not many years ago, when it
contained the fresco portrait of Esther Johnson, said to be from
Mrs. Delany's hand. It is another of the odd tokens of the freshness of the Dean's memory amongst the Irish people, that his ghost
is still believed to haunt the place.

[2] *Swift to Pope*, February 13, 17¾⅞.

tains them often and liberally; they pass the evening with him at cards, with plenty of good meat and wine, eight or a dozen together: he loves them all and they him." "Is not this," he asks, "the truly happy man?" Yet he is obliged to confess that he is not altogether to his taste. Unbroken complacency, such as Helsham's surroundings bred, was not likely to attract Swift's warmest regard.

Patrick Delany, born in a humble position, had pushed himself into prominence, as Fellow of Trinity, and as a preacher of some note. Like Swift, he was a Tory, and carried his Toryism at one time to the very extreme of High Churchism. He became obnoxious to Archbishop Boulter, and was for long barred of promotion: but as Swift's influence waned, Delany made terms with the Government, moderated his extreme partisanship, and became indebted to Boulter for promotion to a deanery. He bore a share, like Sheridan, in the Dean's lighter sallies of wit: but, unlike him, he was careful not to allow his dignity to suffer loss by submitting to be a butt. With all his admiration for the Dean, his respect was mixed with criticism: and the volume in which he comments on Lord Orrery's Remarks contains estimates of Swift's genius in which the Church dignitary is more prominent than the literary critic. If Sheridan pleased the Dean by his careless wit, joined with much lack of worldly wisdom, Delany pleased him, as the vigorous opponent of the Whigs, as the wary companion of his whims and jests, and as the shrewd and keen-eyed man of the world.

There were others of humbler position, who moved on the edge of Swift's circle. Charles Ford, who had occasionally arranged for the publication of Swift's works, and whom he had helped to the post of Gazetter, was now settled not far off. We have an amusing picture of the complacency with which the little man, on the strength of his official authorship, and of some knowledge of foreign countries, took upon himself to dogmatize even in the presence of the Dean,[1] and, strange to say, did so unrebuked. Faulkner, Swift's Irish bookseller, was another of his butts. He "out-caricatured caricature," says one reminiscence of him, which speaks of his "solemn assiduity of absurdity."[2] But absurd as he was, he was one of the notabilities of Dublin. His lameness —caused, as he himself averred, in escaping from a jealous husband, or, as his enemies alleged, in falling down an area when a butcher's boy—became a common topic in the satirical replies to the lampoons that issued from his press. He kept open house, and the gatherings there were so strange that Cumberland tells us how he met in the room on the same evening a criminal who had been reprieved at the gallows, and the judge who had condemned him. Amongst Faulkner's absurdities one was the habit of satisfying an instinct to temperance, by drinking copiously with a strawberry at the bottom of his glass, the cooling properties of which were to be a sufficient protection to sobriety. His conceit was proof against

---

[1] Mrs. Pilkington's *Memoirs*, i. 65.
[2] Cumberland's *Memoirs*.

the sarcasm of the Dean. On one occasion of which Sheridan tells us,[1] Faulkner came to Swift, it appears, in a laced waistcoat, a bag-wig, and other fopperies. Swift affected ignorance as to his visitor, and when poor Faulkner gave his name, threatened to commit him to the House of Correction for imposture. Faulkner presently returned in more becoming guise, and was greeted heartily, with the story of a scoundrel who had tried to pass himself off on Swift for the honest bookseller before him. "If you had dined with Dean Swift, you would have eaten as he bid you,". said Faulkner in after years, when some one twitted him for the poverty of spirit that made him eat his asparagus stalks as the Dean commanded him.

Beyond Dublin, Swift had friends in plenty. A few miles off lay Howth Castle, where he was a welcome guest, and whose surroundings he has celebrated in the verses on the cloud-covered Cape of Howth. Its mistress was Lady Howth, the "Blue-eyed nymph" of more than one poem, and her husband, Lord Howth, so prized his guest, as to procure the picture by Bindon, that now hangs in the Castle, and that tells us so much of Swift as he appeared in his last decade. The gleam of liveliness and humour that lightens up the picture of his prime, has vanished, and in its place has come a sullen haughtiness, the hurtful pride of a social magnate who disdains the applause that was actually his, but that was so different from what he would have

---

[1] Sheridan's *Life of Swift*, p. 376.

chosen.   In keeping with the expression is the tawdry design of the picture, where Wood is grovelling at the Dean's feet as a sort of Caliban.   The picture fitly symbolizes the worst side of Swift, in this, the latest part of his career; the larger meaning of his half-tragic humour, the keenness of his cynicism with its background of sensitive tenderness, the melancholy of his own inner story with its depths of human interest, all narrowed down, as it were, into the hard austerity of the local potentate, who accepts, with disdainful pride, the homage of a circle too small to allow his genius its fitting scope.

There were others who fill up the background of Swift's life, not as friends, or submissive followers, but as the adherents of the Government to which he was opposed.   One of the chief of these was the domineering Provost of Trinity College, Dr. Baldwin, whose strict rule of his university did not prevent him from giving so much point to Swift's satiric address to "Dear Baldwin chaste," that the students are said to have driven his mistress from the college bounds.   Baldwin's violent Whiggism was sufficient, however, to rouse the hatred of Swift without the help of scandal : and between the two there was constant enmity.   James Arbuckle, who wrote as "Hibernicus" in the *Dublin Weekly Journal*, was a hack of the Government who employed his feeble pen to meet Swift's attacks.   Ambrose Philips, the Namby Pamby of the Scriblerus circle, was now secretary to Archbishop Boulter, and was pursued by parodies of the jingling and meaningless rhymes with which he flattered those in power—parodies to which Swift may have lent his aid—

> "Let your little verses flow,
>   Gently, sweetly, row by row,
>   Let the verse the subject fit,
>   Little subject, little wit."

Almost out of the dark, as it were, there comes to us a curious indication of the attitude Swift presented to an outsider during these years. Thomas Amory, the Unitarian, the author of that half-insane medley called the Life of John Buncle, wrote a volume called "*Memoirs of Ladies.*" In the preface he tells us that in a future publication he is to give an account of Dean Swift and (another Dublin celebrity) Mrs. Constantia Grierson. The promised publication never came : but a few of the words in which he anticipates it, are not without interest.

"I know the Dean well," says Amory, "though I never was within-side of his house, because I could not flatter, cringe, or meanly humour the extravagances of any man. . . . . I had him often to myself in his rides and walks, and have studied his soul when he little thought what I was about. As I lodged for a year within a few doors of him, I knew his time of going out to a minute, and generally nicked the opportunity. He was fond of company on these occasions, and glad to have any rational man to talk to ; for whatever was the meaning of it, he rarely had any of his friends attending him at his exercises. . . . What gave me the easier access to him was my being tolerably well acquainted with our politics and history, and knowing many places, etc., of his beloved England. . . . We talked generally of factions and religion, states, revolutions, leaders, and parties: sometimes we had other subjects. Who I was he never knew. Nor did I seem to know he was Dean for a long time, not till one Sunday evening that his verger put me into his seat at

St. Patrick's prayers, without my knowing the Doctor sat there. . . . The Dean was proud beyond all other mortals that I have seen, and quite another man when he was known."

Few readers are likely to believe the whole of Amory's story : but it is not needful to do so, in order to extract some interest out of what he says. It is by gathering such stray glimpses that we are able to fill in the outlines of Swift's life during these years, and to picture him as he was, moving out and in amongst that motley Dublin society; in the plenitude of fame and influence, holding all who came near him under the thraldom of his will, but yet, to all intents and purposes, a lonely and a disappointed man.

The oracle of Dublin tradesmen, the organizer of poor law arrangements, the dispenser of a charity upon which those who could interest few others, had learned to depend,[1] Swift was also an encourager of the literary aspirants of Dublin.   These were not a few; and in the number there were comprised three learned ladies, whose fame, such as it was, extended beyond the bounds of their own island.   One of these was a Mrs. Sican,[2] a sprightly lady for whom Swift had some kindly feeling, and in whose lively, if somewhat

---

[1] A number of old women, afflicted with various ailments, and pursuing such chance vocations as were open to them, were in receipt of regular aid from Swift. Cancerina, Stumpanympha, Fritterilla, and the like, were the names he bestowed on these nymphs who composed, according to Delany, the seraglio which Lord Orrery ascribes to him.

[2] Swift wrote a letter introducing Mrs. Sican (or Sykins, as it is sometimes spelt) to Pope.   "She has," he says, "a very good taste of poetry, has read much, and *as I hear*, has writ one or two things with applause."—*Swift to Pope*, Feb. 6, 17⅞⅞.   Printed by Mr. Elwin (*Letters*, vol. iii. p. 177).

restless wit, he found a subject of half-bantering compliment. More notable still was young Mrs. Grierson,
who seems to have been possessed of more real learning
than the exaggerations of her friends would lead us
to suppose.   Born in 1706, she died when only 27
years of age : and in spite of adverse fates in her
earlier years, she had managed, so it was said, to become a perfect adept in Hebrew, Greek, Latin,
Mathematics, History, Philosophy, and Divinity. The
cycle of her knowledge was large enough to make us
fancy the whole to be fabulous : but she gave evidence
of the partial truth of the reports in editions of
Tacitus and Terence, by means of which she secured
the patronage of Lord Carteret and the friendship of
Swift. The last of the three, whose fame cast a
lustre on Dublin, was Mrs. Barber : and in her, too,
absurd as were the praises lavished on her, we are
bound to believe that there was some ability.   She
possessed none of the scholarship of the encyclopædic
Mrs. Grierson : but the latter, in some complimentary
verses, finds a skilful and sufficient reason for the
want. Apollo, she says, had ordered that Mrs. Barber
should not write in the universal language of Rome,
so that Roman poets might have a chance.   Had he
not taken this precaution

> " *Their* matchless fame, through many ages run,
>   *Her* sex might boast, would be in one outdone."

Mrs. Barber published a volume of poems, for
which Swift wrote a friendly introduction. Not once
does the volume rise above the frigid conceits and

affectations of school exercises.　But she managed to catch a passing breeze of literary fame; and even when old, and ill, and in poverty, she had enough of worth about her to make Mrs. Pendarves say that, in a visit to Bath, she found nothing that would give her more pleasure than the society of Mrs. Barber.

Literary jealousy had, indeed, so little part in the composition of Swift, that he scarcely cared to practise literary discrimination.　A kindly thought, a desire to help a modest effort, a friendly personal feeling— these were quite enough to win from Swift a verdict of unstinted praise.　He took under his protection a young literary aspirant, of the name of William Dunkin, and pressed his advancement with un- grudging labour.　Dunkin had a claim on Trinity College, to whose authorities one of his kinswomen had left an estate: Swift helped him to press the claim.　By his aid Dunkin was made teacher of the Latin school, under the patronage of St. Patrick's chapter: was introduced to Barber, the Lord Mayor of London, as "the best English, as well as Latin, poet in this kingdom": and even an imprudent marriage, of all things the most likely to provoke Swift's anger, did not lose him the Dean's regard.

The same want of discrimination led him to give his patronage where it was even less deserved.　A young clergyman named Matthew Pilkington, whose ambition was to shine as a wit, forced himself on Swift's notice.　He had shrewdness enough to offend none of Swift's prejudices at starting: and by a sufficient submission to his whims, as well as by

the more lively humour of his young wife, Laetitia
Van Lewen, he managed to ingratiate himself with the
Dean.   The connexion eventually came to be one of
the troubles of Swift's later years : but in spite of the
misdoings of the couple, there was clearly something
in the wife that might have turned to good.   Of the
husband, nothing but what is bad can be said : and
the story of his wrong-doings is again to force itself
on our attention.   But Laetitia Pilkington at least
deserves our thanks for having given us, in her
Memoirs, a picture of the Dean which is probably
more true to the life than many that are more
pretentious.   Poor as are her literary efforts, they
have more smartness than those of Mrs. Grierson and
Mrs. Barber.   Her sprightliness amused the Dean : he
watched her literary freaks much as a mastiff might
watch the gambols of a kitten.   She showed none of
that affectation which was the most unpardonable of
sins to Swift : and he admitted her to such intimacy
as gives her reminiscences the value which they have
for us.   As a specimen, the following is sufficiently
graphic to deserve quotation.   She has described his
manner at service, and goes on :

"Service being over, we met the Dean at the church door
surrounded by a crowd of poor, to all of whom he gave charity,
excepting one old woman, who held out a very dirty hand to
him : he told her gravely, 'that though she was a beggar,
water was not so scarce but she might have washed her hands.'
And so we marched with the silver verge before us to the
Deanery House. When we came into the parlour, the Dean
kindly saluted me, and without allowing me time to sit down,
bade me come and see his study : Mr. Pilkington was for
following us, but the Dean told him merrily, he did not desire

his company : and so he ventured to trust me with him into the Library.   'Well,' says he, 'I have brought you here to show you all the money I got when I was in the ministry ; but do not steal any of it.'   'I will not indeed, sir,' says I : so he opened a cabinet, and showed me a whole parcel of empty drawers ; 'Bless me,' says he, 'the money is flown': he then opened his bureau, wherein he had a great number of trinkets of various kinds, some of which, he told me were presented to him by the Earl and Countess of Oxford, some by Lady Masham, and some by Lady Betty Germaine."[1]

It is Mrs. Pilkington who tells us of Swift's manners with his servants : of his dealings with roguish workmen :[2] of the slight but not uncharacteristic trait—a habit "of sucking in his cheeks to prevent laughter": of his memory of *Hudibras*, so accurate that "he could repeat every line from beginning to end of it "; and of his saying about Pope, that has a curious interest in the biography of both men, "that Pope was not so candid to the merits of other writers as he ought to be."   These and other similar traits of the Dean, we owe to her : and his biographers, though they have either affected to

---

[1] Mrs. Pilkington's *Memoirs*, vol. i. p. 53.

[2] "I watched them very close," he told her, "while they were building the wall, and as often as they could they put in a rotten stone, of which I took no notice till they had built three or four perches above it : now as I am absolute Monarch and King of the Mob, my way with them was, to have the wall thrown down to the place where I observed the rotten stone, and by doing so five or six times, the workmen were at last convinced that it was their interest to be honest."   Curiously enough, the story has confirmation in a ermark which Swift himself makes to Bolingbroke (March 21, 17¾), putting, as usual, a bad construction on his own acts, and substituting a motive of pure mischief for good sense.   "I built a wall five years ago, and when the masons played the knaves, nothing delighted me so much as to stand by, while my servants threw down what was amiss."   Here then, at least, Laetitia Pilkington spoke the truth.

ignore an authority so scandalous or have doubted her truth, are yet indebted for more than one of their anecdotes to no other source.

A much more pleasant figure amongst Swift's surroundings in these years, is that of Mary Granville, then Mrs. Pendarves, and at a later day Mrs. Delany. She first met him in 1731, during a visit to Dublin. The sight of her must have brought back to him the memory of very different days, and of meetings in the house of her uncle, Lord Lansdowne, Swift's "brother" of the Club. She was fourteen when the crash came that destroyed the hopes of the Tories in 1714. She herself tells how her uncle, in the full tide of political and social success, suddenly found himself with reduced resources, a prisoner in the Tower : how she and her infant sister, roused from their sleep to be carried by soldiers to the Tower, were prevented sharing the imprisonment, only by coming under the protection of their aunt, Lady Stanley, the wife of Swift's friend Sir John. She lost her hopes of becoming a Maid of Honour : and, instead, was wed, when little more than a child, to a coarse and dull old man, with whom she spent seven years of her youth in a lonely mansion in Cornwall. Scarcely was she free from the bondage of this union, by the death of Pendarves, than she was wounded by the heartless triflings of a male flirt, Lord Baltimore : and it was to shake off the memories of the past, that she came on a visit to her friend, Mrs. Donellan, in 1731. She threw herself into the new scene with all the freshness of enjoyment that she retained to a ripe old age : and from her pen we have a series of vivid pictures of the scenes in which Swift moved. She was struck especially, in coming from London, with the ready mutual understanding, the concentration of purpose, and the brisk gaiety of Dublin. In the boisterous hospitality of St. Stephen's Green, she sees the geniality alone without its worse side. In the evenings at Dr. Helsham's, Dr. Delany's, and above all at the Deanery, she finds a bright and unstudied wit that was refreshing after the fashionable monotony of London. To Swift she came as a bright reviver of scenes in which he had once moved with applause. She had played with him when he visited her uncles : she had sat on Bolingbroke's knee to look at a puppet show : and she reverenced those whom Swift admired. As yet she found him bright in society, though a few years later she had to lament his increasing gloom. She was happy to find him assume the name of her "master," and, after his manner, correct the faults of her pronunciation. She had not missed the first stepping stone to his regard—a readiness to submit to his rebukes : and the real worth she added to her grace and bright intelligence, soon gave her a far stronger hold on his attachment than poor Laetitia Pilkington or Mrs. Barber was able to retain. When he writes to her next year it is with no sarcastic cynicism. He tells her how ill he is : but how much pleasure her letter brought to him, in his ill-health and loneliness. More fully to her than to almost any one else he explains his idea of the place of women : his repugnance to both the types on this day—those who dwindled into frivolous ignorance, and those who hardened into the eccentricity of the professed blue-stocking.[1]

In 1728, Swift's jealousy on behalf on his Cathedral involved him in a dispute that might have led to serious consequences. The monuments in the Cathedral had in some cases been allowed by relatives to fall into disrepair, while in other cases the burial-place of the great was left without note or mark. Amongst those unmarked tombs was that of the Duke of Schomberg, the brave Dutch general of William III. Swift now applied to Lady Holderness, as the Duke's representative, to erect a fitting monument. The request met with a refusal : and, indignant at such heartless disregard, Swift erected the monument from the Cathedral funds, but made it, at the same time, a memorial of the ingratitude of the Duke's descendants.[2] The act was resented at the Prussian Court : it increased the suspicions of Swift at that of St. James's : and even as late as 1734, we find him complaining to Pulteney that the epitaph has involved him in the displeasure of the Court.[3]

---

[1] *Swift to Mrs. Pendarves*, Oct. 7, 1734 and January 29, 173⅘.

[2] " *Saltem ut scias, hospes, ubinam terrarum Sconbergensis cineres delitescunt.*" Swift had it at first " *ut sciat viator indignabundus, quali in cellulâ tanti ductoris cineres delitescunt.*" More prudent friends prevailed to soften the phrase.

[3] In an unpublished letter at Longleat, for which I am indebted to Mr. Elwin, I find the following curious reference to the incident, giving, at the same time, another trait in Swift's conduct. Writing to Lord Bathurst in 1735, he says : "My Lord, you are to know that this kind of procedure is a practice I have followed some years ; for if a Tradesman cheats me, I put him immediately into

In 1733, Swift revived his slumbering hatred against the Dissenters, in a poem which ridiculed their pretensions to be called by Churchmen "Brother Protestants and Fellow Christians." Swift had no taste for the association : and he satirizes it by a comparison with the impudence of " the booby Bettesworth," a serjeant-at-law, whose principles were unpleasing to Swift, and who had nevertheless the presumption to speak of himself and Singleton, a friend of Swift's, as " brethren." The reference so enraged the Serjeant, that, perhaps inflamed by wine, he swore to cut off Swift's ears, and hastened to find him in order to execute the threat. Swift was not to be found at the Deanery : but Bettesworth followed him to Mr. Worrall's house in Bride Street, and there sought an interview. Swift professed ignorance of his visitor : when Bettesworth announced his name and title, Swift only answered, with provoking coolness, "Of what regiment, pray ?" and refused either to admit or deny the paternity of the satire. Swift was safe enough from Bettesworth's revenge : but the learned Serjeant's threats still pursued him : and so indignant

a newspaper, with the bare matter of fact, which the Rogues are grown so afraid of that they are often ready to fall on their knees for pardon. I began this scheme with a long record upon a large piece of black marble in my own Cathedral, on the north side of the Altar, whereon I put a Latin inscription, which I took care to have published in seven London newspapers. The grand-daughter of the old Duke of Schomberg would not send me the £50 to make him a monument over his burying-place, upon which I ordered the whole story to be engraved, and you must have seen the writing, several years ago, to the scandal of the family, particularly because His present M —— said 'G—d—Dr. Swift, whose design was to make him quarrel with the King of Prussia.' Thus I endeavour to do justice to my station, *and give no offence*." The last words repeat the demureness of the Drapier.

were Swift's neighbours, that thirty-one of the
"nobility and gentry" of his Liberty banded themselves together in an association for his defence.   The
story spread to London: it came back exaggerated
to Swift: and the pens of a dozen followers were
pressed into the service against the luckless Bettesworth.   He became known as Serjeant Kite, and his
practice was, on his own admission, injured.   But it
was not long before he gave Swift new ground of
offence.   In 1735, Hort, the Bishop of Kilmore, wrote
a satire, of no great point or wit, on *Quadrille*, in which
it was suggested, by way of ridicule, that disputes
should be referred to Serjeant Bettesworth.   Under
Swift's auspices the piece was sent to Faulkner to be
printed:[1] and Bettesworth, again provoked, this time
used his privilege as Member of Parliament to have
Faulkner thrown into prison.   Swift turned his anger
upon Bettesworth, whom he gibbeted in the lines
beginning,

> "Better we all were in our graves,
>   Than live in slavery to slaves."

And it is clearly Bettesworth that he is describing in
the *Legion Club* as one of those whom he heard

> "Roaring till their lungs are spent
> 'Privilege of Parliament.'"

Little was needed to rouse Swift against one who
was at once a fomenter of Dissent, and an adherent of
the little clique through whom Walpole was ruling
Ireland.

---

[1] Hort, in sending this tract to him, asked Swift to "prune the
rough feathers, and send the kite to the Falconer to set it a-flying."

But ready as he was for the fray, disputes like these, combined with his ill-health, did not pass without leaving their impression. Year by year his gloom becomes more settled, his cynicism more abiding and more deep. "Life is not a farce," he says to Pope,[1] "it is a ridiculous tragedy, which is the worst kind of composition." He did not neglect society : he did not omit acts of kindness : he bore with Mistress Dingley, and never forgot the pension which he continued to pay her; he helped Mrs. Barber : he comforted the last days of poor Miss Kelly, the daughter of an Irish Jacobite, who was dying of consumption, neglected by her profligate of a father : but all this did not prevent the clouds from gathering more thickly over his own head. His powers were growing weaker. He could write nothing, he says, but trifles fit only to amuse an hour, and to be burned the next morning. More sad perhaps than all, any hopes he had ever formed for Ireland were passing away. The momentary energy with which he had inspired the country was ebbing, and, as Alberoni said of Spain, the corpse he had resuscitated was about to sink again into the grave. "Oppressed beggars," Swift says, "are always knaves : and I believe there are hardly any other among us. . . . This is our condition, which you may please to pity, but never can mend. I wish you success with all my heart. I have always loved good projects, but have always found them to miscarry."[2]

---

[1] *Swift to Pope*, April 20, 1731.
[2] *Swift to Mr. Grant*, March 23, 17¾. "Looking upon this

Thus hopelessly he writes to one who was taking up, with more feeble hands, the torch that he had borne so well.

Amongst his new correspondents of these later years was the Earl of Orrery, whose acquaintance with him began about 1732. Orrery's *Remarks* have left no pleasant impression of his relations to Swift, and his desire to secure a certain kind of literary fame by means of his acquaintance was sufficiently transparent. Through the veil of literary foppery, and amidst all the tawdry and futile vanities of the *Remarks*, there pierces an almost constant gleam of petty rancour against Swift. Various stories have been told to account for this. Orrery, it was said by some, was offended by the superscription on one of his letters, found in Swift's desk—"This will keep cold." But so far as their correspondence goes, Swift's intercourse with him during these years seems to have been easy, pleasant, and affectionate. The laboured vanity of the man, his prim and priggish industry, the sedulous care with which he treasured up each scrap of his correspondence, and annotated his private memoranda so as to point out their niceties of style, had something not unamiable and not unpleasing, possibly, to Swift.

It is from unpublished letters to Orrery that we learn the truth as to Swift's Will, the provisions of which now occupied so much of his attention. The

kingdom's condition as absolutely desperate," he says elsewhere, "I would not prescribe a dose to the dead."—*Swift to the Countess of Suffolk* (October 26, 1731).

first Will was made in 1735.[1] It bequeathed the whole of his savings to the Lord Mayor and Aldermen of Dublin, for the foundation of a Hospital for Idiots and Lunatics. What may have been the motive we know not: possibly, in the words of his own poem, it may have been

> "To show by one satiric touch,
> No nation needed it so much."

But it is more likely that Swift, lonely as he was, and with no claims to meet, may have bethought him of the calamity that had clouded his uncle's last days, under the dread of which he had himself lived, and under the shadow of which he was to die: and may have felt that such sufferers had most claim upon his sympathy. Much of his thought was given to the settlement of the plan. "I have been some months," he writes to Lord Orrery,[2] "settling my perplexed affairs, like a dying man: and, like a dying man, pestered with continual interruptions as well as difficulties. I have finished my Will in form, wherein I have settled my whole fortune on the City, in trust for building and maintaining an Hospital for Idiots and Lunatics, by which I save the expense of a chaplain and almost of a physician." In a later letter,[3] he asks Lord Orrery whether he can sell him the land in which he is anxious to invest the bequest. If he could, Swift says, "it would remove a great load from my shoulders, and be an ease to my mind, since years

---

[1] Scott had conjectured this: but the letters to Orrery make it certain.

[2] *Swift to Lord Orrery*, July 17, 1735 (Lord Cork's MSS.)

[3] *Ibid*, October 19, 1735 (Lord Cork's MSS.)

and ill-health have got possession of me, and I cannot long struggle with either." The bequest had brought him new consideration: and with a certain amusement he tells Lord Orrery, in the earlier letter, that he is invited to dine with the Lord Mayor: a prodigious honour, which he believes he has earned "as Drapier and builder of a future hospital." But something occurred to change his purpose in one point. In 1737, he tells Lord Orrery,[1] "upon the City's favouring Fanatics (Presbyterians) I have altered my Will, and not left the Mayor, Aldermen, etc., my trustees for building my hospital." This evidently refers to the making of the Will, which was printed by Scott, from the papers which came to him through Theophilus Swift, and which named a certain number of selected trustees. It was finally superseded by the later Will of May, 1740, which named a different body of trustees.[2]

His last purpose thus accomplished, there seemed nothing left for Swift but to await the oncoming of death. Before we see what the manner of that waiting was, we must first turn to another aspect of Swift's life, and to the part which he plays, during these years, in the sphere of literature, and as the correspondent of those old friends, who still occupied a large place in the literary arena of London.

---

[1] *Swift to Lord Orrery*, March 31, 1737 (Lord Cork's MSS.) Some of these hitherto unpublished letters are printed in Appendix XII.

[2] It must have been in one of these earlier Wills that he ordered that his body should be buried at Holyhead, " being cured of Irish politics by despair."—*Swift to Pope*, February 26, 17$\frac{3}{2}\frac{0}{8}$.

CHAPTER XVII

LATER LITERARY WORK AND CORRESPONDENCE

1727–1737

ÆTAT. 60–70

The circle of Swift's friends in London—Their attitude towards the
Government—The *Beggars' Opera*—Its rapid popularity—Gay
and his new fame—The *Dunciad*—Swift's hopes of rejoining
the circle—Gaps by death—Congreve—Gay—Arbuthnot—
Swift's correspondence with Bathurst—Relations with Boling-
broke and Pope—Swift's contempt for their philosophy—
"*Orna me*"—Lady Betty Germaine—The Countess of Suffolk
—Swift's complaints against her—Petty annoyances—Mrs.
Barber and the counterfeit letter to the Queen—The Pilkingtons
—Later literary efforts—*Verses on the death of Dr. Swift*—*The
Beasts' Confession*—*The Place of the Damned*—*The Day of
Judgment*—*The Rhapsody on Poetry*—*Polite Conversations*
—*Directions to Servants*—Faulkner's edition of the Works—
Verses to a Lady—Walpole's irritation—Swift's increasing
melancholy—The remnants of the old circle—The *History of
the Four Last Years*, and its reception by his friends—Swift's
work closed.

BESIDES these occupations in Ireland, Swift was
leading a second life in his correspondence, and in his
connexion with the literary arena of London.   It was
towards that centre that he felt himself drawn with
deepest interest : and the visits of 1726 and 1727 had
served to revive its hold upon him.   From that time
his letters to the London circle became more constant,

his interest in the literary schemes of his friends more quick, and his interchange of thought with them more frank and open. The confirmation of Walpole's power in 1727, involving, as it did, the discomfiture of Tory hopes and the lack of patronage for a literature of Tory sympathies, drove that circle into steadier opposition to the all-powerful Minister. Their political ideals became more definite, their literary pessimism more intense: they stood more closely together as a forlorn hope against what they maintained to be the total corruption of public life, and the utter degeneracy of public taste. Swift long continued to look forward to a time when he too would rejoin that band, and fight amongst them : but though that time never came, his old supremacy was not lost. The schemes in which he had borne a share were yielding new fruits, and his comments on these throw fresh light upon his later life.

Just after Stella had been laid in her grave, there appeared upon the London stage a play which attracted all men's notice, which served as a sort of landmark in literature, and which has been a household word ever since. This was the *Beggars' Opera*. Thriftless, improvident, and vain, with no fixed or definite purpose to guide his scintillating wit, Gay had now, under the guidance of Swift and Pope, produced a play which struck, with skill, a happy and novel vein of humour. We are told how the play was nearly damned : how it was saved by the charms of the leading actress : and how, at the turning point, this actress caught the fancy of the audience by her happy rendering of one of the songs. But, in truth, it would have been strange had the play not succeeded. The idea, suggested by Swift, of an "idyll of low life," had been most happily developed by Gay. The taste for the Italian opera, which Gay ridiculed, was already on the wane. All were tired of the dreary frivolity of the ordinary comedy whose frail wit and monotonous immorality were constructed on lines so faithful to one type. A political meaning, real or fancied, was soon fastened on the play : the portrait of Walpole was seen in Macheath : and the violence of party feeling that had saved *Cato* completed the success of Gay's comedy. It became the first direct challenge of the wits to the Minister, who ventured to govern without their aid, and heedless of their opposition.

Suddenly Gay found himself a new man. Timid of giving offence to a Court which he had at first fawned upon, and then secretly abused, Gay had let other and abler hands put the finishing strokes to his play. From embarrassment and obscurity, he found himself rising to comparative ease and fame. The way in which Gay's friends accept his triumph is characteristic of each. Pope speaks of it, but scarcely with what we could call real warmth. He tells, no doubt, of his "extreme satisfaction" at the success : but there is at the same time a certain sneer in the reference to Gay's being "occupied with the elevated airs of his opera." Arbuthnot speaks of it with the humour that was his chief trait.[1] When Gay was ill, he says, he strove for his recovery, with more than

---

[1] *Arbuthnot to Swift*, March 19, 17$\frac{2}{8}$.

professional eagerness.   "I took the same pleasure in saving him as Radcliffe did in preserving my Lord Chief Justice Holt's wife, whom he attended out of spite to the husband who wished her dead."   Gay, he continues, is "one of the destructions to the peace of Europe, the terror of Ministers, the chief writer in the *Craftsman*. . . . He is the darling of the city.   If he should travel about the country, he would have hecatombs of roasted oxen sacrificed to him."   But Swift, least of all, grudged any part of his friend's triumph.   When the morality of the play was attacked by Dr. Herring (afterwards Archbishop of Canterbury), Swift took up the cudgels on Gay's behalf. The battle was waged pretty fiercely : and Swift maintained in the *Intelligencer* [1] that "nothing but servile attachment to a party, affectation of singularity, lamentable dulness, mistaken zeal, or studied hypocrisy, could have the least reasonable objection against this excellent moral performance."   Such praise of the *Beggars' Opera* undoubtedly sounds strange : but Swift never measured his words when he was fighting for a friend : and to have rejected the test of salutary moral teaching as a criterion for a work of pure humour, though probably the defence for Gay which our own age would have deemed most appropriate, would scarcely have suited the literary canons of the day.

---

[1] This was a Dublin weekly paper, which was got up, on the model so popular in England, by Swift and Sheridan.   They wrote almost all that appeared in it : but it soon languished, from the want of a younger and more active editor—perhaps, also, of a larger public.

But, with his usual wisdom, Swift is even more solicitous about the use Gay will make of his gains, than of the ultimate judgment to be passed upon his work. After seeking long for Government patronage, Gay had refused, as an indignity, the offer of the place of usher in the royal family. He had no certain provision, and Swift knew how likely it was that his sudden gains would slip through the poet's thriftless fingers. "Providence," he says to Pope,[1] "never designed Gay to be above two-and-twenty, by his thoughtlessness and gullibility. He has as little foresight of age, sickness, poverty, or loss of admirers, as a girl of fifteen." Gay was neither wise in keeping his money, nor very lofty in his conceptions of its use.[2] "Edit ergo est," was the parody of Descartes' dictum which Congreve applied to Gay; and even with such a character Gay never lost hold on the affection of Swift, nor irritated him further than to raise an occasional wish "that Gay was more disengaged from his intentness on his own affairs."

Gay's opera was taken as a challenge from the wits to Walpole. But a new and more weighty defiance was soon to be launched, and this time against the larger company of dunces. In May, 1728, the *Dunciad* appeared. Swift describes the progress of the poem, and claims his share, only because he did not interrupt the muse ;

---

[1] *Swift to Pope*, July 16, 1728.

[2] "Wealth is liberty," Swift says in the same letter to Pope, "and liberty is a blessing fittest for a philosopher—and Gay is a slave." The words explain not a little as to the motives of that parsimony which has been charged against Swift.

> " Yet to the Dean his share allot,
>   He claims it by a canon ;
> That without which a thing is not
>   Is *causa sine quâ non.*"

Pope's debt was indeed more than negative. The dedication to himself had been prized by Swift, and he feels some disappointment when the first edition creeps out without that preface. But he welcomes the poem none the less. " The *Beggars' Opera*," he writes to Gay, " has knocked down *Gulliver :* I hope to see Pope's *Dulness* knock down the *Beggars' Opera*, but not till it has fully done its job." He cannot follow all the allusions : but none the less, " after twenty times reading, he never saw so much good satire, or more good sense, in so many lines." Whatever Swift may have thought, beforehand, of the prudence of Pope's plan,[1] he was not likely to stay his hand or withdraw his sympathy when the fight had once begun. Pope was now entering on the period when his genius was most ripe, and when its fruition was most ample ; and throughout the years that followed, when the Satires and Epistles were ever winning for him new enemies, there was no one who followed Pope's career with more interest, or who judged its many faults with more charity, than Swift. And yet to him, even as to other men, these faults must have been visible.

Swift long refused to relinquish hopes of mixing

---

[1] And from the passage out of his private Journal in 1727 (see chapter xiv.) we know that Swift believed Pope to have committed an error in conferring immortality on obscure scurrility.

once again in the company he prized.[1] Gay had a
plan that he and Swift should meet at Goodrich, to
which the memory of his stout royalist grandfather
gave an enduring attraction for Swift. But as years
go on, the hopes of this visit fade away. In its stead,
Swift urges Pope to come to Dublin, and tells him
what honours will be paid him there.[2] Gradually
even the hope of meeting vanishes. Apathy and
listlessness come with paralysing effect. "I find all
inclination is gone," he tells Pope;[3] "I awake so
indifferent to everything which may pass either in
the world or in my own little domestic, that I hardly
think it worth my time to rise."

But though this hope was relinquished, the outlook on the larger scene was still keen. The old
intimates enter fully into Swift's life, each having his
own part in that world which existed for Swift only
by sympathy and memory. Each brings something
to what Swift called "the usufruct" of his sunken
capital: and as each one drops away, he leaves a
distinct blank in Swift's life.

The first gap in this circle came by Congreve's
death. "I loved him," says Swift, when he hears

[1] *Swift to Lord Oxford*, Sept. 21, 1728. "I intended to have
passed this winter in London. . . . But my health is so uncertain,
I am forced to prefer a home where I can command people."

[2] "Dr. Delany shall attend you at Chester, and your apartment
is ready. I have a most excellent chaise, and about sixteen
dozen of the best cider in the world : and you shall command the
town and Kingdom, and *digito monstrari*, &c."—*Swift to Pope*,
March 6, 17$\frac{2}{8}$. It is curious to find Swift baiting his invitation
with the temptation that he knew to be most likely to attract
Pope, protests notwithstanding—that of flattery and admiration ;
the old and common longing, "*dicier, Hic est.*"

[3] *Swift to Pope*, Jan. 15, 173$\frac{1}{2}$.

the news in February, 1728,[1] "from my youth; and surely besides his other talents he was a most agreeable companion." Swift had known him in the old school-days at Kilkenny, then at Trinity College; and one of his earliest efforts had been a laboured ode in Congreve's honour—Congreve, though a younger man than Swift, being even then the leading light amongst the wits. In the later days of Swift's greatness, Congreve had found Swift's help stand him in good stead when likely to lose place through his own Whig connexions. When at last Congreve passed away, wrecked by ill-health, by dissipation, and by a course of flattery that would have made a lesser man intolerable, Swift keenly felt his loss, though he could not wish that his friend had lived to endure longer torture. "Years have not yet hardened me," he says to Pope; "and I have an addition of weight on my spirits since we lost him: though 1 saw him so seldom, and possibly, if he had lived on, should never have seen him more."[2]

---

[1] *Swift to Pope*, Feb. 13, 172⅞.

[2] That Swift had an affection, and even respect, for Congreve, is certain; but Congreve, as we have seen, did not appreciate *The Tale of a Tub*. In the Journal to Stella, there is a passage which may be read as if Swift, too, had a want of appreciation for that wherein his friend most excelled. Coming back to his lodgings on Oct. 29, 1711, he finds a volume of Congreve's plays which his servant Patrick had got hold of. "I looked into it," he goes on, "and in mere loitering read in it till twelve, like an owl and a fool: if ever I do so again I never saw the like!" But the last sentence may well be taken as a protest against his own loitering reading, rather than as depreciatory of Congreve. We may often feel provoked with ourselves for desultory and aimless reading, even though we feel the book we read deserves more respectful treatment. And it is scarcely conceivable that, in 1711, Swift should have made his first acquaintance with Congreve's plays.

Of those that remained, the most akin to Congreve was Gay. Early in the next year, Swift's attention was claimed by a new effort of Gay's in the shape of a second part of the *Beggars' Opera*, under the title of *Polly*. It might have attracted little attention, had not the Ministry been foolish enough to proscribe it; but, as it was, Gay's reputation became still more inflated: and he found new friends amongst the great. For his sake the witty and eccentric Duchess of Queensberry braved the anger of the Court, and carried her protests to the verge of indecent rudeness. From this time till his death Gay became a constant member of her establishment. In her train he passed from London to Amesbury, and from the "Bath" to Scotland. Repeatedly, on behalf of his patroness, he pressed Swift to share the hospitality which he himself enjoyed so liberally. The invitation pleased Swift. He had known the Duchess when a child, as Lady Catherine Hyde, and had been her father's and mother's friend. He enjoyed the tact by which the Duchess caught the tone in which it suited him to be addressed—one of mingled deference and banter. Her character attracted Swift. The puzzle of staid circles, the admiration of the wits, the toast of more than one generation of gallants, and the centre of an endless whirlpool of gossip, she retained even to extreme age that notoriety for which she thirsted, by keeping up the fashion that had been current in the heyday of her triumphs. Beyond almost any of her contemporaries, she attracted, in the words of Mrs. Pendarves, "the animadversion, the censure, and the admiration" of her time. An invitation from her had some piquancy; and Swift played with it, even though he never was able to accept it.

When Gay makes an attempt of a new kind in the *Fables*, Swift's interest in it is greater than in the proscribed *Polly*. He sees in it exactly what suited the genius of his friend, and candidly confesses that his own attempts in the same kind had failed.[1] But it was destined to be Gay's last effort. In the following December (1732) he was suddenly cut off by a fever. It was Pope who sent the news to Swift : and with a presage of the ill-tidings, Swift could not bear to open the letter for five days. "He was indeed the most amiable by far, his qualities were the gentlest," says Pope. In the midst of his last agony, Gay had asked for Swift. No two men could have been more unlike. Yet their love was such as made Pope see that one of Swift's "principal calls to England is at an end." The blow involved, for Swift, the loss of one more ray of the fast-receding brightness that was left in his life. He receives it almost with an attempt at callousness. "I am only concerned," he says, "that long living has not hardened me."

A calmer spirit, and one whose sympathy with Swift was more deeply rooted, in opinion, in humour, perhaps also in association, than that of any contemporary, was also nearing his end. This was

---

[1] He explains his own method. "I found a moral first, and studied for a fable, but could do nothing that pleased me, and so left off that scheme for ever."—*Swift to Gay*, July 10, 1732.

Arbuthnot.   Conscious of their mutual love, the two friends sometimes remained silent to one another for years.   When Gay died Arbuthnot wrote to Swift,[1] and received a reply in the old tone, but with added sadness.   Arbuthnot was bowed down by bereavements and ill-health.   Like Swift, he feels the world to be out of joint.   The two friends are ready to enter into the efforts and aims of their younger contemporaries : but it is with a sense of being spectators rather than actors.   The banter, the sarcasm, the glimmer of affectation so visible in the letters of Bolingbroke and Pope, and in which Swift sometimes instinctively follows them, drop away when he and Arbuthnot speak to one another.   In a letter written after a period of silence,[2] Swift, as it were, greets Arbuthnot on the very threshold of death. He explains, with a confidence he would have used to no other, the various reasons of health that prevent his coming over : and adds with something of mild sarcasm, "I could not live with Lord Bolingbroke, or Mr. Pope : they are both too temperate and too wise for me, and too profound and too poor." There is doubtless much overdrawn gloom in the later letters of Swift and Arbuthnot.   Swift suffers from a disease of sadness.   He despises his fellows in

---

[1] It is in this letter that Arbuthnot applies to Curll, the biographical bird of prey, a phrase whose authorship is often wrongly attributed to others, "that he has added a new terror to death."

[2] Printed first from the MS. in the British Museum, by Mr. Cunningham in his edition of the *Lives of the Poets* (1854).   Mr. Cunningham dates it conjecturally 1733 ; but it seems to have been written at the close of 1732, in reply to Arbuthnot's postscript to Pope's letter of Dec. 5, 1732.

Ireland, he says, yet he cannot live without them. Arbuthnot thinks the world is going apace to destruction. Ireland may be bad; but it is better than England: "for religion may exist over there for some twenty or thirty years longer; here it is dead and gone." All this was morbid, narrow, and doubtless false in feeling. But we cannot forget that it was only what others, younger, brighter, and with more of life before them than either Swift or Arbuthnot, also felt.

The last letter which Swift received from Arbuthnot was in October, 1734. He had sought a little health in the breezes of Hampstead: but the hand of death, as he knew well, was upon him.

"I am going out of this troublesome world," he says, "and you amongst the rest of my friends shall have my last prayers and good wishes. . . . I most earnestly desired and begged of God (in a recent severe attack) that he would take me. . . . I am in the case of a man almost in harbour and then blown back to sea. . . . I am afraid, my dear friend, we shall never see one another more, in this world."

In such a spirit Arbuthnot waited for death, which released him in the following spring, his piety mingled to the end with much of his half-humorous half-philosophical, apathy, which suggests to old Alderman Barber the saying of Garth, as applicable to Arbuthnot, "that he was glad to die, being weary of having his shoes pulled off and on." [1]

The news of his death "struck me," says Swift, "to the heart." The kindly moderator of bitterness, the easy spirit that had brightened so many lives,

[1] *Barber to Swift*, April 22, 1735.

whose insight was so keen though his charity was so large, was gone from amongst them. "If the world had but a dozen Arbuthnots," Swift had written long before,[1] "I would burn my *Travels*." Arbuthnot had been raised above the envy of others by his carelessness of ambitious aims, as much as Swift by his surpassing power.

Other friends lived on. Lord Bathurst, whose peerage was a memorial of the crisis which had cost Swift so much anxiety in 1711, when the Ministry had been saved only by a desperate expedient, was now, with Bolingbroke, Pope's chief literary friend; and the sprightly wit and gaiety that delighted three generations of literary men brought not a little brightness also to Swift. Bathurst's letters are perhaps somewhat forced in their style of lavish compliment, but they pleased Swift so far as to bring him to copy something of their style in his replies. After a long silence, Bathurst renewed their correspondence in 1729, by some lively banter on Swift's *Modest Proposal for Preventing the Children of the Poor from being a Burden*. Swift's answer seems to have been drawn in the same vein : and writing again in September, 1730, Bathurst threatens to take revenge by showing that Swift has borrowed his numbers from Dryden and Waller, his thoughts from Virgil and Horace, and his humour from Cervantes and Rabelais. He is sure, at least, that he has seen something like them all in Swift's books. By seeming depreciation, he emphasizes Swift's claims to praise. As to Swift's power of

---

[1] *Swift to Pope*, Sept. 29, 1725.

writing English—well, that was only a matter of style. If Swift is a patriot, there have been patriots before. He can doubtless kindle men's passions. But surely he, a clergyman, can have little cause for boasting if, by an hour's work in his study, he has often made three kingdoms drunk at once.

To this banter, lively enough in its way, Swift replies in much the same tone. From the kingdom "whither Lord Bathurst and his crew sent him sixteen years before," and where, since then, he has been " studying as well as practising revenge, malice, envy, and hatred, and all uncharitableness," he reports some of the puny efforts by which " they strive to keep up their spirits "—Sheridan's Collection of Jests, Pilkington's complimentary poems, Mrs. Barber's literary ambitions : and he repays Lord Bathurst's irony thus : [1]—

"When Sir William Temple writ an essay preferring the ancient learning to the modern, it was said that what he writ showed he was mistaken ; because he discovered more learning in that essay than the ancients could pretend to. This, I think, was too great a compliment, but it is none to tell you that I would give the best thing I ever was supposed to publish in exchange to be author of your letters. I pretend to have been an improver of the irony on the subject of satire and praise : but I will surrender up my title to your Lordship. Your injustice extends further. You accuse me of endeavouring to break off all correspondence with you, and at the same time de-

---

[1] The letter is from an unpublished MS. amongst the Bathurst papers at Longleat. It is undated, but is clearly a reply to Lord Bathurst's of Sept. 9, 1730. The reference to Sir William Temple, especially with the reserve as to the exaggerated compliment, is not without interest, as evidence of Swift's real opinion of his early patron.

monstrate that the accusation is against yourself; you threaten to pester me with letters if I will not write. If I were sure that my silence would force you to one letter in a quarter of a year, I would be wise enough never to write to you as long as I live. I swear your Lordship is the first person alive that ever made me lean upon my elbow when I was writing to him, and by consequence this will be the worst letter I ever writ. I have never been so severely attacked, nor in so tender a point, nor by weapons against which I am so ill able to defend myself, nor by a person from whom I so little deserved so cruel a treatment, and who in his own conscience is so well convinced of my innocence upon every article. I have endorsed your letter with your name and the date, and shall leave it to my executors to be published at the head of all the libels that have been writ against me, to be printed in five volumes in folio after my death ; and among the rest a very scrub one in verses lately written by myself. For having some months ago much and often offended the ruling party, and often worried by libellers, I was at the pains of writing one in their style and manner, and sent it by an unknown hand to a Whig printer, who very faithfully published it. I took special care to accuse myself but of one fault of which I am really guilty, and so shall continue, as I have done these sixteen years, till I see cause to reform ; but in the rest of the satire I chose to abuse myself with the direct reverse of my character, or at least in direct opposition to one part of what you are pleased to give me."

Bathurst writes again in April, 1731, in a series of rather forced epigrams based on the irony so cultivated by the circle amongst whom he moved, the wit of which is so apt to pall from repetition. The tone of the whole letter is summed up in the words with which it closes : "In this farce of life, wise men pass their time in mirth, while fools only are serious. Adieu. Continue to be merry and wise : but never turn serious, or cunning."

To witticisms such as these, Swift, with all his gloom, is always ready to make a happy reply. As in his earlier friendship with Prior, so now with Lord Bathurst, he accepted the careless cynicism that called itself a philosophy of life, as a relief from heavier thoughts. He allowed it to turn his mind from disappointment, from the thought perhaps of wasted opportunity; from the loneliness of his present life, and from the fear of calamity to come.

We dwell on the record of friendships like these, with men so different, because it helps us to define to ourselves somewhat more clearly Swift's attitude during these later years. Side by side with the almost despairing struggle for Ireland, and beyond the narrow circle of Dublin society, that intercourse gave Swift a wider outlook. It helped him to live in the past, and afforded him an escape from the gloom of the present.

Literary history, as has been said, assigns a larger place to the later friendship of Swift, Bolingbroke, and Pope. These three stood, alone, at a height which none of their contemporaries reached. More than all others, they had chosen parts which gradually drew them out of harmony with their age, which placed them in sharp antagonism to the powers that now prevailed, and which made them look on one another as the leaders of a forlorn hope. Something of the same spirit that spoke in the *Dissertations upon Parties* spoke also in *Gulliver*, in the *Dunciad*, and in the *Epistles*. But, after all, the bond was an intellectual more than a personal one. Swift had no doubt been attracted by the early brilliancy of St. John. But even in old days their personal sympathy had not been strong. Swift had been repelled by St. John's caprices, by his unabashed debaucheries, above all by the affectation which was the canker-worm to his genius. He had repudiated with indignation the Jacobite leanings ascribed to himself and to the Ministry whom he served : but a few years had shown him how deeply Bolingbroke was involved with the Pretender. Over all that episode Swift was obliged to drop a veil ; and when he accepted Bolingbroke's later view of his own lot, as that of a persecuted patriot, Swift must have been content to ignore all in Bolingbroke's action that had given warrant to the most bitter accusers of the Queen's last Ministry.

The same flaw has already been noticed in his relations with Pope. He had become the patron of Pope in the days when his patronage could earn for the poet the attention of the great. By his influence Pope had at first refrained from joining the triumphant Whigs, and latterly had cultivated the Tories. Swift had sympathized with Pope in his dislike of the monied classes. He had sympathized with him still more in his indignation against Walpole's encouragement of the dunces. Their political position, their literary sympathies, the circle of their friends, their intellectual partnership, had all brought them near to one another. But there were always some grains of dissatisfaction in their friendship. Swift was alive to the pettiness, the vanity, the lack of generosity, in Pope. He was ready to greet the *Dunciad* with applause, and to accept Pope's heralding of its approach with the words,

> Cedite Romani scriptores, cedite Graii,
> Nescio quid majus nascitur Iliade.

But it was no real sympathy of nature which bound together Pope and Swift. Pope borrowed or imitated the mood of Swift, just as he did that of the friend of each season of his life. But a shrewd observer thought it was well that their later intercourse became no closer than it was. The sudden breaking away from Pope's house in 1727 may have had some motive more deep than that which Swift assigned. Swift very probably never fully admitted to himself any real distrust of Bolingbroke and Pope. It is to them that he owed the keenest incitement to renewed endeavours on a greater stage. At times, from their prompting, he was ready to break from his banishment, to come back to the old scenes, to set the world stirring again. He is wearied of the "smaller game": he will return to England and "send for the Dictator from the plough."[1] Again he would fain be assisting Pope in his literary schemes, or riding between Twickenham and Dawley, or discussing Polybius over his wine. He would like to take part "in a new entertainment"—to crush Walpole's Ministry : and by their help he would get into a better world before he has done with it, and

---

[1] *Swift to Bolingbroke*, March 21, 17$\frac{3}{4}$. The date, wrongly given by Scott, is corrected by Mr. Elwin in his edition of Pope's *Letters*, vol. ii. p. 188.

"not die here, like a poisoned rat in a hole." But the mood is short. He soon relapses into listlessness, and feels how unfit he is, broken in health, to ask these younger friends to bear with his infirmities. Their nearer intercourse implied an effort and a strain for which he felt himself unequal. To the last, indeed, he addresses them in language of warm affection. But he could not avoid seeing their affectation, and the insincerity of many of their boasts. "I renounce your whole philosophy," he says, "because it is not your practice." They have adopted their maxims of "*contemptus mundi*" too easily and too young. The gloom which Swift felt eating into his own heart and poisoning his life, the misanthropy for which he sometimes despised himself, but from which he could not escape, was in Pope's mouth, as Swift well knew, nothing but an affectation. The poet's dislikes were of those who hurt him, or who came athwart his path: those of Swift were of human nature as a whole. But it was no unkindly trait in Swift that none of the weaknesses he saw in Pope, lessened his feeling of habitual regard. "Farewell, my dearest friend," are the words with which he closes almost every letter, even as the gloom was becoming more settled, and the shadow of coming calamity deepening.

There was nothing inconsistent with Swift's dignity, in the desire he expresses more than once to find a place in the creations of his friends. The fame that his own works had earned, was cast aside by him with something of contempt. Any profits that they might have brought him, he had uniformly neglected : and, with some cynicism, he declares that his object in cultivating literature had been to gain that social distinction which was not his by birth. But the honour which his friends might bring him, he did not despise. " *Orna me*," he says to Pope in 1735, "I have the ambition, and it is very earnest as well as in haste, to have one Epistle inscribed to me while I am alive, and you just in the time when wit and wisdom are in the height." So he had before said to Gay, "I sometimes reproach you for not honouring me by letting the world know we are friends." And so again, as late as 1738, he begs of Bolingbroke, if he writes a history of his own time, " that my name may be squeezed in amongst the few subalterns, *quorum pars parva fui.*" If the desire is faulty, it is, at least, not on the side of insufficient modesty, or of undue depreciation of his friends' powers of assigning immortality.

Amongst the less famous correspondents of Swift's later years, it would be unjust to omit one whose frank and outspoken advice served him in better stead, perhaps, than the elaborate affectations of his more brilliant literary compeers. This was Lady Betty Germaine, a daughter of Lord Berkeley, and the friend of Swift in the early days of Dublin Castle and of Cranford. Lady Betty had, if we are to believe the story told by the Duchess of Marlborough, got into some trouble in her youth. But these irregularities had been covered by a subsequent marriage with Sir John Germaine, who had left her a wealthy widow in 1718. She now lived at Drayton in Northamptonshire : and the scandals that were caused by early errors did not prevent her mixing with the best society of England down to a ripe old age.   Of all Swift's later correspondents, she shows the most integrity, the most outspoken condemnation of his faults, the most of that sincerity of friendship, which eschews flattery.   She sought to soothe his misanthropy; but when her efforts fail, she is not slow to rebuke his petulance; and it might have been well for Swift if he had more often heard words as plain as these from Lady Betty :—

"As to your creed in politics, I will heartily and sincerely subscribe to it, (that I detest avarice in Courts, corruption in Ministers, schisms in religion, illiterate fawning betrayers of the Church in mitres).   But at the same time, I prodigiously want an infallible judge to determine when it is really so : for, as I have lived longer in the world, and seen many changes, I know those out of power and place always see the faults of those in, with dreadful large spectacles. . . . So experience has taught me how wrong, unjust, and senseless, party factions are ; therefore, I am determined never wholly to believe any side or party against the other : and to show that I will not, as my friends are in and out of all sides, so my house receives them altogether : and those people meet here, who have, and would fight in any other place."[1]

It was one of the symptoms of Swift's fretfulness during these years, that comparatively small annoyances told on his spirits in a degree that to a healthy man would have been impossible.   One of these sources of annoyance arose from Lady Betty's friend, the Countess of Suffolk.   In common with the Opposition faction, Swift had, in the later days of George

---

[1] *Lady Betty Germaine to Swift*, Feb. 28, 17$\frac{32}{33}$.

the First, cultivated the friendship of Mrs. Howard
(as she then was) as a probable counterpoise to
the influence of Walpole. The favour which Mrs.
Howard enjoyed, however, was undermined by the
tactics of the Princess of Wales—tactics so strange in
the domestic annals even of royalty that shrewd
observers may well have been blind to them until the
clue to the secret was obtained. The Princess, even
after she became Queen, ruled her husband by means
of a favourite who was at once the instrument of her
dishonour and of her ambition. Through the Queen,
Walpole's influence continued: and that of Mrs.
Howard, created Countess of Suffolk, was absolutely
set at nought. Upon her therefore fell the brunt of
the Opposition anger. By her they felt themselves
deceived, disappointed, and misled. Her insincerity,
her courtier-like promises, her indifference to friendship—all these became their theme; and Swift was
not the least prominent in the denunciation, refusing
to listen to the apologies of Lady Betty Germaine.
He had wrongs of his own—partly owing to the non-
payment of the thousand pounds, which had waited
since the days of Lord Oxford, and which he had
hoped might now have been secured. Still worse,
Swift fancied that she had misled him by a suggestion
of a settlement in England. The advice seems to
have been as honestly given by Mrs. Howard as she
herself avers. "If I cannot justify the advice I gave
you," she writes in answer to his reproaches,[1] "from
the success of it, I gave you my reasons for it : and it

---

[1] *The Countess of Suffolk to Swift*, Sept. 25, 1731.

was your business to have judged of my capacity
from the solidity of my arguments. If the principle
was false, you ought not to have acted upon it."
The retort is unanswerable : and nothing but the irritation of disappointment and ill-health could have
led Swift to charge his mistake upon another rather
than himself. A more worthy, if not a more reasonable ground of ill-will, was due to the fancied neglect
of Gay. Gay had written his *Fables* for one of the
royal children : and the appointment of Gentleman-
Usher, which was offered as his reward, was deemed
by himself and his friends—Swift amongst the rest—
unequal to his deserts. All these causes served to
feed Swift's anger. Even as early as 1727 he had
written a character of Mrs. Howard, which, with some
flattering phrases, contains sarcasm in much greater
quantity. The key-note of it is her excellence as a
courtier. "In all other offices of life she acts with
justice, generosity, and truth." "If she had never
seen a Court, it is not impossible that she might have
been a friend." "Her talents as a courtier will
spread, enlarge, and multiply to such a degree, that
her private virtues, for want of room and time to
operate, will be laid up clean (like clothes in a chest),
to be used and put on whenever satiety, or some
reverse of fortune, or increase of ill-health (to which
last she is subject) will dispose her to retire."

That Swift was not without his suspicions, when
he wrote these words, is clear. But they were probably intended, and read, as a warning of possible fail-
ings rather than as an actual picture of the reality.

In 1730 and 1731, however, their anticipations seem to Swift to be realized: and he turns upon the false promises of the favourite with an anger which she did not deserve, and which Swift had earned no right to show. It is some satisfaction that the indignation showed itself chiefly in letters to Lady Suffolk herself, and that although it cooled, it did not end, their friendship.[1]

A trifling occasion still further complicated his relations to the Court. In 1731, a counterfeit letter was sent to the Queen, purporting to be from Swift, and praising, in terms so lavish as to be absurd, the Irish poetess, Mrs. Barber, whom Swift had taken under his patronage and who was now in London, seeking to extend her literary fame. The letter seems to assume that the neglect of Mrs. Barber was a new instance of that disregard for Irish claims which distinguished England. Such a travesty of his work as Drapier was enough to irritate Swift: but still more was he annoyed at the supposition that he had sought for any one the patronage of the Queen. Both through Pope and the Countess of Suffolk, he hastens, with almost needless eagerness, to disavow the authorship of the obnoxious letter. Its concoction still remains a mystery. Of all possible solutions that is most unlikely which would ascribe it to Swift: that most likely which would suppose it to be the work of some

---

[1] From certain expressions it has sometimes been supposed that Swift changed from open flattery to something of concealed abuse. But nothing is more bitter than the letters addressed to the Countess herself. Swift was peevish from disappointment, age, and ill-health: to be deceitful, either in praise or blame, was to him impossible.

foolish or indiscreet admirer of Mrs. Barber. Even the poor authoress herself, much as her genius was overrated even in Swift's estimate, was scarcely capable of conduct so damaging to her own reputation as such a forgery.

Another annoyance of these later years was the result, not of Swift's proneness to irritation, but of his helpfulness to those who sought his aid. We have seen how the curate, Matthew Pilkington, and his wife, another of the aspiring authoresses of Dublin, had managed to push themselves into his favour. Over-estimating their literary pretensions, and deceived as to their honesty, Swift had pressed Matthew Pilkington on the notice of his London friends. Alderman Barber,[1] whom Swift had helped to fortune in the days of his power, was in 1732 on the eve of his mayoralty; and Swift, who had brought Pilkington to the notice of Pope and Gay and Arbuthnot, now begs Barber to make him chaplain during his year of office. The request was granted; but Swift soon found cause to repent of his recommendation, when Pilkington showed himself in his true colours, as a coxcomb and a knave.[2]

In these later years Swift's melancholy found

---

[1] Mrs. Pilkington (*Memoirs*, i. p. 159), gives us a description of Barber from the life. "On account of his opposition to the Excise Act, he was then the darling of the people. He was but indifferent as to his person, or rather homely than otherwise; but he had an excellent understanding, and the liveliness of his genius shone in his eyes, which were very black and sparkling."

[2] Barber was obliged to reveal to Swift the knavery of his *protégé:* and Bolingbroke, with even more bluntness, remonstrates: "Pray, Mr. Dean, be a little more cautious in your recommendations."—*Bolingbroke to Swift*, April 12, 1734.

relief nowhere more easily than in those literary occupations that in earlier days he had striven to thrust into the background, amongst the stirring scenes of political activity. In literary fame, too, which he had before neglected and despised, Swift now found a solace amid his gloom. The tribute of that fame was offered from strange sources, and it brought to Swift a content not unmixed with something of irony.

In one of his latest letters to her, Swift tells Lady Suffolk that he is resolved to have a hand "in state scribble no more." The words referred to that angry fight that was now being waged against Walpole's Ministry, under the guidance of Bolingbroke, Wyndham, and Pulteney; and it was well for Swift's fame and for his comfort that in the main he refrained. The anger against the Minister had lost even the dignity of a party struggle, and had dwindled into the attacks of a selfish faction, backed up by the exaggerated anathemas of a literary clique. Swift's combats were now fought on Irish soil; and the time he could spare from his struggles there, was given to work in which his genius found a much more fitting channel. "I have been several months," he writes to Gay,[1] with probable exaggeration of his aversion to sustained effort, "writing near five hundred lines on a pleasant subject, only to tell what my friends and enemies will say of me after I am dead." "My poetical fountain is drained," he tells Pope;[2] but it

[1] *Swift to Gay*, Dec. 1, 1731. Scott has misdated the letter.
[2] *Swift to Pope*, June 12, 1732. Again the date is wrongly given by Scott.

continued nevertheless to flow copiously enough. The words to Gay described one of his most characteristic pieces—the *Verses on the Death of Dr. Swift*. Never attempting to rise into great heights of poetry—studiously keeping himself to the note of ironical humour which he has chosen, and which admits hints of bitter cynicism, though it never allows these to break its equanimity—Swift has here achieved a success which more elaborate poetry would have missed. Keen observation, subtle irony, and bitter cynicism, never took a lighter or an easier dress.

> " Here shift the scene, to represent
> How those I love my death lament ;
> Poor Pope would grieve a month, and Gay
> A week, and Arbuthnot a day ;
> St. John himself will scarce forbear
> To bite his pen, and drop a tear.
> The rest will give a shrug, and cry,
> ' I'm sorry—but we all must die ! '
> Indifference, clad in wisdom's guise,
> All fortitude of mind supplies :
> For how can stony bowels melt,
> In those who never pity felt ?
> When we are lashed, they kiss the rod
> Resigning to the will of God."

The defence of his own political attitude, which the piece contains, is bold enough ; but, as giving his own conception of his task in satire, the lines that follow have even more of interest, and that interest is all the deeper when we contrast their sincerity with the pompous vapourings of Pope, at such times as he is in the humour of advancing his frequent claims to magnanimity :

> " Perhaps I may allow the Dean
> Had too much satire in his vein ;
> And seem'd determined not to starve it,
> Because no age could more deserve it.
> Yet malice never was his aim ;
> He lash'd the vice, but spared the name :
> No individual could resent,
> Where thousands equally were meant ;
> His satire points at no defect,
> But what all mortals may correct ;
> For he abhorr'd that senseless tribe
> Who call it humour when they gibe :
> He spared a hump, or crooked nose,
> Whose owners set not up for beaux.
> True genuine dulness moved his pity,
> Unless it offer'd to be witty.
> Those who their ignorance confest,
> He ne'er offended with a jest ;
> But laugh'd to hear an idiot quote
> A verse from Horace learn'd by rote. "

Shorter poetical pieces followed one another profusely during these years, each telling us something of the restless and fierce misanthropy and contempt that were extending their thraldom day by day. The *Beasts' Confession* pictures the transparent affectations of humanity, by similitudes of brutes. He duly apologises for a comparison only too complimentary to men ; but he has done his best by giving only the lowest orders of brutes—in describing the ass, who blames nature that " he is a wit both born and bred " ; the swine, who feels it needful to ask pardon if he " in diet was perhaps too nice ; " the ape, who

> " Found his virtues too severe
> For our corrupted times to bear " ;

and the goat, whose vow of chastity must excuse his prudish nicety.

In 1731, the stirring lines on the *Place of the Damned*, appeared, as a broadsheet, in Dublin. Hell, he says, is where the damned do mostly congregate. A catalogue, too clearly embracing the very plagues of Irish society, so often satirised by Swift, is given, and he closes thus :—

> "Then let us no longer by Parsons be flammed,
>   For we know by these marks the place of the damned ;
>   And Hell to be sure is at Paris or Rome :
>   How happy for us that it is not at home."

To the same period most probably belong those verses, *On the Day of Judgment*, which have come down to us only through Lord Chesterfield's quotation of them in a letter to Voltaire.[1] Short as they are, and although we may perhaps accept the reason at which Chesterfield hints, as that of their suppression by Swift himself, they yet serve as a condensed specimen of Swift's skill of grim humour at its highest pitch:

> " With a whirl of thought oppress'd,
>   I sunk from reverie to rest.
>   An horrid vision seiz'd my head ;
>   I saw the graves give up their dead !

---

[1] *Chesterfield to Voltaire*, Aug. 27, 1752. "La pièce," says Chesterfield, "n'a jamais été imprimée, vous en devinerez bien la raison, mais elle est authentique. J'en ai l'original écrit de sa propre main." The reason we are meant to divine, is clearly the sarcasm on an accepted dogma : and certainly it would be hard to produce another passage in which Swift is, *intentionally,* so outspoken in his ridicule of a common belief as he is here. The effect of what he says is often the same ; but he is unconscious of the bearing of his words. Here the ridicule is conscious and avowed.

> Jove, arm'd with terrors, burst the skies,
> And thunder roars, and lightning flies!
> Amaz'd, confus'd, its fate unknown,
> The world stands trembling at His throne!
> While each pale sinner hung his head,
> Jove, nodding, shook the heavens, and said:
> ' Offending race, of human kind,
> By nature, reason, *learning*, blind,
> You who through frailty step'd aside,
> And you who never fell—*through pride;*
> You who in different sects were shamm'd,
> And come to see each other damn'd;
> (So some folks told you, but they knew
> No more of Jove's designs than you),
> —The world's mad business now is o'er,
> And I resent these pranks no more.
> —I to such blockheads set my wit!
> I damn such fools!—Go, go, you're *bit.*[1] ' "

The year 1733 saw the *Rhapsody on Poetry*,[2] which stands side by side with Pope's *Epistle to Augustus*, and transcends the latter in its force of sweeping sarcasm. Comparing the two poems, Pope's, with all its marvellous skill, all its command of metre and language, all the subtlety of its satire, yet falls short of the other in variety. There is in the poem a reminiscence of *Gulliver*, in its contempt of humanity; a reminiscence of the *Drapier*, in its obstinate independence; a reminiscence of the *Tale of a Tub*, in the grasp and yet the simplicity of its methods. As poetry, perhaps as a pure literary effort, it is inferior

---

[1] In the common language of the time a "bite" was a hoax: to be "bit" was to be gulled.

[2] It was published anonymously in London in 1733. "Your method of concealing yourself," says Pope, "puts me in mind of the Indian bird I have read of, who hides his head in a hole, while all his feathers and tail stick out."—*Pope to Swift*, Jan. 6, 173$\frac{3}{4}$.

to Pope ; but its power and resistless force of sarcasm
hold us in a grasp compared with which Pope's highest
efforts seem weak and almost tame.　Quotation would
mar the force of the satire.　But, looking back to
the days of the Pindaric odes, and to the dread with
which Swift once regarded his muse, there is not a
little of biographical interest in the two maxims that
follow :

> " Not empire to the rising sun
> By valour, conduct, fortune won :
> Not highest wisdom in debates,
> For framing laws to govern states :
> Not skill in sciences profound
> So large to grasp the circle round ;
> Such heavenly influence require
> As how to strike the Muses' lyre.
> 　Not beggar's brat on bulk begot,
> Not bastard of a pedlar Scot ;
> Not boy brought up to cleaning shoes
> The spawn of Bridewell or the stews ;
> Not infants dropped, the spurious pledges
> Of gypsies litter'd under hedges,
> Are so disqualified by fate
> To rise in Church, or law, or state,
> As he whom Phœbus in his ire,
> Has blasted with poetic fire."

Besides these, he tells Gay in 1731,[1] that he has
" two great works in hand—one to reduce the whole
politeness, wit, humour, and style of England into a
short system, for the use of all persons of quality,
and particularly of all maids of honour.　The other
is of almost equal importance : I may call it the

---

[1] *Swift to Gay*, Aug. 28, 1731.

whole duty of servants, in about twenty several stations, from the steward and waiting woman, down to the scullion and pantry boy." These two were the *Polite Conversations*, and the *Directions to Servants*. The first of these has a special biographical interest. Swift was now interested, more than he ever had been, in the fate of his books. Keenly striving to increase his store of savings, he was perhaps more ready now than before to make them yield some gain. But poor Mrs. Barber wrote to him, in extreme distress. Her literary projects had failed, her health was broken, and debt was accumulating. Kindly as she had been received by Swift's friends, the kindness did not feed her. To help her in these straits, Swift, in one of the last years of his activity, sends her the manuscript of the *Polite Conversations*, that she may make of it what she can. The avarice, the mercenary aims, the cynical selfishness of Swift had, at least, the quality of singular inconsistency.

The other "great work," the *Directions to Servants*, has had to stand the brunt of much severe criticism, from the days of Orrery down to our own. Orrery found it trifling : others have dilated upon its grovelling view of human nature, and the coarseness with which it is stained. Any discussion of these traits must be reserved for our general estimate of Swift's genius. To almost every part of that genius, doubtless, something of the same coarseness clings ; but without the keen insight, without the deliberate and relentless dissection, without the plain and homely humour, without the contempt for conventional grades of dignity, which are so distinctive of the *Directions to Servants*, that genius could not exist.[1]

Efforts so vigorous as these told of the old power, that for thirty years had "inflamed nations," and that could on occasion be re-awakened and shake off its lethargy. But Swift felt that the end of his activity was near. The thought was none the more welcome because he knew that his genius had not always been turned to the best account—that it had often, indeed, been wofully wasted. Now it was less in his power than ever to guide his work into the proper channel, to concentrate his energies, or to keep

[1] Though unprinted during Swift's life, the *Directions to Servants* was handed about and discussed ; and this may have procured for Swift the doubtful honour of the dedication of a translation of a coarse Latin poem written in Germany, which seems not to have been without suggestion for Swift's own book. The Latin version was entitled "*F. Dedekindi Ludus Satyricus de morum simplicitate et rusticitate, vulgo dictus Grobianus ;*" and is dated 1552. The purpose of this book may be gathered from the author's own description :—

> Quae fuerant facienda veto, fugiendaque mando
> Ut doceam gestus foeda per acta bonos ;
> Forsitan haec aliquis jocularia scripta revolvens
> His speculum vitae cernet inesse suae.

He defends himself against the possible harm his book may do, by a principle not flattering to human morals :

> Omnia quae possunt scribi, plerique magistro
> Turpia jam nullo facta docente tenent.

From the name (taken from Saxon *Grob*) the title of the Grobians, for coarse, dirty fellows, became common. There was an English verse translation in 1739 which was dedicated to Swift, and it had been preceded by another in 1605. On the whole this later English version, which is free, bears off the palm from the Latin for filth. There is a superficial similarity to his own satire which makes it almost certain that Swift knew the work : but the deeper meaning of his sarcasm, and the lessons on human nature that it contains, are, of course, wanting in the verses of Dedekindus.

himself from straying into trifles. "His imagination,"
he tells Pope, "was ever at fisticuffs with his judgment." At one time he would be stung to compunc-
tion at the trifles on which he was engaged ; at another,
he flung all such prudence to the winds, and diverted
his gloom by trivialities which he knew would live
only to damage his reputation.

It was perhaps this very sense of waning powers
that led him to busy himself now in putting into shape
some fragments that lay by him, and in revising with
something of personal care the new edition of his
works which Faulkner began to issue in 1735. Swift's
part in that edition has been doubted and even
denied ; but there can be little hesitation, in spite of
his natural disclaimers, in holding it to be that which
received most of his own revision.[1] The state of the
copyright law between England and Ireland, was such,
that Faulkner, had he been so minded, might have
published the edition without the leave of Swift ; and
some of Swift's own expressions would lead us to suppose that this was done.[2] When Motte, his London
bookseller, remonstrated, Swift disclaimed all responsibility. It may well be, that he had some unwillingness

---

[1] This is indeed distinctly stated in a note by Deane Swift to a
letter of Lord Oxford (Aug. 8, 1734). "These were the first four
volumes in octavo which were actually revised and corrected by Swift
himself, as indeed were afterwards the two subsequent volumes,
printed by Faulkner in 1738." This is confirmed by internal evidence, though denied by some subsequent editors.

[2] *Swift to Motte*, Nov. 1, 1735, " Mr. Faulkner in printing these
volumes did what I much disliked and yet what was not in my
power to hinder ; and all my friends pressed him to print them,
and gave him what manuscript copies they had occasionally
gotten from me."

to let an edition appear under his auspices, when he had enjoyed the freedom of anonymity so long.   But when the publication was resolved upon, he probably thought it best to acquiesce, and to do what he could, at least through his friends, to secure its correctness. It did not, certainly, forfeit, for Faulkner, the friendship of the Dean ; and not long after we find him using a letter of introduction from Swift to Pope and Barber.   A year later we find Swift defending Faulkner's action to Motte, as a fair reprisal on the oppressive trade policy of England, and as an offence " neither against the laws of God, nor of the country he lives in," and therefore no sin.   It is tolerably certain, then, that the edition is Swift's own.   He even wrote for it Gulliver's introductory letter to Sympson. To him was probably due the omission of the *Tale of a Tub*, which was notoriously his own, but about which it pleased him to keep up a mystery more complete than about any of his other works.

During this same year a curious, though trifling, literary trouble came to annoy Swift.   Perhaps with some further thought of her necessities, he had sent over to Mrs. Barber the manuscript of his *Rhapsody on Poetry* and of his *Poem to a Lady who had asked him to write on her in the heroic style.*   The latter poem defended his method of scourging vice by humour and ridicule, rather than by the weight of serious denunciation.   He refused to pitch his wit in a higher strain, and showed how well fitted his looser style had been to scourge the vices of a corrupt Ministry.   Like the red rag to the bull, the mere thought of the Ministry had roused Swift's indignation.   As he makes his interlocutor in the poem say :

> Mention Courts, you'll ne'er be quiet
> On corruptions running riot.

To point his description of his own satiric method, Swift drags in a reference to Walpole, under the transparent nickname of Sir Robert Brass.   Strangely enough, for one usually so hardened against attack, Walpole seems to have thought the poem worthy of prosecution ; and though the matter was soon dropped, both Mrs. Barber, as the person responsible for the lines, and Motte and Lawton Gilliver, as concerned in the publication, were subjected to examination before the Privy Council.   If we may gather anything from an obscure reference to the circumstances in Mrs. Pilkington's Memoirs,[1] Matthew Pilkington seems to have been concerned in betraying the Dean's authorship to the Government.   This ill-judged show of irritation did not tend to reconcile the Dean to Walpole's dealing with literature, which, to indifference, seemed thus to add repression.

Oppressed by deep-rooted discontent with the state of affairs, stricken by the loss of friends and by his own ill-health, conscious that his powers were passing with their harvest not fully reaped, Swift sank from apathy to complete silence.   Another of his old friends passes away in Peterborough, the " hang-dog whom Swift loved dearly."   A new election only confirms Walpole's power.   Every circumstance was

[1] Vol. i. p. 171.

tortured by Swift into a new reason for despair. "You are to look upon me," he says to Pope, "as one going very fast out of the world." He seemed to himself stranded in a world where corruption was to rule, where liberty was dead, and where even personal independence was gone. In 1736, Bolingbroke retired to France; and his retirement, the mixed effect of baffled intrigue, diminished resources, and possible apprehension of prosecution, was magnified by his friends, and by Swift amongst them, into a dignified scorn for the miry ways of English politics. Swift and Pope seemed to themselves to be left alone, to struggle against the universal decay around them. Very few of the old circle remained. Erasmus Lewis was still lingering in his former haunts, nursing a wife who was sinking into the grave. Lord Masham was now obscure in station : he had buried, in 1734, the wife of whose health Swift had once spoken as a thing on which the fate of empires hinged : and his son was vexing his old age by misconduct. It would have been but a melancholy journey for Swift even had his health now permitted the attempt, to have come back to London to find the very shadows of the past forgotten.

Through his kinsman, Deane Swift, who was now at Oxford, Swift renewed his acquaintance with William King, the witty Principal of St. Mary Hall.[1] It was through King that he endeavoured to arrange for the publication of the *History of the Four Last Years of the*

---

[1] Not to be confounded with the William King of Swift's younger days, whose rough criticisms Swift had repaid by procuring for him the post of Gazetteer.

Queen. By the aid of the Journal to Stella, Swift had revised the history, which he had written at Windsor in 1712, and its publication may have seemed to him a means of reviving scenes whose memory was so pleasant. The project excited alarm amongst all those concerned. Lewis, the old official, dreaded the revelations which the history might make. Lord Oxford, who, as the son of Swift's old patron, had a right to be heard, eagerly pressed him to refrain from publication. Bolingbroke had read it, but was not favourable. King endeavoured to temporize and dissuade, and ultimately Swift abandoned the intention for a time. But he did so with some ill-will. It is easy to see why, in old age and ill-health, he should have been anxious to tell the story of those times, when "he was a part of all that he had known."[1] But, with something of disgust, he threw aside the scheme, and left the publication for a later hand.[2]

[1] Compare what he says to Bolingbroke, quoted above, p. 219.

[2] For arguments establishing the authenticity of the work published in 1758, see Appendix III.

CHAPTER XVIII

THE CLOSING SCENE

1738-1745

ÆTAT. 71-78

Added gloom and loneliness of Swift's later years—Removal and death of Sheridan—Increase of disease—Waste of bodily strength—Longing for death—Swift and Samuel Johnson—A fruitless request—Swift's interest in his last literary ventures—A final struggle for his Church—Clouds and thick darkness—Pope's dishonesty to Swift—The publication of the letters—The last glimmerings of reason—Outbursts of violence—Curators appointed—Wilson and his insults—The crisis of the disease—The long struggle over—The repose of apathy—Death in life—The final seizure—The end—The nation's grief—Estimate of Swift's character and genius.

ALREADY Swift had lost almost all his old associates, and loneliness was now added to his other burdens. Revered by the Dublin mob, who were ready to obey his orders as those of a dictator; regarded, if not with liking, at least with awe and respect, even by the governing class in Ireland; troubled no longer by the gnawing cares of poverty—Swift yet wanted, now more than at any other time of his life, the solace of a friend. Delany, with whom he had much pleasant intercourse, and between whom and Swift there were

many sympathies in common, was drawn away from
Swift by his keen worldly wisdom, and by his prudent inclination to make friends of the powers that were.
The truest, the kindliest, the easiest of Swift's later
friends had been Sheridan; but Sheridan, too, was
soon lost to him. The story of the breach tells us
something of Swift's later mood. Much as he was
attracted by Sheridan's careless bonhomie, Swift had
seen its dangers, and warned him of them with more
sincerity than was used by kindlier-seeming friends.
When the endowed school of Armagh fell vacant, Swift
not only procured the offer of the appointment for
Sheridan, but also strongly urged him, trying as the
parting would have been to Swift himself, to accept
a post which would secure a safer provision than that
of his Dublin school, and which was removed from
the temptations of Dublin life. Other friends, more
prone to flattery, and more careless of Sheridan's
future, persuaded him to refuse an offer which would
have removed from their midst one whose extravagant
hospitality they enjoyed : and the result was that
Sheridan waited on, to find his income lessening, his
family and his expenses increasing ; and was at length
obliged to accept the much less profitable post of
master of Cavan School. When he left Dublin, the
Dean, to use his own words, found "his right hand
gone." The two had fitted one another in all those
lesser offices of friendship that do so much to make
life run smooth. Sheridan changed the bright society
of Dublin, the comforts of an ample income, the close
intimacy of Swift, for the dreariness of Cavan, the

drudgery of a smaller post, the burden of debt, and the torment of a shrewish wife. The Dean was left without the friend who might best have soothed his passage through old age, to death. The loneliness became more marked, the gloom more abiding and more deep.

During the few years that followed, there had been some attempt at intercourse between the friends. The Dean went to Cavan; and Sheridan spent his vacations at the Deanery. But a friendship such as theirs could only subsist if constant. All the little allowances that had to be made, all the concessions to the temper, the caprices, or the weaknesses of one another, ceased to be endurable when the soothing aid of habit was removed. The younger Sheridan, then only a boy of fourteen or fifteen, professes to remember some incidents of the Dean's last visit to his father at Cavan. He was fretful, morose, and capricious : his parsimony was exaggerated : his pride was offended by a jesting repartee : and the proffered compliments of Cavan he rejected with disdain. Disease, loneliness, and gloom, had told heavily on Swift: and without accepting implicitly all that the younger Sheridan tells us of his morose temper, and capricious anger, we may yet believe that the old friends found that a few months of absence had made each less fitted for the other. The "fierce indignation," that had torn so many of Swift's enemies in the past, was rending his own soul now. On the other hand, Sheridan, seeing the decay that was taking hold of Swift, seemed inclined to act as his Mentor, and doubtless from kindly motives, to assume the office which is, of all others, most likely to strain the bonds of friendship. Years before, Swift had begged Sheridan to warn him when he might seem to fall under the sway of that avarice that often comes, or increases, with old age. Sheridan fulfilled the request with more fidelity than tact. Swift listened to the recital of his own weaknesses. He knew their reality: but the time was past when he might look with boldness on the picture, or feel the gratitude due for the advice. "Did you never read Gil Blas?" he asked Sheridan. The words were significant of what Swift felt: that he was rightly rebuked, but that the rebuke came too late to do aught but break their friendship. They saw one another no more; and a few months removed for ever the friend whose kindliness had not been proof against the bitterness which age, ill-health, and disappointment had bred in Swift.

The year which followed was one, not of gradual, but of rapid, decay. Disease had long been there: but old age was now opening the way for its fiercer inroads. The strong brain that had so long resisted the attack, was now too weak to maintain the struggle: memory was going: the tenacity of his clear logic had dwindled into the loose and broken peevishness of senility. The decline into absolute ruin was quick and striking: but we can, nevertheless, trace with some certainty the separate stages in that downward course. Even when worsted in the fight, Swift yet retains that which is the greatest of his characteristics in his prime, his grim earnestness: even when the struggle is over, and the strong man lies defeated, he yet preserves his dignity, in absolute decay.

In the years 1738 and 1739, he still struggles against his fate. This is the time of the direst and most prolonged torture. The body suffers first. As if to tame the indomitable will, to drive into submission the passion of anger that was too strong for him, he strove to pursue a regimen that only aggravated the disease. He was restless in physical exercise. He wore his body to skin and bone, and even when he could not venture beyond his own house, he sought for violent exercise by hurrying up and down the stairs of the Deanery, or pacing through his empty rooms. He refused, Delany tells us, to use spectacles: and so impaired his sight as to lose the solace of reading. He seemed above all things afraid of sinking into the feebleness of old age: determined, as it were, to wear out quickly, by strained effort, the vital energies whose gradual decay might be prolonged and pitiful. "There is no such thing," said he to a friend, who had praised an old man, "as a fine old gentleman: if the man had a mind or body worth a farthing, they would have worn him out long ago." His efforts were hopeless, and in the struggle, the mind suffered with the body. His misanthropy was exaggerated into a disease. His anger with his kind, his indignation at wrong, burned in upon him with the torture of physical pain; and doubtless it magnified, by imagination, that on which it fed.

The only desire now left to Swift was for death. When he parted from a friend it was with the expressed hope that they might never meet again.[1] When a large pier-glass fell one day on the spot where the Dean had been speaking to a friend a few minutes before, he met the congratulations on his escape only by a regret—"I wish the glass had fallen upon me." For years he had marked the anniversary of his birth by reading the third chapter of the book of Job, praying that the day whereon he was born might be darkness : that he might have lain still and been quiet : "then had I been at rest." The anniversary, so sad for him, was kept with rejoicing by the mob of Dublin. The shouts of the Kevin Bail echoed through the lonely rooms of the Deanery : but it was an incense that he now refused : "'Tis all folly," he said, when told of the rejoicings : "better let it all alone."

Tortured in mind and body, Swift still maintained a firm front against the inevitable encroachments of decay. His final insanity was of a peculiar kind. According to the most recent and most careful medical analysis, it was no slowly developing disease of the brain itself, gradually deepening from partial into confirmed insanity. Until the actual injury came to the brain, Swift, however morbid his mood, however bitter his cynicism, and however unmeasured his anger, was as far from insanity as could be conceived. Structural malformation was there, affecting the nerves of the ear, and producing giddiness and deafness,

---

[1] Deane Swift's *Essay*, p. 217.

which often rendered life a torture. It was not, however, till his waning strength left his brain at the mercy of physical disease, and not till a paralytic stroke had supervened, that the eclipse of reason, which he had long dreaded, actually came. His enemies were planted too near the citadel of reason to permit him to forget the probable end of their attack: but till that citadel fell, the reason itself was unimpaired. Even yet, although decay was already breaking down his defences, he still strove to hold his place among men : still gathered round him the intimates who yet remained, and carried on, as best he might, some fragments of conversation with them. But the conversation was broken and tangled: the memory had failed, the perception was confused and blunted.[1] He still continued to transact business : after the last of these years he revised his Will : and he did not forget the small offices of kindly interference for his friends which are like bright spots amid the gloom of his misanthropy. But he felt and expressed, even at times with a sort of melancholy humour, the decay that was creeping over him. "I

---

[1] In one of the unpublished letters in Lord Cork's MSS. we have a detailed account of this. "In August and September, 1739, his memory was still in such a condition that by the assistance of an intimate friend, who was acquainted with the current of his politics and conversation, so far as they regarded his own times, he could have entertained with pleasure any stranger whatever, but not without the help of such an assistant : for, in the rapidity of his discourse, his memory would frequently fail him : yet by turning to his friend, and asking him with a seeming carelessness, 'What was I going to say?' he would, upon the least hint, recollect his ideas."—Transcript of letter from Deane Swift to Lord Orrery, amongst Lord Cork's MSS.

have been many months," he writes to Lord Orrery,[1]
"the shadow of the shadow of the shadow of etc. etc.
of Dr. Swift. Age, giddiness, deafness, loss of memory,
rage, and rancour against persons and proceedings—
I have not recounted the twentieth part—*I nunc et
versus tecum meditare canoros.*"

It was in the year 1738, when his friend Pope, at
the height of his fame, was still following up the
Dunciad and the *Epistles* with new efforts, and when
Swift, weary and worn with the fight, was sinking to
his rest, that an incident, interesting rather for what
it might have been, than for what it was, occurred.
A new genius, not unlike Swift in mood, not far removed either from Swift or Pope, in political sympathy, was rising in our literary horizon. After a
youth of hardship, of self-distrust, of angry discontent,
of almost hopeless struggle, Samuel Johnson had now
achieved a success of a kind with his *London*. It had
brought him some little fame : but it had not given
him the wherewithal to rise above poverty : and now
at twenty-nine, he was tied hand and foot as a bookseller's drudge, holding nobly to his work, and withal,
not unwilling to profit by such patronage as might
fall to his lot; ignorant as yet how ill his own spirit
was to suit the conditions on which such patronage
was granted. He had fixed his thoughts on a very
humble ambition : and strangely enough it seemed
either to himself or a friend that Swift might help him
to realize his object. The letter which was written
so as to reach Swift must tell its own tale :—

----

[1] *Swift to Lord Orrery*, February 2, 173⅞.—Lord Cork's MSS.

LORD GOWER TO A FRIEND OF DEAN SWIFT

TRENTHAM, *Aug.* 1, 1738.

SIR,

Mr. Samuel Johnson (author of *London*, a satire, and some other poetical pieces) is a native of this country, and much respected by some worthy gentlemen in this neighbourhood, who are trustees of a charity school now vacant: the certain salary is £60 a year, of which they are desirous to make him master; but, unfortunately he is not capable of receiving their bounty, which *would make him happy for life*, by not being a Master of Arts: which, by the statutes of the school, the master of it must be.

Now these gentlemen do me the honour to think that I have interest enough with you, to prevail upon you to write to Dean Swift, to persuade the University of Dublin to send a diploma to me, constituting this poor man Master of Arts in their University. They highly extol the man's learning and probity: and will not be persuaded that the University will make any difficulty of conferring such a favour upon a stranger, if he is recommended by the Dean. They say he is not afraid of the strictest examination, though he is off so long à journey: and will venture it, if the Dean thinks it necessary: choosing rather to die upon the road, *than be starved to death in translating for booksellers*, which has been his only subsistence for some time past.

I fear there is more difficulty in this affair than these good-natured gentlemen apprehend, especially as their election cannot be delayed longer than the 11th of next month. If you see this matter in the same light as it appears to me, I hope you will burn this, and pardon me for giving you so much trouble about an impracticable thing; but, if you think there is a probability of obtaining the favour asked, I am sure your humanity, and propensity to relieve merit in distress, will incline you to serve the poor man, without my adding more to the trouble I have already given you, than assuring you that I am, with great truth, sir,

Your faithful servant,

GOWER.

The application came to nothing: and the fears that Lord Gower expresses of its hopelessness were probably well founded. Even had such a grant been possible, it seems unlikely that Swift would either have been a suitor to the authorities of Dublin University, or that his recommendation would have been very favourably accepted by them. That the failure of a request, conveyed so indirectly as this, formed any part of the ground for Johnson's prejudice against Swift, is absolutely without foundation. A far more likely, and, indeed, a far more worthy, cause of that prejudice was the very similarity of temperament. Genius is not prone to make allowances. Its possessors are not drawn to one another because they are alike in their haughtiness, in their cynicism, in their intolerance. Johnson knew, and shrank from, the bitterness that was bred in Swift as it was in himself, of hardship, of early poverty, of disappointed hopes, and of the ceaseless burden of ill-health. He had struggled too long against the fatal influences, not to know and dread their strength; and just in proportion as the effort to school himself was painful, so his judgment on another suffering from the same enemy was severe. Even if Swift neglected to afford aid which it was in his power to bestow, the neglect was one entirely impersonal to Johnson. Swift knew nothing of him: he could not have read his poem: he could have borne no grudge against its author. Had the benefit been conferred, it might have constrained Johnson to a more lenient judgment: that it was not, could scarcely have given to his judgment its severity.

While the power to work, and even to think, is passing away from him, it is strange to find Swift dwelling, with something of senile weakness, on the fate of the latest products of his pen. More than once he asks after the manuscript of the *Polite Conversations*. He is vexed about the repression of his *History*. He is eager about the small addition that might, by this or that work of his old age, be brought to his fame, and how they might swell his store of savings.[1] We have Swift's own word for it that never, except on one occasion, when Pope arranged matters for him,[2] had he been a gainer by his writings. When, on another occasion, one of his pieces was deliberately published for gain, it was only that he might thereby aid poor Mrs. Barber, in poverty and ill-health. Now, in old age and decay, when his possessions were far greater than his utmost needs, he sought by this unwonted means, to increase them ; partly, it may be, from the mere obstinate tenacity with which old age pursues an object on which it has concentrated all its energy : but we are surely entitled to say, partly from the not unworthy motive of making greater his last gift to the country for which he had toiled so bravely, even under the tragic gloom of his own life.

---

[1] He writes, as he tells Lord Orrery, " to increase my reputation : and besides I should have been glad to have seen my small fortune increased by some honest means."—*Swift to Lord Orrrey*, February 2, 173⅞. Lord Cork's MSS.

[2] Probably the case was that of *Gulliver's Travels*.

Before his life's work closed, it is characteristic of Swift, that one of his latest struggles was for his Church. The fidelity with which he had clung to her cause, did not desert him at the last. A contest for the representation of Dublin University was impending in the summer of 1739: and the issue lay between one who supported the dominant faction, and one who, as a Tory, was believed to be more friendly to the Church. Swift was convinced that the majority of the Irish House of Commons, if they had their way, would strip his Church of her privileges, and his fellow-clergy of their livelihood. In the *Legion Club* he had shown what he thought of that House: it was now his object to deal one more blow at their power. The Church candidate was a certain Macaulay: and for him Swift did his utmost. He strove to enlist on his side the Duke of Devonshire, who was then Lord-Lieutenant. His old friend, Richardson, the agent of the Londonderry Society, was employed to prosecute the same object in London. Pope was appealed to on behalf of Macaulay: and finally, through Lyttleton, then " the rising genius of his age," Swift sought to enlist in the cause the sympathies even of the Prince of Wales, who was then Chancellor of the University. Swift's last struggle fails: but it is interesting, not only for the glimpse it gives us of his fidelity to his Church, but also as it brings him in old age into contact with the central hope of the band that was to be the harbinger of better things, whose youthful patriotism was to crush out the noisome pollutions of the age: that band, of whom

Pope wrote that "with them he would never fear to hold out against the corruption of the world."

A few more friends aided : a few more charities done : a few more groans against the degeneracy of mankind indulged in—and Swift's work was over. Clouds and thick darkness were coming on, and in their midst he descended into the valley of death.

Before we pass to the closing scene, there is one episode of these last years, that gives no pleasing picture of Swift's treatment by professing friends. He was already losing all grasp upon the past, his sense even of the present was as the blurred vision of one whose sight is failing, when his name was dragged into a degrading squabble, pushed on by Pope in one of those freaks of deceitful vanity to which he was so prone. Pope's passion for giving to the world every scrap of his literary work, led him to desire that even the frigid conceits of which his letters were composed,[1] should not be allowed to perish. The desire was a capricious and morbid one : but still more morbid was the chicanery by which more than once he sought to attain this end. Editions of these letters were concocted, in order to be afterwards

---

[1] It is scarcely possible, without special study of it, to credit the contemptible artificiality that was current in the so-called friendly letters of Pope's day. These unburdenings of the heart were performed on certain models, embraced certain stock conceits, and turned their expressions of affection after certain fashionable rules. Thus Lord Orrery, in his careful transcripts of his own letters, in Lord Cork's MSS., often adds chapter and verse for his model, and points out the elegance of his own conceits. In this, as in much else, Swift was superior to his age.

indignantly disavowed, at the same time that they served as an excuse for the issue of authorized versions, only, it was to be understood, in self-defence. At a plan of this kind Pope was now working with even more than his usual trickery. The correspondence between him and Swift had been published with his own connivance in England.[1] Through his agency a copy found its way to Ireland. Having thus laid the train, he began to scream out against the wrong already done him, and the greater wrong that would be done if a new Irish edition should appear. The Dean, he hinted, careless as to his own fame, indifferent as to his acts, sunk in hopeless imbecility, was being misled by treachery into authorizing what would injure both himself and his friends. All this was meant only to hide Pope's own stratagems to secure publication, and at the same time to give him an opportunity of correcting the letters as he pleased, and of completing the collection. But, meanwhile, Pope professed profound alarm. His affection for the Dean : his fear of the freedom of remark which the letters contained : his pretended ignorance of the printed matter—all were called in aid of this well-simulated panic. But one deceit involves another. Faulkner, who was about to reissue the letters, agrees to abide by Pope's own decision, whatever that might be. With singular deliberation, so as not to interfere with any intention on the part of Faulkner, Pope writes to refuse. In spite of the delay, Faulkner, to

---

[1] The series of letters which establish Pope's fraud, has been published by Mr. Elwin from the MSS. of Lord Cork.—Pope's Works : *Letters*, vol. iii.

Pope's disappointment, submits readily to the presumed refusal. A new ground has then to be chosen. Pope does not believe that suppression is now possible. The folly of the Dean, so he professes to think, the mercenary motives of Mrs. Whiteway, the dishonesty of Swift's friends, have exposed Pope to serious danger. But he will be magnanimous. He is ready to forgive. There is no avoiding publication : but as the volume must come out, it had better be revised, and the letters still in the Dean's possession had better be added to it. As he goes on, he gets entangled more deeply in the deceit. At one time he writes with strained civility to Mrs. Whiteway : at another time, he accuses her to Lord Orrery of absolute theft. While he is lavishing on Swift expressions of the most endearing friendship, he is bestowing on him, to others, the contemptuous pity which we reserve only for idiocy. He enlists on his own behalf, Lord Orrery, whose chief ambition was for the regard of genius, and who for that reward was ready to lend himself to Pope's dishonesties. The treachery drags on, with all its infinite littleness, for many months, while Orrery and Pope were plying Mrs. Whiteway with alternate threats and promises. The key to the deception has been furnished by Mr. Elwin : and now that it stands exposed before us in all its naked deformity, the only result of the correspondence is to prove the hollow pretences of Pope's friendship, the despicable vanity of the man, and the sincerity of Swift's latest guardian, his cousin Mrs. Whiteway, whose honesty was so unscrupulously attacked. We are glad to turn from the episode, even though it be to the closing scene that now awaits us.

Whatever may be the correct medical theory of Swift's malady,[1] the story of these last years stands out, in its main features, clearly enough. During 1738 and 1739, as we have seen, the irritation greatly increased: in 1740, it rendered him scarcely capable of seeing strangers; and to his morbid gloom was now added either loss, or absolute confusion, of memory. It was during this year that the miserable wrangle about the correspondence, bred of Pope's vanity and deceit, was dragging on its course: and Swift was as unheeded and unheeding in the midst of the attacks upon him, as if he had been dead. In July of that year, he wrote thus to Mrs. Whiteway, in tones that sound as if uttered on the brink of the grave:

"I have been very miserable all night, and to-day extremely deaf and full of pain. I am so stupid and confounded, that I cannot express the mortification I am under both in body and mind. All I can say is, that I am not in torture: but I daily and hourly expect it. Pray let me know how your health is and your family. I hardly understand one word I write. I am sure my days will be very few: few and miserable they must be.

"I am, for those few days, yours entirely,
"JON. SWIFT.

If I do not blunder, it is Saturday, July 26, 1740."

With broken accents such as these, heard painfully

---

[1] For some discussion of the latest theories as to this, see Appendix XIII.

as it were, through a thick curtain of pain, disease, and baffled memory, Swift's voice drops into silence. The years that follow have little incident: and such as they have, is soon told. During 1741, the decline was rapid: each month made him less fit for the society of his fellows. To the last he sought to carry on his religious exercises: and even when his memory was a blank to all else, his faithful servant, Richard Brennan, told how he still repeated the only part of them he could remember—the Lord's Prayer. Another prayer was also overheard, when he cried in his agony "to be taken away from the evil to come." [1] In January, 17$\frac{4}{4}\frac{2}{1}$, his behaviour, we are told, "was grown perfectly intolerable." [2] Even poor Mrs. Whiteway, who in the midst of troubles and ill-health of her own, bore gently with the racked spirit longing for rest, but finding none,—even she was forced to visit the Deanery by stealth in order to see that he was cared for. Unseen by him, she watched the Dean, as in his restless agony he paced the room, ceaselessly walking, as she tells us, for ten hours a day. He would eat only when alone: and even after it had been left in his room for hours, his food was often taken away untouched. [3] In March, 17$\frac{4}{4}\frac{2}{1}$, guardians were appointed for him, by the Court of Chancery. It was feared that he might lay violent

---

[1] Lyon's MS. notes on Hawkesworth's *Life.*

[2] The expression is taken from the unpublished letter of Deane Swift to Lord Orrery, of March 23, 1750, already quoted, which gives the dates of Swift's decline with somewhat more detail than other narratives.

[3] *Mrs. Whiteway to Lord Orrery*, November 22, 1742.

hands upon himself. On one occasion, it was said, he was found threatening his own image in a mirror. When his kinsman, Deane Swift, called, he was met only by the words "Go, go!" and yet with the ineffectual relenting of baffled reason, the Dean strove again to speak, and then pointing to his head, could only utter the words, "My best understanding—" and then sink into apathy. During the summer of 1742, he was subjected to gross indignity by a scoundrel who had secured a place in the Cathedral, and who attempted to extort from Swift the post of sub-dean, by insults at least, if not by actual violence.[1]

In this state of absolute gloom, shunning the company of his fellows, escaping from pain only by frenzied physical exertion, and at times breaking out into actual violence, Swift lingered through the summer. In September, 1742, his illness came to an acute crisis. The pressure on the brain produced, or

---

[1] The story is told by Faulkner, of this miscreant Wilson having rendered the Dean intoxicated, and then endeavoured by actual blows, while they were driving together, to extort the promise of the place. This story is confirmed by an unpublished letter from Deane Swift to Lord Orrery of December 19, 1742 (in Lord Cork's MSS.) So serious was the indignation aroused in Dublin that Wilson found it needful to make an affidavit (published by Scott) which ascribed the actual violence to Swift. In Lord Cork's MSS., there is a further affidavit from Richard Brennan, Swift's servant, which gives some countenance to this version, without, however, lessening Wilson's barbarity. Brennan says he was riding behind the carriage, when he heard Wilson demand the sub-deanship. Swift refused : when Wilson began to curse, and in loud tones swore that "no man should strike him." Brennan interfered, and rescued his master by force from the scoundrel's abuse. Even if Wilson's abuse was in answer to some violence offered by old age and imbecility, it scarcely alters the case.

was itself increased by, violent inflammation, which at first extended over his body, and finally settled into a painful abscess in the eye.   For weeks his agony was so great that it sometimes required the strength of five men to prevent this enfeebled old man of seventy-three from tearing his eyeball from his head.   At length the torture did its work.   The swelling in the eyeball sank, and the pain ceased. The last struggle of the long combat was over : and the strong man, so long invincible even in decay, sank into apathy and silence for ever.   In this state he spent three years of living death.   There was no longer any frenzied resistance to the mental decay. The fierce exercise by which he had striven to defy his torture was now over: he could scarcely be persuaded to move from his chair; and his body, which had shrunk to skin and bone, now recovered its plumpness : the wrinkles left his face, which now, in spite of the thick snow-white hair that overhung it, had an aspect of almost childlike gentleness.[1]   Still, his state was one where controlling and guiding power was wanting, rather than one of ordinary insanity.   He "never talked nonsense nor said a foolish thing."[2]   He was very "quiet and peaceful."

---

[1] So it is described by Mrs. Pendarves.

[2] *Deane Swift to Lord Orrery*, April 4, 1744.   Deane Swift adds in another unpublished letter (March 23, 1750, Lord Cork's MSS.) : " Sometimes, perhaps once or twice in a week, he would say two or three words which, as far as could be observed, always carried meaning in the sense of them."   Swift seems to have suffered from that form of aphasia, the result of paralysis, which does not prevent the clear utterance of words, but breaks the connexion between the brain and the organs of speech so far, as to make the words no longer answer to the meaning intended.

He seemed to know old friends—(Deane Swift, Mrs. Whiteway, and his housekeeper, Mrs. Ridgway.) At times there was some sign of irritation : after a vain attempt to express his meaning, he broke off with the words "I am a fool."   Looking at himself in the glass, he was said to have exclaimed in pity, "Poor old man !"   When a knife was removed from his reach, he shook his head as if to deprecate the caution, and whispered "I am what I am." (On the whole, so far as comfort could be associated with such a state, Swift's last days were peaceful, and even if the story is true, which finds support from the experience of Scott's friend, Lord Kineddar, that the servants admitted strangers to see the living wreck of former greatness, this probably had little effect upon the list-less apathy of the Dean.   But) it is vain to attempt to gauge his state too exactly : we cannot penetrate behind the veil of that mysterious, and withal not undignified silence, nor tell how much of the man's reason was still living, though cut off from all his fellow-men.

Before the close came, there seems to have been another short but sharp agony. (The epileptic tend-ency to which so many of the Dean's symptoms point, appears to have broken out fiercely at the last.) For thirty-six hours, we are told, he lay in strong convulsive fits.   But these passed away : and the final exhaustion came on.   The cup of misery, that had been drained to the last dregs, was now taken from his lips.   The long struggle, the torture, the morbid restlessness, all he had suffered from himself and from the world, were now ended. Death that had lingered so mercilessly, had come at last as if in answer to his prayers.

(He died on the 19th of October, 1745.) The passion and the earnestness: the cynicism and the tenderness: the strength, the pride, and the prejudice: the stern enmity and the faithful friendship; the stinging sarcasm and the far-reaching humour: the hatred of cant, and the hatred of tyranny—all were hushed for ever. They had made many suffer: but none more direly than their possessor. He had spent his power lavishly: had despised the efforts of lesser men in their thrifty economy of strength: and now he found rest where the bitterness of anger might tear that torn heart no more.

When it became known that the Dean had breathed his last, the nation's love and veneration, hushed to silence during these years of living death, broke out once more. The people crowded to the Deanery, to take a last look of him who had been their idol for five-and-twenty years, to "beg a hair of him for memory," and to pay to him in death that tribute of enthusiastic worship which, living, he had accepted with half-pitying disdain. According to the precise instructions of his Will, Swift was buried privately,[1] on the 22nd of October, at twelve o'clock at night: and, likewise by his own instructions, on a tablet of black marble over his

---

[1] In a letter to the executors, written on the morning of the 22nd, Mrs. Whiteway expressed her fear that Swift's instructions might be too literally interpreted. But they could scarcely have been more express.

grave in the Cathedral, in "large letters, deeply cut, and strongly gilded," there were inscribed the words—

HIC DEPOSITUM EST CORPUS

JONATHAN SWIFT, S.T.P.

HUJUS ECCLESIÆ CATHEDRALIS

DECANI :

UBI SÆVA INDIGNATIO

ULTERIUS COR LACERARE NEQUIT.

ABI VIATOR

ET IMITARE, SI POTERIS,

STRENUUM PRO VIRILI LIBERTATIS VINDICEM.

OBIIT ANNO (1745)

MENSIS (OCTOBRIS) DIE (19)

ÆTATIS ANNO (78).

The amount of his bequest for the Hospital for Lunatics and Incurables was between ten and eleven thousand pounds. By subsequent gifts from others, the endowment was greatly increased: and from 1757, when it was opened, St. Patrick's, or Swift's Hospital, as it was called, continued long to do a work which national effort did not then recognise as its own. To the vicars of Laracor he leaves the tithes of Effernock, "so long as the present Episcopal religion shall continue to be the national established faith and profession in this kingdom." "Whenever any other form of Christian religion shall become the established faith in this kingdom, then the proceeds are to go to the poor of Laracor, always excepting Jews, atheists, and infidels; and even this destination is to be maintained only so long as "Christianity in any shape shall be tolerated among us." Mistress Dingley was to have an annuity of twenty pounds out of the Hospital funds;[1] pecuniary bequests were made to Mrs. Whiteway, and her sons, and to Mrs. Ridgway, the daughter of his old housekeeper; and other friends, such as Pope,[2] Delany, the Grattans, Lord Orrery, and Macaulay, were remembered by gifts to which something of interest or of whimsical meaning was attached.   Bolingbroke is not named in the Will.

Looking back over the record of Swift's life, the task remains of forming some estimate of the man and of his genius.

Very early in his career, Swift wrote two letters, which have only recently become accessible, and which for the first time appear in his biography. The following extracts throw a curious light upon his later life.   The first is dated 3rd May, 1692.[3]

"I esteem the time of studying poetry to be two hours in a morning (and that only when the humour fits), which I esteem to be the flower of the whole day, and truly I make bold to employ them that way, and yet I seldom write above two stanzas in a week.   I mean such as are to any Pindaric ode; and yet I have known myself to be in so good a humour as to make two in a day, but it may be no more in a week after; and when all done, I alter them a hundred times, and yet I do not believe myself to be a laborious writer: because if the fit comes

---

[1] Mrs. Dingley did not survive Swift, dying in 1743.   Her Will, of which the executor was Swift's friend, Mr. Lyon, left nothing to Swift.

[2] Pope had died during the Dean's unconscious state, on the 30th of May 1744.

[3] It is printed in the *Hist. MSS. Commissioners' Report*, vol. vii. p. 680.

not immediately I never heed, but think of something else. I have a sort of vanity or foibless, I do not know what to call it, and which I would fain know if you partake of. It is (not to be circumstantial) that I am overfond of my own writings (I would not have the world think so), and I find when I write what pleases me, I am Cowley to myself, and can read a hundred times over. I know 'tis a desperate weakness, and has nothing to defend it but its secrecy, and I know I am wholly in the wrong, and have the same pretence the baboon had to praise her own children."

The second is dated 6th December, 1693.[1]

"I myself was never very miserable while my thoughts were in a ferment, for I imagine a dead calm is the troublesomest part of our voyage through the world."

The letters from which these are extracts were written to his cousin Thomas Swift, whom the Dean afterwards found reason to despise and ridicule : and it is odd that he, of all men, should have been the recipient of confidences contrasting, at first sight, so strongly with the traits most marked in Swift's later career. The youth, uncertain of his own power, ashamed of, yet morbidly alive to, his own vanity, nervous as to the verdict of others on his work, became the one author of his day whose indifference to the fame which his genius might have brought him was most marked : the aspirant after "ferment," sank into his grave wearied out with many a long fight, and seeking there a calm which his own life had never yielded to him. But strange as the words at first appear from the pen of Swift, they throw such light on his biography, as to make us long for more of these early

---

[1] Also printed by the Hist. MSS. Commissioners.

confidences.   They show how soon the power of self-inspection came, and how pitiless it was ; they explain the anxiety with which each work was thrown out, under such disguise as was possible ; they testify to that inherent restlessness which, _even in old age, made him feel " a dead calm " more irksome than the fiercest strife.   But these hints of early doubt, and effort, and satisfied achievement, tell us something more.   Was there not, in the original bent of that genius, something which the accomplished work of Swift does not contain ?   We cannot claim for any of his verses the qualities of real poetry.   We find in them no flights of imagination : no grandeur either of emotion or of form : and even the deftness of his rhythmical skill never attains to the harmony of poetic utterance.   But when we search through the tangled mazes of the Pindaric odes : when we watch their tensity and earnestness in the light of these early confidences : when we place side by side with them the fierce energy of the later verses,—evident as is the severe repression therein of any poetic fancy, —we feel that Swift, though he never attained to true poetic utterance, had a temperament, which in his own words, was " blasted with poetic fire."   The fire was indeed checked by untoward experiences, smothered under a burden of contending faculties, and done to death.   But how much of Swift's cynicism, how much of his waste of power, how much of his apparent indifference to fame, was due to the withering of those early aspirations, and to the repression of a temperament of surpassing keenness, forced to utter itself only in the language of satire, and not of poetry?

We must not forget this early impulse in judging of Swift's later work, with its union of contrasting qualities. By nothing did he affect men more than by his marvellous combination of the grimmest earnestness with the most mocking humour. The two are ever at combat, but the combat is maintained on almost equal terms. The mocking laugh never sounds without telling of the earnestness behind; the fury of denunciation never speaks but as the humour rules it, and with such sense of repression as doubles its effect. In himself Swift seems to sum up the two instinctive tendencies ever striving for the mastery in the thoughts of humanity—the tendencies which seem to make of life what he has called it, "a ridiculous tragedy."

Such is the ruling feature of Swift's work. It repeats itself in an idiom which, to use his own words, is "his own English" as no man's ever was. Free from all tricks and peculiarities, it holds to its purpose with absolute directness and lucidity. It has no balanced periods; no ornaments; even grammatical regularity is sometimes wanting. But with dramatic nicety it suits the character in which he speaks, and he bends it to his purpose with the unconscious skill with which a well-trained fencer turns his foil.

Besides his strength of idiom, besides his combined earnestness and humour, Swift has another power as rare. It is that of presenting thought in lucid metaphor or allegory sustained through a long train of implicit reasoning. It is by such travesty of metaphysics that he avenged himself on what seemed to him the wordy triflings of philosophy; and it is this which gives at once its chief subtlety, and much of its interest, to his most characteristic work.

In the verse of Swift's mature years we strike upon a vein quite different from his prose. It astonishes us by its varying range, from the lightness of sportive fancies to the grim earnestness of the *Rhapsody on Poetry;* by the combined perfection and simplicity of its workmanship; by the accuracy with which it hits its mark. But only in isolated passages does it show Swift's power at its highest. For the rest, it seems to be thrown to the world not as the best product of its author's genius, but as all that his cynicism would permit him to give, as the utmost freedom with which his poetic faculty could be indulged.

From the salient features of Swift's genius, we pass naturally to the marked traits in his character. Here, too, we find the same contradiction. It is built upon a double foundation of keen sensitivity and fierce indignation, that give to his life at once its interest and its mystery. Others might smooth down contending forces by conventional rules; in Swift the forces were too keen to be held in check, the combat too lasting to permit of words of peace.

Two sets of conditions affected the development of a character thus strangely framed. Born to poverty, nursed in dependence on a grudging charity, entering upon the world under ungenial and chilling patronage, Swift's experience was the worst possible for such a character as his. And he lived a slave to strange physical conditions. With a physique so powerful as to prompt him to ceaseless exertion; with a disease that caused life-long torture and threatened an end still worse; with an intellectual fierceness that made his physical temperament seem cold,—Swift could feel only that he was not as other men.

This made him above all things a lonely man. Partly he misunderstood his fellow-beings; partly with the abnormal distinctness of vision of the solitary, he saw clearly what to other men was hidden, by social habit, in a healthy and convenient blurredness of perception. The infinite littleness of humanity; the endless and hopeless reign of disorder and injustice: the ludicrous incongruity between principle and practice—all lay exposed before him as a nightmare from which he found no escape. The degrading conditions of physical existence obtruded themselves before him with disgusting plainness. He could not save himself from seeing with an unveiled accuracy: but the vision was for all practical purposes as unhealthy and as unsympathetic as that of one whose gaze has been too long fixed upon a microscopic lens.

It was this loneliness that produced his harsh and yet unconscious trampling upon feelings which he did not share. The abnormal coarseness that stains his work, and on which it would be waste of time to dwell, has its root in this apathetic callousness. Not

once is he guilty of the deliberate pandering to lewdness which stains the pages of Pope : the noisomeness
has for him no attraction : he dwells upon it only
because it is one side of the picture that makes
humanity loathsome in his eyes.

The same absence of sympathy with his fellow-men
explains the unconscious irreverence with which he
often treats religion.　Strict as was the discipline
that Swift imposed on himself, yet the greater part of
the world of ordinary religious ideas was a region
where there was no resting-place for him.　Unquestionably Swift's was a nature, in the highest
sense, religious : and in the passionate earnestness
with which he forces himself to conform to the conventional religious creed, there is something of a
longing to escape from his loneliness and solitude to
the kindly ways of men.

Behind the veil of that inner religion, of which
Swift, like all men who are framed after his type,
bore the secret in his own heart, we cannot hope to
penetrate.　But his inability to appreciate the religious
feelings which his own words might irritate, in no
way rendered him the less strict in his avowed
adherence to his Church and its creed.　What that
creed involved to him, we cannot know.　But that he
held to it with rigid firmness, that he permitted
himself no conscious relaxation from it, that he would
have repelled any suggestion tending to diminish its
authority, is as certain as anything can be.　He had,
indeed, a curious dread of exposing his religious
exercises to the world.　He read prayers to the

servants of his household, but concealed this from his visitors : he attended early services in London, in order that he might escape the observation of the world on his devotions.[1] He concealed this, much as he would have concealed an act of charity. On the other hand, he made no secret of his creed : and the very fact of its open avowal shows us that he considered such orthodoxy not as a positive merit, but as the natural result of his mental bias, and as harmonizing with the political attitude which he had assumed.

Swift was scrupulous about entering the Church as a mere means of livelihood. His scruples may have proceeded as much from pride as from conscience : but, be that as it may, when he did adopt her orders, he bound himself to practise the discipline of a sentinel at his post. According to Delany, Swift was wont to speak of his early hopes of attaining such ecclesiastical eminence as might prompt men occasionally to ask the sexton on a Sunday morning, "Pray, does the doctor preach to-day?" The reminiscence had more of sarcasm in it than Delany seems to perceive : but it was with all earnestness that Swift strove to fulfil his clerical duties, and with real regret that he found how his political battling had turned his sermons into pamphlets. If he felt doubts as to the dogmas of the Church, he never permitted himself to utter them. "The want of a belief," he says, "is a defect which ought to be concealed when it cannot be overcome." In what way he held that dogma,

---

[1] Delany's *Observations*, p. 44.

what it really represented to his inmost soul, how far its acceptance was a part of that refusal to follow the mazes of metaphysical speculation to which he steadfastly adhered, were questions which Swift probably never asked himself, and to which the world can find no answer. The self-repression was the easier because it suited with his contempt for the affectations of current scepticism, with his impatience of the claims to free thought advanced by those who "could no more think than fly." For their complacent rationalism he had no tolerance : the creed that would shape itself to suit what they called their reason would only lose his sympathy. The same tyranny which he imposed on them he would impose upon himself; unconscious, perhaps, of the independence which his own pride kept in reserve.

Much the same motives penetrated into the political convictions of Swift. By political convictions we understand, of course, something different from the mere phases of his party allegiance. His political creed was built upon the same foundation as his creed in religion, his hatred of abstract reasoning. In his contempt for the metaphysics of politics he anticipated Burke. The expedient was the only rule for the government of men. To dogmatise upon abstract rights, to frame constitutions upon a basis of theoretic justice, was to him only so much solemn trifling, worthy of the sages of Laputa. But the expedient he judged not according to the catch-words of any party, not with any of the limitations of conventional habit. Piercing straight to the heart of a question, impatient of the laboured methods of political platitude and commonplace, he had nothing but contempt for the more timid intellects that refused to accept his conclusions, or to keep pace with his reasoning. Purblind and narrow, they seemed to him steeped to the lips in dishonesty, and he drove home the more keenly against them that tyrannical supremacy that it was his to wield.

This was the central point of his political creed, and in the main it determined his political attitude amid the accidents of party. The point at which he aimed was seldom selected with impartial judgment. Pride, prejudice, anger, or misanthropy too often stepped in and made him choose his line of action in very derision of the opinion of his fellow-men. But once chosen, no power on earth could bring anything of shiftiness or dishonesty into Swift's pursuit of it. When he first joined the Whigs he did so from the natural bias that his connexion with Sir William Temple and his association with the leading members of the Whig party, together with the virulent factiousness of the Tories, gave to him. But from the first his mouth refused to shape itself to their Shibboleths. The Revolution was not to him valuable as an assertion of the hypothetical terms of the Original Contract. To him it was no epoch in politics, and marked the establishment of no ideal constitution. It was simply an episode, necessary at the moment, shaped by the accidental conditions of the time, and liable to revision whenever that seemed expedient. He believed in no divine mission of the Whigs, and credited them with no monopoly of political prescience. The very care with which he searches for reasons to support the Revolution settlement, proves that its advantages were to him no matter of political axiom, as they were to the orthodox Whig. He never ceased to judge his party, not by their professed principles, but by their acts.

A breach was, from the first, not unlikely: and we admit no imputation against the honesty of Swift, in allowing that personal offence first suggested its occasion. But this would have carried him only a little way had not more cogent arguments come to clinch the change. The Whigs neglected his efforts in the mission with which he had been entrusted. But he soon found that their neglect extended to the Church, whose sworn defender he was. Once begun, the breach became rapidly wider. Swift could not rest half-way. In escaping from the bonds of one party, he seemed to be breaking down what had long been to him an irrational and artificial fiction which it suited the exigencies of professional politicians to preserve. The change did not precede, it lagged after, his inclination. But once it was made, he found new vices in his former associates day by day. He saw, or fancied he saw, the insincerity of their specious claims to be the maintainers of toleration and of liberty: he saw their encouragement of the latitudinarianism which his soul abhorred—partly because it satisfied those whom he despised, partly, perhaps, because it did *not* satisfy uneasy doubts which he strove to hide from himself: he saw the oligarchical monopoly that the Whigs had drawn out of the Revolution. The Tories had been violent, factious, and forgetful of all judgment in the maintenance of impossible extremes : but Swift forgot or condoned their faults for the support they gave his Church, for the opposition they maintained to the abstract political theories on which the Whigs based their claim to virtue. When he broke his long silence to speak on behalf of Ireland, the keynote of all his denunciations was the repudiation of those specious "maxims" by which it was sought to experiment upon her woes—"maxims" which his knowledge of Ireland told him were there "controlled."

Great as his influence must necessarily have been, this predominant bias in his opinions enhanced it. It gave directness and force to his arguments: it made his convictions for the time part and parcel of himself, held with the tenacity of personal traits, of which he seemed no more able to divest himself than to cast off his own being. Cavil and paradox have sought to minimize the hold which Swift had upon men of his own time. He exaggerated, it has been said, his own influence with the Government of Harley : he was never really trusted in the conduct of affairs : he mistook the fair speeches by which his help as a Government hack was conciliated, for confidences and deference paid to an adviser and a guide. To such fancies history gives the lie. It was not merely help that his so-called patrons sought from Swift ; it was to him they looked to shape their policy, to write out their credentials to the people, to interpret for them the history of their time. More than this, no man in England had before appealed to such a constituency as that aroused by Swift : for the first time a mass of opinion beyond the purview of Court and Parliament was asked to judge between the merits of parties. In Ireland he stirred a feeling which not even the red hand of rebellion has been able to awaken either before or since. He anticipated the force of democracy : and he was the first to put into shape that political ideal which has never since failed to find an hereditary line of supporters,—that of so-called Tory principles resting upon popular support.

The secret of his after-influence is akin to this. Of all the writers of last century, there is none that remains so much of a living force and personality as Swift. The questions agitated in his day are forgotten; its party struggles and its political theories have passed away : but his genius is for us no mere historic memory. Some reasons for this lie on the surface. We are attracted by the commanding calmness of his humour, with its back-ground of grim earnestness. The mystery and the romance of his life, the story of its love and of its anger, of its pride and of its ruin, can never lose their hold on human interest. Even in the gloom, in the loneliness of one "dwelling in the wilderness," he is intensely English to the very centre of his being.

But beyond and above all this, he commands our attention by the stern earnestness with which he has dealt with problems that are as living for us, as when he wrote. Others have dwelt upon the same problems, have expressed something of the same cynicism, have attempted to denounce in something of his tone. The theme is an old and an inexhaustible one; the "*ludibrium rerum humanarum*" with its tragedy behind, the thought of which makes humour strive to be something more than mockery or laughter, and which gives another aspect to the cynic's sneer. But Swift stands on a different level from all these others, in that, while his humour is never forced or thin, his earnestness never forgets the supreme quality of self-command. He is never, but by implication, a preacher. But were we to choose a name for the one chief topic of his denunciation, it would be that given by Johnson to the object of his hatred, which he called Cant. A preacher of our own day, with a misanthropy less scathing, but more fretful, than that of Swift, has chosen what might appear a kindred topic in the energy of his invective against Shams. But the Sham is soon fathomed and exposed. Its shell is easily pierced, and the nickname is left to suggest to weak imaginations the depreciation of all that we do not understand. The Shams of one generation are forgotten by the next, or remembered only as the dress in which it pleased our predecessors to masquerade. But who can place bounds to the dominion of Cant? Who can say into what specious theories it does not enter, over what sphere it fails to leave its trail? And yet, though the preacher cannot rid us of it, it must still blanch in all time coming, before the calm irony of Swift's humour, before the relentless tragedy of the picture that his genius has drawn.   If his pride was boundless, if his anger was consuming, they have at least left to us a rich inheritance, in the discomfiture which that ever-present foe suffered at his hands.

APPENDICES

    I. Fragment of Autobiography.

   II. Note on *A Tale of a Tub*.

  III. Authorship of *Four Last Years of the Queen*.

  IV. The Marriage of Swift and Stella.

   V. Swift's Offer to Announce the Marriage.

  VI. Wood's Halfpence.

 VII. Proclamation against the Drapier.

VIII. Editions of *Gulliver's Travels*.

  IX. Journal of 1727.

   X. The Will of Esther Johnson.

  XI. *Character of Mrs. Johnson*.

 XII. Letters from the MSS. of the Earl of Cork.

XIII. Swift's Disease.

APPENDICES

APPENDIX I

FRAGMENT OF AUTOBIOGRAPHY

[This fragment, written about 1727, and first printed by Deane Swift, from a copy now in Trinity College Library, is reproduced here with the alterations, which are apparently authoritative, contained in a copy of the MS. to which Mr. Forster had access.]

THE family of the Swifts are ancient in Yorkshire. From them descended a noted person, who passed under the name of Cavaliero Swift, a man of wit and humour. He was created an Irish Peer by King Charles the First, 20 March 1627, with the title of Viscount of Carlingford, but never was in that kingdom. Many traditional pleasant stories are related of him, which the family planted in Ireland hath received from their parents. This lord died without issue male ; and his heiress, whether of the first or second descent, was married to Robert Fielding, Esquire, commonly called handsome Fielding. She brought him a considerable estate in Yorkshire, which he squandered away, but had no children. The Earl of Eglinton married another co-heiress of the same family.

Another of the same family was Sir Edward Swift,

well known in the times of the great Rebellion and Usurpation, but I am ignorant whether he left heirs or no.

Of the other branch, whereof the greatest part settled in Ireland, the founder was William Swift, prebendary of Canterbury, towards the last years of Queen Elizabeth, and during the reign of King James the First. He was a divine of some distinction. There is a sermon of his extant, and the title is to be seen in the catalogue of the Bodleian Library, but I never could get a copy, and I suppose it would now be of little value.

This William married the heiress of Philpot, I suppose a Yorkshire gentleman, by whom he got a very considerable estate, which however she kept in her own power, I know not by what artifice. She was a capricious, ill-natured, and passionate woman, of which there have been told several instances. And it hath been a continual tradition in the family, that she absolutely disinherited her only son Thomas, for no greater crime than that of robbing an orchard when he was a boy. And thus much is certain, that Thomas never enjoyed more than one hundred pounds a year, which was all at Goodrich, in Herefordshire, whereof not above one-half is now in the possession of a great great grandson, except a church or chapter lease which was not renewed.

His original picture was in the hands of Godwin Swift, of Dublin, Esq., his great grandson ; as well as that of his wife, who seems to have a good deal of the shrew in her countenance ; whose arms as an heiress are joined with his own ; and by the last he seems to have been a person somewhat fantastic ; for he altered the family coat of arms and gives as his own device, a Dolphin (in those days called a Swift) twisted about an anchor, with this motto, *Festina lente.*

There is likewise a seal with the same coat of arms (his, not joined with the wife's), which the said William commonly made use of ; and this was also in the possession of Godwin Swift above mentioned.

His eldest son Thomas seems to have been a clergyman before his father's death. He was vicar of Goodrich, in Herefordshire, within a mile or two of Ross : he had likewise another church living, with about one hundred pounds a year in land (part whereof was by church leases), as I have already mentioned. He built a house on his own land in the village of Goodrich, which by the architecture denotes the builder to have been somewhat whimsical and singular, and very much towards a projector. The house is above an hundred years old and still in good repair, inhabited by a tenant of the female line ; but the landlord, a young gentleman, lives upon his own estate in Ireland.

This Thomas was much distinguished by his courage, as well as his loyalty to King Charles the First, and the sufferings he underwent for that prince, more than any person of his condition in England. Some historians of those times relate several particulars of what he acted, and what hardships he underwent for the person and cause of that martyr'd prince. He was plundered by the Roundheads six and thirty, some say above fifty, times.

The author of *Mercurius Rusticus* dates the beginning of his sufferings so early as October, 1642. The Earl of Stamford, who had the command of the Parliament army in those parts, loaded him at first with very heavy exactions ; and afterwards at different times robbed him of all his books and household furniture, and took away from the family even their wearing apparel ; with some other circumstances of cruelty too tedious to relate at large in this place. The Earl being asked why he committed these barbarities, my author says "he gave two reasons for it : first, because he (Mr. Swift) had bought arms and conveyed them into Monmouthshire, which, under his Lordship's good favour, was not so ; and secondly, because, not long before, he preached a sermon in Ross upon the text Give unto Cæsar the things that are Cæsar's, in which his Lordship said he had spoken treason in endeavouring to give Cæsar more than his due. These two crimes cost Mr. Swift no less than £300."

About that time he engaged his small estate, and having quilted all the money he could get in his waistcoat, got off to a town held for the King : where, being asked by the Governor, who knew him well, what he could do for his Majesty, Mr. Swift said he would give the King his coat, and stripping it off, presented it to the Governor ; who observing it to be worth little, Mr. Swift said, Then take my waistcoat, and bid the Governor weigh it in his hand ; who, ordering it to be unripped, found it lined with three hundred broad pieces of gold, which as it proved a seasonable relief, must be allowed an extraordinary supply from a private clergyman of a small estate, so often plundered, and soon after turned out of his livings in the Church.

At another time being informed that three hundred horse of the rebel party intended in a week to pass over a certain river, upon an attempt against the cavaliers, Mr. Swift having a head mechanically turned, he contrived certain pieces of iron with three spikes, whereof one must always be with the point upward ; he placed them over night in the ford, where he received notice that the rebels would pass early the next morning, which they accordingly did, and lost two hundred of their men, who were drowned or trod to death by the falling of their horses, or torn by the spikes.

His sons, whereof four were settled in Ireland (driven thither by their sufferings, and by the death of their father), related many other passages, which they learnt either from their father himself, or from what had been told them by the most credible persons of Herefordshire, and some neighbouring counties : and which some of those sons often told to their children ; many of which are still remembered, but many more forgot.

In 1646 he was deprived of both his Church livings sooner than most other loyal clergymen, upon account of his superior zeal for the King's cause, and his estate sequestered. His preferments, at least that of Goodrich, were given at first to one Giles Rawlins, and after to William Tringham, a fanatical saint, who scrupled not however to conform upon the Restoration, and lived many years, I think till after the Revolution.

The Committees of Hereford had kept Thomas Swift a close prisoner for a long time in Ragland Castle before they ordered his ejectment for scandal and delinquency (as they termed it), and for being in actual service against the Parliament. On the 5th July 1646 they ordered the profits of Gotheridge (Goodrich) into the hands of Jonath : Dryden, minister, until about Christmas following ; and on 24th March they inducted Giles Rawlins into this parish : who in 1654 was succeeded by Tringham. His other living of Bridstow underwent the same fate. For he was ejected from this on 25th Sept. 1646, and it was given to the curate, one Jonath : Smith, whom they liked better, and ordered to be inducted into his Rector's cure. What became of him afterwards I know not, but in 1654 one John Somers got this living.

The Lord Treasurer Oxford told the Dean of St. Patrick's, the grandson of this eminent sufferer, that he had among his father's (Sir Edward Harley's) papers, several letters from Mr. Thomas Swift writ in those times, which he promised to give to the Dean ; but never going to his house in Herefordshire while he was treasurer, and Queen Anne's death happening in three days after his removal, the Dean went to Ireland, and the Earl being tried for his life, and dying while the Dean was in Ireland, he could never get them.

Mr. Thomas Swift died May 2nd 1658, and in the 63rd year of his age. His body lies under the altar at Goodrich, with a short inscription. He died before the return of King Charles the Second, who by the recommendations of some prelates had promised, if ever God should restore him, that he would promote Mr. Swift in the Church, and other ways reward his family for his extraordinary services, zeal, and persecutions in the royal cause. But Mr. Swift's merit died with himself.

He left ten sons and three or four daughters, most of which lived to be men and women. His eldest son Godwin Swift, of Goodridge, Co., Hereford, Esq., one of the Society of Gray's Inn (so styled by Guillym in his Heraldry) was called to the bar before the Restoration. He married a relation of the old Marchioness of Ormond, and upon that account, as well as his father's loyalty, the old Duke of Ormond made him his Attorney General in the palatinate of Tipperary. He had four wives, one of which, to the great offence of his family, was co-heiress to Admiral Deane, who was one of the Regicides. She was Godwin's third wife. Her name was Hannah, daughter of Major Richard Deane, by whom he had issue Deane Swift, and several other children.

This Godwin left several children, who have all estates. He was an ill pleader, but perhaps a little too dextrous in the subtle parts of the law.

The second son of Mr. Thomas Swift was called by the same name, was bred at Oxford, and took orders. He married the daughter of Sir William D'Avenant, but died young, and left only one son, who was also called Thomas, and is now rector of Putenham in Surrey. His widow lived long, was extremely poor, and in part supported by the famous Dr. South, who had been her husband's intimate friend.

The rest of his sons, as far as I can call to mind, were Mr. Dryden Swift (called so after the name of his mother, who was a near relation to Mr. Dryden the Poet), William, Jonathan, and Adam, who all lived and died in Ireland. But none of them left male issue, except Jonathan, who besides a daughter left one son, born seven months after his father's death ; of whose life I intend to write a few memorials.

Jonathan Swift, Doctor of Divinity, and Dean of St. Patrick's, was the only son of Jonathan Swift, who was the seventh or eighth son of Mr. Thomas Swift abovementioned, so eminent for his loyalty and his sufferings.

His father died young, about two years after his marriage : he had some employments and agencies ; his death was much lamented on account of his reputation for integrity, with a tolerable good understanding. He married Mrs. Abigail Erick, of Leicestershire, descended from the most ancient family of the Ericks, who derive their lineage from Erick the forester, a great commander, who raised an army to oppose the invasion of William the Conqueror, by whom he was vanquished, but afterward employed to command that prince's forces; and in his old age retired to his house in Leicestershire, where his family hath continued ever since, but declining every age, and are now in the condition of very private gentlemen.

This marriage was on both sides very indiscreet; for his wife brought her husband little or no fortune, and his death happening so suddenly before he could make a sufficient establishment for his family, his son (not then born) hath often been heard to say, that he felt the consequences of that marriage not only through the whole course of his education, but during the greatest part of his life.

He was born in Dublin, on St. Andrew's day, in the year 1667; and when he was a year old, an event happened to him that seems very unusual; for his nurse who was a woman of Whitehaven, being under an absolute necessity of seeing one of her relations, who was then extremely sick, and from whom she expected a legacy, and being at the same time extremely fond of the infant, she stole him on shipboard unknown to his mother and uncle, and carried him with her to Whitehaven, where he continued for almost three years. For, when the matter was discovered, his mother sent orders by all means not to hazard a second voyage, till he could be better able to bear it. The nurse was so careful of him, that before he returned he had learnt to spell; and by the time that he was three years old he could read any chapter in the Bible.

After his return to Ireland, he was sent at six years old to the school of Kilkenny, from whence at fourteen he was admitted into the University of Dublin, a pensioner, on the 24th April, 1682; where by the ill treatment of his nearest relations, he was so discouraged and sunk in his spirits that he too much neglected his academic studies; for some parts of which he had no great relish by nature, and turned himself to reading history and poetry : so that when the time came for taking his degree of bachelor of arts, although he had lived with great regularity and due observance of the statutes, he was stopped of his degree for dulness and insufficiency ; and at last hardly admitted in a manner little to his credit, which is called in that college *speciali gratiâ*, on the 15th February 1685, with four more on the same footing : and this discreditable mark, as I am told, stands upon record in their college registry.

The troubles then breaking out, he went to his mother, who lived in Leicester; and after continuing there some months, he was received by Sir William Temple, whose father had been a great friend to the family, and who was now retired to his house called Moor Park, near Farnham in Surrey; where he continued for about two years. For he happened before twenty years old, by a surfeit of fruit, to contract a giddiness and coldness of stomach that almost brought him to his grave ; and this disorder pursued him with intermissions of two or three years to the end of his life. Upon this occasion he returned to Ireland in 1690, by advice of physicians, who weakly imagined that his native air might be of some use to recover his health : but growing worse, he soon went back to Sir William Temple ; with whom growing into some confidence, he was often trusted with matters of great importance.

King William had a high esteem for Sir William Temple, by a long acquaintance, while that gentleman was ambassador and mediator of a general peace at Nimeguen. The King, soon after his expedition to England, visited his old friend often at Sheen, and took his advice in affairs of greatest consequence. But Sir William Temple, weary of living so near London, and resolving to retire to a more private scene, bought an estate near Farnham in Surrey, of about £100 a year, where Mr. Swift accompanied him.

About that time a Bill was brought into the House of Commons for triennial parliaments ; against which the

King, who was a stranger to our Constitution, was very averse, by the advice of some weak people, who persuaded the Earl of Portland that King Charles the First lost his crown and life by consenting to pass such a Bill. The Earl, who was a weak man, came down to Moor Park by his Majesty's orders to have Sir William Temple's advice, who said much to show him the mistake. But he continued still to advise the King against passing the Bill. Whereupon Mr. Swift was sent to Kensington with the whole account of the matter in writing to convince the King and the Earl how ill they were informed. He told the Earl, to whom he was referred by his Majesty (and gave it in writing), that the ruin of King Charles the First was not owing to his passing the Triennial Bill, which did not hinder him from dissolving any Parliament, but to the passing of another Bill, which put it out of his power to dissolve the Parliament then in being, without the consent of the House. Mr. Swift, who was well versed in English history, although he was under twenty-one years old, gave the King a short account of the matter, but a more large one to the Earl of Portland : but all in vain. For the King by ill advisers was prevailed upon to refuse passing the Bill. This was the first time that Mr. Swift had ever any converse with Courts, and he told his friends it was the first incident that helped to cure him of vanity.

The consequence of this wrong step in his Majesty was very unhappy ; for it put that prince under a necessity of introducing those people called Whigs into power and employments, in order to pacify them. For, although it be held a part of the King's prerogative to refuse passing a Bill, yet the learned in the law think otherwise, from that expression used at the coronation, wherein the prince obligeth himself to consent to all laws, *quas vulgus elegerit.*

Mr. Swift having lived with Sir William Temple some time, and resolving to settle himself in some way of living, was inclined to take orders. But first commenced M.A. in Oxford as a student of Hart Hall on 5th July, 1692. However, although his fortune was very small, he had a scruple of entering into the Church merely for support, and Sir William, then being Master of the Rolls in Ireland, offered him an employ of about £120 a year in that office ; whereupon Mr. Swift told him, that since he had now an opportunity of living without being driven into the Church for a maintenance, he was resolved to go to Ireland, and take holy orders. In the year 1694 he was admitted into deacon's and priest's orders by Dr. William Moreton, Bishop of Kildare, who ordained him priest at Christ Church the 13th January that year. He was recommended to the Lord Capel, then Lord Deputy, who gave him a prebend in the north worth about £100 a year, called the Prebend of Kilroot in the Cathedral of Connor, of which growing weary in a few months he returned to England, resigned his living in favour of a friend who was reckoned a man of sense and piety, and was besides encumbered with a large family. After which he continued in Sir William Temple's house till the death of that great man, who beside a legacy left him the care, and trust, and advantage of publishing his posthumous writings.

Upon this event Mr. Swift removed to London, and applied by petition to King William upon the claim of a promise his Majesty had made to Sir William Temple, that he would give Mr. Swift a prebend of Canterbury or Westminster. Col. Henry Sidney, lately created Earl of Romney, who professed much friendship for him, and was now in some credit at Court, on account of his early services to the King in Holland before the Revolution, for which he was made Master-General of the Ordnance, Constable of Dover Castle, Lord Warden of the Cinque Ports, and one of the Lords of the Council, promised to second Mr. Swift's petition ; but said not a word to the King. And Mr. Swift, having totally relied on this lord's honour, and having neglected to use any other instrument of reminding his Majesty of the promise made to Sir William Temple, after long attendance in vain, thought it better to comply with an invitation, given him by the Earl of Berkeley, to attend him to Ireland, as his chaplain and private secretary ; his lordship having been appointed one of the Lords Justices of that kingdom, with the Duke of Bolton and the Earl of Galway, on the 29th June, 1699. He attended his lordship, who landed near Waterford ; and Mr. Swift acted as secretary the whole journey to Dublin. But another person had so far insinuated himself into the earl's favour, by telling him that the post of secretary was not proper for a clergyman, nor would be of any advantage to one who aimed only at Church preferments, that his lordship after a poor apology gave that office to the other.

In some months the Deanery of Derry fell vacant ; and it was the Earl of Berkeley's turn to dispose of it. Yet things were so ordered that the secretary having received a bribe, the Deanery was disposed of to another, and Mr. Swift was put off with some other Church livings not worth above a third part of that rich Deanery ; and at this present time, not a sixth : namely, the Rectory of Agher, and the Vicarage of Laracor and Rathbeggan in the Diocese of Meath ; for which his letters patent bear date the 24th of February following. The excuse pretended was his being too young, although he were then thirty years old.

The next year, in 1700, his grace Narcissus Lord Archbishop of Dublin was pleased to confer upon Mr. Swift the prebend of Dunlaven in the Cathedral of St. Patrick's, by an instrument of institution and collation dated the 28th of September. And on the 22nd of October after, he took his seat in the chapter.

From this time he continued in Ireland ; and on the 16th of February, 1701, he took his degree of Doctor of Divinity in the University of Dublin. After which he went to England about the beginning of April, and spent near a year there.

He appeared at the Dean's visitation on the 11th of January, 1702 ; at a chapter held the 15th of April ; and at the visitation on the 10th of January, 1703. He attended a chapter on the 9th of August, and the visitation of 8th of January, 1704. He was at two chapters held the 2nd of February and the 2nd of March following, and at the visitation the 7th of January, 1705.   Also in April, August, and January, 1706 ; and in April, June, July, and August, 1707.   Set sail for England 28th of November, 1707 ; landed at Darpool ; next day rode to Parkgate ; and so went to Leicester first.

He was excused at the visitation in. 1707 and 1708 ; and on the 9th of January 1709 expected at the visitation, but did not come.   He spent 1708 in England, and set sail from Darpool for Ireland 29th of June, 1709, and landed at Ringsend next day, and went straight to Laracor.   Was often giddy and had fits this year.

He attended a chapter held the 15th February, 1709 ; also at a chapter 29th July and 11th August, 1710. Excused at the visitation 8th of January, 1710.   He was not in Ireland after this till his instalment as Dean on the 13th of June, 1713.   On the 27th of August he nominated Dr. Edward Synge to act in his absence as sub-dean ; and came no more to Ireland until after the Queen's death.   He set out to Ireland from Letcombe in Berkshire August the 16th, 1714 ; landed in Dublin the 24th of the same month ; and held a chapter on the 15th of September, 1714.

APPENDIX II

NOTE ON THE *TALE OF A TUB*

THE *Tale of a Tub* was first issued in April or May, 1704. During that year three editions appeared (besides those that were pirated, or published in Ireland, where no English copyright was secured by law).   In 1705, a fourth edition was issued by John Nutt, who had been the authorized publisher from the first.   The demand then fell off, or was met by unauthorized editions : and the next, or fifth, authorized edition was that issued, also by Nutt, in 1710, with the *Author's Apology* prefixed. After this the copyright seems to have passed into the hands of Benjamin Motte and Tooke. In 1711, I find an unauthorized version, without the *Apology:* but the sixth and seventh editions appear only in 1724 and 1727. In 1747 there appeared an eleventh edition, published by Bathurst.

The differences between the editions are very slight, except for a few notes, taken from the adverse critiques of Wotton and others, introduced in the fourth and later editions.

A fact so well ascertained as Swift's authorship of the *Tale*, would not be worth discussion, were it not for the half paradoxical doubt cast on it by Johnson. That doubt clearly arose from Johnson's wish to disparage Swift, by denying the authenticity of his greatest work. But setting aside the overwhelming intrinsic evidence, it may be well to state shortly the proof positive. First, Swift's letter to Tooke (June 29, 1710) is only intelligible as written by the author of the *Tale*. Secondly, in a list of those of his pieces that are suitable for a miscellany, written in his own hand, the *Apology* occurs ; and if he wrote the *Apology*, he necessarily wrote the *Tale*. Thirdly, in the Journal to Stella, he clearly refers to it as "*you know what*," which might help him with his new Tory friends. Fourthly, he treasured amongst his papers a letter from a Quaker in Philadelphia, in which the writer thanked him—truly the strangest thanks that any of his sect ever gave—as the author of the *Tale*. So generally accepted did the authorship at length become, that Pulteney in a letter to Swift himself (June 3, 1740) actually names the book in some Latin verses, as one of the manifestations of his genius.

Seu levis a vacuo fabula sumpta cado.

Lastly, in the period of almost speechless apathy which preceded his death, Swift was heard by Mrs. Whiteway to mutter, as he turned over the leaves of the book,

"Good God, what a genius I had when I wrote that book!"

APPENDIX III

THE AUTHORSHIP OF THE *HISTORY OF THE FOUR LAST YEARS OF THE QUEEN*

As is the case with several particulars in Swift's life, doubts, proceeding from what was at first a mere suspicion, have been cast on his authorship of this work : and these doubts have grown until they gave rise to a positive denial. I must begin the discussion of the subject, by expressing my indebtedness to Mr. Elwin, for the evidence and arguments bearing on it which he has enabled me to adduce.

We know for a certainty, from the published correspondence of Swift, that the work, written long before, was revised and sent to Dr. William King, the Principal of St. Mary's Hall, Oxford, for publication in 1737. The bearer of the MS. was Lord Orrery. Swift was deeply interested in the work : but much to his vexation, it was strongly objected to by those who represented the very Ministry whose defence it undertook. Remonstrances came to him from Erasmus Lewis, the old official : from Lord Bolingbroke : and from Lord Oxford as representing his father, the special patron of Swift.

This prevented its appearance at the time ; but, in 1758, what claimed to be this work was published by Dr. Lucas, into whose hands a transcript had fallen, and who, while professing it worth publication from its interest and ability, was careful to disclaim any sympathy with the opinions it professed ; and who, in particular, strives to exaggerate the dangerous interpretation which might be placed on certain casual words in it.[1]

[1] *E.g.*, the use of the phrase "abdicated King" of James II. Had Lucas been forging a subject of accusation against Swift, he

The author's preface prefixed to some of the editions, tells us that the treatise was written at Windsor, and that he had resolved to publish it in 1713, but was kept back owing to the alterations desired by Lord Oxford, and Lord Bolingbroke, to which the author refused to submit. This supposes 1712, or early in 1713, as the date of its being written, the narrative beginning in January $17\frac{12}{11}$. Now we know from the Journal, which was not published in 1758, that Swift was at Windsor in September 1712. The supposed forger thus hit upon the truth : and he is further corroborated by the account given in Swift's letter to Lord Oxford of June 14, 1737—which was also unpublished in 1758.

This so-called forgery was published in 1758, and received universally as genuine. It attracted much notice. Dr. King, to whom it had been entrusted, lived till 1763 : he was a man of letters, yet he published no denial : he was a man widely known, yet he said nothing against it, or we should certainly have had his doubts repeated. Lord Orrery had carried over the MS. : had read the work ; and was a man much inclined to literary talk. Yet he also lived till 1762, and never allowed any denial to escape him. Deane Swift, who was at St. Mary's Hall, and intimate with King, tells us that his cousin handed the MS. about in Ireland. Yet no one amongst all these readers of the MS. ever convicted or accused the publication of being a forgery.

This evidence is in itself surely strong enough : and the internal evidence of the piece tells the same way. It is not indeed equal to the great efforts of Swift : no genius is ever equal to himself throughout all his work. But it has conclusive and inimitable marks of Swift's manner in every page : and it has no real marks of forgery. Its resemblances to his style are natural : not of the pronounced and forced type which would certainly have appeared had the forger been at work.

But Mr. Elwin has enabled me to adduce another and

would have invented something a little more conclusive of guilt than this careless phrase.

almost conclusive piece of evidence. It is the following abstract of the history by the historical collector, Dr. Birch, which is amongst his manuscripts in the British Museum.

"June 30, 1742."

"From ye manuscript of Dr. Swift's History of the last Parliament of Queen Anne : written at Windsor in 1713.

"It begins with the characters of Lord Sommers, Lord Godolphin, Lord Sunderland, Lord Wharton, Lord Cowper, Duke and Duchess of Marlborough, Earl of Nottingham, and Duke of Somerset, and Prince Eugene.

"Lord Sommers—a man of strong passions, though a great master of them, he frequently discovered great rage in his countenance, at the same time that his words and the tone of his voice were full of softness—extremely civil in his whole behaviour, even in private conversation, though it appeared there like formality ; of excellent parts, well cultivated by polite learning, but had no great relish for conversation, spending his leisure hours in thinking and reading, except when he relaxed himself with an illiterate chaplain, an humble friend, or a favourite domestic.

"Lord Godolphin, said to be designed for a trade before he was a page at court ; faithful to his master King James II. to a degree beyond many persons, who had much greater obligations ; corresponded with his queen, and made little presents to her, with the leave of K. William, though he concealed it from her lest she should be offended, and wrote to her in a style of *double entendre*, between *Love* and *Respect*. Had a turn for gallantry, and would write songs to his mistress with a pencil on a card. Had a passion for the Duchess of Marlborough. Negligent of the public accounts, but not corrupt.

"Lord Sunderland received his religion, that is, his indifference for any form of it, from his father, and his politics from his tutor, Dr. Trimnell, afterwards Bishop of Winchester. A Republican in his notions, and so zealously so, while his father was living, that he refused often to be styled lord and chose to be called Charles Spencer, declaring that he hoped to see the time when the name of a lord should be extinguished. Moderate in his parts, and no scholar either in reality or even in the opinion of the public, notwithstanding his vast library.

"Lord Wharton, perfectly indifferent to all real religion, though exclusive of this, in all other respects, a firm Presbyterian. Of great address in the management of elections, and bringing over young men of quality to his schemes by engaging them in his parties of pleasure, but of so prostitute a character, that it was infamous even to be seen with him. By his administration of Ireland liable to an impeachment, at least for high crime and misdemeanours.

"Lord Cowper, ignorant in all foreign affairs, as appeared in council, and brought into the high station of Chancellor, without any of the intermediate steps to it, by those who wanted a person in it, that would give no obstruction to any of their designs, though his character was blemished with such irregularities as rendered him by no means a fit keeper of her Majesty's conscience. *A piece of a scholar*, and a tolerable logical reasoner, but accustomed to disguise a cause by sophistry and false glosses.

"Duke of Marlborough, of good understanding, though absolutely uncultivated by education or study; had a prodigious command of his passions upon all occasions, except after he was dismissed from being general: his character for personal courage doubted by many, though it might justly be supposed consistent with the prudence of a general. Avaricious, and resolved to continue the war for the immense profits he made of it.

"Duchess of Marlborough, a woman of unbounded avarice, infinite pride, and ungovernable rage; affecting the character of wit, though supporting it chiefly by the fashionable humour of ridiculing the doctrines of Christianity and religion in general.

"Earl of Nottingham declared at first against the Government of K. William, though he afterwards took a post under him—a conduct to be excused only from his numerous family. Took great pains to run down Lord Godolphin and the Junta, but being disobliged by the refusal of the post of Lord President of the Council, became a zealous enemy of the new Ministry. His countenance not at all hypocritical, nor unsuitable to his temper. Of very slender acquisitions in learning, and from his facility of speaking persuading himself that he was master of an extraordinary eloquence, and affecting to show it on all occasions.

" Duke of Somerset, of immeasurable pride, with a very bad judgment, though at first an enemy to the old Ministry, soon quarrelling with the new, because they could not be governed by him ; and at last lost his favour with the Queen, which himself and his duchess had gained by the respect which they showed her Majesty while she was Princess of Denmark.

"Prince Eugene, a lover of war, a science in which alone he could make any figure ; cruel to a degree, that he would at any time have sacrificed 20,000 men to any point which he had in view ; and resolved, while he was in England, to have taken off the Earl of Oxford *à la negligence*, as he styled it, for which purpose he encouraged those parties who did so much mischief in the streets of London in the night.

" Lord Oxford's passion, ambition, without pride, cruelty or avarice, and though negligent of his friends' interests on some occasions, yet still more so of his own. Too patient under scandalous imputations, though thoroughly innocent of them. Those thoughts occurred at first to him which long deliberation alone suggests to others.

" Mr. Robert Walpole engaged to his party by his absolute indifference to any principles, and secured to them by the loss of his place ; whose firmness of countenance, which set him above that infirmity which makes men bashful, and readiness in speaking, made him esteemed by them one of their leaders of the second form.

" The history sets forth the reasons of the changes of the Ministry, which were—I. Their bad policies in refusing the terms offered by the King of France at Gertruy-denberg, and imposing such upon him as neither that monarch nor his kingdom would submit to, and which, being published by him, united all his subjects in a re-solution to support him at all hazards, and with the sacri-fice of their whole property, and particularly the clergy, who offered to melt down their consecrated plate for that purpose.   II. Their principles with regard to government and religion, which were extremely disagreeable to her Majesty.   III. And the superior way in which they dictated to her upon all occasions, and the shocking treatment which she received from the Duchess of Marl-borough.   IV. That among other instances of ill-conduct they were highly blameable in inviting over so vast a number of Palatines, an useless idle body of men, from whom we could expect no advantage : upon which occasion Dr. Swift examines in what sense a nation may be said to be richer for the number of its inhabitants.

"That the Dutch were clandestinely treating with the French on their own separate account.

"Reflections on Buys the Dutch Minister, and the whole Dutch nation.

"Reflections on the French nation, with an invective against the injustice of their Salic Law.

"Abusive character of Count Bothmar, whose memorial he says in the first draught to have been unknown to his master, though in his correction of that passage he seems to suppose it was known.

"The history ends with the peace of Utrecht."

Now, in the first place, this abstract, which is in Dr. Birch's own handwriting, is dated in June, 1742,—nearly three years before the death of Swift.   It was clearly taken from a manuscript *substantially* identical with that from which the book was published in 1758. We might, indeed, guess that the MS. which Lucas followed had received some alterations and additions as compared with that which Birch's abstract sums up.   But this apparent discrepancy actually helps to establish the genuineness of the book : for Birch says his abstract was taken from *the* manuscript, meaning thereby, as we must reasonably infer, the manuscript written by Swift himself. A man accustomed as he was to literary accuracy must otherwise have said that he followed a copy. On the other hand the publisher of the book in 1758, says that he followed "the last manuscript copy, corrected and enlarged by the author's own hand."

If, then, we suppose the book to be a forgery, we must suppose also that so careful a collector as Dr. Birch accepted without question a forgery which he had every opportunity of detecting : we must suppose that the forger courted detection by allowing his work to get abroad while Swift was still alive : [1] and that he concocted a counterfeit work when the genuine MS. was certainly in existence and might at any time have appeared to confute him.

It would clearly require powerful arguments to meet these proofs that the work is Swift's own. But the evidence to the contrary really amounts to nothing at all. The first doubt was raised by Dr. Johnson, in his *Life of Swift* (written more than twenty years after Lucas's book was published). The History, he says, was " after Swift's death in the hands of Lord Orrery and Dr. King.[2] A book under that title was published with Swift's name by Dr. Lucas, of which I can only say, that it seemed by no means to correspond with the notions that I had formed of it, from a conversation which I once heard between the Earl of Orrery and old Mr. Lewis." The doubt, it is only fair to say, is hesitatingly expressed ; and Johnson must have known how deceptive the memory as to such matters is, and how feeble a guide is the recollection of others' report of what they recollected. But even this hesitating doubt is completely dissipated

---

[1] Doubtless his mind was gone : but the world could not know that recovery was impossible.

[2] This is inaccurate. It was in their hands for a certain time during Swift's life. What became of it after his death we have no means of knowing.

as evidence when we find Johnson himself, twenty years before, fully accepting the book as genuine. In the *Idler* (No. 65, July 14, 1759) Johnson says, "with hopes like these, to the executors of Swift was committed the history of the last years of Queen Anne, and to those of Pope, the works which remained unprinted in his closet. The performances of Pope were burnt by those whom he had, perhaps, selected from all mankind as most likely to publish them : and the history had likewise perished, had not a straggling transcript fallen into busy hands."

With Johnson any doubt that is worth listening to, begins and ends. It was revived again by Lord Stanhope,[1] who in the text of the *History of the Reign of Queen Anne* speaks of "great reason to doubt" : and in the index names the work as "falsely ascribed to Swift." He tells us also that Macaulay had "more than once expressed (to Lord Stanhope) the conviction that it was not his." This is doubtless confirmed by a note which Macaulay has placed opposite the title of the book in the copy of Lord Orrery's *Remarks*, annotated by him in pencil, which the British Museum possesses—"Wretched stuff ; and, I firmly believe, not Swift's." But Macaulay's casually expressed convictions are belied by the fact that he actually quotes a description given in the book, of Lord Somers's manner, as written by one of his enemies.[2] But a forger, who was at work half a century later, was neither a good authority on the peculiarities of Lord Somers, nor could he be called one of his "enemies."

So much for the growth of doubts which, once started, are apt to be pursued from mere love of paradox. They were revived in 1873, when Mr. Disraeli, in a speech at Glasgow, referred to the work as Swift's, and for so doing

---

[1] 4th edition, ii. 176.

[2] The words in the book are : "His breast has been seen to heave, and his eyes to sparkle with rage in those very moments when his words, and the cadence of his voice, were in the humblest and softest manner." Macaulay writes, as the description of his enemies, "Sometimes while his voice was soft, and his words kind and courteous, his delicate frame was almost convulsed by suppressed emotion."—*History*, iv. 448, edit. 1855.

was accused by a correspondent in the *Times*, of surprising ignorance.   The controversy which ensued threw no new light whatever on the subject.

APPENDIX IV

THE MARRIAGE OF SWIFT AND STELLA

RATHER than encumber the narrative of Swift's life with a discussion so long as this must be, I have deemed it best to state separately the arguments in favour of his marriage.   I must again acknowledge the invaluable aid which I have received from Mr. Elwin in weighing the evidence and in arranging the arguments.   Much of what follows I might attribute entirely to him, were it not that by so doing I should impute to him, not only the merit of his own arguments, but the defects which may belong to my method of stating them.

For seventy years after the death of Swift, his marriage to Stella had come to be accepted, after the amount of doubt and discussion which was inseparable from a matter so mysterious, as a fact.   But in 1820 Mr. Monck Mason published his *History and Antiquities of the Cathedral Church of St. Patrick.*   A large part of that volume is devoted to the life of Swift : and the principal, if not the only, novelty in that life is its maintenance of the proposition that the marriage, so long accepted, had no foundation at all in fact.   Mason's book was published between the first and second editions of Scott's Swift : and in the latter edition (1824), while Scott notices the arguments which Mason had brought against him, he refuses to change his view in deference to them.   Mason's view, however, was accepted by the late Mr. Dilke : and Mr. Forster, although he did not reach the point in Swift's life where a full discussion was possible, yet states (*Life of Swift*, p. 140) that he "can find no evidence of a marriage that is at all reasonably sufficient." Since the first edition of the present book was published Mr. Churton Collins, in a recent volume on Swift, expresses, even more strongly, the same view.

I regret that a student of literature so enthusiastic and accomplished as Mr. Collins does not agree with my view ; and still more that he has ignored many of the arguments I have adduced. I can only say that my opinion on all the evidence remains unchanged.

Now, undoubtedly, it must be admitted that the course of Swift's biography would run more smoothly, and that expressions used in his letters would be more naturally and simply brought into accord with the facts, were it possible to set aside this marriage as a fabrication. Were it not so, the matter would need no argument at all. But to argue as Mr. Collins does, that if we believe Swift to have gone through this ceremony, we are bound to condemn him as utterly base, "all that his enemies would represent "—"cruel and mean," "cowardly and treacherous," "lying and hypocritical," seems to me a position entirely untenable.

Swift found himself in a position of the most painful sort possible. The question simply is what course did he follow to satisfy Stella. That he acted wisely or rightly, no one can pretend. But it is equally absurd to say that the concession he made was either heartless, cruel, or base.

It must be admitted, further, that some of the evidence adduced is absolutely worthless, depending upon no more than the idle stories of those who sought to gain attention by inventing gossip. The truth must be reached by testing the more valid evidence adduced, and the arguments with which Monck Mason attempts to set this evidence aside.

To begin with the earliest in the order of time. Lord Orrery, in his *Remarks* on Swift, published in 1752, states (Letter II.), "Stella's real name was Johnson. She was the daughter of Sir William Temple's steward, and the concealed, but *undoubted*, wife of Dr. Swift. . . . I cannot tell how long she remained in England, or whether she made more journeys than one *to* Ireland after Sir William Temple's death, but, *if my informations are right,* she was married to Dr. Swift in the year 1716, by Dr. Ashe, then Bishop of Clogher."

Next Dr. Delany, Swift's old and intimate friend, in his *Observations on Lord Orrery's Remarks,* published in 1754, writes (p. 52), "Your Lordship's account of his marriage is, *I am satisfied,* true." He then turns to an explanation of Swift's conduct in a matter the truth of which he thinks beyond doubt : and tells, on the authority of an intimate friend of his own, whose informant was Stella herself, the story of her refusal, as "too late," of Swift's offer to own the marriage about six years after the ceremony had taken place.

Before going into any further evidence, let us see how Mason deals with these two witnesses. "The first person," says Mason (p. 299), "that mentions it is John, Earl of Orrery, who relates 'that they were married in the year 1716, by Dr. Ashe, then Bishop of Clogher.' This however he is far from asserting positively : rather doubtingly he adds, 'if my informations are right'; so that this testimony, when we consider the temper and disposition of the narrator, the faltering manner in which it is advanced, and the weak arguments with which it is supported, becomes at length very feeble evidence indeed. The earl's account is, however, supported by that of Dr. Delany, who in his *Observations on Lord Orrery's Remarks,* declares his opinion of its truth. That Dr. Delany's acquaintance with this matter should go no further than opinion, furnishes argument against rather than for it, and yet the belief of this intimate friend of Swift is the best evidence we have in favour of the marriage, and that which most deserves our attention."

Mason adds the following note : "Dr. Delany does not, in his own work, give us any additional proof of the marriage ceremony having been performed, neither does he say that he received any direct communication upon the subject ; this would have been more to the purpose than all his reasoning, nor can we suppose, had he any such direct proof, that he would have recourse to such weak arguments as he employs."

From these comments we can gather some idea of the dishonesty with which Mason conducts the controversy, and the flagrant misrepresentation of evidence by which he imposes upon any one credulous enough to trust him. He quotes only the words in which Lord Orrery gives the detailed circumstances of the ceremony, the date and the person by whom it was performed. He suppresses altogether the previous assertion of Orrery that Stella was "the concealed, but *undoubted* wife" of Swift. This assertion is positive enough : it contains no doubt or faltering, and Orrery applies a qualifying phrase only to the further information about the details. But by quoting only this last, Mason is able to misrepresent the statement and dishonestly to attach the qualification to the main and central fact. As to the "weak arguments by which Lord Orrery supports it," these are only invented by Mason to serve his purpose. Orrery adduces no arguments, either weak or strong. He simply states that the fact was undoubted : and the value we place upon his assertion depends upon our estimate of his competence to form an opinion, and of his honesty in stating the degree of certainty which attached to the evidence upon which he depended.

Next as to Mason's description of Delany's evidence, which is just as dishonest. "The Earl's account," he says, "is supported by that of Delany, who declares his opinion of its truth." "Your *account* of the marriage is, *I am satisfied*, true," are Delany's actual words. The "account" referred clearly to the circumstances of the marriage : the fact was accepted as an undoubted truth. Delany does not express "an opinion" of its truth : he writes from first to last as if it were certain : and even as to the details, it is not an "opinion" of the truth of Lord Orrery's statement which he avows, but that "*he is satisfied*" of its truth.

Having thus twisted the statements, Mason affirms that Delany's acquaintance with this matter goes no further than opinion ; that "he does not in his own work give us any additional proof of the marriage ceremony having been performed "; that "he does not say that he received any direct communication upon the subject" : and that we cannot suppose "had he any such direct proof, that he would have recourse to such weak arguments as he employs." But Delany does tell us of the testimony of his own "well-known" friend, to whom Stella imparted her story, although Mason makes no reference to the fact. Just as in the case of Lord Orrery, Mason imputes to Delany arguments, to which Delany never has recourse. Delany accepts the evidence as sufficient, and then proceeds to suggest explanations of the conduct of Swift : but he does not even suggest that these explanations should be accepted as additional proofs : the evidence was too strong, to his mind, to require them.

To misrepresent statements is the surest proof of being unable to meet them. By deliberately suppressing and twisting what Lord Orrery and Delany said, Mason virtually threw up his case.

But to proceed to additional evidence. The next is that of George Monck Berkeley, in the Inquiry into the Life of Dean Swift, prefixed to his *Literary Relics*, published in 1789. "In 1716," he says (p. xxxvi.), Swift and Stella "were married by the Bishop of Clogher, who himself related the circumstance to Bishop Berkeley, by whose relict the story was communicated to *me*." Of this Monck Mason says : "What has been adduced by Mr. Monck Berkeley, in his *Literary Relics*, is certainly without foundation, viz. 'that the Bishop of Clogher himself related the circumstance to Bishop Berkeley, by whose relict, he says, it was communicated to him.' The Bishop of Clogher never could have had any communication with Berkeley upon the subject, for the former died in the year (1717) following that in which the marriage is reported to have been celebrated, and the latter was at that time in Italy, where he had resided during several preceding years."

Now Berkeley *was*, no doubt, abroad at the time. But Mason does not state that he was abroad in the capacity of tutor to the Bishop of Clogher's son, and that communications not only may, but must have passed between the bishop and his son's tutor. The circumstance need not have been related by word of mouth, as Mason assumes.[1] The essential fact, which was all that Monck Berkeley cared for, was that the communication took place : how it took place, is a matter of no moment. Berkeley was the respected friend both of the bishop and of Swift. To him, perhaps, sooner than to any other man, would the secret have been entrusted. So much for the intrinsic probability of the story. And who are the witnesses on whose authority we are to accept it ? Not the faintest suspicion could attach either to the Bishop of Clogher or to Berkeley. Could Berkeley's wife be mistaken ? The fact was a very simple one : that the Bishop of Clogher married Swift to Stella. How could she have misconceived, or misreported it, unless of set purpose ? And is it likely that she would put into her husband's mouth, after his death, a deliberate falsehood which she had invented herself, and in which she could have no sort of interest ? The same reasoning applies to the credibility of Monck Berkeley, who was a man of high integrity and whose narrative is marked by a full sense of responsibility.

Next there is the evidence of Thomas Sheridan in his *Life of Swift*, published in 1784, in which he speaks (p. 311 of 2nd edition) of the story of Swift's refusal to acknowledge the marriage, even at Stella's dying request. From an examination of the evidence dealt with in the next appendix I am compelled to reject the authenticity of this anecdote. But although Sheridan might have been mistaken as to the particular course which the interview took, from an imperfect recollection of his father's narrative, yet I do not think it is possible that he could have been mistaken as to the main fact, attested by his father's testimony, that the marriage had actually taken place. And his evidence becomes all the more difficult

---

[1] Mr. Collins repeats Monck Mason's assumption, and entirely ignores this explanation.

to set aside, from the fact that the elder Sheridan's authority is adduced by others as supporting their version of the story—a version which, while it differs from that of the younger Sheridan, is still based upon the same primary fact, that the marriage actually took place.

Another proof of the marriage, which might not in itself be strong, but which, as corroborative of the others, acquires much weight, is the assertion of Dr. Madden as quoted by Johnson in his "Life of Swift," (*Lives of the Poets*, Cunningham's edition, 3, 186). Johnson says that doubts have lately been thrown upon the marriage : "but alas !" he goes on, "poor Stella, as Dr. Madden told me, related her melancholy story to Dr. Sheridan when he attended her as a clergyman to prepare her for death." Johnson's information must have been received from Dr. Madden, most probably about 1745, when he was correcting and cutting down Madden's poem, called "Boulter's Monument," for which service Madden paid him ten pounds. The evidence was thus entirely independent of the testimony which the younger Sheridan gives at a later day of his father's knowledge of the story. We can scarcely believe that a man so masculine in intellect, and so conscientious in his adherence to strict accuracy as Johnson, would have quoted Madden's testimony as conclusive evidence, had he not known that Madden had drawn his information from Sheridan himself. From Sheridan also, in all probability, was derived that further evidence which Johnson quotes on Madden's authority : "Soon after, in his forty-ninth year, he was privately married to Mrs. Johnson, by Dr. Ashe, Bishop of Clogher, as Dr. Madden told me, in the garden" (*Lives of the Poets*, 3, 177). Monck Mason discredits the idea that Sheridan could have been Madden's informant, because they were different in politics. When, however, we remember that they were both clergymen, both frequenting Dublin society, both much connected with Trinity College, both men of kindly and sociable habits, the balance of probability is very decidedly the other way.

Such are the arguments in favour of the marriage. The witnesses all agree with one another (though the sources of their information are clearly independent) both in regard to the date, and in the other details of the ceremony. Though the report was published almost immediately after Swift's death, and had long been accepted by his most intimate friends, it never was contradicted either by Swift or Stella, or by any one whose authority would even be worth attention, except Dr. Lyon. As Dr. Lyon was only Swift's attendant in his later and feeble years, it may be questioned whether his evidence on the point would be of much value. But it is so vague in its character as to be even on this ground alone valueless. The story, Dr. Lyon says in his MS. notes in a copy of Hawkesworth's Life, now in the Forster Library at South Kensington, was "founded only on hearsay": and he adds a second-hand testimony to its falsity that proves how little he could trust to his own knowledge. "It is certain," he goes on, "that the Dean told one of his friends whom he advised to marry, 'that he never wished to marry at the time that he ought to have entered into that state : for he counted it as the happiest condition, especially towards the decline of life, when a faithful and tender friend is most wanted.' While he was talking to this effect his friend expressed his wishes to have seen him married. The Dean asked 'Why?' 'Because,' replied the other, 'I should have had the pleasure of seeing your offspring. All the world would have been pleased to have seen the issue of such a genius.' The Dean smiled, and denied his being married in the same manner as before : and said 'he never saw the woman he wished to be married to.' The same gentleman, who was intimate with Mrs. Dingley for ten years before she died, in 1743, took occasion to tell her, that such a story was whispered of her friend Mrs. Johnson's marriage with the Dean ; but she only laughed at it, as an idle tale founded on suspicion."

It is scarcely necessary to point out how small is the weight to be attached to this. Clearly Swift, even if the conversation occurred as stated, was speaking only in generalities. To any one on the distant terms in which the interlocutor clearly stood, it was certain that Swift would enter upon none of the secrets of his life. As to Mrs. Dingley, it is not likely that she would be entrusted with the secret at all. Her character and temper were troublesome, and her position was much more that of the companion, necessary for appearance, than that of the confidante. But if she had the secret in her keeping, she could choose no other way of turning aside an impertinent question than that which is reported. The whole paragraph could have been written only by one whose knowledge of Swift was based upon second-hand reports of his mere casual acquaintances. The utter baselessness of Lyon's testimony becomes even more evident when he adduces the disbelief of Swift's housekeeper, Mrs. Ridgway —an uneducated drudge—as an argument against the reality of an occurrence which, admittedly, was entrusted only to one or two of Swift's oldest and closest friends.

As flimsy is the argument against the marriage, which Lyon and Monck Mason adduce, viz. that Stella used her maiden name in her ordinary signatures and finally in her will. This was clearly only a part of the bargain : and after it had been finally settled between them, that no publication of the marriage should take place beyond a very limited circle of friends, it remained for Stella, both out of fidelity to their original bargain, and out of a regard for her own dignity, to use that name, and to exercise those free testamentary powers with which she was quite confident that Swift would never, on the strength of his legal rights, seek to interfere.

It is perhaps worth adding, as some confirmation of the stronger evidence given above, the testimony of Deane Swift. He had considerable opportunities for reaching the truth, although not always the best judgment for testing it ; and while he acknowledged, in one of the letters written to Lord Orrery during the lifetime of Swift, and transcribed in a volume now in Lord Cork's possession, that to many the marriage seemed based only "on a buzz and rumours," yet in his own volume on the Dean, published in 1755, he unhesitatingly expresses his conviction of its truth.

In connexion with a point which affects so nearly the relations between Swift and Stella, it may be well to say a word of what is the chief literary record of their love. This is the *Journal to Stella*, so-called, although the letters which make it up were addressed jointly to Esther Johnson and to Rebecca Dingley, and although the former did not yet bear to Swift the name of Stella. Of these letters the last twenty-five were published by Hawkesworth, and placed for reference in the British Museum: the earlier letters were published subsequently and less faithfully by Deane Swift, and of them only one remains to aid in verification. One of the chief features of these letters is the so-called "little language" which occurs in them: a language partly made up of the kindly and easy tricks of phrase in which Swift gave his confidences to Stella; partly of the childish and broken verbiage which recalled the prattle of her infancy, and in writing which Swift says "he makes up his mouth as if he was speaking it"; and partly of certain tokens which they used in a cypher of their own, and which we can occasionally interpret with fair certainty. M.D. seems to stand for Esther Johnson and her friend: PDFR. for Swift: Ppt. for Stella alone, and so on. Mr. Forster has spent some care not only in the useful labour of collating the letters which still exist, but in hazarding translations for such cyphers as these. Not a few may deem that such secrets lose in charm more than they yield of biographical interest, by a too painful nicety of interpretation.

APPENDIX V

SWIFT'S OFFER TO ANNOUNCE THE MARRIAGE

THE evidence which bears on the question of when, and by whom, any proposal to own the marriage, was made, is involved and inconsistent, and in one version tells more severely against Swift than any other incident of his life. On what basis rests a charge of callousness which, if true, would almost amount to barbarity?

Three stories have hitherto been given.

Writing in 1754, Dr. Delany says :—

" This (the Dean's increasing gloom of temper) gave Stella inexpressible uneasiness; and I well knew a friend to whom she opened herself upon that head, declaring that the Dean's temper was so altered, and his attention to money so increased (probably increased by his solicitude to save for her sake); her own health at the same time gradually impaired : that she could not take upon herself the care of his house and economy ; and therefore refused to be publicly owned for his wife, as he earnestly desired she should. It was then, she said, 'too late : and therefore better that they should live on, as they had hitherto done.' "

This refers to the year 1722 or thereabouts : since the paragraph which follows speaks of her resolution as confirmed, *not very long after*, by the publication of " Cadenus and Vanessa," just after the death of Vanessa in 1723.

Next Sheridan, the son of Swift's intimate friend, writing in 1784, says :—

" A short time before her death a scene passed between the Dean and her, an account of which I had from my father, and which I shall relate with reluctance, as it seems to bear more hard on Swift's humanity than any other part of his conduct in life. As she found her final dissolution approach, a few days before it happened, in the presence of Dr. Sheridan, she addressed Swift in the most earnest and pathetic terms to grant her dying request. That as the ceremony of marriage had passed between them, though for sundry considerations they had not co-habited in that state, in order to put it out of the power of slander to be busy with her fame after death, she adjured him by their friendship to let her have the satis-faction of dying at least, though she had not lived, his acknowledged wife. Swift made no reply, but turning on his heel, walked silently out of the room, nor ever saw her afterwards during the few days she lived. This behaviour threw Mrs. Johnson into unspeakable agonies, and for a time she sank under the weight of so cruel a disappointment. But soon after, roused by indignation, she inveighed against his cruelty in the bitterest terms ; and, sending for a lawyer, made her Will, bequeathing her fortune, by her own name, to charitable uses."

Lastly, on the authority of Theophilus Swift, the son of Deane Swift, Sir Walter Scott gives the following story, in which the words reported by Delany are transferred to the dying scene, but with a widely different purport from that of the story told by Sheridan. Theophilus Swift claimed to have his information from Mrs. Whiteway.

" When Stella was in her last weak state, and one day had come in a chair to the Deanery, she was with diffi-culty brought into the parlour. The Dean had prepared some mulled wine, and kept it by the fire for her refresh-ment. After tasting it she became very faint, but, having recovered a little by degrees, when her breath (for she was asthmatic) was allowed her, she desired to lie down. She was carried upstairs and laid on a bed ; the Dean sitting by her, held her hand, and addressed her in the most affectionate manner. She drooped, however, very much. Mrs. Whiteway was the only third person present. After a short time, her politeness induced her to withdraw to the adjoining room, but it was necessary, on account of air, that the door should not be closed : it was half shut— the rooms were close adjoining. Mrs. Whiteway had too much honour to listen, but could not avoid observing that the Dean and Mrs. Johnson conversed together in a low tone : the latter, indeed, was too weak to raise her voice. Mrs. Whiteway paid no attention, having no idle curiosity, but at length she heard the Dean say, in an audible voice, " Well, my dear, if you wish it, it shall be owned " ; to which Stella answered, with a sigh, ".It is too late."

With regard to these stories, this much may be said with confidence, that Delany is almost certain to be right, so far as his narrative goes : that Sheridan was at least honest, though the information he got from his father (who died in 1738) was too remote from the date when he wrote his book to let us accept, without hesitation, all he says : while Theophilus Swift, the hair-brained son of a very foolish father, was almost certain to be wrong even when professing to report the words of so trustworthy an authority as Mrs. Whiteway. His story is clearly a mere garbled version of that told by Delany, except that Delany's belongs to 1722, when it was probable, and Theophilus Swift's to 1727, when it was scarcely possible. Delany's story we may therefore accept as true : Theophilus Swift's we may pronounce false.

With regard to Sheridan's story, we must first look at its intrinsic probability. Swift, it may be allowed, had motives for refusing the acknowledgment in 1727, even though willing to propose it, according to Delany in 1722. Since 1722 the story of his connexion with Vanessa had come out by the publication of the poem " Cadenus and Vanessa." Had he acknowledged Stella as his wife in 1727, the precautions he had taken in their intercourse must have made him ridiculous ; we know, also, that in 1726 and 1727 he was exceedingly careful that no rumours should get abroad by Stella's dying at the Deanery. At that time he evidently avoided anything that could give the least confirmation to the report absurdly circumstantial in his imputing of motives and describing of conversations. His story might, no doubt, be reconciled with that of Delany, by supposing that the Dean had changed his mind in the interval between 1722 and 1727. But had the incident happened as described at the later date, Swift would have felt a resentment against Stella, which might no doubt have passed away with time, but which would probably have prevented his writing as he did of her, in terms of the most earnest affection, immediately after her death. Lastly, if Stella was so roused by indignation, why should she have acted, with regard to her Will, just as Swift had, more than a year before, suggested she should do ?[1] Would it not have been a more complete revenge to have published to the world the evidence of her marriage which she doubtless possessed, rather than have acquiesced in the refusal by using her maiden name, in a legal document ?

But here a new fragment of evidence helps us. Amongst the MSS. belonging to Lord Cork, I find a transcript of a letter from Deane Swift to Lord Orrery— one of a series written in the last years of the Dean's life, in which the following occurs :—

"I must correct myself again. What I writ of Stella from the best of my memory was not right exactly. Mrs. Whiteway says, he did not acknowledge her to be his wife in the presence of Dr. Sheridan, but that Stella told Dr. Sheridan he had offered to declare his marriage to the world, which she refused, alleging that it was then too late."

Here, then, is a fourth version of what probability would lead us to think was one and the same story at bottom. Deane Swift would not himself be entitled to a great deal of weight : but here he is almost certain to be right. Mrs. Whiteway was strictly honest and had the best means of information. She was intimate with Sheridan. Deane Swift, as her son-in-law, was in constant communication with her : and both were trying to amass all

<hr>

[1] Letter to Mr. Worrall, July 15, 1726.

the facts they could for Lord Orrery's book, which was already in preparation. The story was told even before the Dean's death. It is not a mere careless version, but is evidently carefully corrected after consultation with Mrs. Whiteway. The corrected version would seem to make the story less important, since it made Sheridan's evidence less direct ;[1] and Deane Swift would not readily or lightly have stript his story of any importance that it seemed to possess.

Now we have to see how it suits with the other versions. It is quite enough to account for, and dispose of, the flimsy superstructure that Theophilus Swift built on it, and that Sir Walter Scott accepted. But as the story brings in the elder Sheridan, it is absolutely inconsistent with the story told by Sheridan's son, attributing to his father an opposite version. We must believe one to be mistaken : and of the two, surely the younger Sheridan was most liable to mistake. He— when a boy of seventeen, too young to understand the real bearing of the question—had discussed the matter with his father at least forty-six years before he wrote. The discussion would necessarily involve the fact of Swift's original condition of secrecy. Is it impossible that this condition, imposed by Swift, may have led Sheridan to think that the refusal to remove it was Swift's also ?

The story, finally, agrees perfectly with that of Delany, and it would fix the friend of whom Delany speaks as the elder Sheridan himself. The relations between Delany and Sheridan were not very cordial : and this fact may have prompted Delany's omission of the name. An apparent difficulty in the way of this theory arises from the fact that Delany's story refers to 1722, while both the younger Sheridan and Dr. Madden, as reported by Johnson, represent Sheridan's information as given him

---

[1] The statement which Deane Swift corrects occurs previously in the same letter. "It is said, he acknowledged her to be his wife in the presence of Dr. Sheridan, some little time before she died."

by Stella only on her death-bed. But the difficulty is only apparent; although Delany's friend spoke of 1722, it does not follow that it was not on Stella's death-bed that he received the account of an occurrence which took place five years before.

APPENDIX VI

WOOD'S HALFPENCE

To attempt a complete explanation of this transaction is a hopeless task; but there are certain misrepresentations of it which it is well to clear away. Scott, whose notes to the *Drapier's Letters* repeat the impressions of earlier editors who were more conversant with the facts, treats the whole affair, in his *Life*, as a sort of portentous joke on the part of Swift. But it is Lord Stanhope whose version of the affair is most unfair.

He begins by describing the financial part of the patent as " directed by Walpole with his usual skill." Unless the word is used in a sarcastic sense, it is hard to say wherein this skill was shown. Lord Stanhope forgets to state that the proposed amount of copper coinage was from six to ten times more than independent and competent writers declared to be necessary. In what he calls "this clear and well-conducted transaction," Lord Stanhope finds only one, and that a trifling, flaw, which " could not materially affect the quantity or quality of the coin to be issued." This was the payment to the Duchess of Kendal of £10,000—or about 10 per cent of the whole coinage—as a preliminary bribe. Lord Stanhope omits to state the further deductions, in payments to the Crown and the Comptroller, amounting to £1000 a year.[1]

---

[1] This is the statement of the Government Report. The payment was apparently, as a fact, only £300. But the mis-

That Irish susceptibilities should have been aroused by the insulting manner of carrying out the transaction, seems to Lord Stanhope only a proof of the nation's folly. When the vote of the Parliament declares that the terms of the Patent had not been carried out, and that, even if they had been, the nation would have lost 150 per cent, Lord Stanhope meets the statement by quoting the impartial authority of Walpole. But Walpole's words, so far as they are intelligible at all, do not touch the fact that copper worth 12d. was to count for two shillings and sixpence in Ireland. His talk of the cost of coinage in the English mint, of the exchange, of "allowances," and so on, is all beside the question. England no doubt paid something for her copper coinage : Ireland was to pay a great deal more.

The Report of the Committee of Privy Council, which Lord Stanhope thinks clear and conclusive, has already been shown to be, in material points, fallacious. He praises Wood's conduct in consenting that $5\frac{1}{2}$d. should be the limit which any one could be compelled, in one payment, to receive : forgetting that in the multitude of petty payments in Ireland, this sufficiently ensured the speedy currency of the coin.

By arguments so weak as these Lord Stanhope maintains that Swift, for the purposes of a simulated indignation, traded on a popular delusion, and he further believes that Swift attacked this " clear and well-conducted transaction " with no ulterior purpose : that he had no tyranny and no misgovernment to expose, but only a childish love of mischief to indulge : and that, when the outcry against the halfpence was over, " the whole edifice of indignant patriotism crumbled to the ground ! "

statement represents either further error or more intricate dishonesty.

APPENDIX VII

PROCLAMATION AGAINST THE DRAPIER

Oct. 27th, 1724.

A PROCLAMATION for discovering ye Author of ye Pamphlet intituled A letter to ye whole people of Ireland, by M. B. Drapier, author of the Letter to the shopkeepers, etc.

£300 Reward.

BY THE LORD-LIEUTENANT AND COUNCIL OF IRELAND

A Proclamation.

CONTENT :

Whereas a wicked and malicious pamphlet, intituled A Letter to the whole people of Ireland, by M. B. Drapier, author of the Letter to the shopkeepers, etc., printed by John Harding, in Molesworth's Court, in Fishamble Street, Dublin, in which are contained several seditious and scandalous paragraphs highly reflecting upon his Majesty and his Ministers, tending to alienate the affections of his good subjects of England and Ireland from each other, and to promote sedition among the people, hath been lately printed and published in this kingdom : We, the Lord-Lieutenant and Council do hereby publish and declare that, in order to discover the author of the said seditious pamphlet, we will give the necessary orders for the payment of three hundred pounds sterling, to such person or persons as shall within the specified six months from this date hereof, discover the author of the said pamphlet, so as he be apprehended and convicted thereby.

Given at the council chamber in Dublin, this twenty-seventh day of October, one thousand seven hundred and twenty-four.

(Signed) Midleton *Cancer.* Shannon ; Donneraill ; G.

Fforbes ; H. Meath ; Santry ; Tyrawly ; Fferrars ; William
Conolly ; Ralph Gore ; William Whitshed ; B. Hale ;
Gust. Hume ; Ben Parry ; James Tynte ; R. Tighe ; T.
Clutterbuck.

God save the King.

APPENDIX VIII

EDITIONS OF GULLIVER

THE bibliography of *Gulliver's Travels* belongs to the
commentary on Swift's works, rather than to the account
of his life.   But there are one or two points regarding it,
to which it may be well to refer.

The book was first published about the 7th of November,
1726.   When the first edition was issued Swift got a
large-paper copy, in which he entered from time to time
his MS. corrections.   That large-paper copy is now in
South Kensington Museum, and it is of great importance
in helping us to trace the comparative authority of each
edition and the reasons for the later changes.

Before the close of 1726 there was a re-issue of the
first volume, along with a new edition of the second
volume, the latter only being designated as a second edition.
The first volume seems to have been re-issued as it stood,
in consequence of the wish to consult Swift as to the
so-called commendatory verses, which it was proposed to
print before it in any new edition.[1]   The second volume
professes to be a second edition : but it contains none of
the MS. changes of the large-paper copy.   In 1727 there
appeared the first new edition of both volumes : the first
volume being designated "Second edition," and the second
volume "Second edition, *corrected.*"   In spite of the

---

[1] *Pope to Swift*, March 8, 17$\frac{2}{7}$.

different designation, an examination of all accessible copies makes it certain that they belong to the same issue.

Now both volumes of this new edition embody, not all, but a certain number, of Swift's own MS. corrections. The changes are not very important, but they are not merely typographical, and the printer must necessarily have had access to Swift's MS. corrections so far as these had been made at that date.

But the edition which embodies the greatest number of these MS. corrections is Faulkner's Dublin edition of 1735.[1]   It was in that edition, too, as has not been noticed by the editors, that the *Letter from Gulliver to his cousin Sympson* was for the first time printed.   The letter is dated April 27, 1727 : but its date is only a part of the mystification which Swift intended that the letter should produce.

This conclusively settles the question of Swift's watchful interest over the new editions.   However much he allowed others to act for him, to regulate the issue, and probably to draw the profits, he yet took care that such changes as he wished to make in the text should not be overlooked.   It proves, further, the supervision which he gave to Faulkner's edition of his works.

The changes were chiefly in *Laputa*, on which criticism had been least favourable ; and Swift seems even to have added further changes after those embodied in the edition of 1735.   At p. 70 of *Laputa*, in the large-paper copy, he has inserted an addition of some length, which has never yet been printed.

The reasons for the letter to Sympson are plain enough.   Swift desired to sit loosely to the responsibility of authorship.   He suggests in 1726 that probably parts are garbled : and throughout he uses this loophole for disclaiming what he or his friends might afterwards condemn.   If he wished in 1735 to embody changes and

---

[1] The following passages may be noted where this edition embodies changes which are not made in "the 2nd edition corrected" (1727) of the 2nd volume :—*Laputa*, pp. 42, 90, 101 ; Houyhnhnms, pp. 65, 69, 77, 97.

yet to make them appear to be what he originally wrote,
he could have chosen no better means to help the design
than such a letter. In it he referred at once to material
and to trifling changes. He speaks of them with the
seriousness of a narrator who finds his veracious history
confused and disturbed by the mistakes of the editor.
To carry out the delusion, he dates the letter eight years
before it was written.[1] Further, the letter helped to give
circumstantiality to the whole book. Who would not be
persuaded by a traveller, that showed himself anxious
that there should be no mis-spelling of such veracious
nomenclature as that of Brobdingrag, which has hitherto
been wrongly printed Brobdingnag?[2]

A further proof of Swift's interest in *Gulliver* is
supplied by an unpublished letter of his own to Benjamin
Motte, of Dec. 28, 1727 (now in South Kensington
Museum), in which he gives minute suggestions as to the
engravings which may be selected for pictures in a new
edition. The little men, he thinks, will bear illustration
better than the great. In one sentence of some interest,
he gives his opinion of the hold the book has gained and
is likely to retain. "The world," he says, "glutted itself
with that book at first, but now it will go off but soberly,
but I suppose will not be soon worn out."

[1] One small fact shows the date to be a false one. Gulliver
speaks of the book as having appeared seven months before. But
it had appeared only five months before April, 1727. Such a slip
was very likely in 1735; it would have been impossible, in 1727.

[2] The question has been raised whether Swift really intended
that the name should be Brobdingnag or (as Gulliver insists in his
letter) Brobdingrag. The point is not of much importance, but
we certainly need not make the change on the authority of Gulliver,
whose letter is quite sufficiently accounted for as a device for
giving additional circumstantiality to the narrative. Swift had,
at least, allowed one edition after another to appear, for eight
years, without suggesting an alteration. He has not introduced
it into the copy which contains his own MS. alterations. He
makes it only in a mock letter addressed by himself in one
character to himself in another. And, finally, the letter tells
us that he "cannot stand to the corrections," but must leave the
matter to his candid readers, "to adjust it as they please."

APPENDIX IX

THE JOURNAL OF 1727

THIS Journal having come into the hands of the late Mr. Forster, was by him bequeathed to South Kensington Museum, where it now is. On the inside of the cover of the little book in which it is written, there is the following note :—

"This Book I stole from the Right Honble. George Dodington, Esq., one of the Lords of the Treasury, June, 1727. But the Scribblings are all my own."

Then follow some memoranda relating to commissions which Swift had to perform—the providing of a clock for the Cathedral, the purchase of spectacles, investments, the care of his grandfather's tomb, etc.

Next come the following fragments of verse.

HOLYHEAD, *Sepbr.* 25, 1727.

Lo here I sit at holy head,
With muddy ale and mouldy bread :
I'm fastened (?) both by wind and tide,
I see the ships at anchor ride.
All Christain vittals stink of fish,
I'm where my enemyes would wish.
Convict of lies is every Sign,
The Inn has not one drop of wine.
The Captain swears the sea's too rough,
He has not passengers enough.
And thus the Dean is forc'd to stay
Till others come to help the pay.
In Dublin they'd be glad to see
A packet though it brings in me.
They cannot say the winds are cross :
Your Politicians at a loss
For want of matter swears and fretts—
Are forced to read the old Gazettes.
I never was in haste before,
To reach that slavish hateful shore.

Before, I always found the wind
To me was most malicious kind,
But now the danger of a friend,
On whom my fears and hopes depend,
Absent from whom all Climes are curst,
With whom I'm happy in the worst,
With rage impatient makes me wait
A passage to the Land I hate.
Else, rather on this bleaky shore,
Where loudest winds incessant roar,
Where neither herb nor tree will thrive,
Where Nature hardly seems alive,
I'd go in freedom to my grave
Than Rule yon Isle, and be a slave.

IRELAND.

Remove me from this land of slaves,
Where all are fools, and all are knaves ;
Where every knave and fool is bought,
Yet kindly sells himself for nought ;
Where Whig and Tory fiercely fight
Who's in the wrong, who in the right ;
And, when their country lies at stake,
They only fight for fighting sake,
While English sharpers take the pay,
And then stand by to see fair play.
Meantime the Whig is always winner,
And for his courage gets—a dinner.
His Excellency, too, perhaps
Spits in his mouth and stroaks his Chaps.
The humble whelp gives ev'ry vote—
To put the question strains his throat.
His Excellency's condescension
Will serve instead of place or pension.
When to the window he's trepan'd—
When my L^d shakes him by the hand,
Or, in the presence of beholders,
His arms upon the booby's shoulders—
You quickly see the gudgeon bite.
He tells his brother fools at night
How well the Governor's inclined—
So just, so gentle, and so kind.
He heard I kept a pack of hounds,
And longs to hunt upon my grounds,
He s^d our Ladyes were so fair,
The land had nothing to compare ;

But that indeed which pleased me most,
He call'd my Dol a perfect toast.
He whispered public things at last,
Asked me how our elections past.
Some augmentation, Sir, you know,
Would make at least a handsome show.
Now kings a compliment expect ;
I shall not offer to direct.
There are some prating folks in town,
But, Sir, we must support the Crown.
Our letters say a Jesuit boasts
Of some invasion on your coasts.
The king is ready, when you will,
To pass another Popery bill ;
And for dissenters, he intends
To use them as his truest friends.

.   .   .   .   .

I think they justly ought to share
In all employments we can spare.
Next, for encouragement of spinning,
A duty might be laid on linen.
An Act for laying down the plough—
England will send you corn enough ;
Another Act that absentees
For licences shall pay no fees.
If England's friendship you would keep,
Feed nothing on your lands but sheep ;
But make an Act, severe and full,
To bring up all who smuggle wool.
And then he kindly gave me hints
That all our wives should go in chintz.
To-morrow I shall tell you more,
For I'm to dine with him at four.
 This was the speech, and here's the jest—
His arguments convinced the rest.
Away he runs, with zealous hotness,
Exceeding all the fools of Totness,
To move that all the nation round
Should pay a guinea in the pound ;
Yet should this blockhead beg a place,
Either from Excellent or Grace,
'Tis pre-engaged, and in his room
Townshend's cast page or Walpole's groom.

On Ld Carteret's arms given, as the custom is, at every
Inn where the L^d L^t dines or lies, with all the bills in a
long parchment.

'Tis twenty to one,
When Carteret is gone,
These praises we blot out ;
The truth will be got out,
And then we'll be smart on
His l^dship as Wharton ;
Or Shrewsbury's duke,
With many rebuke ;
Or Bolton the wise,
With his Spanish flyes ;
Or Grafton the deep,
Either drunk or asleep.
These titles and arms
Will then lose their charms,
If somebody's grace
Should come in his place.
And thus it goes round—
We praise and confound.
They can do no good,
Nor would if they could.
To injure the nation
Is recommendation ;
And why should they save her
By losing their favour ?
Poor kingdom, thou would'st be that governor's debtor,
Who kindly would leave thee no worse nor no better.

Then comes the Testament to Posterity, quoted on p. 339, and finally the Journal, as follows :—

Friday, at 11 in the morning I left Chester.   It was Septr. 22, 1727.

I bated at a blind ale-house 7 miles from Chester.   I thence rode to Ridland,[1] in all, 22 miles.   I lay there, had bad meat, and tolerable wine.   I left Ridland at a quarter after 4 morn. on Saturday, slept on Penmenmawr, examined about my sign verses : the Inn is to be on t'other side, therefore the verses to be changed.   I baited at Conway, the Guide going to another Inn.   The Maid of the old Inn saw me in the Street, and said that was my Horse, she knew me ; there I dined and sent for Ned Holland, a Squire famous for being mentioned in Mr. Lyndsay's verses to Davy Morice.   I there again saw

---

[1] *I.e.* Rhudlan.

Hook's Tomb, who was the 41st Child of his Mother, and had himself 27 Children ; he died about 1639.   There is a *nota bene* that one of his posterity new furbished up the Inscription.   I had read in A. B^p William's Life that he was buryed in an obscure Church in North Wales.   I enquired, and heard it was at ——[1] Church, within a mile of Bangor, whither I was going : I went to the Church, the Guide grumbling.   I saw the Tomb with his Statue kneeling (in marble).   It began thus :—[Hospes lege et relege quod in hoc obscuro sacello non expectares. Hic jacet omnium præsulum celeberrimus].   I came to Bangor, and crossed the Ferry a mile from it, where there is an Inn, which, if it be well kept, will break Bangor. There I lay—it was 22 miles from Holyhead.   I was on horseback at 4 in the morning, resolving to be at Church at Holyhead, but to shew Wat Owen Tudor's Tomb at Penmarry.   We passed the place (being a little out of the way) by the Guide's knavery, who had no mind to stay. I was now so weary with riding, that I was forced to stop as Langueveny, 7 miles from the Ferry, and rest 2 hours. Then I went on very weary, but in a few miles more Watt's Horse lost his two fore-shoes, so the Horse was forced to limp after us.   The Guide was less concerned than I.   In a few miles more, my Horse lost a fore-shoe, and could not go on the rocky ways.   I walked above 2 miles to spare him.   It was Sunday, and no Smith to be got.   At last there was a Smith in the way ; we left the Guide to shoe the Horses, and walked to a hedge Inn 3 miles from Holyhead.   There I stay^d an hour, with no ale to be drunk, a Boat offered, and I went by Sea and sail in it to Holyhead.   The Guide came about the same time.   I dined with an old Inn-keeper, Mrs. Welch, about 3, on a loyn of mutton, very good, but the worst ale in the world, and no wine, for the day before I came here, a vast number went to Ireld after having drunk out all the wine.   There was stale beer, and I tryed a receit of Oyster shells, which I got powdered on purpose ;

---

[1] Blank left in MS.

but it was good for nothing. I walked on the rocks in
the evening, and then went to bed, and dreamt that I had
got 20 falls from my Horse.

Monday, Septr. 25. The Captain talks of sailing at
12. The talk goes off; the Wind is fair, but he says it
is too fierce ; I believe he wants more company. I had
a raw chicken for dinner, and Brandy with water for my
drink. I walkt morning and afternoon among the rocks.
This evening Watt tells me that my Landlady whispered
him that the Grafton packet boat, just come in, had
brought her 18 bottles of Irish Claret. I secured one,
and supped on part of a neat's tongue, which a friend at
London had given Watt to put up for me—and drank a
pint of the wine, which was bad enough. Not a soul is
yet come to Holyhead, except a young fellow who smiles
when he meets me, and would fain be my companion ;
but it is not come to that yet. I writ abundance of
verses this day ; and several useful hints (tho' I say it).
I went to bed at 10, and dreamt abundance of nonsense.

Tues. 26th. I am forced to wear a shirt three days,
. . . I was sparing of them all the way. It was a mercy
there were six clean when I left London ; otherwise Watt
(whose blunders would bear an history) would have put
them all in the great Box of goods which goes by the
Carrier to Chester. He brought but one cravat, and the
reason he gave was because the rest were foul, and he
thought he should not put foul linnen into the Portman-
teau. For he never dreamt it might be washed on the
way. My shirts are all foul now, and by his reasoning,
I fear he will leave them at Holyhead when we go. I
got anoth^r loin of mutton, but so tough I could not
chew it, and drank my 2^d pint of wine. I walked this
morning a good way among the rocks, and to a hole in
one of them from whence at certain periods the water
spurted up several foot high. It rain'd all night, and
hath rained since dinner. But now the sun shines, and I
will take my afternoon's walk. It was fairer and milder
weather than yesterday, yet the Captain never dreams of
sailing. To say the Truth Michaelmas is the worst season

in the year. Is this strange stuff? Why, what *would*
you have me do? I have writt verses, and put down
hints till I am weary. I see no creature, I cannot read
by candle-light. Sleeping makes me sick. I reckon my
self fixed here : and have a mind like Marcchall Tallard
to take a house and garden. I wish you a merry Christmas, and expect to see you by Candlemas. I have walked
this evening again about 3 miles on the rocks; my
giddiness, God be thanked, is almost gone, and my
hearing continues ; I am now retired to my Chamber to
scribble or sit hum-drum. The night is fair, and they
pretend to have some hopes of going to-morrow.

Septr. 26. Thoughts upon being confined at Holyhead.
If this were to be my settlement, during life, I could
caress myself a while by forming some conveniences to be
easy ; and should not be frighted either by the solitude,
or the meanness of lodging, eating or drinking. I shall
say nothing upon the suspense I am in about my dearest
friend ; because that is a case extraordinary, and therefore
by way of amusement, I will speak as if it were not in
my thoughts, and only as a passenger who is in a scurvy
unprovided comfortless place without one companion, and
who therefore wants to be at home, where he hath all
conveniences there proper for a gentleman of quality. I
cannot read at night, and I have no books to read in the
day. I have no subject in my head at present to write
on. I dare not send my linnen to be washed, for fear of
being called away at half an hour's warning, and then I
must leave them behind me, which is a serious point. I
live at great expense, without one comfortable bit or sup.
I am afraid of joining with passengers for fear of getting
acquaintance with Irish. The days are short, and I have
five hours at night to spend by myself before I go to bed.
I should be glad to converse with farmers or shopkeepers,
but none of them speak English. A dog is better
company than the vicar, for I remember him of old.
What can I do but write everything that comes into my
head. Watt is a Booby of that species which I dare not
suffer to be familiar with me, for he would ramp on my

shoulders in half an hour. But the worst part is my
half-hourly longing, and hopes and vain expectations of a
wind ; so that I live in suspense, which is the worst
circumstance of human nature. I am a little risky (?)
from two scurvy disorders, and if I should relapse, there
is not a Welsh house-cur that would not have more care
taken of him than I, and whose loss would not be more
lamented. I confine myself to my narrow chamber in
all unwalkable hours. The Master of the pacquet boat,
one Jones, hath not treated me with the least civility,
altho' Watt gave him my name. In short I come from
being used like an Emperor to be used worse than a Dog
at Holyhead. Yet my hat is worn to pieces by answering
the civilities of the poor inhabitants as they pass by.
The women might be safe enough, who all wear hats yet
never pull them off, if the dirty streets did not foul their
petticoats by courtseying so low. Look you ; be not
impatient, for I only wait till my watch marks 10, and
then I will give you ease, and myself sleep, if I can.
On my conscience you may know a Welsh dog as well as
a Welshman or woman by its peevish passionate way
of barking. This paper shall serve to answer all your
questions about my Journey ;[1] and I will have it printed
to satisfy the Kingdom. *Forsan et hæc* then is a damned
lie, for I shall always fret at the remembrance of this
imprisonment. Pray pity poor Wat, for he is called
dunce, puppy, and liar 500 times an hour, and yet he
means not ill, for he means nothing. Oh for a dozen
bottles of deanery wine and a slice of bread and butter.
The wine you sent us yesterday is a little upon the sour.
I wish you had chosen better. I am going to bed at ten
o'clock, because I am weary of being up. Wednesday.
Last night I dreamt that Ld Bolingbroke and Mr. Pope
were at my Cathedral in the Gallery, and that my L^d
was to preach. I could not find my surplice ; the Church
Servants were all out of the way ; the doors shut. I
sent to my L^d to come into my stall for more conveniency

---

[1] Swift is addressing only an imaginary correspondent.

to get into the Pulpit.   The Stall was all broken; they
s^d the Collegians had done it.   I squeezed among the
Rabble, saw my L^d in the Pulpit.   I thought his Prayer
was good, but I forget it.   In his sermon, I did not like
his quoting Mr. Wycherley by name, and his Play.   This
is all, and so I waked.   To-day we were certainly to sail;
the morning was calm.   Wat and I walked up the mon-
strous mountain properly called Holyhead or Sacrum
Promontorium by Ptolemy, 2 miles from this town.   I
took breath 59 times.   I looked from the top to see the
Wicklow hills, but the day was too hazy, which I felt to
my sorrow; for returning, we were overtaken with a
furious shower.   I got into a Welsh cabin, almost as bad
as an Irish one.   There was only an old Welshwoman
sifting flour who understood no English, and a boy who
fell a roaring for fear of me.   Wat (otherwise called
unfortunate Jack) ran home for my coat, but stay^d so
long that I came home in worse rain without him, and
he was so lucky to miss me, but took care to carry the
key of my room where a fire was ready for me.   So I
cooled my heels in the Parlor till he came, but called for
a glass of Brandy.   I have been cooking myself dry, and
am now in my night gown; and this moment comes a
Letter to me from one Whelden who tells me he hears I
am a lover of the Mathematicks, that he has found out
the Longitude, shown his discourse to Dr. Dobbs of y^r
College, and sent letters to all the Mathematicians in
London 3 months ago, but received no answer, and
desires I would read his discourse.   I sent back his
Letter with my answer under it, too long to tell you,
only I said I had too much of the Longitude already, by
2 projectors, whom I encouraged, one of which was a
cheat and the oth^r cut his own throat, and for himself
I thought he had a mind to deceive others, or was deceived himself.   And so I wait for dinner.   I shall dine
like a King all alone, as I have done these 6 days.   As
it happened, if I had gone straight from Chester to
Parkgate, 8 miles, I should have been in Dublin on
Sunday last.   Now Mich'lmas approaches, the worst time

in the year for the Sea, and this rain has made these
parts unwalkable, so that I must either write or doze.
Bite ; when we was in the wild cabin, I ordered Wat to
take a cloth and wipe my wet gown and cassock—it
happened to be a meal bag—and as my Gown dryed, it
was all daubed with flour well cemented with the rain.
What do I, but see the Gown and cassock well dried in
my room, and while Wat was at dinner, I was an hour
rubbing the meal out of them, and did it excell^y ; He is
just come up, and I have gravely bid him take them
down to rub them, and I wait whether he will find out
what I have been doing. The Rogue is come up in six
minutes with my gown, and says there were but few
spots (tho' he saw a thousand at first), but neither wonders
at it nor seems to suspect me who laboured like a horse
to rub them out. The 3 Pacquet boats are now all on
this side ; and the weather grows worse, and so much
rain that there is an end of my walking. I wish you
would send me word how I shall dispose of my time. If
the Vicar could but play at back-gammon I were an Emperor ; but I know him not. I am as insignificant here
as Parson Brooke is in Dublin. By my conscience, I
believe Cæsar would be the same without his army at his
back. Well, the longer I stay here, the more you will
murmur for want of packets. Whoever would wish to
live long should live here, for a day is longer than a
week, and if the weather be foul, as long as a fortnight.
Yet here I could live with two or three friends, in a
warm house, and good wine—much better than being a
Slave in Ireld. But my misery is, that I am in the
worst part of Wales under the very worst circumstances ;
afraid of a relapse, in utmost solitude ; impatient for the
condition of our friend ; not a soul to converse with,
hindered from exercise by rain, cooped up in a room not
half so large as one of the Deanery Closets. My room
smokes into the bargain, and the other is too cold and
moist to be without a fire. There is or should be a Pro-
verbe here, "When Mrs. Welsh's Chimney smokes, 'Tis a
sign she'll keep her folks. But, when of smoke the room

is clear, It is a sign we sha'nt stay here." All this is to divert thinking. Tell me, am not I in a comfortable way? The Yacht is to be here for Ld Carteret on the 14th of Octb^r. I fancy he and I shall come over together. I have opened my door to let in the wind that it may drive out the smoke. I asked the wind why it is so cross, he assures me 'tis not his fault, but his cursed Master Æolus's. Here is a young Jackanapes in the same Inn waiting for a wind, who would fain be my companion; and if I stay here much longer, I am afraid all my pride and grandeur will truckle to comply with him, especially if I finish these leaves that remain; but I will write close, and do as the Devil did at mass—pull the paper with my teeth to make it hold out.

Thursday. 'Tis allowed that we learn patience by suffering. I have now not spirit enough left me to fret. I was so cunning these 3 last days, that whenever I began to rage and storm at the weather, I took special care to turn my face towards Ireland, in hopes by my breath to push the wind forward. But now I give up. However, when, upon asking how is the wind, the people answer, Full in y^r teeth, I cannot help wishing, worse were in theirs. Well, it is now 3 afternoon. I have dined and invited the Master. The wind and tide serve, and I am just taking boat to go to the Ship: so adieu till I see you at the Deanery.

Friday, Mich's day. You will now know something of what it is to be at sea. We had not been half an hour in the ship till a fierce wind rose directly against us. We tried a good while, but the storm still continued. So we turned back, and it was eight at night, dark and rainy, before the ship got back, and at anchor. The other passengers went back in a boat to Holyhead, but to prevent accidents and broken shins I lay all night on board and came back this morning at 8: am now in my Chamber, where I must stay, and get in a new stock of patience. You all know well enough where I am, for I wrote thrice after your Letters that desired my coming over. The last was from Coventry, 19th instant, but I brought it with me to Chester, and saw it put into the Post, on Thursday 21st, and the next day followed it myself, but the Pacquet boat was gone before I could get here, because I could not ride 70 miles a day.

APPENDIX X

THE WILL OF ESTHER JOHNSON

Esther Johnson's Will has been printed at full length by the late Sir W. Wilde, in his *Closing Years of Dean Swift*. It is only necessary here to notice some of its important points.

It is dated December 30th, 1727, and begins thus :—

"In the name of God. Amen. I, Esther Johnson, of the city of Dublin, spinster, being of tolerable health in body, and perfectly sound in mind, do here make my last Will and testament, revoking all former wills whatsoever. First, I bequeath my soul to the infinite mercy of God with a most humble hope of everlasting salvation, and my body to the earth, to be buried in the great aisle of the Cathedral Church of St. Patrick's, Dublin, and I desire that a decent monument of plain white marble may be fixed in the wall, over the place of my burial, not exceeding the value of twenty pounds sterling, and that the charges of my funeral may not exceed the said sum."

She next provides for the investment of £1000 of her property in land, to be purchased, exactly according to the directions of Swift's own Will, in any province of Ireland, except Connaught. The proceeds of such investment are to go, during their lives to her mother and sister, and thereafter to the payment of a salary to a chaplain in Dr. Steevens's hospital.[1]

---

[1] This was exactly the disposition of her property which Swift had urged, in a letter from London, to Mr. Worrall, of July 15,

The next stipulation of her Will again bears a striking resemblance to the Will of Swift. "If it shall happen," she says, "(which God forbid) that at any time hereafter the present Established Episcopal Church of this kingdom shall come to be abolished, and be no longer the national Established Church of the said Kingdom, I do, in that case, declare wholly null and void the bequest above made . . . and my will is, that, in the case aforesaid, it devolves to my nearest relation then living."

As in the Will of Swift, there is a clause preventing rack-renting on the lands to be purchased and held in trust, under her Will.

After some specific legacies, the Will proceeds :—

"Lastly I make and constitute the Rev. Dr. Thomas Sheridan, of the City of Dublin, the Rev. Mr. John Grattan, the Rev. Mr. Francis Corbet, and John Rochfort, Esq., of the City of Dublin, executors of my last Will and testament. I desire likewise that my plate, books, furniture, and whatever other moveables I have, may be sold to discharge my debts : and that my strong box, and all the papers I have in it or elsewhere, may be given to the Rev. Dr. Jonathan Swift, Dean of St. Patrick's.

"*Item.* I bequeath to the Rev. Dr. Jonathan Swift a bond of thirty pounds, due to me by Dr. Russell, in trust for the use of Mrs. Honoria Swanson."

She designates herself as a "Spinster," and she signs herself "Esther Johnson." But this, as has already been pointed out, is no argument against the marriage : it was obviously a necessary part of the compact of secrecy ; and she had no reason to fear that Swift would use his legal powers as her husband, to interfere with, or to invalidate, the terms of a Will, so made.

1726, that she should make. She adds the condition that the chaplain should be unmarried : and this Monck Mason conceives to be an argument in favour of his contention that she had not herself gone through the ceremony. The cause is weak that requires to be supported by such a puerility.

APPENDIX XI

THE CHARACTER OF MRS. JOHNSON [STELLA]

[This character gives us so clear a picture of the qualities which Swift found to admire in her whom he had
chosen from amongst all women, that the bond between
him and Stella is not to be understood without it: and
it is printed here as essential to his own biography.]

THIS day, being Sunday, January 28, 1727-8, about
eight o'clock at night, a servant brought me a note, with
an account of the death of the truest, most virtuous, and
valuable friend, that I, or perhaps any other person, was
ever blessed with. She expired about six in the evening
of this day; and as soon as I am left alone, which is
about eleven at night, I resolve, for my own satisfaction,
to say something of her life and character.

She was born at Richmond, in Surrey, on the 13th
day of March, in the year 1681. Her father was a
younger brother of a good family in Nottinghamshire, her
mother of a lower degree; and indeed she had little to
boast of her birth. I knew her from six years old, and
had some share in her education, by directing what books
she should read, and perpetually instructing her in the
principles of honour and virtue; from which she never
swerved in any one action or moment of her life. She
was sickly from her childhood until about the age of
fifteen; but then grew into perfect health, and was
looked upon as one of the most beautiful, graceful, and
agreeable young women in London, only a little too fat.
Her hair was blacker than a raven, and every feature of
her face in perfection. She lived generally in the country,
with a family where she contracted an intimate friendship with another lady of more advanced years. I was

then, to my mortification, settled in Ireland ; and about a year after, going to visit my friends in England, I found she was a little uneasy upon the death of a person on whom she had some dependance.[1] Her fortune, at that time, was in all not above fifteen hundred pounds, the interest of which was but a scanty maintenance. Under this consideration, and indeed very much for my own satisfaction, who had few friends or acquaintance in Ireland, I prevailed with her and her dear friend and companion, the other lady, to draw what money they had into Ireland, a great part of their fortune being in annuities upon funds. Money was then ten *per cent* in Ireland, besides the advantage of returning it, and all necessaries of life at half the price. They complied with my advice, and soon after came over ; but I happening to continue some time longer in England, they were much discouraged to live in Dublin, where they were wholly strangers. She was at that time about nineteen years old, and her person was soon distinguished. But the adventure looked so like a frolic, the censure held for some time, as if there were a secret history in such a removal ; which, however, soon blew off by her excellent conduct. She came over with her friend on the —— in the year 170 – ; and they both lived together until this day, when death removed her from us. For some years past, she had been visited with continual ill health ; and several times, within these last two years, her life was despaired of. But, for this twelvemonth past, she never had a day's health ; and, properly speaking, she has been dying six months, but kept alive, almost against nature, by the generous kindness of two physicians, and the care of her friends. Thus far I writ the same night between eleven and twelve.

Never was any of her sex born with better gifts of the mind, or who more improved them by reading and conversation. Yet her memory was not of the best, and was

---

[1] The omission of Sir W. Temple's name is clearly due to Swift's strained relations with the family.

impaired in the latter years of her life. But I cannot call to mind that I ever once heard her make a wrong judgment of persons, books, or affairs. Her advice was always the best, and with the greatest freedom, mixed with the greatest decency. She had a gracefulness, somewhat more than human, in every motion, word, and action. Never was so happy a conjunction of civility, freedom, easiness, and sincerity. There seemed to be a combination among all that knew her, to treat her with a dignity much beyond her rank; yet people of all sorts were never more easy than in her company. Mr. Addison, when he was in Ireland, being introduced to her, immediately found her out; and, if he had not soon after left the kingdom, assured me he would have used all endeavours to cultivate her friendship. A rude or conceited coxcomb passed his time very ill, upon the least breach of respect; for, in such a case, she had no mercy, but was sure to expose him to the contempt of the standers-by, yet in such a manner, as he was ashamed to complain, and durst not resent. All of us who had the happiness of her friendship agreed unanimously, that, in an afternoon or evening's conversation, she never failed, before we parted, of delivering the best thing that was said in the company. Some of us have written down several of her sayings, or what the French call *bons mots*, wherein she excelled beyond belief. She never mistook the understanding of others; nor ever said a severe word, but where a much severer was deserved.

Her servants loved, and almost adored her at the same time. She would, upon occasions, treat them with freedom; yet her demeanour was so awful, that they durst not fail in the least point of respect. She chid them seldom, but it was with severity, which had an effect on them for a long time after.

January 29. My head aches, and I can write no more.

January 30. Tuesday.

This is the night of the funeral, which my sickness will not suffer me to attend. It is now nine at night;

and I am removed into another apartment, that I may
not see the light in the church, which is just over against
the window of my bed-chamber.

With all the softness of temper that became a lady,
she had the personal courage of a hero. She and her
friend having removed their lodgings to a new house,
which stood solitary, a parcel of rogues, armed, attempted
the house, where there was only one boy. She was then
about four-and-twenty; and having been warned to
apprehend some such attempt, she learned the management of a pistol; and the other women and servants
being half dead with fear, she stole softly to her dining-
room window, put on a black hood to prevent being seen,
primed the pistol fresh, gently lifted up the sash, and
taking her aim with the utmost presence of mind, discharged the pistol, loaden with bullets, into the body of
one villain, who stood the fairest mark. The fellow,
mortally wounded, was carried off by the rest, and died
the next morning; but his companions could not be
found. The Duke of Ormond had often drunk her
health to me upon that account, and had always a high
esteem for her. She was indeed under some appre-
hensions of going in a boat, after some danger she had
narrowly escaped by water, but she was reasoned
thoroughly out of it. She was never known to cry out,
or discover any fear, in a coach or on horseback; or any
uneasiness by those sudden accidents with which most of
her sex, either by weakness or affectation, appear so much
disordered.

She never had the least absence of mind in conversation, or given to interruption, or appeared eager to put in
her word, by waiting impatiently until another had done.
She spoke in a most agreeable voice, in the plainest
words, never hesitating, except out of modesty before new
faces, where she was somewhat reserved; nor, among her
nearest friends, ever spoke much at a time. She was but
little versed in the common topics of female chat; scandal,
censure, and detraction, never came out of her mouth;
yet, among a few friends, in private conversation, she

made little ceremony in discovering her contempt of a coxcomb, and describing all his follies to the life ; but the follies of her own sex she was rather inclined to extenuate or to pity.

When she was once convinced, by open facts, of any breach of truth or honour in a person of high station, especially in the Church, she could not conceal her indignation, nor hear them named without showing her displeasure in her countenance ; particularly one or two of the latter sort, whom she had known and esteemed, but detested above all mankind, when it was manifest that they had sacrificed those two precious virtues to their ambition, and would much sooner have forgiven them the common immoralities of the laity.

Her frequent fits of sickness, in most parts of her life, had prevented her from making that progress in reading which she would otherwise have done. She was well versed in the Greek and Roman story, and was not unskilled in that of France and England. She spoke French perfectly, but forgot much of it by neglect and sickness. She had read carefully all the best books of travels, which serve to open and enlarge the mind. She understood the Platonic and Epicurean philosophy, and judged very well of the defects of the latter. She made very judicious abstracts of the best books she had read. She understood the nature of government, and could point out all the errors of Hobbes, both in that and religion. She had a good insight into physic, and knew somewhat of anatomy ; in both which she was instructed in her younger days by an eminent physician, who had her long under his care, and bore the highest esteem for her person and understanding. She had a true taste of wit and good sense, both in poetry and prose, and was a perfect good critic of style ; neither was it easy to find a more proper or impartial judge, whose advice an author might better rely on, if he intended to send a thing into the world, provided it was on a subject that came within the compass of her knowledge. Yet, perhaps, she was sometimes too severe, which is a safe and pardonable error. She preserved her wit, judgment, and vivacity, to the last, but often used to complain of her memory.

Her fortune, with some accession, could not, as I have heard say, amount to much more than two thousand pounds, whereof a great part fell with her life, having been placed upon annuities in England, and one in Ireland.

In a person so extraordinary, perhaps it may be pardonable to mention some particulars, although of little moment, farther than to set forth her character. Some presents of gold pieces being often made to her while she was a girl, by her mother and other friends, on promise to keep them, she grew into such a spirit of thrift, that, in about three years, they amounted to above two hundred pounds. She used to show them with boasting ; but her mother, apprehending she would be cheated of them, prevailed, in some months, and with great importunities, to have them put out to interest ; when the girl, losing the pleasure of seeing and counting her gold, which she never failed of doing many times in a day, and despairing of heaping up such another treasure, her humour took quite the contrary turn ; she grew careless and squandering of every new acquisition, and so continued till about two-and-twenty ; when, by advice of some friends, and the fright of paying large bills of tradesmen who enticed her into their debt, she began to reflect upon her own folly, and was never at rest until she had discharged all her shop bills, and refunded herself a considerable sum she had run out. After which, by the addition of a few years, and a superior understanding, she became, and continued all her life, a most prudent economist ; yet still with a stronger bent to the liberal side, wherein she gratified herself by avoiding all expense in clothes (which she ever despised) beyond what was merely decent. And, although her frequent returns of sickness were very chargeable, except fees to physicians, of which she met with several so generous that she could force nothing on them, (and indeed she must otherwise have been un·done,) yet she never was without a considerable sum of ready money. Insomuch, that, upon her death, when her nearest friends thought her very bare, her executors found in her strong box about one hundred and fifty pounds in gold. She lamented the narrowness of her fortune in nothing so much, as that it did not enable her to entertain her friends so often, and in so hospitable a manner, as she desired. Yet they were always welcome; and while she was in health to direct, 'were treated with neatness and elegance, so that the revenues of her and her companion passed for much more considerable than they really were. They lived always in lodgings ; their domestics consisted of two maids and one man. She kept an account of all the family expenses, from her arrival in Ireland to some months before her death ; and she would often repine, when looking back upon the annals of her household bills, that everything necessary for life was double the price, while interest of money was sunk almost to one-half ; so that the addition made to her fortune was indeed grown absolutely necessary.

[I since writ as I found time.]

But her charity to the poor was a duty not to be diminished, and therefore became a tax upon those tradesmen who furnish the fopperies of other ladies. She bought clothes as seldom as possible, and those as plain and cheap as consisted with the situation she was in ; and wore no lace for many years. Either her judgment or fortune was extraordinary in the choice of those on whom she bestowed her charity, for it went farther in doing good than double the sum from any other hand. And I have heard her say, " she always met with gratitude from the poor " ; which must be owing to her skill in distinguishing proper objects, as well as her gracious manner in relieving them.

But she had another quality that much delighted her, although it might be thought a kind of check upon her bounty ; however, it was a pleasure she could not resist : I mean that of making agreeable presents ; wherein I never knew her equal, although it be an affair of as delicate a nature as most in the course of life. She used

to define a present, "That it was a gift to a friend of
something he wanted, or was fond of, and which could
not be easily gotten for money."   I am confident, during
my acquaintance with her, she has, in these and some
other kinds of liberality, disposed of to the value of
several hundred pounds.   As to presents made to herself,
she received them with great unwillingness, but especially
from those to whom she had ever given any ; being, on
all occasions, the most disinterested mortal I ever knew
or heard of.

From her own disposition, at least as much as from
the frequent want of health, she seldom made any visits ;
but her own lodgings, from before twenty years old, were
frequented by many persons of the graver sort, who all
respected her highly, upon her good sense, good manners,
and conversation.   Among these were the late Primate
Lindsay, Bishop Lloyd, Bishop Ashe, Bishop Brown,
Bishop Sterne, Bishop Pulleyn, with some others of later
date ; and indeed the greatest number of her acquaintance was among the clergy.   Honour, truth, liberality,
good nature, and modesty, were the virtues she chiefly
possessed, and most valued in her acquaintance : and
where she found them, would be ready to allow for
some defects ; nor valued them less, although they did
not shine in learning or in wit : but would never give
the least allowance for any failures in the former, even to
those who made the greatest figure in either of the two
latter.   She had no use of any person's liberality, yet her
detestation of covetous people made her uneasy if such a
one was in her company ; upon which occasion she would
say many things very entertaining and humorous.

She never interrupted any person who spoke ; she
laughed at no mistakes they made, but helped them out
with modesty ; and if a good thing were spoken, but
neglected, she would not let it fall, but set it in the best
light to those who were present.   She listened to all that
was said, and had never the least distraction or absence
of thought.

It was not safe, nor prudent, in her presence, to offend

in the least word against modesty ; for she then gave full employment to her wit, her contempt, and resentment, under which even stupidity and brutality were forced to sink into confusion ; and the guilty person, by her future avoiding him like a bear or a satyr, was never in a way to transgress a second time.

It happened, one single coxcomb, of the pert kind, was in her company, among several other ladies ; and in his flippant way, began to deliver some double meanings ; the rest flapped their fans, and used the other common expedients practised in such cases, of appearing not to mind or comprehend what was said. Her behaviour was very different, and perhaps may be censured. She said thus to the man : "Sir, all these ladies and I understand your meaning very well, having, in spite of our care, too often met with those of your sex who wanted manners and good sense. But, believe me, neither virtuous nor even vicious women love such kind of conversation. However, I will leave you, and report your behaviour: and whatever visit I make, I shall first inquire at the door whether you are in the house, that I may be sure to avoid you." I know not whether a majority of ladies would approve of such a proceeding ; but I believe the practice of it would soon put an end to that corrupt conversation, the worst effect of dulness, ignorance, impudence, and vulgarity ; and the highest affront to the modesty and understanding of the female sex.

By returning very few visits, she had not much company of her own sex, except those whom she most loved for their easiness, or esteemed for their good sense : and those, not insisting on ceremony, came often to her. But she rather chose men for her companions, the usual topics of ladies' discourse being such as she had little knowledge of, and less relish. Yet no man was upon the rack to entertain her, for she easily descended to anything that was innocent and diverting. News, politics, censure, family management, or town-talk, she always diverted to something else ; but these indeed seldom happened, for she chose her company better : and therefore many, who mistook her and themselves, having solicited her acquaintance, and finding themselves disappointed, after a few visits dropped off; and she was never known to inquire into the reason, nor ask what was become of them.

She was never positive in arguing; and she usually treated those who were so in a manner which well enough gratified that unhappy disposition; yet in such a sort as made it very contemptible, and at the same time did some hurt to the owners. Whether this proceeded from her easiness in general, or from her indifference to persons, or from her despair of mending them, or from the same practice which she much liked in Mr. Addison, I cannot determine; but when she saw any of the company very warm in a wrong opinion, she was more inclined to confirm them in it than oppose them. The excuse she commonly gave, when her friends asked the reason, was, "That it prevented noise, and saved time." Yet I have known her very angry with some, whom she much esteemed, for sometimes falling into that infirmity.

She loved Ireland much better than the generality of those who owe both their birth and riches to it; and having brought over all the fortune she had in money, left the reversion of the best part of it, one thousand pounds, to Dr. Steevens's Hospital. She detested the tyranny and injustice of England in their treatment of this kingdom. She had indeed reason to love a country, where she had the esteem and friendship of all who knew her, and the universal good report of all who ever heard of her, without one exception, if I am told the truth by those who keep general conversation. Which character is the more extraordinary, in falling to a person of so much knowledge, wit, and vivacity, qualities that are used to create envy, and consequently censure; and must be rather imputed to her great modesty, gentle behaviour, and inoffensiveness, than to her superior virtues.

Although her knowledge, from books and company, was much more extensive than usually falls to the share of her sex, yet she was so far from making a parade of it, that her female visitants, on their first acquaintance, who expected to discover it by what they call hard words and deep discourse, would be sometimes disappointed, and say, "They found she was like other women." But wise men, through all her modesty, whatever they discoursed on, could easily observe that she understood them very well, by the judgment shown in her observations, as well as in her questions.

APPENDIX XII

ORIGINAL LETTERS FROM THE MSS. IN THE POSSESSION OF THE EARL OF CORK

THESE letters, for which I am indebted to the kindness of the Earl of Cork, have been quoted frequently in the narrative of Swift's last years. But a few additional extracts will have interest, as throwing light on Swift's occupations and moods during these years. Every one of the letters expresses as strongly as possible his regard for Lord Orrery.

The first extract is from a letter of March 22, $17\frac{33}{32}$.

"I had this minute a letter from England telling me that excise on tobacco is passed, 265 against 204, which was a greater number of sitters than I can remember. It is concluded they will go on in another session to farther articles, and then you will have the honor to be a slave in two kingdoms. Here is a pamphlet just come out in defence of the excise, it was reprinted here by a rascal from England, in a great office and at his own charge, to pave the way for the same proceeding here: but I hope our members will think they are slaves enough already: and perhaps somebody or other may be tempted to open folk's eyes.

"I sent the Epitaph[1] on Mr. Gay to Mrs. B—— to be

---

[1] The epitaph by Pope in Westminster Abbey, beginning "Of manners gentle, of affections mild."

copied for your Lordship, and I think there are some lines that might and should be corrected. I am going to write to the author, and shall tell him my opinion. I agree with your Lordship that his imitation of Horace is one of the best things he hath lately writ : and he tells me himself, that he never took more pains than in his *Poem to Lord Bathurst* upon the use of riches : nor less than in this, which however his friends call his *chef d'œuvre*, although he writ it in two mornings, and this may happen when a poet lights upon a fruitful hint, and becomes fond of it. I have often thought that hints were owing as much to good fortune as to invention. And I have sometimes chid poor Mr. Gay for dwelling too long upon a hint (as he did in the sequel of the *Beggar's Opera*, and this unlucky posthumous production).[1] He hath likewise left a second part of fables, of which I prophesy no good. I have been told that few painters can copy their own originals to perfection. And I believe the first thoughts on a subject that occurs to a poet's imagination are usually the most natural. . . . A stupid beast in London, one Alexander Burnet (I suppose the Bishop's son) has parodied Mr. Pope's satirical imitation in a manner that makes me envy Mr. Pope for having such an adversary, than whose performance nothing can be more low and scurrilous."

The next extract is from a letter of July 17, 1735.

"My Lord,
I am like a desperate debtor, who keeps out of the way as much as he can ; and want of health in my case is equal to want of money or of honesty in the other. I have been some months settling my perplexed affairs, like a dying man, and like the dying man, pestered with continual interruptions as well as difficulties. I have now finished my will in form, wherein I have settled my whole fortune on the city, in trust for building and maintaining an Hospital for idiots and lunatics, by which I save the expense of a chaplain, and almost of a physician, so that I now want only the circumstance of health to be very idle, and a constant correspondent, but no further than upon trifles. As to writing in verse or prose I am a real king, for I never had so many good *subjects* in my life ; and the more a king, because like all the rest of my rank (except K. George) I am so bad a governor of them, that I do not regard what becomes of them, nor hath any single one among them thrived under me these three years past. My greatest loss is that of my viceroy Trifler Sheridan. . . . Our Bishop Rundle is not yet come over, and I believe his chaplain

---

[1] The "sequel" was *Polly :* the "posthumous production," the opera of *Achilles.*

Philips is in a reasonable fright that his patron may fall sooner
than any living in the diocese; I suppose it is Trim Tram
betwixt both, for neither of them have three pennyworth of
stamina. If there be any merry company in this town, I am
an utter stranger to the persons and places, except when half a
score come to sponge on me every Sunday evening. Dr.
Helsham is as arrogant as ever, and Dr. Delany costs two
thirteens to be visited in wet weather, by which I should be out
of pocket nine pence when I dine with' him.—This moment
(Wednesday, six o'clock evening, July 16th) Mr. Philips sent me
word that he landed with his bishop this morning, and hath sent
me two volumes of poetry just reeking, by one John Hughes,
Esq.[1] . . . I have been turning over Squire Hughes's poems,
and his puppy publisher, one Duncomb's, preface and life of the
author. This is all your fault. I am put out of all patience to
the present set of whifflers, and their new fangled politeness.
Duncomb's preface is fifty pages upon celebrating a fellow I
never once heard of in my life, though I lived in London most
of the time that Duncomb makes him flourish. Duncomb put
a short note in loose paper to make me a present of the two
volumes, and desired my pardon for putting my name among
the subscribers. I was in a rage when I looked and found my
name; but was a little in countenance when I saw your
Lordship's there too. The verses and prose are such as our
·Dublin third-rate rhymers might write just the same for nine
hours a day till the coming of Antichrist. I wish I could send
them to you by post for your punishment. Pray, my Lord,
as you ride along compute how much the desolation and
poverty of the people have increased since your last travels
through your dominions. Although I fancy we suffer a great
deal more twenty miles round Dublin than in the remoter
parts, except your city of Cork, who are starving (I hope) by
their own villany. Since you left the town there hath not
been one riot either in the University nor among the Cavan
Bail,[2] which causeth a great dearth of news, nay not so much as
a review, and but two or three bloody murders. . . . I called
at my Lady Acheson's and in came Philips very hearty, and
has some excellent stories piping hot from London, which I
have entreated him to send you. His Bishop is full of disease,
but Philips pronounces him the best man alive, and he does
not value the chaplainship the thousandth part so much as the
agreeable manner that it was given. This you will agree to
be a compliment perfectly new, as new as any of my Polite

---

[1] Whom he speaks of, in a letter to Pope, as "too grave a
poet for me."

[2] The mob in St. Patrick's Liberty was called the Cavan or
Kevin Bail.

Conversation.   I will hold you no longer, but remain, My dear
Lord, with more expression than the remainder of this paper
will hold,   Ever your, etc.,
J. S."

On Sept. 25, 1735, he writes :

"Sheridan staid here not above ten days, all which he passed
abroad, and only lay at the Deanery.   He boasts in every letter
of the fine air and meat and ale of Cavan, and the honest merry
neighbourhood.   He writes me English Latinized, and Latin
Englyfied, but neither of them equal to mine, as my very
enemies allow.   It is true indeed, I am gone so far in this
science that I can hardly write common English, I am so apt
to mingle it with Latin.   For instance, instead of writing, *my
enemies*, I was going to spell it *mi en emis*. . . . I was to sign
a report of a committee at the Blue-Coat Hospital just now ;
but would not do it till the words *mob* and *behave* were altered
to *rabble* and *behaved themselves*.   Curse on your new-fangled
London wits, *misti lis*[1] corrupted, and you, out of spite, will in
your next letter torment me with *sho'dn't, wo'dn't, be'n't, can't,
cu'dn't*."

On March 31, 1737, he writes :

"My dear Lord :
      I am so busy a person in State affairs, that I cannot
endure to read country letters.   I have, indeed, some faint
remembrance that I received a letter from you about four days
ago, and another about as many days sooner.   Confound that
jade Fortune who did not make me a lord, although it were of
Ireland ; I should have been above the little embranglements
into which I put myself.   The thing was this.   A great flood
of halfpence from England hath rolled in upon us by the
politics of the Primate.[2]   I railed at them to Faulkner, who
printed an advertisement naming me, and my ill-will towards
them ; for which he was called before the Council, was terribly
abused, but not sent to prison, only left to the mercy of the
common law for publishing a libel, for so they called his
paragraph.   I expected to have the same honour of attending
their——ships ; I sent off all my papers, as I have often done ;
but their——honours have not meddled further, and the halfpence must pass.   I quarrel not at the coin, but at the indignity
of not being coined here, and the loss of £12,000 in gold and
silver to us, which, for aught I know, may be half our store.

---

[1] *I.e.* "my style is."
[2] Archbishop Boulter.   See Vol. II. p. 86.

I am told by others as well as your Lordship that the city of Cork hath sent me my Silver box and Freedom, but I know nothing of it.[1]   I am sorry there are not fools enough in Cork to keep you out of the spleen.   Have you got any money from your tenants?   Can you lend me a thousand pounds?   Are you forced to diet and lodge?   Or, if I visit you about two, can you give me a chicken and a pint of wine?   It was your pride to refuse £100 that I offered to lend you when I thought you were in want; can you now do me the same civility?   But I scorn to accept it?   Mrs. Whiteway found £60 in my cabinet, besides some few (but very small) banker's bills.   When I get my Cork box I will certainly sell it for not being gold. . . . I desire your Aldermen would begin with gold, and if any mischief should happen, let them send another eighteen times and 50 grains heavier in silver."

He turns aside to send some civil messages from Mrs. Whiteway, and to ask Lord Orrery to come and see him, that he may take "an eternal farewell" of him : and thus describes his own state.   "I am daily losing ground, both in health and spirits.   I am plagued this month with a noise in my head which deafens me, and some touches of giddiness—my old disorders.   I am fretting at universal public mismanagement."

After some inquiries as to Lord Orrery's health, he goes on :—

"My neighbour Prelate, who politicly makes his court to Sir R. W. by imitating that great minister in every minute pulling up of his breeches—this prelate, I say—as parsons say 'I say'—harangued my neighbours against me under the name of some wicked man about the new halfpence, but received no other answers than 'God bless the ——[2]'"

He has no news, he says, nor can Mrs. Whiteway give him any.

"It is now the last day of March, and I have not one

---

[1] Swift acknowledged the receipt of the Freedom in a silver box on the 15th of August this year.   But he was offended that there was no inscription stating the grounds of the presentation, and returned it accordingly.   His anger was appeased by a suitable inscription being afterwards engraved upon the box.
[2] Presumably the Drapier.

scheme to make a hundred fools to-morrow.[1]   Mrs. Whiteway is
just gone down stairs, but I expect her every moment up : and
that she is gathering materials at the street-door gate.   I had
yesterday a letter from my old friend Lord Carteret, who says
not a syllable to confirm what we hear from England, that
Walpole and Mr. Pulteney are become friends, and both to be
made Lords : which I scarce believe : because the first might
have been a Duke many years ago, if it had been possible to
govern the Parliament without him."

On the 2nd of July, 1737, Swift sends the Preface to
the *History of the Four Last Years* to Lord Orrery, with
this letter :

"My dear Lord :
          I have corrected the enclosed as well as my shattered
head was able.   I entreat your Lordship will please to alter
whatever you have a mind, and please to deliver it, with your
own hand, to Doctor King, at his Chambers in the Temple.
If you sail on Monday, I fear you will not have time to see me,
so I must bid you Farewell for ever.   For although you should
stay a day or two longer you will be in too great a hurry for me
to expect you.   May God protect you in h(*appiness*[2]) and the
continuance in the Love and Esteem of (*all good*) men.   I can
hear something better, but my head is very ill, but in all
conditions I will live and die with the truest Respect, Esteem,
Love, and Attachment, Your most obedient and most
                    Obliged Servt.
                                        J. Swift."

On 26th Nov. of the same year he writes about some
lawsuit in which a friend is interested, and closes thus :

" I am grown an entire Ghost of a Ghost of what I was,
although you left me ill enough.   Pray God bless you in every
circumstance of yourself, your Family and Fortune.
" I could tell you a Million things relating to this country :
of the great plenty of money, by the Primate's scheme of the
lowering of the Gold, which its younger brother silver hath
followed, and neither have been seen since.   I could be more
large upon both Houses and all their good actions.   Pray send
me a silver sixpence by the first opportunity.   Pray God preserve you and your family, my dear Lord, and may you live
till Christian times."

---

[1] The Journal to Stella shows us that All Fools' Day was not
always so unobserved by Swift.

[2] The paper is here torn.

On 22nd Feb. 17$\frac{38}{37}$, he writes again, and in the course of the letter upbraids Lord Orrery with considerable warmth.

"I complain of your Lordship upon one Article.   Mrs. Whiteway assures me, that a correct copy of the *History of the Four Last Years*, &c., was put into your hands to be given to Doctor King of St. Mary Hall in Oxford, to be published as he could agree with some bookseller or printer : but I have never heard a word from the Doctor since.   How will you answer this, my Dear Lord ?   This proceeding is directly against all the Rules of Justice, Honour, Friendship, and conscience.   My chief design in that History was with the utmost truth and zeal to defend the Proceedings of that blessed Queen and her Ministry, as well as myself, who had a greater share than usually falls to men of my level.   I did thorough (*sic*) the whole treatise impartially adhere to Truth.   I had some regard to increase my own Reputation, and besides I should have been glad to have seen my small Fortune increased by an honest means.   I therefore wish that (your) Lordship would please, if your time and leisure permit, to see Doctor King, and desire he would explain himself concerning his long silence, and his very slow, or *no* proceedings in a point which I have so much at heart for a hundred reasons.   I believe you sometimes see my friend, Mr. Pope.   Pray report to him the state of my health, and the disposition of my mind, that I am become good for less than nothing.   He is one of the oldest and dearest friends I have remaining. . . Do you know my old friend Erasmus Lewis ?   If so, I desire your Lordship will present him with my true Love and Esteem.   And if my Lord Bathurst be one of your acquaintance let him know how grateful I desire to be for the continual marks of his Favour and Friendship. Thus I treat you, my Lord, in the phrase of Plautus, as one of my *Pueri Salutigeruli*."

There is not a little of pathos in the sorrow with which he sees the efforts of his old age neglected, and in the eagerness with which he presses himself on the remembrance of his old friends.

APPENDIX XIII

SWIFT'S DISEASE

In the account which I have given of Swift's later years, and in my references to his disease, and to the effect which it had upon his character and ultimately upon his reason, it has been my object to deal with the question from what may be called the biographical, and not the medical, point of view. The most recent medical opinion clearly establishes the fact, which is of main interest in his biography, that Swift's disease was not a case of gradually developing insanity, which might have affected his reason, even while its development was proceeding ; but a case of specific malady, which tortured him during life, and which ultimately produced a definite injury to the brain, but which up to that point in no way obliterated his reason. It may be well to state very shortly one or two of the facts which medical science has proved.

Sir William Wilde, in his *Closing Years of Dean Swift* gave the first careful analysis of Swift's symptoms: and successfully proved that the term insanity had been far too sweepingly applied to Swift. He showed that the Dean suffered throughout life from brain pressure, aggravated by gastric attacks : and that congestion, to which he says the name of *epileptic vertigo* might be applied,. was ultimately accompanied by paralysis, under which the brain sank into lethargy rather than insanity. Dr Bucknill, F.R.S. (to whose inquiries my attention was called by Mr. Churton Collins, to whom belongs the credit of having instigated them) in *Brain*, for January (1882), has carried further Sir William Wilde's inquiries, in the light of the recent discoveries of medical science. He proves that the two maladies of giddiness and deafness from which Swift suffered, sometimes separately, and sometimes conjointly, and for which he himself assigned causes in a surfeit of fruit and in a cold, respectively, really had their common origin in a disease in the region of the ear, to which the name of *Labyrinthine vertigo* has been given. This physical malady, as Dr. Bucknill shows, would have an increasingly depressing effect as years went on, or strength failed, and as other causes for melancholy came to ally themselves with it.   The Dean was, in short, reduced to the state of profound gloom,' apathy, and physical suffering, which his own words repeatedly describe, and which he sums up with more force than metrical accuracy in the Latin line,

Vertiginosus, inops, surdus, male gratus amicis.

But nothing that could be called insanity came on, until this physical and local malady produced paralysis, a symptom of which was the not uncommon one of aphasia, or the automatic utterance of words, ungoverned by intention.   As a consequence of that paralysis, but not before, the brain, already weakened by senile decay, at length gave way, and Swift sank into the dementia which preceded his death.

DATES OF SWIFT'S WORKS

1689. Ode to Archbishop Sancroft.
„ Ode to Temple.
1691. Ode to Athenian Society.
1693. Verses to Congreve.
„ Verses on Temple's illness.
1700. Mrs. Frances Harris's Petition.
„ Publication of Temple's Letters.
1701. Dissensions in Athens and Rome.
„ Publication of Temple's *Miscellanea*.
1704. Tale of a Tub.
„ Battle of the Books.
„ Mechanical Operation of the Spirit.
1706. Baucis and Philemon.
1708. Bickerstaff's Predictions.
„ Letter on the Sacramental Test.
„ Sentiments of a Church of England Man.
„ Argument against Abolishing Christianity.
„ Remarks on Tindal's *Rights of the Christian Church*
1709. Advancement of Religion.
„ Publication of Temple's Memoirs.
1709-10. Contributions to *Tatler*.
1710. Character of Earl of Wharton.
1710-11. Contribution to *Examiner*.
1712. Proposals for improving the English Tongue.
„ Conduct of the Allies.
1713. Importance of the *Guardian*.
„ Public Spirit of the Whigs.
„ Abstract of Collins's *Discourse*.

1713. Cadenus and Vanessa.

1714. Free Thoughts on the Present State of Affairs.

1715. Memoirs relating to the Change in the Queen's Ministry.

,, Inquiry into the Behaviour of the Queen's Last Ministry.

1719. Letter to a Young Clergyman.

1720. Letter of Advice to a Young Poet.

,, On the Universal Use of Irish Manufactures.

1723. Against the Power of Bishops.

1724. Drapier Letters.

1726. Gulliver's Travels.

1727. Short View of the State of Ireland.

1728. Contributions to *Intelligencer* (Dublin).

1729. Modest Proposal as to Children of Irish Poor.

1730 (about). Essay on Modern Education.

,, Essay on Conversation.

,, Polite Conversation.

1731. Presbyterian Plea of Merit.

,, Verses on the Death of Dr. Swift.

1732. Advantages Proposed by the Repeal of the Sacramental Test.

,, The Beasts' Confession.

1733. Rhapsody on Poetry.

,, Roman Catholic Reasons for Repealing the Test.

1736. On the Universal Hatred against the Clergy.

,, The Legion Club.

Published after Death.

Directions to Servants.
The Last Four Years of the Queen.

INDEX

A Long History of a Short Parliament, in a Certain Kingdom, Delany, ii. 11

Academy, Swift's proposal to found an, i. 329 and note

Academy, of France, i. 81

Academy, Royal Irish, Proceedings of the, i. 61 note

Acheson, Sir Arthur and Lady, Swift's visit to, ii. 170 and note

Addison, and Swift, i. 167, 168 note, 175 ; his alterations in *Baucis and Philemon, ib.* and note ; Under-Secretary to Lord Sunderland, 190, 205, 207, 227 ; Swift's parting with, Sept. 1709, 236 and note ; leaves Ireland Aug. 1710, 249, 255, 260, 261, 287, 337 ; ii. 3, 18 ; "Addison's Walk," i. 236 note

Addresses, Swift's, to William III., i. 46 ; to William Congreve, i. 50

Æolists, Sect of, i. 139

Æsop, i. 85

Agher, Living of, given to Swift, i. 100

Allen, Lord ("Traulus"), ii. 158

Almanac, Partridge's, for 1709, i. 223

Amory, Thomas, *Memories of Ladies,* ii. 185 ; account of Swift, *ib.*

Anne, Queen, i. 121 ; construction of the Ministry under, 1702, *ib.* ; the ministry of 1703, 125 ; prejudice against Swift, 147 ; differences with the Duchess of Marlborough, 244 ; celebration of the, anniversary of accession, 275 ; illness, 356, 358 ; last council, 376 ; death, 377

Annesley, Dr. Samuel, marriage of daughters of, to John Dunton and Samuel Wesley, i. 43

Arbuckle, James, ii. 184

Arbuthnot, quoted, i. 32 ; appointed Physician to Queen Anne, 162, 260, 288, 361, 364 ; to Swift, June 26, 1714, 365 ; Swift to, July 3, 1714, 366 ; letter from Pope to, 368, 374, 378 ; his place among the wits, ii. 97 ; sympathy with Swift, 98 ; and Gay, 202 ; last letter to Swift, Oct. 1734, 211 ; death of, *ib.*

Argyll, the Duke of, offer to take Marlborough prisoner, i. 243 ; heads a petition to the Crown against the *Public*

Spirit of the Whigs, 359, 376

Armagh, Archbishop of. *See* Boyle, Marsh

Armagh, Endowed School of, ii. 239

Armagh, Records of, i. 185 note

Ashburnham, Lord, i. 320 note

Ashburnham, Lady, daughter of the Duke of Ormond, i. 326

Ashe, Dilly, i. 182, 285

Ashe, Dr. St. George (afterwards Bishop of Clogher), i. 20, 182, 247 ; death 1717, ii. 16 note ; and Stella, 41, 42, 300, 302

Asparagus, Dutch way of cutting, i. 48

Athenian Society, The, 1689, Swift's letter to, quoted, i. 35 note ; address to, 41, 43, 45 ; aims of, 43

Atterbury, Francis, Archdeacon of Totnes, i. 88, 89 ; as leader of the High Church party in Convocation, 124 ; *Vindication of the Rights of Convocation, ib.* ; character of, *ib.*, 125 and note, 144 and note ; his part in the Church struggle, 1705, 164 ; and Sacheverell's Defence, 243 and note ; (Dean of Carlisle) elected Prolocutor of Convocation, 270 ; Swift's intimacy with, 284 ; appointed Bishop of Rochester and Dean of Westminster, 348 ; Swift to, *ib.* ; Swift to, April 18, 1716, ii. 8, 94 note, 102, 124 and note

Attorney-General of the Palatinate of Tipperary, Office of, given to Godwin Swift by first Marquis of Ormond, i. 9

Author's Apology, prefixed to 1710 ed. of the *Battle of the Books*, i. 90 note

Autobiographical Anecdotes, references to, i. 2, 7 note, 25, 33, 49 note, 59 note, Appendix i.

BALDWIN, Dr., Provost of Trinity College, Dublin, i. 20 note ; ii. 184

Bandbox Plot, The, i. 324

Bank, National, of Ireland, proposal to establish a, ii. 63

Barber, Alderman, i. 313 and note, 359 ; ii. 211, 224 and note

Barber, Mrs., ii. 187, 223 ; Swift's assistance to, 231, 235

Barrett, Dr., Essay on Swift's Early Days, i. 17 ; ii. 152 note

Barton, Mistress, niece of Sir Isaac Newton, i. 228

Bathurst, Lord, i. 285 ; ii. 103 ; correspondence with Swift, 1730, ii. 212, 214

Bavaria, Elector of, i. 156

Beaumont, Joe, from Trim, i. 285

Bedell, Bishop, i. 62 ; death, 1641, *ib.* note

Beggar's Opera, The, reception of, ii. 201 ; attacked by Dr. Herring, 203 ; Swift's defence of, *ib.* ; its political bearing, 204

Benevolence, Swift's, i. 77 note

Bentley, and the Christ Church Society, i, 39, 85 ; dispute with Charles Boyle, 87 ; attack on Sir William Temple's defence of Phalaris, *ib.* ; *Dr. Bentley's Dissertations Examined*, 88 note, 89

Bequests, Swift's, ii. 259

Berkeley, Bishop, of Cloyne, with Judge Marshall, appointed Vanessa's executor, ii. 34 ; his reported evidence of Swift's marriage, Appendix iv.

Berkeley, Lord, i. 26 note, 98 ; Swift's satire on, 99 ; end of office, April 1701, 102, 107, 108 and note ; 201, 227 and note ; Lord Lieutenant of Gloucestershire, 258

Berkeley, Lady, i. 101, 173, 213

Berkeley, Lady Betty, i. 101 and note. *See* also Germaine

Berkeley, Lady Mary, i. 101

Berkeley, Lady Penelope, i. 101

Berkeley, Mr. Monck, his evidence as to Swift's marriage, Appendix iv.

Berkeley, *Literary Relics*, i. 148 note

Bernier, author of the *Grand Mogul* read by Swift, i. 72 note

Berwick, Mr., friend of Sir W. Scott, ii. 34

Bettesworth ("Sergeant Kite"), Swift's attacks on, ii. 194, 195

Bickerstaff, Isaac, Swift as, attacks John Partridge, i. 220 ; *The Tatler*, 224

Bill to suspend the laws for security of the King's person, 1696, i. 64

Bindon, Portrait of Swift by, at Howth Castle, i. 230 and note

Birch, Dr., his abstract of the *Four Last Years*, Appendix iii.

Blackmore, attack on the *Tale of a Tub*, i. 147

Blenheim, Battle of, i. 156

Boileau, i. 81

Bolingbroke, Henry St. John, Viscount, i. 146, 157, 188, 258, 271, 276, 334 ; Treaty of Commerce Bill defeated, 343, 366 ; the Schism Bill, 371, 378 ; joins the Pretender, ii. 6, 13 ; invitation to Swift, July 1721, 94 ; return from exile 1723, 94 ; character of, 96 and note, 215, 225 ; retirement to France, 236. *See* also St. John

Bolingbroke, Lady, to Swift, ii. 7

Bolton, Duke of, i. 98

Bolton, Dr. Theophilus, appointed Dean of Derry, i. 99 and note

Bouchain, Fall of, i. 296

Boulter, Dr. Hugh (Archbishop), i. 169 note ; *Letters*, ii. 55 note ; appointed Archbishop of Armagh, 86 ; character of, *ib.* ; opposition to emigration, 89 ; and Swift, *ib.* ; *Letters*, reference to, 155 note ; 160 note

Boyer, Abel, *Political State*, i. 355

Boyle, Charles, afterwards Earl of Orrery, i. 86 and note ; cause of quarrel with Bentley, 87

Boyle, Michael, Archbishop of Armagh, i. 62

Brennan, Richard, ii. 254, 255 note

Brent, Mrs., i. 25 and note

Brentford, "Kings of," i. 100

Bristow, Living of, i. 7 note

Brobdingnag, or Brobdingrag, Appendix viii.

Broderick, appointed Lord Chief Justice, i. 247 and note

Bromley, William, elected Speaker, i. 269 ; defeated by Sir Thomas Hanmer, 358

Brook, Henry (the Fool of Quality), ii. 170

Brouncker, Lord, and Sir William Temple, i. 32

Browne, Dr., Bishop of Cork, ii. 10, and note

Browne, John, *Scheme of the Money Matters of Ireland*, 1729, ii. 64 note, 149 note

Brydges, afterwards Duke of Chandos, i. 258

Buckingham, John Sheffield, Duke of, i. 121 ; Lord Steward, 258, 306. *See* Normanby

Buncle, John, i. 247 note

Burdy's *Life of Skelton*, reference to, i. 20 note ; ii. 156 note

Burgess, Dissenting preacher, i. 245 and note

Burnet, Alexander, Appendix xii.

Burnet, Gilbert, Bishop of Salisbury, i. 64, 110, 111, 112, 127 ; action in the Church differences, 1705, 165, 241 ; *History of his Own Time*, 245 note, 303 note

Bush, Swift's attack on, i. 99

Butler, Lady Betty, i. 326

Caermarthen, Marchioness of, death, i. 355

Callières, François de, i. 90 note, 91, 92 note

Capel, Lord, Lord Deputy of Ireland, i. 62

Cardonnel, Marlborough's secretary, i. 307

Carlingford, Viscount (*see* Barnam Swifte), i. 4

Carlyle, Dr. Alexander, i. 295 note

Carroll, Mr., of St. Bride's, Dublin, i. 105 note

Carteret, Lord, Secretary of State, and the Coinage question, ii. 66 ; appointed Lord Lieutenant, April 1724, 76 ; character of, *ib.* ; Swift's letter to, 77 ; intimacy with Swift and other Tories, 172 ; resignation, May 1730, 173

Carteret, Lady, her letter to Lady Sundon, i. 159 note

Cashel, Archbishop of. *See* Marsh', Bolton

"Castilian language," i. 183 and note

Castledurrow, Lord, anecdote of Swift, i. 51 note

Catherine Hall, Cambridge, Wotton a student at, i. 84

Celbridge, Vanessa at, ii. 23

Certificate of Conduct for ordination, Swift's, i. 60, 61

Chandos, Duke of. *See* Brydges

Charles I., Barnam Swifte created Lord Carlingford by, i. 4

Charlton, Chiverton, letter to Swift, May 22, 1714, i. 362 and note

Chartres, Colonel, ii. 116

Cherbury, Lord Herbert of, *History*, read by Swift, i. 72 note

Chesterfield, Lord, ii. 116, 228 and note

Christchurch wits, i. 39, 85, 86

Church, The : in *Tale of a Tub*, i. 140 ; Memorial of, 161 ; the struggle of party in, 164 ; Sacheverell and the Church, 237 *seq.* ; favour to, 269, 281 ; Church and Schism Act, 371 ; Irish Church. *See* Ireland

Church, The, in danger, Cry of, i. 160, 162, 163

Cicero, *Epistles*, read by Swift, i. 73

Cleveland, Duchess of, i. 4 note

Clogher, Parnell, Bishop of, i. 236 note

Club, The, i. 284

Coffee-Houses, Wills' and St. James', i. 170, 233; Button's, i. 172 note

"Cold temper" of Swift, i. 47

College Roll, for Easter term, 1685, Dublin, i. 18, 19 and note

Combat des livres, i. 90

Comment on the Sermon of Dr. Hare, by Mrs. Manley, i. 296

Commissioners on forfeited Irish estates, i. 106

Compton, Sir Spencer, ii. 130

Congreve, William, with Swift at Kilkenny, i. 14; literary and dramatic successes, 50; Swift's address to, *ib.*; and the *Tale of a Tub*, 147 and note, 168, 169 and note, 222, 255, 260 and note, 268; ii. 104; death, 1728, 206 and note.

Conolly, Speaker, Irish House of Commons, ii. 68 and note

Considerations for promoting the Agriculture of Ireland, Viscount Molesworth, ii. 54, note

Considerations upon Considerations for promoting Agriculture, 1724, ii. 146

Convocation, The Houses of, struggles in, i. 124, 158; and Atterbury, 124

Cooksey, *Life of Lord Somers*, quoted, i. 146 note

Copper Coinage, The, ii. 64; the patent passed, July 12, 1722, 65; comparative value of, 68; Swift's arguments against, 69; Report of the Committee on inquiry on, 70. *See* Wood

Correspondents, Swift's list of his, i. 228

Cowley's Pindaric odes, and their popularity, i. 40; Swift's

comparison of himself to, ii. 261

Cowper, Lord, i. 243, 257

Craftsman, The, and Swift's reply to, ii. 155

Craggs, i. 373

Cranford, seat of Lord Berkeley, i. 227 and note

Crisis, The, by Steele, i. 357

Crooksbury Hill, near Moor Park, i. 28

Cunningham's edition of *Lives of the Poets*, i. 34 note, 199 note, 235 note

Curll, and the *Tale of a Tub*, i. 148 and note; a "new terror to death," ii. 210 note

DARTINEUF, i. 274

Davenant, Sir William, daughter of, married to Thomas Swift, i. 9 note

Davenant, Dr., i. 145

Davies, Sir John, author of *Nosceteipsum, or the Immortality of the Soul*, read by Swift, i. 72 note

Davis. *See* Macky

Dawes, Sir William, i. 367 and note

Dawley House, Lord Bolingbroke's seat, ii. 106 and note

Deacon, Swift ordained, i. 61

Deane, Admiral, kinswoman of, married to Godwin Swift, i. 9

Defence of Eating and Drinking in Remembrance of the Dead, by the Bishop of Raphoe, ii. 10 note

Degree of Bachelor of Arts taken by Swift, i. 15

Degree, Doctor's, taken by Swift, i. 102

Delafaye, Charles, letter of, to Archbishop King, ii. 12

Delany, Mrs., i. 350 note. *See* Pendarves *and* Granville

Delany, Dr. Patrick, his account of Swift's college days, i. 16, 236 note ; *Observations,* i. 168 note, 175 note, 181 note, 183 note, 190 note, 344 note ; *A Long History of a Short Parliament in a Certain Kingdom,* ii. 10, 29 ; *Observations,* ii. 35 note, 180, 181, 238, 267

Delville, Traditions of, ii. 67 note, 180 note

Denmark, Prince George of, Lord High Admiral, i. 184 ; his death, 194

Derry, Bishop of. *See* King

Derry, Deanery of, i. 99

Devonshire, Duke of, Lord Lieutenant of Ireland, ii. 249

Diaper, Swift's assistance to, i. 314

Dilke, Mr., author of *Papers of a Critic,* i. 316 note

Dingley, Rebecca, with Stella in Ireland, i. 114, 120, 148 ; in London, 226 ; ii. 196, 259 ; her death, 260 note ; evidence as to the marriage of Swift and Stella, Appendix iv.

Dissertation, Bentley's, on Phalaris, i. 87

Dobbs, Arthur, *Essay on the Trade and Improvement of Ireland,* 1729, ii. 54 note, 146

Dolben, Mr., i. 241

" Dorinda," Lady Giffard, i. 53 and note, *ib.*

" Dorothea," Lady Temple, i. 53 note

Dorset, Duke of, appointed Lord Lieutenant, ii. 173

" Dragon," The (Lord Oxford), i. 366, 367

Dragoons, Captaincy of, offered to Swift, i. 48, 59

Drake, Dr., i. 161 note, 255 note

Drapier, M. B., letters by, ii. 67, 71, 73 ; Proclamation against the author, 75 and note ; fifth letter, 82 ; seventh letter, 84 and note. *See* Swift

Dryden, Elizabeth, married to Rev. Thomas Swift, Vicar of Goodrich, i. 5 and note

Dryden, John, opinion of Swift's verse, i. 45

Dryden, Rev. Jonathan, received living of Goodrich, 1646, i. 7 note

Dublin, Archbishop of. *See* Marsh, King

Dunciad, The (May 1728), ii. 204 ; Swift and, *ib.* 217

Dunkin, William, Swift's assistance to, ii. 188

Dunkirk, Importance of, Steele's, i. 357

Dunlaven, Prebend of, given to Swift, i. 101

Dunton, John, originator of the Athenian Society, i. 43 ; account of, 44 and note

Eadric the Forester, ancestor of Abigail Erick, i. 10

Edwyn, Sir Humphrey, Presbyterian Lord Mayor, i. 127 note

Eglinton, Lord, married to daughter of Barnam Swifte, i. 4

Elizabeth, Queen, celebration of birth of, i. 305

Elwin, Rev. W., ii. 252

Epistles of Phalaris, i. 85, 86

Epsom, Swift at, i. 193

Erick, Abigail, married to Jonathan Swift (the elder), i. 10 ; Appendix i. ; *see* Swift, Abigail

Essays, Divine, Moral, and Political, Steele (?), ii. 4 and note

Essay on the Trade of Ireland (Dobbs, 1729), ii. 146

Eugene, Prince, i. 156 ; visit to England, Jan. 1712, i. 315 ; his character, Appendix iii.

Examiner, The, i. 217 note, 260, 263, 336, 354 note

Exercise, Physical, practised by Swift, i. 74

FAME, Swift's description of, i. 46 note

Fanatic, The Modern, i. 240

Farnham, i. 27, 28

Farnham Castle, i. 28

Faulkner, Character of, ii. 182 ; anecdote of Swift and, 183 ; imprisoned, 195, 233, 234, 251, 255 note ; his edition of Swift, Appendix viii.

Fenton, Elijah, quoted by Warton, i. 45 note

Fenton —, husband of Jane Swift, i. 105

Fielding ("handsome Fielding ") married to daughter of Barnam Swifte, i. 4 and note

"First Fruits," i. 184

Fishpond, Swift's, at Laracor, i. 120

Floyd, Biddy, i. 101

Flying Post, The, i. 322 and note ; Wood's defence of the Coinage in, ii. 66

Fontenelle, i. 81

Ford, Charles, i. 320 note; ii. 182

Forster's *Life of Swift,* references to, i. 18, 19 notes, 35 note, 61 notes, 96 and note, 97 note, 118 note, 167 note, 178 note, 183 note, 185 note, 186 notes, 226 note

Fountaine, Sir Andrew, i. 174 note ; intimacy with Swift, 182

Fowle, Rev. T., rector of Islip, i. 235 note

Freind, Dr., i. 260

GALWAY, Lord, i. 98

Garth, Dr. (afterwards Sir Samuel), author of the *Dispensary,* i. 255 and note, 306

Gaulstown, Swift at, ii. 169

Gay, John, i. 361 ; Swift's assistance to, ii. 102 ; production of the *Beggar's Opera,* 201 ; *Polly* proscribed, 208 ; the *Fables,* 209 ; death, Dec. 1732, 209 ; epitaph on, Appendix xii.

Gent, Thomas, i. 243 note

George, Prince, death (Oct. 28th, 1708), i. 194. *See* Denmark.

George I., death (June 11th, 1727), ii. 130

Germaine, Lady Betty, her influence with the Duke of Dorset in favour of Swift, ii. 174 ; her friendship with Swift, 219. *See* also Berkeley, Lady Betty.

Gery, Rev. Mr., Swift's visit to, i. 363

Gery, Molly, i. 363

Giddiness and deafness, Swift's sufferings from, i. 34, 56

Giffard, Lady, sister of Sir William Temple, i. 30 note ; her position at Moor Park, 32 ; and Swift, *ib.* ; as "Dorinda," 53 ; and note *a,* 77, 96, 113

Gilliver, Lawton, printer, ii. 235

Gloucester, the Duke of, death of, i. 106

Godolphin, Lord, appointed Lord Treasurer under Queen Anne, i. 121, 124, 126 ; Swift's interview with, 191 ; as "Valpone" attacked by Sacheverell, 241 ; political opposition to, 246 ; dismissed, 251 ; Swift's lampoon on, 259 ; death, Sept. 1712, 312 and note

Goodrich, i. 1, 5 *seq.*, 510 *seq.*; ii. 206 ; Appendix i.

Goodrich, Castle of, held by the Parliamentarians, 1642, i. 6

Gower, Lord, letter on behalf of Johnson, ii. 246

Grafton, Duke of, Lord Lieutenant of Ireland, stops the action against Waters, ii. 60 ; and the inquiry into the Coinage question, 66 ; recalled, 75 ; Walpole's opinion of, 76 note

Granville, George, Secretary of War, 1710, i. 258

Granville, Mary (Mrs. Delany), ii. 180 ; friendship with Swift, 191. *See* Pendarves *and* Delany

Greg, William, clerk to Robert Harley, charge of treason against, i. 187 and note

" Gresham, Men of," i. 85, 136, 137, 138

Grierson, Mrs. Constantia, ii. 187, 189

" Grub Street," i. 136, 147, 322

Gualtier, Abbé, negotiations with France through, i. 309

Guardian, The, i. 335, 353

Guiscard, Marquis de, i. 275 ; quarrel with St. John, 276 ; attack on Harley, 277 ; death, 278 and notes

Halifax, Lord, proposed impeachment of, i. 108, 112 and note, 162, 185, 186 and note, 199, 206, 227 ; letters from Swift to, 234 and note, 255, 257, 258, 259

Hamilton, Duke of, Lord Lieutenant of the County Palatine, 1710, i. 258 ; part in the Peace negotiations, 323 ; death, 325

Hamilton, Duchess of, i. 324

Hanmer, Sir Thomas, elected Speaker, i. 358

Hannibal at our Gates, i. 317 and note

Harcourt, Sir Simon, Attorney-General, i. 121 ; resignation, 188 ; Lord Chancellor, 257, 271

Harding, the Drapier's Second Letter to, ii. 71 ; imprisoned, 75 ; throwing out of the bill against, 81

Hare, Dr., chaplain to the Duke of Marlborough, i. 296

Harley, Robert, i. 75 ; elected Speaker, 107 ; Secretary of State, 187 and note ; dismissed from office, *ib.*, 244, 249 ; Chancellor of the Exchequer, 251, 259, 262, 271 ; Guiscard's attack on, 277 ; illness and recovery, 279 ; made Earl of Oxford and Lord Treasurer, 282 ; Swift's estimate of, *ib. See* Oxford

Harley, Thomas, i. 363

Harrison, i. 260 ; appointed secretary to Lord Raby's embassy, 274 ; death, 327

Hart Hall, or Hertford College, Oxford, i. 36 note ; Swift at, Appendix i.

Hartstong, Dr., Bishop of Ossory, i. 367 and note

Haversham, Earl, i. 162, 184

Hawkesworth's Life. See Lyons

Heathcote, Sir Gilbert, i. 250

Helsham, Dr., i. 236 note ; ii. 180 ; Swift's description of, *ib.*

Hemp and Flax manufacture in Ireland, Proposal for the improvement of, i. 158

Henley, Anthony, i. 227

Herodotus, cited by Swift, i. 143

Hill, Abigail, i. 244. *See* Masham, Mrs.

Hoadley, Miss, letter from Swift to, i. 228 note

Hobbes, i. 217, 239

Hoey's Court, birthplace of Swift, i. 11

Holderness, Lady, granddaughter of the Duke of Schomberg, ii. 193

Homer, cited by Swift, i. 143

Horace, Ode of, paraphrased by Swift, i. 39 and note

Horse, bought by Swift at Kilkenny, i. 13

Hort, Bishop of Kilmore, author of *Quadrille*, 1735, ii. 195 and note

Howard, Mrs., afterwards Countess of Suffolk, correspondence with Swift, ii. 118 ; to the author of *Gulliver's Travels*, 127, 130, 220, 223 and note

Howe, Jack, joins the Ministry under Queen Anne, i. 121

Howth, Lord and Lady, ii. 183

Howth Castle, Swift at, ii. 183 ; portrait of Swift at, *ib.*

Hudibras, Butler's, compared with *Tale of a Tub*, i. 138, 139 note ; reference to, 142, 143

Hue and Cry after Dean Swift, ii. 3

Hunter, Colonel, Swift's letters to, i. 225 note, 227, 229

Hyde, Lady Catherine. *See* Queensberry, Duchess of

INCOME, Swift's, from his livings, i. 118 note

Intelligencer, The, Swift's defence of the *Beggar's Opera* in, ii. 203 and note

Ireland, the Parliament of 1705, i. 157 ; causes of trouble in, ii. 50 ; forfeitures of absentee landlords in, *ib.* ; life in, 52, 53 notes ; condition of lower classes in, 54 ; emigration from north of, 55 and note ;

restrictions on exports, 57 ; Swift's ridicule of the idea of a National Bank for, 63 ; Parliament of, presentation of a memorial against the copper coinage patent from, 66

Ireland, Church of, the state of, when Swift entered it, i. 62 ; struggles of, *ib.*, 63, 64, 65 ; Swift's mission for, 184 *seq.*, 198 ; defence of, ii. 16 ; last struggle for, 162

Ireland, Works on, *List of Absentees*, ii. 52 ; *On the Conduct of the Purse of Ireland*, 1714, 53 note ; *Scheme of the Proportion which the Protestants of Ireland may probably bear to the Papists*, *ib.*, note ; Swift's *Proposal for Universal use of Irish manufactures*, 54 note ; *Considerations for promoting the Agriculture of Ireland*, *ib.* ; *Essay on the Trade and Improvement of Ireland*, Arthur Dobbs, *ib.* note, 55 note ; *Essay on the Trade of*, 146, 147 notes ; Proposals for meeting the evils of, 147 ; Swift's *Tracts* on, 150, 160. *See* also Swift

Irenæus, read by Swift, i. 72 note ; cited by him, i. 143

Irish Academy Pamphlets referred to, ii. 11

Irishman, Wild, exhibition of a, in London, ii. 80 note

Irreverence, apparent in the *Tale*, i. 141

Italian Travels, Addison's, i. 167

JAMES II., Death of, Sept. 17, 1701, i. 111

Jervas, Portrait of Swift by, i. 229 and note ; ii. 3

Johnson, Dr. Samuel, on Pindaric verse, i. 40, 45 note, 58

note, 90 note, and the authorship of the *Tale of a Tub*, 145 and note, 146 and note ; on Swift's charity, ii. 177 note ; dawning fame, 245 ; *London, ib.* ; letter concerning, from Lord Gower, 246 ; his doubts as to Swift's authorship of the *Tale of a Tub*, Appendix ii. ; and *Four Last Years of the Queen*, Appendix iii. ; contradiction to doubts in *Idler, ib.*

Johnson, Mrs., mother of "Stella," i. 32, 74 note ; marriage with Mr. Mose, 114 note ; ii. 139

Johnson, Ann (afterwards Mrs. Filby), ii. 139

Johnson, Esther, "Stella" (born March 13, 1681), i. 33 ; sympathy with Swift, 78 ; personal appearance, 79 ; her position in Sir W. Temple's household, 80, 113 ; in Ireland, 114, 120, 148 ; proposal of Dr. Tisdall to, 150 ; in London, 226 ; and Addison, 236 and note ; Swift to, Sept. 9, 1710, 254, 288 ; ii. 20 ; marriage with Swift, 26 and note, 33 ; her love for Swift, 35 ; confidences to Bishop Ashe, 41 ; illness, 108 ; increasing illness, 131 ; Swift's reticence as to, 137 note ; Sheridan's story of Swift and, 138 ; her Will, 139 ; death of, Jan. 28, 1728, 140 and note ; evidences of her marriage to Swift, Appendix iv. ; character of, Appendix xi.

Jollivet, Mons. *Poésies chrétiennes de*, i. 206 note

Jonson, Ben, his use of the name Volpone, i. 241

Journal to Stella, *References to, throughout* ; publication of, Appendix iv. ; Journal and Notebook of 1727, Appendix ix.

KEALLY, Congreve's letter to, i. 148 note

Kelly, Miss, Swift's assistance to, ii. 196

Kendall, Duchess of, ii. 65 and note, Appendix vi.

Kendall, Rev. John, Swift's letter to, quoted, i. 25 note, 26 note, 38 note

"Kevin Bail," ii. 90 and note

Kildare, Bishop of. *See* Moreton

Kilkenny, Swift at, i. 13 ; civic division of, 14

Killaloe, Bishop of, i. 254

Kilroot, Prebend of, i. 62 ; Swift settled at, 65 ; resignation of, 76

King's Inns, Dublin, *History of*, by Duhigg, quoted by Sir W. Scott, i. 10 note

King, William, Bishop of Derry, afterwards Archbishop of Dublin, i. 63, 64, 117 note, 146 and note ; correspondence with Swift, 158 and note ; Swift's letter to, 6th December 1707, 185, 201 note ; advice to Swift, 293 ; Swift to, 331 ; letter to Swift, 340, 352 ; ii. 6 ; appointed Lord Justice, 10 ; misrepresentations of Swift, 15 ; letter to Archbishop of Canterbury, opposition to the Presbyterian Toleration Bill, 16, 156 and note

King, Dr. William, i. 226 and note ; appointed Gazetteer, 313 and note

King, Dr. William (Principal of St. Mary's Hall, Oxford), intercourse with Swift, ii. 236 ; connection with *Four Last Years*, Appendix iii.

Knightsbrooke, river, at Laracor, i. 120

Kirle, Captain, i. 7 note
Königsmark, Count, tried for the assassination of Thomas Thynne, i. 287 note

LANDLORDS, Absentee, in Ireland, ii. 50
Laracor, Living of, i. 100 ; Swift at, and description of, 117 and note ; Swift's return to, 1704, 128, 347, 348 ; ii. 5, 6
Leicester, i. 23, 25 note, 35, 60, 185, 207
Leicester House, ii. 118 and note
Letcombe, Swift's visit to, i. 363
Letters, Swift to Addison, 22nd August 1710, i. 249, and 314 note ; to Arbuthnot, i. 364, 366, 374 ; ii. 210 ; to Atterbury, i. 348 ; ii. 8 ; to Lord Bathurst, ii. 213 ; to Bolingbroke, ii. 19, 92, 217 note ; to Lord Carteret, ii. 77 ; to Gay, ii. 209 note, 225, 230 ; to Lady Betty Germaine, ii. 114 ; to Mr. Grant, 23rd March 1735, ii. 196 ; to Lord Halifax, November 1709, i. 187 note, 235 and note ; to Miss Hoadley, 4th June 1734, i. 228 note ; to Mrs. Howard, ii. 127 ; to Colonel Hunter, 1709, i. 225 note ; to Mrs. Johnson, i. 74 ; to Archbishop King, i. 117 note, 160, 185 and note, 186 note, 188 note, 191 note ; 30th November 1708, 197 note, 198 note, 200 note, 201 note, 205 and notes ; 1711, 282 note ; 1713, 331, 342 ; ii. 13 ; to Archbishop Marsh, i. 206 note ; to Lord Midleton, ii. 78 ; to Lord Orrery, ii. 198, 199, 245, 248 ; to Lord Oxford, i. 373 ; ii. 206 ; to the 2nd Lord Oxford, ii. 95 note ; to Lord Palmerston, ii. 104, 113 ; to Mrs. Pendarves, ii. 193 note ; to Lord Peterborough, ii. 113 ; to Ambrose Phillips, October 1709, i. 236 note ; to Pope, 1729, i. 170 note ; to Pope, 1720, i. 219 note ; ii. 9, 18, 56, 60, 93, 99, 117, 186 note, 196, 204, 206, 207, 212 note ; 1735, 219, 225 and note, 236 ; to Pulteney, 1735, i. 171 note ; to the Duchess of Queensberry, i. 228 note ; to Dr. Sheridan, ii. 131 ; to Dean Sterne, i. 117 note, 191 note, 196 note ; 15th April 1708, 227 ; ii. 162 ; to Dr. Stopford, ii. 108 ; to Lady Suffolk, ii. 112, 225 ; to Sir W. Temple, 6th October 1694, i. 60 ; to John Temple, i. 178 ; to Tickell, ii. 106 ; to Dr. Tisdall, i. 127 notes, 128 note, 149 note, 151 note, 202 notes ; to Vanessa, i. 347 ; to Archdeacon Walls, i. 186, 188, 189 note, 201 note, 350, 351, 352, 355, 356, 360, 364, 370, 375 ; ii. 9, 14, 39 ; to Miss Waring, i. 66, 67 ; to Mrs. Whiteway, ii. 253 ; to Mr. Winder, 1698, i. 76 note ; to Mr. Worrall, ii. 109, 131
Lewis, Erasmus, i. 288, 333 ; letter to Swift, 342, 343, 366, 372, 378 ; ii. 236, 237
Lexiphanes, Lucian's, quoted, i. 92 note
Library, Royal, at St. James's, i. 87
Life and Errors, of John Dunton, i. 44 note
Lille, Siege of, i. 193
Lindsay, Archbishop of Armagh, ii. 10, 86

List of Absentees, Prior, ii. 146
" Little Language," The, i. 345,
  Appendix iv.
Locke, i. 39, 181 ; ii. 83
Locker's *Patchwork*, i. 61 note
Long, Mistress Anne, i. 228 ;
  correspondence with Swift,
  292 ; death, *ib.*
Louis XIV., Age of, i. 81 ; and
  the Pretender, 111, 237
Lucas, Dr., publishes the *Four
  Last Years of the Queen*,
  Appendix iii.
Lucretius, read by Swift, i. 73 ;
  quoted, i. 143, 144
Lyons, Dr., MS. notes on
  Hawkesworth's *Life*, i. 12
  note, 13 note, 25 note, 71
  note, 94 note ; on Swift's
  marriage, Appendix iv.
Lyttleton, " the rising genius of
  his age," ii. 249

MACAULAY, Lord, i. 58 note ;
  criticism of Temple's *Ancient
  and Modern Learning*, 82,
  83 ; doubt of authenticity of
  Four Last Years of the Queen,
  Appendix iii.
Macaulay, Alexander, candidate
  for the representation of Dublin University, ii. 249
Macky's *Remarks on the Characters at the Court of Queen
  Anne*, i. 98 and note. *See*
  Davis
Mainwaring, conductor of the
  Medley, i. 322 note
Manley, Mrs. de la Rivière, i.
  278 note ; *A Vindication of
  the Duke of Marlborough*,
  297, 314 and note, 336
*Mant's History of the Church
  in Ireland*, Reference to, i.
  64, 341
Manton, Dr., folio of 119 ser-
  mons, i. 123 note
Market Hill (seat of Sir Arthur

Acheson), Swift's life at, ii.
  170
Marlay Abbey, Vanessa at, ii.
  23, 32 ; description of, 33
  note
Marley, Judge, ii. 34
Marlborough, Duke of, i. 121,
  124, 126 ; success at the
  Battle of Blenheim, 1704,
  156 ; at the Hague and victory of Ramillies, 179 ; letter
  to Queen Anne, 243, 262,
  266, 271 ; Mrs. Manley's
  Vindication of, 297, 304 ; in
  London, November 1711, 305 ;
  dismissed, 307 ; Swift and
  the dismissal of, 311 ; entry
  into London, 4th August
  1714, 378
Marlborough, Duchess of, i. 244 ;
  quits the Queen's service, 271 ;
  and *Gulliver's Travels*, ii. 126 ;
  character of, Appendix iii.
Marriage ceremony between
  Swift and Stella, 1716, ii.
  41 ; Swift's offer to publish
  in 1723, 46
Marsh, Narcissus, Archbishop
  of Cashel, of Dublin and of
  Armagh, i. 63 ; presents
  Swift with the Prebend of
  Dunlavan, 1700, 102, Appendix i.
Marshall, Judge, with Bishop
  Berkeley, appointed Vanessa's
  executors, ii. 34
Masham, Mr. (afterwards Lord),
  i. 285 ; ii. 236
Masham, Mrs. (afterwards Lady),
  i. 187, 249 and note, 286,
  366 ; ii. 236
Mason, Monck, his arguments
  to disprove Swift's marriage,
  Appendix iv.
Meath, Bishop of, i. 100 note
Medley, The, i. 322 note
Memoirs of the New Atalantis,
  by Mrs. Manley, i. 278 note

Memorial of the Church of England, etc., by Dr. Drake and others, i. 161 and note

Mercurius Rusticus, or Country's Complaint, 1685, i. 7 note

Merlinus Liberatus, published by Partridge, i. 220

Mesnager, visits to England, i. 309

Midleton, Viscount, ii. 68 note ; letter from Swift, 78

Milles, Dr. Thomas, i. 186

Miln, Rev. William, i. 65 and note

Miscellanies, by Swift and Pope, i. 171 note

Modern Fanatic, The, attack on Sacheverell in, i. 240

" Mohawks " or " Hawkubites," Brutal frolics of, i. 316

Mohun, Lord, death of, i. 325

Molesworth, Viscount, the fifth Drapier letter addressed to, ii. 82 and note ; and Irish reform, 144 and notes

Montague, Charles. *See* Halifax

Moor Park, Description of, i. 27 ; Swift at, 29, 30 note, 35 and note, 48, 60, 74, 77, 94

Moral Meditations by Robert Boyle, i. 173

Mordaunt. *See* Peterborough

Moreton, Dr., Bishop of Kildare, Swift ordained by, i. 61 and note, Appendix i.

Morphew, publisher, i. 201 note, 260 note, 359

Morris, Lady Catherine, i. 279

" Mother Ludlam's Cave," i. 28

Motte, Purchase of copyright of *Gulliver* by, i. 171 note ; ii. 233, 234, 235

Mountjoy, Lord, i. 249

Mulgrave, John Sheffield, Earl of, Marquis of Normanby, i.

121 note. *See* Normanby *and* Buckingham

NARFORD, Norfolk, residence of the Fountaine family, i. 173 and note, 175, 183 note

New House Farm, Goodrich, built 1636, description of, i. 2 ; sacking of, by the Parliamentary troops, 6

Newspaper Tax, 1712, i. 322

Newton, Sir Isaac, ridiculed by Christ Church wits, i. 85

Nichols, i. 96 note, 146 note

Normanby, Marquis of, created Duke of Buckingham and appointed Privy Seal, in Queen Anne's ministry, i. 121 and note. *See* Buckingham

Norwich, Bishop of, i. 164

Nottingham, Lord, Secretary of State under Queen Anne, i. 121, 162, 184 ; opposition to the Tory Peace policy, 300 ; joined by Shrewsbury, *ib.* ; Swift's attack on, 301, 306, 336

Nurse, Swift's, i. 11, 12

Nutley, Judge, i. 349

OBSERVATIONS on Coin in General, etc., Prior, ii. 63 note

Occasional Conformity, Bill against, i. 123 and note, 124, 150, 157, 162

October Club, i. 262, 271

Odes, Swift's, to Archbishop Sancroft, i. 41 ; to Sir W. Temple, 42 ; to the Athenian Society, 43, 45, 46 ; on Sir W. Temple's recovery from illness, 51, 53, 54

Of drinking in Remembrance of the Dead, by the Bishop of Cork, 4th November 1713, ii. 10

Ogle, Earl of (Henry Cavendish), i. 287 note

Orders, Holy, Swift's condition of taking, i. 47 ; scruples as to, 59

Orford, Earl of, i. 108

Original Contract, i. 110

Orkney, Lady, i. 325 and note

Ormond, Marchioness of, kinswoman to Godwin Swift's first wife, i. 9

Ormond, Duke of, appointed Lord-Lieutenant of Ireland, 1703, i. 125 ; resignation, 181, 258 ; reception in Ireland, 295 ; replaces Marlborough, 316, 333, 334 ; flight of, ii. 6

Ormond, Duchess of, i. 376 ; ii. 7

Orrery, Lord, statement as to Swift's degree, i. 16, 58 note, 119 note, 159 note ; ii. 164 and note ; *Remarks*, i. 160 note, 230 and note ; ii. 29, 164, 197, 231, 252

Osborne, Dorothy. *See* Temple, Lady, i. 32

Ossory, Bishop of, i. 254

Oudenarde, Victory of, i. 188

" Outliers," or absentee landlords, the cause of Irish troubles, ii. 50

Oxford, Swift a graduate of, i. 36

Oxford, Lord, and the Occasional Conformity Bill, i. 300, 306, 333, 354, 359, 361 ; address to Queen Anne, 371 ; dismissal, 372 ; letter from Swift to, 373 ; sent to the Tower, ii. 6 ; Swift's letter to (19th July 1715), *ib.* ; acquittal, 1st July 1717, 19 ; death, 95. *See* Harley

Oxford, Lord, son of the above, ii. 237

Palmerston, Lord, i. 30 note ; Swift's letter to, 1726, ii. 104

Parker, Chief Justice, i. 310 and note

Parliament : Bill against Occasional Conformity, 1702, i. 123 ; dissolution of, 1705, 157 ; Whig majority, 1705, 161 ; meeting of, 1709, 237 ; Tory triumph, 269 ; defeat of the Ministry, 306 ; Treaty opposed, 343 ; election, 353 ; new Speaker, 358 ; Steele expelled, 360 and note ; the new parliament under George I., ii. 6

Parliament, Irish, meeting of, February 1705, i. 157

Parnell, Dr., Bishop of Clogher, i. 236 note, 351

Parnell (the poet), i. 286, 327

Partition, Treaty of, i. 106, 107

Partridge, John, i. 219, 222

Parvisol (Swift's agent), i. 370

Pastorals, The, by Ambrose Philips, i. 169

Pembroke, Earl of, i. 121, 181, 182, 184, 196

Pendarves, Mrs. (Mary Granville), *Autobiography of,* i. 230 note ; ii. 188, 191, 256 note. *See* Delany, Mrs.

Percy, Bishop, on Dr. Salter, i. 198 note

Perkin's Cabal, or the Mock Ministry, ii. 11

Perrault, *Le Siècle de Louis le Grand*, i. 81, 91

Peterborough, Lord, i. 127, 273 and notes, 290 and note ; ii. 104, 127, 235

Phalaris, Epistles of, i. 85, 86

Philips, Ambrose (Namby Pamby), i. 169 and note, 172, 193 note, 287 ; ii. 184

Philips, John, i. 144 and note

Philosophy, Swift's dislike of, i.
43
Philosophy of clothes, i. 139
Philpot, Miss, married to William
Swift, i. 4
Phipps, Sir Constantine, i. 295,
349, 352
Pilkington, Matthew, ii. 188,
224, 235
Pilkington, Mrs. Letitia, i. 328
note ; ii. 180 note, 189 ;
Memoirs of, quoted, i. 18 note,
120 note, 138 note ; ii. 224
Pindar, Imitations of, i. 40
Polly, by Gay, proscribed, ii.
208
Pope, Alexander, i. 274, 330,
361, 365, 368, 369 ; ii. 3, 9,
17, 93, 94, 99, 107, 118, 127,
129, 132, 133, 167, 190, 196,
202, 205, 209, 210, 215, 218,
229, 245, 249, 250, 260
Popery, Bill for preventing
growth of, i. 125
Portland, Earl of, i. 49, 108,
Appendix i.
Post, The Flying, of 8th October
1723, ii. 66
Prebend, Swift's hopes of a, i.
60
Pretender, The, attempt of, i.
187, 367
Price, Dr., Bishop of Meath,
afterwards Archbishop of
Cashel, ii. 27 and note
Prince Posterity, Dedication to,
in the *Tale of a Tub*, i. 133
Prior, Matthew, i. 108, 169,
227, 260, 274 ; mission to the
French court, 298 ; ii. 18
Prior, Thomas, *Observations on
Coin, etc.*, ii. 63 note ; *List
of Absentees*, 146
Proclamation, The, against the
Drapier, text of, Appendix vii.
" Pug," Stella's dog, i. 227
Pulteney, William, i. 373 ; ii.
115, 165, 167 note, 225

Puttenham, Thomas Swift rector of, i. 9 note

Queensberry, Duchess of, i.
228 note ; ii. 208
Quilca, Swift's visits to Dr.
Sheridan at, ii. 169

Rabelais, Swift's debt to, i. 144
Raby, Lord, i. 274, 317
Raglan Castle, held by Lord
Worcester for the Royalists,
1642, i. 6, 7
Ramillies, Victory of, i. 179
Rantavan, seat of the Brook
family, ii. 170
" Raps," in Irish currency, ii.
64
Rathbeggan, Living of, i. 100
Raymond, Dr., of Trim, i. 120,
183, 228, 285, 344
Reading, List of Swift's, i. 71
note
Records of Armagh, i. 65 note
*Reflections on Ancient and
Modern Learning*, by William
Wotton, 1694, i. 84, 87
Remains, Sir W. Temple's,
edited by Swift, i. 96, 112
Resolutions for Old Age, Swift's,
i. 97 note
Resumption Bill, carried, i. 106
Revolution, Swift a sound ad-
herent of, i. 47
Richardson, agent of the Lon-
donderry Society, ii. 249
Richardson, Samuel, letter on
Swift, i. 17
Ridgway, Mrs., i. 25 note ; ii.
260
Ridpath, conductor of the *Fly-
ing Post*, i. 322 note
Ringsend, Swift lands at, June
30, 1709, i. 207
Rivers, Lord, i. 313
Robinson, Dr., Bishop of Bristol
and Dean of Windsor, ap-
pointed Privy Seal, i. 294, 317

Rochester, Earl of, i. 107, 162, 184, 257, 281

Rochfort family, Swift's visits to, ii. 169 and note

Roger, the clerk of Laracor Church, i. 119 and note

Rolls, Office of, at Dublin, clerkship in, offered to Swift, i. 59

Roman Catholics, Penal legislation against, i. 63; proportion of, in Ireland, ii. 53 note

Romney, Earl of, and Swift, i. 97, 98, Appendix i.

Rotherham Church, brass in memory of Robert Swifte and wife, i. 3 and note.

Roubiliac, Bust of Swift by, i. 231

Rowe, Nicholas, i. 222, 260

Rundle, Bishop, ii. 176 note

Ryder, Mr., master of grammar school, Kilkenny, i. 13

SACHEVERELL, Dr., of St. Saviour's, Southwark, i. 145, 237 note, 238·; impeachment, 241; trial and suspension, March 23, 1710, 242; and Atterbury, 243; presented with a living in Shropshire, and progress thither, 246; payment of the Tory debt to, 289

Sæva indignatio, Swift's, i. 141; ii. 44

St. James's Coffee-House, the Whig resort, i. 170

St. John, Henry (Lord Bolingbroke), i. 123 and note, 188; Secretary of State, 1710, 258; quarrel with Guiscard, 276; Swift's opinion of, 282, 316 note; his part in the Peace negotiations, 317; created Viscount Bolingbroke, 321. *See* Bolingbroke

St. Mary's Ladies, Swift's name for Stella and Dingley, i. 344 and note

Salmon, Dr., *Non-Miraculous Christianity*, reference to, i. 19 notes

Salter, Dr., his story of Swift and Lord Wharton, i. 197, 198 and notes

Sancroft, Archbishop, Swift's address to, i. 41

Scheme of the Money Matters of Ireland, Browne, 1729, ii. 64 note

Schism Bill, i. 371

Schomberg, Duke of, Swift's monument to, ii. 193

Scott, Sir Walter, i. 10 note; 77 note, 90; his edition of Swift, 118 note; 119 note, 197 note, 198 note, 199 notes, 213 note, 229 note, 230 note, 253 note, 255 note, 256 note, 351 note; ii. 77 note, 84 note, 148 note; and the Irish Tracts, ii. 151 note, 157 note, 198 note; and the Vanessa correspondence, ii. 31

Scriblerus Club, The, foundation of, and members, i. 284; meetings at St. James's Palace, 361 and notes, 362

Shaftesbury, third Earl, letter on Enthusiasm, 1708, i. 225 and note

Sharp, Archbishop, i. 147

Sheen, Sir W. Temple at, i. 26, 27, 29

Sheffield, John (Marquis of Normanby), i. 121 note. *See* also Buckingham

Sheridan, Bishop of Kilmore, i. 111 and note

Sheridan, Dr., and Stella, ii. 46; in Drapier controversy, 82; in Stella's illness, 108; Swift's visit to, 169; friendship of Swift and, 178 ; his character, *ib.* ; Master of Cavan School, 239 ; breach with Swift, 241 ; his death, 180, 241, Appendices iv. v. xii.

Sheridan, the younger, i. 17, 99 note ; ii. 240, Appendix v.

Shippen "Honest" and the Wood controversy, ii. 84

Shrewsbury, Duke of, i. 146, 300, 350 and note, 376

Sican, Mrs., ii. 186

Sidney, Edward, brother of Algernon Sidney. *See* Romney

Siècle de Louis le Grand, by Perrault, i. 81, 91

Skelton's *Some Proposals for the Revival of Christianity,* ii. 165 note. *See* Burdy

Smalridge, Dr., i. 88, 145 and note, 270

Smith, Edmund, "Captain Rag," i. 144 and note

Some Considerations for the Promoting of Agriculture and Employing the Poor, Viscount Molesworth, 1723, ii. 144 note

Somers, Lord, i. 107, 108, 109, 110, 112 and note, 127, 132, 146, 147, 162, 184, 185, 186, 191, 196, 198, 241, 257, Appendix iii.

Somerset, Duke of, i. 188 note, 376

Somerset, the Duchess of, i. 147 ; and the *Windsor Prophecy,* 286, 287 and note, 310, 333

Sophia, Princess, death, May 28, 1714, i. 365

South, Dr., i. 187 note, 235

South Sea Company, ii. 63

Southey's *Doctor,* i. 243

Southwell, Sir Robert, Sir

William Temple's letter to, i. 34 and note

Southwell, Mr., ii. 70 note

Specialis gratia, i. 15, 17 and note, 19

Stamford, Earl of, commanding for the Parliament at Hereford, 1642, i. 6, 7

Stanhope, Lord, i. 373 ; doubts authenticity of *Four Last Years,* Appendix iv. ; his account of Wood's Halfpence, Appendix vi.

Stanley, Sir John, i. 350 and note

Steele, Sir Richard, i. 169, 213 note, 215, 224, 255, 260, 261, 287, 306 ; quarrel with Swift, 335, 337, 353, 357, 358, 360 ; ii. 4 note

"Stella." *See* Johnson, Esther

"Stella's Cottage," i. 33

Sterne, Dr., Dean of St. Patrick's, afterwards Bishop of Dromore and of Clogher, i. 182, 190, 334 ; ii. 16

Stewardship of King's Inns, Dublin, i. 10

Stopford, Dr., Swift to, July 20, 1726, ii. 110

Strafford, Lord. *See* Raby

Stratford, a schoolfellow and friend of Swift, i. 14 and note

Subjects of examination for degree, Dublin, Feb. 1686, i. 18

Suffolk, Countess of. *See* Howard

Suffolk, MSS., The, ii. 127 note

Sunderland. First Lord, i, 75, 76 ; dismissal of, 76 ; dismissed, June 1710, 250 ; Lord Lieutenant of Ireland, ii. 9

Sundon MS., i. 159 note

Surfeit of fruit, in Swift's childhood, i. 57

Swanson, Mrs., daughter of Willoughby Swift, i. 22 note

Swift, Abigail (mother of Jonathan), i. 10, 24 and note, 25, 247, 248 and note, Appendix i.

Swift, Adam, i. 22 and note, Appendix i.

Swifte, Barnam, "Cavaliero Swifte," i. 4; created Viscount Carlingford, 1627, *ib.*

Swift, Deane, son of Goodwin Swift, i. 22 and note, 60 note

Swift, Deane, i. 17 and note, 22 and note, 24 note, 71 note, 74, 100, 150, 344 note; ii. 164 note, 233 note, 236, 243 note, 254 note, 255, 256 note, 257

Swift, Godwin, son of Rev. Thomas, vicar of Goodrich, i. 8; his marriages and success, 9; residence, 11; losses, 13; death, 1688, 22

Swift, Jane, birth, i. 10, 74 note; marriage, 104; death, 105, 248 note

Swift, Jonathan (the elder), birth, 1640, i. 6; marriage with Abigail Erick, 10; death, 1667, *ib.*, Appendix i.

Swift, Jonathan (Dean), birth Nov. 30, 1667, i. 11; at Whitehaven, 12; return to Ireland, 12; at the grammar school, Kilkenny, 13; at Trinity College, Dublin, 15; academic struggles, *ib.*; evidence as to his degree, 18; course of study, 19; intimacy with Dr. St. George Ashe, 20; death of Godwin Swift, 22; assistance from Willoughby Swift, *ib.*; new plans, 23; leaves Dublin for Leicester, *ib.*; engagement with Sir William Temple, 1689, 26; at Moor Park, 29; attacks of giddiness and deafness, 34; return to Ireland, 1690, *ib.*;

again at Moor Park, 35; at Oxford, 36; Bachelor's degree, June 14th, and Master of Arts, July 5th, 1692, *ib.*; new position with Sir William Temple, *ib.*; first poetic efforts, 39; Pindaric imitations, 41; addresses to Archbishop Sancroft, Sir William Temple, and the Athenian Society, *ib.*; contribution to the Athenian Society, 43, 45; address to William III., 46; commissioned to attend William III. on the Triennial Bill, 49; address to Congreve, 50; ode on Sir William Temple's recovery from illness, 1693, 51; forebodings of mental disease, 55; thoughts of the Church, 59; leaves Moor Park, May 1694, 60; at Leicester, and in Ireland, June 1694, *ib.*; letter to Sir William Temple, October 6, 1694, 60 and note; ordained deacon, Oct. 25, 1694, 61; priest, Jan. 13, 169$\frac{4}{5}$, 62; obtains prebend of Kilroot, *ib.*; Swift and Miss Waring, 66; invitation to Moor Park, 1696, 67; leaves Kilroot for England, May 1696, 68; at Moor Park, 1696, 70; first design of the *Tale of a Tub*, 71; course of reading, *ib.* and note; and Lord Sunderland, 76; resignation of Kilroot, 76 and note; and Esther Johnson, 78; *Battle of the Books*, 80; defence of Temple, 88; literary advance, 93; Journal of Temple's illness, 95; edits Temple's Essays, etc., 96 and notes; in Ireland, 1699, 98; chaplain to Lord Berkeley, *ib.*; appointed to the livings of Laracor, Agher, and Rathbeggan, Feb. 1700, 100 and note; obtains prebend of Dunlaven, 1700, 101; Doctor's degree, 1701, 102; letter to Miss Waring, *ib.*; return to England, 105; visit to Leicester, April 1701, 108; in London, *ib.*; *Dissensions at Athens and Rome, ib.*; interview with William III., 112; return to Ireland, Sept. 1701, 117; home at Laracor, *ib.*; in England, April 1702, 120; return to Ireland, Oct. 1702, 123; in England, November, 1703, 125; on the Occasional Conformity Bill, 126; political waverings, 128; return to Laracor, June 1704, *ib.*; *Tale of a Tub, Battle of the Books,* and *Discourse on the Mechanical Operation of the Spirit,* 129; incident of Dr. Tisdall and Stella, 150; Irish politics, 157; correspondence with Archbishop King, 158; Election in England, 160; Whig majority, 161; Convocation prorogued, 165; in London, 1705, *ib.*; and Addison, 167; literary friends, 168; Swift's position amongst them, 170; indifference to literary gains, 171; story of, at St. James's Coffee-House, 172; *Baucis and Philemon,* 175; invitation to Moor Park, 1706, 177; comes to England with Lord Pembroke, Nov. 1707, 182; his circle in Dublin, 183; at Leicester, 1707, 185; hopes of preferment, *ib.*; efforts to obtain the Bishopric of Cork, 186; checks to Church advancement, 187; with Sir Andrew Fountaine, 188; " *The Triti-*

cal Faculties of the Mind," 1708, 190; his first interview with Lord Godolphin, June 1708, 191; disgust with the Whigs, 197; further efforts for the Church, 200; *Letter on the Sacramental Test,* 201 and note; offer of Secretaryship to the Embassy to Vienna, 1708, *ib.*; signs of illness, 205; increasing friendship with Addison, *ib.*; interview with Halifax, May 3, 1709, 206; last visit to his mother, May 1709, 207; return to Laracor, *ib.*; *Argument against Abolishing Christianity, Project for the Advancement of Religion,* and *Sentiments of a Church of England Man,* 1708, 208 seq.; *Predictions for the Year* 1708, 219; *Letter to a Person of Honour,* 1708, 221; *Apology* for the *Tale of a Tub,* 225; portrait of, by Jervas, 229 and note; Roubiliac's bust of, 231; at Laracor, 1709, 234; parting with Addison, Sept. 1709, 236; return to England, Sept. 1710, 247 and note; *Letter to a Member of Parliament in Ireland on Choosing a new Speaker there,* 247 note; news of his mother's death, 248 and note; correspondence with Tooke, *ib.*; the *Journal,* 253; further efforts for the Irish Church, 254; *Tatler* and *Spectator* contributions, 255 note; *Description of a City Shower,* 256; received by Lords Wharton and Halifax, 257; the Tories in power, 258; *Sid Hamet's Rod,* 259; *Miscellanies in Prose and Verse,*

1711, 260 note ; circle of friends, 1710, 260 ; differences with Addison and Steele, 261 ; the *Examiner* papers, 263, 269 ; admitted to Cabinet meetings, 271 ; and Lord Peterborough, 273 and note ; in favour of a Peace policy, 275 ; solicitude for Harley, 279 ; and the vote to the Church, 281 ; estimate of Harley, *ib.* ; opinion of St. John, 282 ; at Chelsea, 284 ; intimacy with Atterbury, *ib.* ; foundation of the Scriblerus Club, *ib.* ; leaves Chelsea for Suffolk Street, July 1711, 285 ; at Windsor, *ib.* ; and Irish friends, 285 ; friendship with Arbuthnot, 288 ; society at Windsor, 289 ; at St. Martin's Street and Panton Street, 291 ; visits to Lord Peterborough at Parson's Green, 291 ; intimacy with the Vanhomrighs, 291 ; note on Mrs. Anne Long, 292 ; further efforts for the Peace, 297 ; attack on Dissenters on the acceptance of the Occasional Conformity Bill, 301 ; the *Hue and Cry after Dismal,* *ib.* ; *Conduct of the Allies,* Nov. 27, 1711, 302 ; misgivings on Marlborough's dismissal, 310 ; *Remarks on the Barrier Treaty,* 316 note ; *Letter to the October Club,* 319 ; position in society, 319 and note ; illness, 320 ; *Fable of Midas,* *ib.* ; *Letter to a Whig Lord,* *ib.* note ; Grub Street and the Paper Tax, 322 and note ; at Windsor, Sept. 1712, 323 ; *History of the Four Last Years of the Queen, ib.* ; the Bandbox plot, 324 ; and the Duchess of

Hamilton, *ib.* ; and Lady Ashburnham, 326 ; *A Proposal for correcting, improving, and ascertaining the English Tongue,* 328 and note ; Dean of St. Patrick's, 334 ; quarrel with Steele, 335 ; quits London, June 1st, 1713, 339 ; reception in Dublin, 344 ; at Laracor with Stella, *ib.* ; to Vanessa, 347 ; summoned to London, Aug. 1713, 350 ; the Prolocutorship of Convocation, 351 ; Whig attacks on, 355 ; *Importance of the Guardian,* Dec. 1713, 357 ; *The Public Spirit of the Whigs,* 358 ; quits London for Letcombe, May 1714, 363 ; *Free Thoughts on the Present State of Affairs,* 365 ; application for post of Historiographer, 369 ; Letter to Lord Oxford, July 1714, 373 ; news of Queen Anne's death, 377 ; his part in the Wagstaffe volume, 379 ; satires on, ii. 3 ; troubles in Dublin and at Laracor, 5 ; letter to Lord Oxford, 6 ; renewal of old friendships, 17 ; at work on *Gulliver's Travels,* 18 note ; to Bolingbroke, 19 ; Stella and Vanessa, 20 ; *Cadenus and Vanessa,* 28 ; last interview with Vanessa, 33 ; retires to the south of Ireland, 35 ; marriage, 41 ; the Irish troubles, 56-58 note ; *Proposal for Universal Use of Irish Manufactures,* 1720, 57 ; letter to Pope, 1722, 60 and notes ; views as to National Bank for Ireland, 63 ; the copper coinage, *ib.* and note ; the first Drapier Letter, 67 ; arguments against

the coinage, 69 ; the second
Drapier Letter, Aug. 4, 1724,
71 ; third Drapier Letter,
Aug. 25, 1724, *ib.* ; fourth
Drapier Letter, Oct. 13, 1724,
73 and note ; letters to Lord
Carteret, 77, 78 note ; Proclamation against the author
of the Drapier Letters, 78
and note ; *see* also Appendix
vii. ; letter to Lord Midleton,
ib. ; popularity of Drapier,
82 ; fifth Drapier Letter, *ib.* ;
seventh (so - called) Drapier
Letter, 84 ; Swift and Archbishop Boulter, 89 ; longings
for England, 91 ; invitations
from Bolingbroke and Gay,
94 ; leaves Ireland for London,
March 1726, 95 ; reception in
London, March 1726, 104 ;
letter to Lord Palmerston,
ib. ; to Tickell, 106 ; literary
work and intercourse, 107 ;
anxiety about Stella, 108,
109 and note ; Swift and
Walpole, 111 and note, 112,
113, 116 ; return to Ireland,
Aug. 15, 1726, 117 ; reception
in Dublin, *ib.* ; *Gulliver's
Travels,* published Nov. 1726,
118 ; return to England, April
9, 1727, 129 ; news of Stella's
second illness, 131 ; last of
England, Sept. 1727, 132 ;
Note - book and Journal of
1727, *ib.* ; reticence regarding
Stella, 137 note ; Stella's
death, 140, 141 notes ; the
Irish Tracts, 148, 150, 151
and notes ; The *Modest Proposal,* 1729, 152 ; *Answer to
the Craftsman,* 1730, 155 ;
later friendship with Archbishop King, 156 ; presented
with the freedom of the City
of Dublin, 1729, 157 ; reply
to Lord Allen, 158 ; speech
at the Guildhall, April 24,
1736, 159, 160 note ; *Advice
to the Freemen of Dublin,*
etc., 160 ; *The Legion Club,*
1736, 164 ; continued opposition to Walpole, 165 ; *Proposal
for Virtue,* 166 ; visit to the
Rochfort family, 169 ; visits
to Dr. Sheridan, *ib.* ; with
Sir Arthur Acheson, 170 ;
return to Dublin, 1729, 171 ;
Swift and Lord Carteret, 172 ;
Dublin surroundings, 174 ;
money affairs, 176, 178 and
note ; monument to the Duke
of Schomberg, 193 ; attack on
Bettesworth, 194 ; signs of
weakness, 196 ; first Will,
1735, 198 ; second Will,
May 1740, 199 and note ;
literary correspondence with
London friends, 200 ; defence
of the *Beggar's Opera,* 203 ;
death of Congreve, 206 ;
invitation to Pope, 206 ; invitation from the Duchess of
Queensberry, 208 ; interest in
Gay's *Polly* and the *Fables,*
209 and note ; last letter
from Arbuthnot to, 211 ;
letter to Lord Bathurst, 213 ;
later friendship with Pope
and Bolingbroke, 215 ; to
Bolingbroke, March 21, 1730,
217 and note ; to Pope,
1735, 219 ; friendship with
Lady Betty Germaine, *ib.* ;
quarrel with Mrs. Howard,
220 ; counterfeit letter to the
Queen about Mrs. Barber,
223 ; interest in Matthew
Pilkington, 224 ; *Verses on
the Death of Dr. Swift,* 226 ;
The *Beasts' Confession,* and
other pieces, 227 ; engaged
on new edition of his works,
1735, 233 ; to Motte, *ib.*
note ; *Poem to a Lady,* etc.,

234 ; *History of the Four Last Years of the Queen*, publication postponed, 237 ; the parting with Sheridan, 241 ; the fight against disease, 242 ; failure of memory, 244 and note ; Swift and Johnson, 245 ; last efforts for the Church, 249 ; letter to Mrs. Whiteway, 253 ; oblivion, 256 ; death, Oct. 19, 1745, 258 ; bequests, 259 ; review of his life and work, 260-274

——Works :

A Proposal for correcting, etc., the English Tongue, i. 328 and note

A short View of the State of Ireland, 1727, ii. 151 and note

A Vindication of his Excellency, John, Lord Carteret, etc., 1730, ii. 172 note

Advice to the Freemen of Dublin, 1736, ii. 160

An Answer to a paper called a Memorial of the Poor Inhabitants, etc., of the Kingdom of Ireland, 1728, ii. 148

Answer to the Craftsman, 1730, ii. 155

Apology for the Tale of a Tub, i. 225

Argument against Abolishing Christianity, 1708, i. 208 and note, 210, 229 note

Battle of the Books, 1697, i. 80, 88, 92, 93, 124, 129

Baucis and Philemon, i. 175 and note

Beasts' Confession, The, ii. 227

Cadenus and Vanessa, 1713, ii. 28 and note ; published 1723, ii. 35

Change in the Queen's Ministry, i. 237 note

Conduct of the Allies, i. 302, 309 note, 315, 318 note

Description of a City Shower, i. 256 and note

Directions to Servants, i. 100 ; ii. 231, 232 note

Discourse on the Mechanical Operation of the Spirit, i. 129, 142 note

Drapier's Letters, 1st (1724), ii. 67 ; 2nd (1724), 71 ; 3rd (1724), *ib.* ; 4th (1724), 73 ; 5th (1724), 82 ; 7th (1735), 84

Fable of Midas, i. 320

Free Thoughts on the Present State of Affairs, i. 365 note

Gulliver's Travels, Nov. 1726, i. 171 note ; ii. 18 note, 118 ; object and meaning of the work, 119-126 ; popular reception of, 126 ; Pope and, 127 and note ; dramatized in France, ii. 129 notes, Appendix viii.

History of the Four Last Years of the Queen, i. 237 note, 296 note, 323 ; ii. 236, Appendix iii.

Hue and Cry after Dismal, i. 301

Importance of the Guardian, Dec. 1713, i. 357

Letter concerning the Sacramental Test, 1708, i. 113 note ; 201 and note, 202 note, 215

Letter of "Seasonable Advice" to the Grand Jury, Nov. 11, 1724, ii 81

Letter to a Member of Parliament in Ireland, i. 247 and note

Letter to a Whig Lord, i. 320 and note

Letter to the October Club, i. 319

Maxims controlled in Ireland, 1724, ii. 150 and note

Meditation on a Broomstick,
i. 101, 173
*Memoirs relating to the Change
in the Queen's Ministry,* i.
112 note
*Miscellanies in Prose and
Verse,* 1711, i. 260 note
*Modest Proposal for Prevent-
ing the Children of Poor
People in Ireland from
being a burden, etc.,* 1729,
ii. 152
*Mrs. Francis Harris's Peti-
tion on the loss of her Purse,*
i. 100
On the day of Judgment, ii.
228 and note
*On the Dissensions at Athens
and Rome,* 1701, i. 108 ;
aims and argument of, 109
Place of the Damned, The,
ii. 228
*Poem to a Lady who had asked
him to write on her in the
heroic style,* ii. 234
Polite Conversations, ii. 231,
248
Predictions for the year 1708,
i. 219
*Project for the Advancement
of Religion,* 1708, i. 208
and note, 213, 227 note
*Proposal for Universal use of
Irish Manufactures,* 1720,
ii. 54 note, 57
Proposal for Virtue, ii. 166
*Proposal that the Ladies wear
Irish Manufactures,* ii. 152
note
Public Spirit of the Whigs,
March 1714, i. 358
Rhapsody on Poetry, 1733,
ii. 229 and note, 264
*Remarks on the Barrier
Treaty,* i. 316 note
*Sentiments of a Church of
England Man,* 1708, i. 208
and note, 216

Sid Hamet's Rod, i. 259
Tale of a Tub, 1696, i. 21, 46
note, 71 and note, 162
note ; review of, 128-144 ;
issue of the fifth edition
and the *Apology* by Tooke,
1710, 225, Appendix ii.
The Legion Club, 1736, ii.
164, 249
Tritical Faculties of the Mind,
i. 190
*Verses on the Death of Dr.
Swift,* ii. 226
Windsor Prophecy, i. 286
Swifte, Robert, memorial brass
to, in Rotherham Church, i. 3
Swift, Rev. Thomas, Vicar of
Goodrich, grandfather of Jonathan, i. 3 ; builder of New
House Farm, *ib.* ; born 1595,
5 ; at Goodrich, and marriage
with Elizabeth Dryden, *ib.* ;
his part with the Royalists,
ib. ; death, 1658, 8 and note
Swift, Thomas, son of Robert
Swifte of Rotherham, at Can-
terbury, 1570, i. 4
Swift, Thomas, second son of
the Vicar of Goodrich, i. 9
note
Swift, Rev. Thomas (cousin of
the Dean), i. 14, 15, 145 ;
ii. 261, Appendix i.
Swift, William (son of Thomas
Swift), at Canterbury, 1592,
i. 4 and note
Swift, William, uncle of the
Dean, i. 22 and note, 47 note
Swift, Willoughby, son of God-
win, i. 22 and note
Swiftiana, by Wilson, i. 118
note
Swiftsheath, family house of the
Ormond family, i. 13
Synge, Dr., Bishop of Raphoe,
afterwards Archbishop of
Tuam, ii. 10 and note, 16,
147 note

TAINE, M., i. 17 note
Tallard, i. 156
Tatler, The, quoted, i. 213 note, 225 and note ; Swift's part in, i. 224, 247, 255 and note, 274
Tax, Newspaper, i. 322
Temple, Sir John, father of Sir William, i. 26 note
Temple, John, i. 61 note, 177
Temple, Sir William, i. 26, 30, 34, 35, 42, 49, 51, 52, 77, 82, 89, 94, 95 and note, 96
Temple, Lady, wife of Sir William, i. 32
Temple, ——, son of Sir William, i. 27
The Last Will and Testament of the Pretender, 1715, ii. 11
Thucydides, Hobbes' Translation of, read by Swift, i. 73
Thynne, Thomas, assassinated Feb. 1682, i. 287 note
Tickell, biographer of Addison, i. 236 note ; Swift to, ii. 106
Tighe, Dick, i. 291
Tisdall, Dr. William, i. 149 ; correspondence with Swift, 150 ; proposal to Stella, *ib.*
Tisdall, of Dublin, i. 291, and note
Tooke, Benjamin, i. 96 note, 248, 313 and note
Treatise on Ancient and Modern Learning, Sir W. Temple's, i. 82, 85
Treatise on the Human Understanding, by Locke, i. 181
Treaty of Commerce between England and France, i. 343, 353
Triennial Bill, The, i. 48
Trim, i. 117
Trinity College, Dublin, i. 15
Turin, Battle of, i. 179
Tyrconnel, i. 23, 113

ULTIMUS ANGLORUM, Bishop Bedell so called, i. 62 and note
Union, The, of England and Scotland, i. 180
Utrecht, Treaty of Peace, signed 1713, i. 331, 357 ; Swift's History of, i. 367 and note

VANBRUGH, i. 169, 173-4
Vanessa.   *See* Vanhomrigh, Hester
Vanhomrigh, Mrs., i. 227, 284
Vanhomrigh, Hester, Swift and, i. 292, 344 *seq.*; ii. 20 ; residence in Ireland, 23 ; the story of her love, 24 ; retirement to Marlay Abbey, 32 ; Swift's interview with, 33 ; death and will, 34, 36 note
"Varina."   *See* Waring (Miss)
Vindication of the Rights of Convocation, Atterbury's, i. 124
Vivian Grey, i. 132 note
Voltaire and Swift, ii. 130
Vossius, Isaac, Canon of Windsor, author of *de Sibyllinus*, read by Swift, i. 72 note

WAGSTAFFE's *Character of Steele*, i. 360 and note
Wagstaffe Volume, note on the, i. 379
Wales, the Princess of, and Swift, ii. 112 and note
Walls, Archdeacon, i. 183 ; letter from Swift to, 22nd January 1708, 186 and note, 285, 349 ; Swift to, 17th Sept. 1713, 350 ; 1st October 1713, 351 ; 11th June 1714, 364 ; ii. 17 note, 39
Walpole, Sir Robert, i. 188, 258, 310, 373 ; *Short History of the Last Parliament*, 354 ; opinion of the Duke of Grafton, ii. 76 note ; his method in Irish politics, 85 ; Swift's visit to, 111, 235

Warburton, note on Swift's letter
    to Pope, 1722, ii. 61
Waring, a fellow-student of Swift,
    i. 21, 66 and note
Waring, Miss "Varina," i. 66,
    74, 77, 78 ; Swift's letter to,
    102, 104
Waterford, Bishopric of, given
    to Doctor Milles, i. 186
Waters, printer of the *Proposal
    for Universal use of Irish
    Manufactures*, prosecution of,
    ii. 60
Waverley Abbey, i. 28
Wesley, Samuel, brother-in-law
    of John Dunton, i, 44
Wharton, Lord, Governor of
    Ireland, i. 162, 184, 196, 197
    and note, 198, 249, 257, 258 ;
    Swift's pamphlet on, 266
    note, 321
Whigs, Swift's formal connection
    with, i. 108
Whitehaven, Swift carried to,
    by his nurse, 1668, i. 12
Whiteladies, in Worcestershire,
    i. 146
Whiteshed, Lord Chief Justice,
    and the prosecution of Waters,
    ii. 60 ; and the trial of Hard-
    ing, 81
Whiteway, Mrs., i. 97 note ;
    ii. 159 note, 252, 253, 254,
    258 note ; her evidence re-
    garding Swift's marriage,
    Appendix v.
Will, Stella's, ii. 139, Appen-
    dix x.
Will, Swift's, ii. 198
William III., visits to Sir Wil-
    liam Temple at Sheen and
Moor Park, i. 29 ; Swift's
    address to, 46 ; and the
    Triennial Bill, 48, 111 ;
    Swift's interview with, 112 ;
    death, 8th March 1702, 121 ;
    Whig custom of drinking to
    the memory of, ii. 10
Willows, Swift's, at Laracor, i.
    128
Wills' (coffee-house), the wits of,
    alluded to, i. 136, 137, 138 ;
    Whigs in, i. 147
Wilson, B., his portrait of Swift,
    i. 230 note
Wilson, personal attack on
    Swift, ii. 255 and note
Winder, Rev. M., i. 66 ; replaces
    Swift at Kilroot, 68 ; suc-
    ceeds him in the living, 76 ;
    letter from Swift to, *ib.* and
    note
Winter, Dean, ii. 27 and note
Witwoulds and *Petulants*, i. 135
Wood, William, and the Copper
    Coinage, ii. 64, 65, 68,
    Appendix vi.
Worcester, Marquis of, holding
    the castle of Raglan for the
    Royalists, 1642, i. 6, 7
Worrall, Rev. Mr., i. 349 ; ii.
    108, 109, 194
Worrall, Mrs., i. 248 note
Wotton, Rev. Henry, author of
    a pamphlet, i. 84
Wotton, William, son of the
    Rev. Henry Wotton, i. 84,
    87, 90, 148 and note, 226
Wyndham, Mr., ii. 225

YALDEN, Rev. Thomas, i. 222
    and note

THE END

The Eversley Series.

Globe 8vo.   Cloth.   5s. per volume.

Essays by George Brimley.   Third Edition.

Chaucer's Canterbury Tales.   Edited by A. W. POLLARD.   2 Vols.

Dean Church's Miscellaneous Writings. Collected Edition.   6 Vols.
  MISCELLANEOUS ESSAYS.
  DANTE : and other Essays.
  ST. ANSELM.
  SPENSER.
  BACON.
  THE OXFORD MOVEMENT.—Twelve Years, 1833-1845.

Emerson's Collected Works. 6 Vols.   With Introduction by JOHN
  MORLEY.
  MISCELLANIES. ESSAYS. POEMS.
  ENGLISH TRAITS AND REPRESENTATIVE MEN.
  THE CONDUCT OF LIFE, AND SOCIETY AND SOLITUDE.
  LETTERS AND SOCIAL AIMS.

Letters of Edward Fitzgerald.   Edited by W. ALDIS WRIGHT.
  2 Vols.   New Edition.

Goethe's Prose Maxims.   Translated, with Introductions, by T. BAILEY
  SAUNDERS.

Thomas Gray's Collected Works in Prose and Verse.   Edited by
  EDMUND GOSSE.   4 Vols.   Poems, Journals, and Essays.—Letters, 2 Vols.
  —Notes on Aristophanes and Plato.

Stray Studies from England and Italy.   By JOHN RICHARD GREEN.

The Choice of Books, and other Literary Pieces.   By FREDERIC
  HARRISON.

R. H. Hutton's Collected Essays.
  LITERARY ESSAYS.
  THEOLOGICAL ESSAYS.
  ESSAYS ON SOME OF THE MODERN GUIDES OF ENGLISH
    THOUGHT IN MATTERS OF FAITH.
  CRITICISMS ON CONTEMPORARY THOUGHT AND THINKERS
    2 Vols.

Thomas Henry Huxley's Collected Works.
  I. METHOD AND RESULTS.
  II. DARWINIANA.
  III. SCIENCE AND EDUCATION.
  IV. SCIENCE AND HEBREW TRADITION.
  V. SCIENCE AND CHRISTIAN TRADITION.
  VI. HUME.   With Helps to the Study of Berkeley.
  VII. MAN'S PLACE IN NATURE : and other Anthropological Essays.
  VIII. DISCOURSES, BIOLOGICAL AND GEOLOGICAL.
  IX. EVOLUTION AND ETHICS : and other Essays.

French Poets and Novelists. By HENRY JAMES.

Letters of John Keats to his Family and Friends. Edited by SIDNEY COLVIN.

Charles Kingsley's Novels and Poems.

WESTWARD HO! 2 Vols.
HYPATIA. 2 Vols.
YEAST. 1 Vol.
ALTON LOCKE. 2 Vols.
TWO YEARS AGO. 2 Vols.
HEREWARD THE WAKE. 2 Vols.
POEMS. 2 Vols.

Charles Lamb's Collected Works. Edited, with Introduction and Notes, by the Rev. Canon AINGER, M.A. 6 Vols.

THE ESSAYS OF ELIA.
POEMS, PLAYS, AND MISCELLANEOUS ESSAYS.
MRS. LEICESTER'S SCHOOL, and other Writings.
TALES FROM SHAKESPEARE. By CHARLES AND MARY LAMB.
THE LETTERS OF CHARLES LAMB. 2 Vols.

Life of Charles Lamb. By CANON AINGER.

The Poetical Works of John Milton. Edited, with Memoir, Introduction, Notes, by DAVID MASSON, M.A., LL.D. In 3 Vols.

I. THE MINOR POEMS.
II. PARADISE LOST.
III. PARADISE REGAINED, AND SAMSON AGONISTES.

John Morley's Collected Works. In 11 Vols.

VOLTAIRE. 1 Vol.
ROUSSEAU. 2 Vols.
DIDEROT AND THE ENCYCLOPÆDISTS. 2 Vols.
ON COMPROMISE. 1 Vol.
MISCELLANIES. 2 Vols.
BURKE. 1 Vol.
STUDIES IN LITERATURE. 1 Vol.

Science and a Future Life, and other Essays. By F. W. H. MYERS, M.A.

Records of Tennyson, Ruskin, and Browning. By ANNE THACKERAY RITCHIE.

Works by James Smetham.

LETTERS. With an Introductory Memoir. Edited by SARAH SMETHAM and WILLIAM DAVIES. With a Portrait.
LITERARY WORKS. Edited by WILLIAM DAVIES.

Life of Swift. By HENRY CRAIK, C.B. 2 Vols. New Edition.

Essays in the History of Religious Thought in the West. By BROOKE FOSS WESTCOTT, D.D., D.C.L., Lord Bishop of Durham.

MACMILLAN AND CO., LONDON.